RUN WILDE

HIS CLAIM

LUNA KAYNE

Run Wilde is the second book in the HIS series. While it can be read on its own, it will be better enjoyed if the first book, **Step Darkly** is read first. While this book follows new characters, Noah was introduced in book one and the storyline continues from the end of that story and updates on the main characters found in that book.

GET STEP DARKLY NOW

Life is what happens to you while you're busy making other plans.

— ALLEN SAUNDERS

1

HAZEL

*L*ooking back, it's funny to me how we make plans for our future at all because life always has a way of showing us who is really in charge.

Going to college at 24, when all of my friends had long since graduated and started their careers, was never the way I imagined my life ending up, but here I am.

I left high school with a scholarship, a boyfriend and lofty hopes of starting college while working with my father at his local veterinary clinic. That was three weeks before we found out life decided to go in a different direction, for all of us.

The news of my father's cancer hit us hard. He was given a year, and he beat the odds and fought for three more years before we lost him, but not before he lost almost everything else. Up until his diagnosis, his veterinary clinic was doing really well. He kept his costs low and never charged his customers more than what was necessary.

Eventually, his illness caught up with him and he couldn't keep his doors open. He made just enough to live comfortably and no other vets wanted to come on at such a low salary.

I tried my hardest to fill in for him but my lack of further education meant there were more things I couldn't do than I could.

One by one we lost our long-time customers because I just couldn't help them beyond annual shots and clipping nails. In the end, I failed him. Many of our clients were loyal but eventually we were muscled out by a series of lies, gossip and a price war around the only services left I could perform.

In the end, my dad ended up taking an extreme lowball offer from one of his competitors and chose to live out his final days with us.

I had long ago said goodbye to my scholarship. Instead, I took on a job in a restaurant to keep up with our bills. With only a high school education, I was lucky to be hired anywhere. My parents ended up selling their house, but the bills kept coming. My father's medical bills drained most of their savings and after he passed away, my mother and I came up with a plan for ourselves.

I worked full time for one year while she took a business administration course and got everything she needed to get back into the workforce as an administrative assistant. She had the skills from working in my father's office, she just needed the certification to make her more competitive. She found a good job but it was a couple of hours away so we moved her into an apartment near her work.

After that, it was my turn. I picked up where I left off. I applied to the college I was supposed to go to and was accepted into their veterinary sciences program. The school is a little too far to commute to everyday from my mom's place so I moved onto campus. I needed the space to study and I picked up extra jobs to cover my expenses.

Now, I'm 26 and I'm at the end of my second year. I've settled into a familiar chaos of sorts. Between my early shifts at the coffee house and my lunch time working at the school library, I rarely have time to study for my finals. Then there are my weekend shifts at The Echo Club, a local bar for the college crowd.

If I can make it through these exams, then I have a quiet summer ahead of me, the thought makes me smile as the bell on the door jingles, catching my attention. The last of our customers have left and the coffee shop is empty.

"Hazel, I haven't taken my last fifteen yet. I need to call my boyfriend. I'll be back before your shift is over." Estelle doesn't wait for my answer as she heads into the back room.

Out of habit, my phone is in my hand before I realize I'm checking my messages.

Nina: Hey.
Nina: A few of us are going out tonight. Wanna come?
Nina: Before you say no, just think about it.
Nina: You've been working and studying non-stop.

Hazel: Can't. Working.
Hazel: Where are you going?

Nina: Ugh. Of course you're working. You never stop.

Hazel: I'm not the one with the trust fund, remember ;)

Nina: Fine...
Nina: Peasant.
Nina: Bwahaha, joking.
Nina: But not really.
Nina: I'm your roommate and I hardly see you.
Nina: That's not good, Hazy.

Hazel: I know but it's only for a couple of weeks.

Nina: I know.
Nina: We're going to The Echo Club.
Nina: Are you at least working there tonight?

Hazel: I am. My shift ends at 11.
Hazel: I'll hang out for a bit after if you are still there.

Nina: Yay, I'll make sure we're there.
Nina: FYI, Paul has been asking about you ;)

Hazel: Srsly?

Nina: I'm not the only one who misses you.

Hazel: Brb. Customers.

Eight men and women file into the shop and make their way to the counter as I plaster a smile on my face and wait for someone to make eye contact. Awkward seconds tick by as eight sets of eyes scan the menu until, one at a time, they place their order and take a seat.

"That'll be $74.86." I say to the last guy and he almost looks surprised.

"Oh, I'm sorry. I thought someone said something. The guy who is buying will be here in a moment." He speaks without looking at me and joins his group around our largest table.

I know it shouldn't bother me, but I hate feeling invisible to these types. The suits here don't see anyone they can't buy or sell. The rest of us are white noise. It doesn't help that I can hear them laughing under their breaths and placing bets to see how many of their drinks I'm going to get wrong.

I know I got every one of them right, and I work quickly at the counter so they don't get a chance to complain about the slow service. Placing each one perfectly on a tray, I hurry around to the front of the counter and lift the heavy tray, turning to deliver the whole order.

As if watching my worst nightmare from outside of my body, my brain registers the person standing directly in front of me before the rest of me does and I hit him head on, spilling everything all around us.

The broken mugs and spilled coffee lands with a sharp

crash that grates into my ears and, as I look up, I see the look of shock and smug horror on each one of the eight faces I was just about to serve.

This couldn't have happened at a worse time. I shouldn't have taken this shift for my coworker today. I only have two hours to study in between this job and my next and now I'm going to miss my bus to the library.

Chuckles from the group at the table hit me the wrong way and I feel my arms begin to vibrate with anger as I set my sights on the man standing before me.

The most intensely beautiful man I've ever seen in my life.

2

NOAH

*T*hese past six weeks have been a blur.

After firing Brent and Sean along with their two buddies in HR and finance, we worked around the clock to refill positions and support our smaller sales staff while we helped our lawyers build their case and now it is in the hands of the court.

Joshua and Emilia have grown together in leaps and bounds during this time and they make me realize I've been missing out in finding someone to explore my own life with— every aspect of my life. Is it too much to ask to find a connection like they have? I once thought it was, but my best friend and his partner have rekindled a new hope in me.

To say the start of their relationship was rocky is an understatement but they fit together like no one I've met before. Well, maybe Adam and Lexa came close, but it is a rare connection.

Like Joshua, after high school, I focused a lot of my energy on my work with Connor Realty. We both saw the potential in working hard and Adam and his team made it easy to learn. *Investing in yourself is the best investment,* Adam used to say. He talked about the importance of always learning, always growing and taking care of ourselves and each other.

Now, I'm running out to meet up with some of our more recent employees to celebrate the end of their probationary period and their official roles in the company. I have to admit, I don't see a lot of potential in this group. While I like to be in charge, I also like to be challenged. I enjoy debate and discussion, and I love to further educate, and this group of recruits are a little too compliant. Maybe it's just the younger age; those who challenge the status quo are often the ones with more life experience behind them.

Regardless, this past month made all of our jobs more challenging and everyone rose to the occasion to complete their tasks and keep our company going strong in light of all of our recent setbacks.

One of the guys on the team suggested a quaint coffee shop down the street and now I'm rushing to meet everyone there. With my increased responsibilities at Connor Realty, Joshua suggested I hire a driver to get around downtown and it was perfect timing that an old acquaintance of mine happened to be looking for work like this. Watching from the back seat, I'm happy not to be the one driving in this madness as Marcus pulls up to the curb and I get out and head for the front door.

Everyone is sitting around the largest table by the front window and I nod as I make my way to the woman standing with her back to me in front of the counter. It looks like she's just finishing everyone's order so I can pay her before she delivers everything.

As I stop behind her and before I catch her attention,

one of the new girls calls my name and I turn to tell her I'll just be a minute, but I'm not fast enough. Before I turn all of the way back, I feel a hard bump and I watch as everything crashes into me then down to the floor and I feel my body heat up as the drinks slowly soak into my shirt and pants.

Everyone around us goes silent and the woman in front of me is frozen in place blinking rapidly at the destruction around us. Waves of auburn hair cover most of her face as she scans the floor and I hear a couple of people from the table laugh to themselves as I notice her tense up and I suddenly feel a pang of guilt for getting in her way.

"Well, I did say drinks were on me?" I shrug at my team, hoping to deflect some of the attention onto myself and it seems to work as I have all of their eyes back on me.

"Are you kidding me? That's all you have to say?" I hear her behind me. Her voice is angry. I understand she must feel embarrassed but she is still the one currently doing the serving in a service industry so I attempt to keep my voice steady.

"You ran into me, remember?" I speak calmly but something goes off inside of me.

"You're standing in an employees only space." She speaks as she begins pointing her finger around the room. "You order over there and you pay over there. What are you doing over here?" Her words continue to taunt whatever is stirring inside of me.

While I want to push back, I sense now isn't the time. There is more than spilled coffee going on for the woman in front of me and I push down my retort and drop my voice so only she can hear my words. "I apologize. I saw you over here and I was coming over to pay for the group and help you carry the drinks over to our table."

As I finish my sentence, her eyes shift to everyone around the table who, I now notice, have gone completely quiet. When she meets my stare again, she looks like she's realized her situation and her bottom lips quivers while she sniffles back her tears.

"I—okay," she tries to steady her voice. "Give me a moment to remake this order." She forces a smile. Embarrassment warms her cheeks and I notice her hands have started to tremble.

Catching her before she leaves, "It's not necessary." As I speak, her brows knit in confusion and I hear the table behind me begin to groan. Turning to the eight waiting, I pull some bills out of my wallet and hand them to Greg. "I promised you after-work drinks. Here, this should cover a couple of rounds at the pub down the street. I'll catch up with you another time." Everyone's eyes light up and they quickly gather their things and mutter their thanks, leaving the two of us alone.

"What do I owe you?" I take a step closer to her and she doesn't back away but she does drop her head and her gaze down.

"I don't want your money." She responds cooly and I decide, now that we are alone, it's time to assert myself a little more.

"I'm not asking if you want my money. I'm telling you, I will pay for the drinks you dropped when you bumped into me." I speak slowly, purposefully. I haven't used my dominant voice in awhile and I watch her chest heave a little deeper in reaction as she backs down.

"Look, we can't accept money for drinks we don't serve." Reluctantly, she sounds like she's quoting directly out of an employee handbook.

"Then who pays for these drinks?" My patience wears thin as she considers my question. I already know the answer. Most places like these make the employees pay for these mistakes out of pocket and this was a large order.

"I asked you a question—Hazel." I notice her name tag and use it to further hold her attention as I continue, "I expect a quick reply."

"I pay for them out of my tips. It's company policy. I'm not allowed to charge you. Look, it's fine. It was my mistake. I'm sorry." Her face falls with every word she says and now we've come to some sort of unspoken understanding and it pleases me.

"Fair enough. As your customer though, I have a right to leave a tip."

"What?" Incredulously, she takes a step back and I feel my words have offended her.

"It's pardon me or, my favorite, I *beg* your pardon. That's if you didn't hear me, but I think you did." I feel my smile turn into something a little darker.

"I told you. I don't want your money." I'm not sure what her reasons are for turning down this tip but I want to find out. I've never met anyone so intent on not taking money. Just as I'm about to ask her another question, a second woman steps out from the back and gasps at the caffeinated carnage laying at our feet.

Turning to her coworker, she raises her hand. "It's okay. It was an accident. I've got this." And her coworker distances herself from the mess as quickly as she can. "Look, my shift is over. I need to clean this up and get out of here." She attempts to shut our conversation down but I'm not ready to leave her just yet.

"Am I keeping you from your boyfriend?" My question

catches her off guard but I'm going to need an answer before I decide to continue.

"Something like that." She mutters as she reaches for a broom from behind the counter.

"Fine, but I'm not leaving until you tell me the amount on the bill so I can leave a proper tip—for your time." She sighs deeply at my words and I shrug telling her that I'm not going to be leaving until I settle this with her.

Setting the broom down, she pulls the receipt out of her apron and reaches out to hand it to me as she echoes the same number I'm reading. "The total was $74.86."

"Here, this should cover it." I hear the door to the back room swivel again as I reach into my wallet and pull out a bill, handing it to Hazel and her eyes bulge.

"This is a hundred dollars."

"Look at you. You're a smart one." I taunt with a smirk.

"I can't accept this." She pushes it back into my hand just as quickly and I refuse to accept it as I slowly shake my head.

"Either I hand it to you, or I hand it to your coworker to cover the loss, but I am the customer and I am always right." I give her the choice as her coworker pretends to clean the counter nearby so she can eavesdrop on our conversation.

"We don't say the customer is always right, here." Crossing her arms, she challenges me.

"You shouldn't say that. The customer isn't always right. My declarations were independent of each other. I am the customer. I am always right. I am not always right because I am the customer. I am always right because I am always right." I end with a wink and I imagine my arrogance is grating on her.

Before she declines again, I end the back and forth.

"Look, I'm not taking no for an answer. I wish to give you a tip, for your time."

She glances over her shoulder at her coworker who is silently telling her to just take the money and she resigns herself to the battle she just lost.

"This is very generous of you. Thank you."

"You are welcome. I found our conversation to be very enlightening, Miss?" I wait for her to fill in my blank and I finally get to see what she looks like when she smiles.

"Masters—Hazel Masters."

"It's nice to meet you Hazel, you can call me N." She snaps her head in surprise at my response.

"Ummm." Is all that comes out of her mouth and I feel myself become heady at her confusion.

"Anyway, I believe you have a boyfriend to get to?" I get back to the question I won't directly ask, further setting her off. In all truth, I'm still waiting to hear if she has someone in her life.

"Great. Thanks." She neither confirms nor denies my statement and I clench my palms into a fist before I notice my hands have become sweaty at the thought of how I'd love to deal with her for beating around the bush.

I'm almost ready to ask her the question outright when her nosy coworker finally answers it for me. "Hazel, when did you get a boyfriend?" Both of us glance at the girl behind the counter.

As my attention slowly moves back to Hazel, my grin turns wicked as I see the defeat in her eyes and I can't help but feel triumphant. I feel it in my bones. This is the exact moment I decide to pursue her further.

"Interesting." I savour the tension.

"What?"

"There you go again with *the whats*."

"What is interesting?" She corrects herself.

"That's better. We've just begun our arrangement and already you're lying to me." I'm in my full dominant mode now and I'd be lying if I wasn't utterly enjoying this.

I hear the door to the backroom open again and I don't care to check to see if we are alone.

"What arrangement? And I'm not lying if you assume something and I don't correct you." She tries to justify her vagueness and I feel the need to take control of the situation.

"Hmmm. Then let me make myself clear. Are you currently in any type of romantic or sexual relationship, Miss Masters?" Her mouth drops wide open at my question.

"I don't have a boyfriend. I need to get to the library to study before my next shift. I have a final tomorrow." She surrenders the information I need quickly and I wonder if this tension I'm feeling is the same for her.

"Forgive me for my assumption, but you look a little older than the college crowd." I state but, again, it's more of a question.

"I started late. I'm 26." She winces at herself. No doubt she realizes how easily she is giving me all of the information I need.

"I see. That's good to know. I'll give you some time to clean this up but I'd like to speak with you before you leave. I'll be outside. Don't leave me waiting." Without waiting for her answer, I turn and walk outside to call Marcus to come around to the front.

I'll know in the next few minutes if this is something that interests her as well.

3

HAZEL

hat the hell just happened?
The chime on the door echoes louder than I ever remember it sounding as the man I only know as N leaves. Scanning the empty coffee shop, my focus jumps from the door to the large empty table, then down to the mess on the floor and back up to the door.

"So, what was that about?" Estelle startles me and I spin around, stepping in the spilled coffee I need to clean up. This is going to take a lot longer to clear than the few minutes I think he just gave me.

"Um, I'm not sure. He wants to talk to me outside. But —" I look down at the broken mugs again.

"*But* nothing. Go. You've covered for me so many times. Your shift is over. I got this." Walking to me, she takes the broom and nods for me to gather my things and I don't waste any time.

Why am I rushing? I just met the guy.

Rush hour traffic is beginning to taper off but this means I've missed my chance to study at the library so my only option is to go back to the dorm rooms after this and, as much as I love her, I hope Nina isn't there so I can study in peace before my shift at the club tonight.

"I appreciate you not making me wait. I'd like to discuss our arrangement." Mr. Stranger gets right down to business and, somehow, I feel better speaking to him among the noise from outside. The silence from inside the shop was a little unnerving.

"What arrangement? I just met you twenty minutes ago when you made me spill my drinks." While I am intrigued, I feel my patience wearing thin and, hottie or not, I don't have all day, literally and figuratively.

"I haven't made you do anything—yet." The hint of a promise in his words makes me blush. "You dropped the drinks when you ran into me. I was standing perfectly still." I feel like we're going around in circles.

"Whatever. What arrangement?" I try to make my voice sound more aloof than I feel.

N stares at me for a long minute and I know what he's doing. He's trying to make me feel uncomfortable. It's working. I feel an urge to move, to create a distraction as his eyes gaze over me and I shuffle a bit to the side then open my mouth but I have no idea what to say.

"I find you interesting, Hazel." Thankfully, he speaks, "I spend most of my days around people who agree with me. Not because they actually agree with me, but because they feel they have to. They are paid to." I barely notice his pause. I can't stop looking at his mouth. "There are two types of people in this world. People who own and people who are owned. Which one are you, Miss Masters?" I sense he isn't talking about his employees anymore.

"I, well, is there a third kind? I'm not owned." I answer cautiously.

"Not yet." There's his smile again.

"P—pardon me?" I fight against my natural tendency to use *what* again.

"Very good. You catch on quick. Give me your phone." He reaches his hand, palm up, toward me.

"Wha—"

"And do not say *what*, again. You don't want me to show you, out here on the sidewalk, how I handle disobedience." His words are a challenge, one I am not willing to take him up on at the moment.

He stays still, palm extended, waiting. I've never had anyone speak to me like this. He's charming, but at the same time demanding but I'm not afraid of him. I glance down to the phone in my hand and slowly reach it out toward him as if on autopilot.

He grumbles to himself as he presses the screen and it opens for him. While he works away, I take a good look at him. I'd say he's a couple of years older than me. His suit probably cost my whole month of wages and tips at all three jobs combined and I spilled coffee all over it. I hope he can get the stains out and there is no way I can offer to pay for it. Now that I'm looking closer, his dress shirt clings rather nicely to his chest.

Lost in my thoughts, I've forgotten to watch what he's done with my phone. As he clears his voice, I'm met with a grin as he holds my phone out to me and I quickly take it and stuff it in my bag as he watches me carefully.

"Thank you. I'm going to let you go but I'm not done with you, Hazel. I want to know more about you but it will have to wait. Your studies are important. For now, I have two rules and you will obey them. First, don't text that number until I contact you and, second, answer me quickly when I do. I don't like to be kept waiting." His words don't sound stern or demanding and I almost sense this is a formality of sorts and I nod in understanding.

He turns and walks over to the sleek black car parked at the side of the road and gets into the backseat.

The guy has a driver.

I don't make enough money to know what kind of car that even is and he has someone driving it for him. I suddenly feel so far out of my league and I have to remind myself he picked me up at my job so he's under no delusion that I am made of money.

But still, I can't help but feel he is on a completely different level than I am in more ways than one. I mean, he has his own driver. Not to mention, all of those people in the store seemed to listen to everything he said and they cleared out pretty fast when he told them to.

Who has their own driver? Criminals, that's who. And I just gave him my first AND last name and access to my phone.

I don't have time to process this. My study time is ticking away and I see the bus to the dorms turn onto the street. I'll have to cram about 20 minutes in, then I need to get ready for my shift tonight.

My stomach grumbles as I step onto the half-full bus and find a seat. It looks like I'll have to skip eating this afternoon as well. As we pull away from the curb, I fish my phone out of my bag and open my text messages.

It looks like N added his contact info and he sent a text off to an unknown number with four words that fill me with butterflies.

In need of spanking.

I'm falling into something I've never been in before and a dark little part of me can't wait to see where it goes. But another part is wary. His methods for asking someone out are unorthodox at best and I feel like he's sizing me up for something more.

Regardless, I have bigger things to focus on. *That exam tomorrow isn't going to pass itself*, I chuckle to myself at the thought then open up my messages on my phone. I'll need to know, before I get home, if Nina is there so I send her a text next.

Hazel: Hey, got a second?

Nina: Where were you? You said BRB.

Hazel: Sorry. It got weird.

Nina: What got weird? Work?

Hazel: Kind of.
Hazel: This guy came in and I dropped a huge order of drinks all over the both of us.

Nina: Oh, no. Did they fire you?

Hazel: No. I think he asked me out.

Nina: Your boss asked you out?

Hazel: No. The guy I spilled drinks on.

Nina: But you're not sure.

Hazel: Um no.

Nina: OK.
Nina: That is weird. I don't even know what to say.
Nina: How did he ask you out?

Hazel: Well, he didn't.

Nina: ???

Hazel: He took my phone and sent himself a message from it.

Nina: Well then text him and ask him.

Hazel: I can't.

Nina: Why?

Hazel: I'm not allowed to.

Nina: What?

Hazel: I told you, it got weird.

Nina: #accurate
Nina: Okay, what's his name?

Hazel: N

Nina: That's an initial. What's the rest of his name?

Hazel: I don't know.

Nina: WHAT?

Hazel: I'm heading to the dorms now. Are you home?

Nina: No, I'm out with the gang grabbing sushi.
Nina: Paul is here, too.
Nina: Speaking of which...
Nina: Why don't you join us?

Hazel: I can't. I'm going to review a couple of chapters, then I'll head into work early.
Hazel: If I'm lucky, they'll have some food leftover from their lunch buffet.

Nina: OK. See you tonight.
Nina: I'll smuggle some sushi in for you ;)
Nina: You know I'll do it.

Nina: Can you still hang out for a bit after your shift?

Hazel: Just a bit.
Hazel: I have about an hour of studying left before my exam tomorrow.
Hazel: I just want to make sure I know my stuff.

Nina: Damn, girl.
Nina: You know your stuff.
Nina: You could teach that class.

Hazel: I wish I had your confidence.

Nina: You just don't see what I see, Hazy.

Hazel: Thanks.

Nina: I mean it.
Nina: Out of our whole little group, you had the biggest odds stacked against you.
Nina: I know we take our money for granted. We all have safety nets.
Nina: But you work so hard.
Nina: You dessert everything that is coming to you.

Hazel: Dessert?

Nina: ?

Hazel: You said I dessert everything.

Nina: Oh.
Nina: Hahaha
Nina: LMAO

Hazel: Are you drunk?

Nina: No. Pfft.
Nina: But I do feel funny.

Hazel: What are you drinking?

Nina: Just a sec. I'll ask Cassie.
Nina: She says it's called Sake.

Hazel: Nina, that's Japanese rice wine.
Hazel: There's alcohol in there.
Hazel: Ask for a big glass of water and cut yourself off or I won't see you tonight.

Nina: OK. Good idea.
Nina: I'm glad you texted.
Nina: I should have known something was up. I feel like singing karaoke.
Nina: I HATE KARAOKE

Hazel: Lol.

Hazel: Only water for the next couple of hours, deal?

Nina: Deal.
Nina: Cassie's laughing at me.
Nina: I'm starting to think that little bitch knew it was alcohol.
Nina: I'm going to get her back for this.

Hazel: Oh no.

Nina: I saw a show where someone baked a bunch of chocolate flavored poop softener into brownies.
Nina: I'm going to do that.
Nina: Remind me about my diabolical plan when I sober up. K?

Hazel: Lol, ok. Or you can just reread your text messages.

Nina: See. Look at all of us assholes out here with our money and shit.
Nina: You're the smartest one out of all of us.
Nina: I'm so proud of you.
Nina: I love you, Hazy.

Hazel: DRINK YOUR WATER, NINA!!!

4

NOAH

"What's up? I was on my way home. Is she in?" I enter through the opened door to Joshua's office and take a seat in front of his desk thankful I had a change of clothes in my office or I'd be explaining the coffee stains down my front.

After everything blew up with Brent and Sean, Emilia came back to work and they moved up to Adam's old office as soon as the renovations were done. In the end, Joshua had the designers adjust their plans to accommodate two offices and an area for their administration team and now both of them have an office of their own along with a common area.

"Emilia? No. She left a while ago. Her and Rosie have plans tonight. I called you back because I need to talk about Brent's defence. It appears he's trying to file some charges of his own and he's fighting, against his lawyers advice, to have some of our charges dropped." Joshua leans back in his chair, dragging his hands over his face.

"Does Emilia know about this?" Unbuttoning my jacket and leaning back in my seat, I ask. Emilia went through a lot in the last couple of months. Between the death of her father and Brent's harassment, it was enough to crush a normal human. Thankfully, Emilia is anything but.

"Oh, yes. She's fine with it. I spoke to our legal team and he said Brent doesn't have a leg to stand on. It's just his way of drawing it out and trying to intimidate us but he isn't doing himself any favors. We're all just going through the motions now. The reason I called you in is because this means we'll be called into court again to go over a few things next week. It's just a formality, but it's going to consume our attention and time over for a bit and I wanted to prepare you for it."

"Ok, thanks. I have some meetings I can either reschedule or have go on without me. Other than that, we are all settling back into business as usual here so it shouldn't be a problem. I'll rearrange everything tomorrow when I get in." I finish and wait for the real reason he called me back.

I've known Joshua long enough to know he would have sent this information to me over text and I force my expression to remain unassuming, but I have a feeling I already know why I'm here.

Joshua doesn't know what to do with himself without Emilia. They've spent the last month getting to know each other and have been inseparable. It makes me happy he's found this and it makes me giddy that she affects him so deeply.

"Great. Hey, what are you doing tonight?" He goes for casual conversation but falls short and I can't help myself. I start laughing. "What's so funny?"

"You don't want to go home without Emilia there, do you? She's grown on you that much, has she?"

"What? No. Shut up. Can't a guy just want to catch up

with his friend?" He looks genuinely offended and I back down.

"Absolutely. And I would love to, but I can't. I'm meeting up with someone tonight. Paige is in town and I told her I'd take her out. How about next week?" I offer as I stand and he rises with me.

"Sure. Pick a day next week and we'll go for drinks." He counters.

"Good. So things are well with Emilia then?" I already know what he's going to say by the look on his face. I've never seen the guy so content. It almost looks awkward coming from him. He does *brooding angry guy* much better.

"Things are good. She's even asked if we can go back to Ravenous together. I think I might take her next weekend. We haven't seen Alexandra in a few weeks and I know they want to catch up. You should come. Lexa tells me there are some new faces now." His suggestion isn't lost on me. He's trying to play matchmaker.

"I'll think about it. I've got to get going." I turn and make my way to the door.

"Enjoy your time and say *hi* to Paige from me." I nod and waive over my shoulder, leaving him to finish his work.

Everyone has gone for the day and I make a note to text Joshua later to make sure he doesn't spend too much time in his office.

I had a moment in our conversation when I considered telling him about the new woman I just met but I need time to absorb everything first. Right now, my focus is on Paige. I have a few hours before I see her and I've got to get ready.

Hazel caught my interest the moment I looked at her and she shied away. There's a depth to her I felt when we spoke. While I don't believe she's ever had the type of relationship I am looking for, I sense it's something she might be a fit for. I also can't deny what she does to me. She had some stellar moments when she challenged me and her attitude is addictive.

When Hazel handed me her phone earlier, I was able to unlock it without a code. I'll deal with her lack of security another time. For now, I'm interested in the message that appeared on the screen when I first opened it. The message she sent to her friend about working a shift at The Echo Club tonight.

I suddenly know where I'm meeting Paige for drinks and, if I'm lucky, I'll see Hazel as well.

5

HAZEL

*A*s the bus bounces over the train tracks at the crossing, I feel my shoulders relax. We missed the train today so that means I'll get into work with about 10 minutes to spare and it's just enough time to go looking for something to eat before my shift starts.

A text from an unknown number makes my heart skip a beat before I realize it can't be from N because he put his information in my phone already.

Unknown number: Hey Hazel

Hazel: Who's this?

Unknown number: Paul
Paul: I hope U don't mind
Paul: Nina gave me ur #

Hazel: Hi. No. I don't mind.

Hazel: Is Nina okay?

Paul: She's good
Paul: She's drinking water and talking
about karaoke

Hazel: Haha. Sounds like everyone
had fun.

Paul: Ya
Paul: We're heading to the club in a bit
Paul: Nina said you were working a shift

Hazel: I am. On the bus over there now.

Paul: Great
Paul: Well I'll see you there later

Paul is a nice enough guy. He's one of Nina's friends and part of the group I hang out with when I manage to get free time. Before I respond, I glance up and see my stop coming up fast so I decide to let the message go.

The first face I see when I get into the club is my frazzled boss. It turns out we're short staffed because too many of us 'college kids' took the time off to study. It was why I couldn't get tonight off, as well. On the bright side, he's asked me to assist on the main bar which means it'll be busier and my shift should go by faster.

I make a stop in our staff area and look over what is left from the afternoon buffet and the only thing that looks remotely edible are some spring rolls that might have been tasty when they were first put out, six hours ago. Just the thought of food poisoning puts me off eating and I gather my apron and head out to the bar a few minutes early.

The dance floor is empty but the bar is filling up when I arrive and make my way across to the main bar. Jackson is behind the secondary bar at the back which is good news. The guy is almost six and a half feet full of muscle and he's hot which means the ladies will flock to him for the complicated frilly drinks and Megs is most likely at the main bar which means that's where the guys will be and I'll be serving up beer for most of the night.

"Hey, stranger. I haven't seen you here all week." Megs hands two beers to the guys in front of her and clears some empty shot glasses from the counter.

"Finals. I got a few days off to study but I had to cover tonight because everyone else is taking time off now." I scan the bar for customers but it looks like we've got a few minutes to ourselves.

"Makes sense. It's been quiet in here—until tonight. I guess most of the exams are done."

"I'm near the end of mine. I have one tomorrow, then one next week."

"Well, this is the busiest Thursday I've seen in a long time. All you young students need to blow off some steam." Megs ends her sentence with a sultry wink and I can see why the guys are always around her bar during the evening. Her long wavy blonde hair and perfectly applied makeup always means the tips will be good.

The volume in the bar increases, a sign that we are about to get busy and the DJ makes some announcements as we both ready ourselves for the first rush. It turns out I was right and, as the night goes on, I lose track of the time until I hear a familiar voice order a Sex on the Beach and look up to see everyone crowded around the bar in front of Megs.

"I think she belongs to you. Tell her Jackson is at the back for the frilly shit." Megs points at Nina and calls over her shoulder. Everyone waves at me.

"I'm just kidding. I'll take a white wine. Whatever you got back there. Hey, Hazy." Nina dances at the bar and I move in to help out.

"I've got this, Megs." She steps back and moves around me to a group of guys who just came up to my side of the bar.

"Hey, Nina. I'm glad you got in. Is it a long line?"

"The longest. Thanks for putting our names on the list." I smile and start taking everyone's orders before I get to Paul, standing just behind the group.

"Hi, Paul. What can I get you?"

"Hey, Hazel. Thanks for adding us to that list. It's crazy out there. I'll have a beer. Does five dollars cover it?" I nod. Sliding the bill across the bar, he takes the bottle and starts walking in the direction the others went.

"Before I forget. Here. I got the sushi past the bouncers." Nina looks over her shoulder like she's going to get caught.

"Thanks, but it's not contraband. I'm so hungry." As I speak, I look at Megs who nods, telling me to eat it quickly at the bar.

"We've got a table. Find us after your shift?" She waits for me to acknowledge I'm staying behind and I agree.

Before Nina is out of sight, I've already eaten half the sushi as I see a group of guys forming around Megs. I pack the rest up and tuck it away, then return to help her and a few of them are asking for rounds of shots as the music beats on. One of the guys in the group looks at me, points his finger in my direction and tells Megs to pour me one, too.

"Thank you, but I can't. I have an early morning." I shrug to a collective grumble among the guys.

"Oh, come on. Just one. Join us for a bit." The same guy asks again and, just as I'm about to say no a second time, Megs catches my attention.

"You can have just one. I'll make them." She finishes her sentence with a wink only I saw, telling me that she'll make mine non-alcoholic and no one will know.

I plaster a big smile on my face and throw my hands up in mock surrender to cheers from the gang in front of the bar. All of the guys speak over each other in a toast to something I can't quite make out. I shoot my drink back and scrunch my face up, pretending the drink was strong and everyone leaves, opening up space for the next customers.

As Megs continues to serve, I decide to start clearing the empties away and I drop my attention down to the mess on the bar in front of me and begin to sort the glasses and wipe up any spills when I hear a customer in front of me.

"Should you really be drinking the night before your exam?"

Confused, I look up to answer him and stop short.

It's *him*.

N is here, standing on the other side of the bar. He's changed clothes since I last saw him. Of course he would, I spilled coffee all over the guy.

"Are you following me?" I blurt out the first thought in my head.

He smiles. "I saw you when I came in. I was going to leave it but then I noticed you drinking and enjoying everyone and thought I'd ask about your studies. They are important, Miss Masters." It isn't lost on me, he didn't exactly answer my question.

"I know they are. What are you doing here?" I attempt a second shot at getting an answer.

"I'm meeting someone for a drink. Speaking of drinks, do you normally share drinks with your customers, or is it just the ones you like, because I ended up wearing mine?" He reminds me of my stellar performance earlier in the day and I sense he is enjoying watching me squirm.

"Right." I have no response but I see Megs watching our conversation and she's getting a line again. "What can I get you to drink? I need to get back to work." I tilt my head in the direction of the line and he takes the cue.

"I'll have a glass of red wine and a shot of whatever you just had." He answers and I feel my face heat up again.

"Oh, um, it was cranberry juice." Sheepishly, I pour his wine.

"Pardon?" His amusement is evident.

"Cranberry juice. I don't usually drink here and she knows I have school tomorrow so she gave me an easy shot."

I watch him for a tense moment as he considers my answer before responding himself. "My aren't you a good girl?"

There is something about the way he just said it that makes me need to push down a giggle as my cheeks warm. My brain fixates on him calling me a good girl. Why does hearing this from him make me feel this way? It's like I want to make him happy and I still don't know the rest of his name.

"I should get back to work. Um, so—" Before I finish speaking a younger girl bounces into his space and throws her arms around N, placing a kiss on his cheek.

6

NOAH

"Sorry I'm late. That line up was crazy. I couldn't get in until I told the bouncer who I was here to meet." Paige jumps into my space, placing a kiss on my cheek and it isn't lost on me, Hazel looks confused.

At 21, Paige is younger than both of us and, as she steps back from me, I notice her top barely covers her tonight. I'll have to talk to her about that later. If I have to tell one guy here to stop gawking at her, my night is going to end badly.

"You're here now. Why don't you grab us a seat and we'll catch up. I thought you'd like a place a little more upbeat. Here, I ordered for you." Passing the glass of wine to Paige, I watch out of the corner of my eye as Hazel takes her in, unaware that I'm doing the same to her.

Paige stops for a hot second and glances awkwardly between the two of us. She knows me too well and she takes the glass and offers Hazel a smile before excusing herself and moving toward the back of the club.

I could offer Hazel more information, but watching her uncertainty is pushing at something dark inside of me and

I'm not ready for it to stop yet. The tension building between us is too delightful to release now.

"What can I get you?" Hazel's demeanor turns cold and she gets back to business.

"I'll have a Cassanova."

"Of course. How fitting." She mumbles, grabbing a glass.

"Tsk, tsk. Is that a hint of jealousy I hear in your tone, Miss Masters?" I test her further. I know she's interested. Everything about her reactions tells me I'm right.

"Of course not. I mean it's fitting that someone as *stylish* as yourself would choose such a rich and smooth bourbon drink." Her well-delivered sarcasm covers for her insecurity nicely.

"Hmmm. Interesting. I'll let your response go this time but only because I have someone else that requires my attention. I'll take my drink now, preferably in a glass this time." I retort and watch as she struggles to keep her irritation hidden behind her pretty smile.

I become too distracted thinking about all of the ways I can help her center herself when she sets my glass down and holds out her hand and I must have missed how much she said I owe her.

"Is there anything else?" My mind goes straight to the double entendre in her question and I feel a war wage between what I want to say and what I should say.

"Not at this moment. Thank you, Hazel." I hand her more than enough to cover the drinks.

I see her go for the register and I turn and make my way through the crowd before she can attempt to give me my change back.

As I move across the bar, looking for Paige, my mind continuously wanders back to Hazel. I have a deep desire to know more about her and it doesn't hurt that every time I see her, I feel like I'm not close enough to her.

I always thought I would meet someone at Ravenous. At least there, people are more open and accepting and there are some things I enjoy that don't always fall into a traditional relationship but small bits of my conversations with Hazel lead me to believe we may have more in common than she realizes.

Still, I wonder about her. I want to know her story. Why did she continue her education later than her friends? And what is her issue about money? Or is it status? I know she's interested in learning more as well but I sense hesitation. Maybe it's just that she's unsure of what I want or she hasn't been exposed to the lifestyle I'm interested in.

I'll give it time. I like where our conversations are heading and I don't want to rush anything. Besides, her focus is on her studies which is where it should be.

Paige catches my attention with a wave and I feel my anger build as the guys at the table beside her have taken notice of her. Staring them down as I approach, one by one, they turn their attention away and Paige rolls her eyes as I take the seat next to her.

"Really?" She crosses her arms to punctuate her challenge.

"I don't know what you're talking about."

"Are you going to stare down everyone who looks at me?" She sips her wine.

"If I have to." I take a drink, Hazel knows her stuff. This is one of the best drinks I've ever had. "And it's not like you're helping anything. Is that even a top or did you just tie a thin scarf around yourself?" I grumble and she giggles which she knows makes me even more irritable.

"She's beautiful." Changing the subject has always been Paige's strength.

"Who?"

"You know who. The pretty one behind the counter. I get the feeling I interrupted something." Paige lifts her accusing eye brows in my direction and now it's my turn to roll my eyes. She isn't going to drop this.

"We were just talking." I shrug and take another gulp.

"Right." She draws out her word. "Well, she looked like she was into you. That's all I'm going to say."

"That's not all you're going to say." I laugh. Paige has never been one to keep her opinions to herself.

"You're right. I'm not done. What's the deal with her?"

I can't answer her question. Mostly because I don't know what the deal is but if I tell Paige as much, she'll march her barely clothed ass right back up to the bar and talk to Hazel herself and I can't let that happen.

"There is no deal—yet." I answer, draining the last of my drink. I make my own attempt at distraction, "Joshua says hello."

"Really? How is he? Still smokin' hot?" She can't contain her giggle. She knows my friends are off limits.

"He's very happily taken."

"And you? Are you happily taken?" Her eyes jump back to the bar and I follow them up to see Hazel making her way back to the main area with a small box.

"Still working on it." I answer and I forget my surroundings for a moment as I watch someone say something to Hazel and she laughs. All I hear is the beat of the music as my ribs vibrate with the deep bass.

I really want to hear what her laugh sounds like.

"Noah?" My own name pulls me back to our conversation and I realize I'm not paying attention.

"Sorry. What did you say?"

"I was just saying, again. Your friend is very pretty." She takes another drink, tilting her head in Hazel's direction and I agree with her in my head.

"So—when are you going to tell her who I am?"

7

HAZEL

"*H*ey, we're out of limes. Can you grab a box from the kitchen?" Megs shouts over the music and I wave at her as I turn back to give N his change only to find he's disappeared.

Of course he did. He's no doubt running off to that girl who *needs his attention*. The girl who probably knows his full name.

The noise in the kitchen is considerably lower than the main area and I need to take a few minutes to compose myself before I return to the floor so I decide to send off a text.

Hazel: He's here.

Nina: Of course he is.
Nina: He's sitting right beside me.
Nina: He's talking about you.

Hazel: Who is?

Nina: Duh... Paul.

Hazel: No.
Hazel: He's here.
Hazel: N

Nina is: Holy shit. No way.
Nina: Where is he?
Nina: I'll go over and get the rest of his name out of him for you.

Hazel: He's here with someone else.

Nina: WHAT?

Hazel: She looks way younger than me.
Hazel: I should have carded her.
Hazel: I need to get back to the bar.

Nina: Where's he sitting?
Nina: I want to see him.

Hazel: I don't know. I lost him in the crowd.

Nina: Describe him.

Hazel: I can't right now. Gotta Go.

**Nina: Fine but if you can, take a pic
of him.**

Hazel: I'll try. But I better not get caught.

Once I'm back at the bar with the limes, the time seems to fly by as the two of us get into a steady rhythm of serving drinks and clearing glasses. It feels like an hour has passed when I look up and watch as N orders a drink from Megs. The girl with him is putting on her jacket and glancing at her watch as Megs hands N a bottle of water and I'm suddenly disappointed he didn't order from me.

They must be getting ready to leave. Nina's request jumps into my head and I fumble with my phone to take a photo before he's gone. I'm too nervous to look as I take the shot, and I hug my phone close to my body and snap a picture under my arm but I feel my hands shaking. I would suck at undercover work.

Quickly, I put the phone down in front of me to pull up the photo. It's too dark in here to get a good enough pic and it's blurry but it's all I've got so I hit send.

Before I pocket my phone and get back to cleaning the counter, the sound of a throat clearing makes my heart race.

Of course N is standing in front of me—again.

"You didn't, by chance, just take my picture? Did you?" He seems too amused with himself.

"What? No. I was just checking my messages." I reach for the dish rag and start moving glasses around as I feel my cheeks heat up.

"Give me your phone, Hazel."

"Wh—why?"

"There's something you should know about yourself, Miss Masters. You are a horrible liar. Now, give me your phone."

Busted. I don't think there's any way out of this except the truth. "Fine. I took your photo."

"Let me see it." His grin grows across his face.

"Why?"

"Well for starters, I want to see it before I delete it. Since I don't think you would like me to punish you at your job for lying to me, I think losing the photo is a good alternative." His words are laced with seduction and I feel entirely too exposed right now.

Without asking again, N simply holds out his hand and waits. I feel my shoulders slump forward in defeat and I place my phone in his palm for the second time today. Repeating his motions from earlier, he taps the phone a few times then chuckles to himself before handing it back.

His photo is still on my screen.

"Your photo is still there."

"You're as good at photography as you are at being covert. I can't even tell that's me. You can keep the photo. Besides, I see you already sent it to your friend. Tell me, is Nina here tonight?" I feel my skin prickle with goosebumps as he learns more about me.

"Yes."

"And is she with your friend, Paul?" The question catches me off guard. How does he know about Paul?

"He's here, too." I answer slowly.

The girl N is with waves at him then taps the imaginary watch on her wrist and he nods once to her as she turns and begins walking to the exit while he focuses his eyes back on me and leans in, lowering his voice just enough that I need to lean toward him to properly hear him.

"Hazel, you may stay and talk with your friends after your shift but make sure you head home, alone, in time to get your studying in. I can send my driver back for you if you need a ride."

My head is still swirling. How does he know about all of my friends?

"Um, I don't need a ride."

"Very well. Good luck on your exam tomorrow." He smiles.

I take a deep breath to respond but Megs surprises me when she reminds me my shift is almost over. I look at her and answer and then turn back to thank N, but he's gone.

The traffic around the bar has died down and my phone vibrates in my hand.

Nina: WTH Hazy!
Nina: That pic is so blurry.
Nina: I can't even tell if you're still in this club.

Hazel: Sorry. It was the best I could do.

Nina: Try again. Just take it while he's distracted.

Hazel: I can't. I think they left.
Hazel: I can't see them anywhere.

Nina: :(

Nina: Ugh
Nina: Fine.
Nina: You almost done?

Hazel: About 10 mins.

I finish cleaning the counter surrounding the bar then do my end of shift meet up with Megs to see if she needs me to do anything else before I'm done and she waves me off, telling me to go see my friends. Pulling my own bill out of my pocket, I slide it to her and get a bottle of water, then make my way to the back to store my apron and grab my bag.

When I get to the table, everyone is still partying and some of our group is on the dance floor. Paul looks up from his conversation and clears a spot beside him and I spend a few minutes getting into their conversation when Nina comes back from dancing.

"How was work?" She asks as I pour my water into her empty wine glass and she winks and takes a drink.

"It was busy but it went by fast."

"Hey, a bunch of us are thinking about going somewhere for dessert. Want to join us?" Paul asks.

My first instinct is to say *no*. I need to get home and cram a bit more in before tomorrow morning. But now that N says he expects me at home, I feel like I should go out. He has some nerve telling me what to do after he paraded that girl in front of me. I only just met the guy.

I nod and Paul smiles while the rest of the table begins to look restless. Nina waves to the group on the dance floor and everyone heads back to the table. I pull out my phone; I can be reckless while still being responsible and getting home at a decent hour and I check the time when a message pops up on my screen.

N: I didn't get the chance to say good night.
N: You looked busy.
N: Good luck on your exam in the morning.
N: I expect you at home and studying tonight like a good girl.

Hazel: Actually, I decided I'm going to go out with my friends instead.

N: And Paul?

Hazel: Yes, and Paul. How do you know Paul?

N: Miss Masters, I expect you at home, alone, and studying in the next 30 minutes.
N: This is non-negotiable.

Hazel: I just met you today.
Hazel: You can't tell me what to do.
Hazel: I don't even know your full name.

N: Some things are earned, Miss Masters.
N: Do you think you'll earn my full name

by going out when you should be
preparing for your exam?

Hazel: No.

N: You're a smart one. You have 30
minutes to get home to study.
N: Is that enough time?

Hazel: No.
Hazel: The bus takes 40 minutes at this
time of night, and that is after I wait
for it.
Hazel: If I even decide to listen to you.

N: Tic toc, Hazel.
N: Would you like me to send my driver
back for you?
N: I am no longer in need of a car tonight.

Hazel: Had to get your date home before
her curfew?
Hazel: Does she have high school in the
morning?

N: Jealousy does not look good on you,
Miss Masters.
N: 29 minutes.
N: If you are interested in seeing where
this goes, and I know you are, you'll get

home and study or this arrangement will
be over before it begins.
N: What will it be?

Hazel: You just want to know my address
so you know where I live.

N: I already know where you live, Hazel.
N: You're in a room on campus.
N: You really shouldn't give your full name
and your phone to strangers.
N: What were you thinking?
N: I should punish you for being so
reckless with your safety.
N: I may still do that.
N: 27 minutes, Hazel.

Hazel: My phone.
Hazel: That's how you knew about Paul
and about me working at The Echo Club.
Hazel: You saw my text message to Nina
at the coffeehouse.

N: 26 minutes.

Hazel: Fine, send your driver.
Hazel: But if I'm late, that's on him.

N: He's already outside.
N: Say your goodbyes and get home.

Hazel: Should I text you when I get there?

N: While it pleases me that you wish to update me, it won't be necessary this time.
N: My driver will inform me.
N: Good night, Miss Masters.

Hazel: Good night.

"Look, I'd like to join you guys but I didn't realize how late it is. I really need to review my definitions before I go to sleep." Most of the group keeps gathering their things as I speak except for Nina and Paul.

"It's okay, really. I know how much you need this. Besides, there's only a couple of weeks left, then we all have more time." Nina smiles and Paul reluctantly nods in agreement.

The last thing I want everyone to see is me getting into some high-end car so I wave and hastily say good night. One of the waitresses hits the table with a late ordered round of shots and it buys me some time to get to N's car.

I know which one it is. The Echo Club is mostly college students on limited budgets and a well-dressed driver standing beside a fancy car is very out of place in the parking lot and I walk right toward it.

"Miss Masters, N has instructed me to make sure you get home safely." The well-dressed man moves to the back and opens the door for me.

"You call him N, too? Is that his name?" Now I feel stupid. Is this guy for real?

"No, Miss Masters. N has instructed me to refer to him as such in your presence until further notice."

"Fine. But you tell your boss I'm just going to start giving him a first name soon." I huff, causing the driver to crack a smile and I stay where I am still trying to decide if I should get in.

"I will inform him of your plans, Miss Masters. But I advise against it."

"I'll take it under consideration. Um, can I at least know your name?" I know I'm grasping at straws and the guy thinks about my request for a few seconds before answering.

"You may. I'm Marcus." I beam. I feel a little triumphant. I got someone's name tonight.

"It's nice to meet you, Marcus. Did N enjoy his date earlier?" I feel a brief moment of satisfaction before I realize N is right; I am totally jealous.

"N mentioned you might say something about that. He told me to tell you he had a wonderful night visiting with his sister. She was in town to meet her boyfriend's family."

"He lied to me? What else did he *allow* you to tell me?" I notice Marcus trying hard not to smile when I ask him what's so funny.

"N told me you would say that and he told me to tell you a wise woman once told him that he's not lying if you assume something and he doesn't correct you."

How does this guy get under my skin so easily? I mean it's like watching a dumpster fire. I just can't look away from him. Hopefully he won't be as destructive.

Defeat settles in as I slide into the backseat and close my eyes as the car pulls out of the club parking lot.

What have I gotten myself into?

8

HAZEL

"*Hazel*, wait up." I hear my name, but I can't focus well enough to see who the voice is attached to. After my three-hour exam, I feel like I can't process anything and the sun is exceptionally bright today, making it difficult to transition from the windowless room I just spent my time in so I decide to stand still and rub my eyes while whoever it is catches up to me.

"Hey. I just finished my last exam. You done, too?" Paul asks as he stops at my side.

"Hi, Paul. I just finished one, but I still have one on Thursday. How did you do?" I ask, staying put.

"I understood the questions, but the instructor is a bit of a stickler so we'll see. Are you free now? Want to grab lunch?" I look at my phone while he asks his question.

"I can't today. I have a shift at the library. They're getting ready to close over the summer and I told them I could help out. I'm heading there now." I sling my bag over my shoulder.

"Can I walk with you?" I shrug and he falls in step as I start walking in the direction of the campus library.

"So you're done then? That must be a great feeling." I prompt.

"It is. Now I can relax and think about the summer. What are you going to do during break? Are you working?"

"Well, that's the thing. The library closes and the club is quiet after the students head home. They may have to lay me off, and I don't make enough to work at the coffee shop alone. I might stay with my mom for the summer if I can't find work. It's only a couple of hours away." I feel my anxiety build. I knew this was coming and Mom and I spoke about it. My studies are my priority so I need to get my last exam over with, then we'll figure it out. "What about you?"

"I'm going to pick up a summer job at my family's resort. It's easy work. Do you want me to ask about getting you a job, too?" I'm hesitant to answer his question.

"No. Thank you though." Paul gets quiet at my answer and we walk for a few minutes before he speaks again.

"Well, before you leave, I was wondering if you'd like to go out for dinner or something? Without everyone else. I mean just the two of us." He adds the last part as more of a hint.

"Do you mean like a date?"

"Well, yes." I hesitate again.

I'm not sure this is a good idea. But at the same time, maybe I should. I know I would be turning Paul down because of N and that isn't fair to me. The guy can't even give me his whole name and I don't want to wait around forever only to find out he was amusing himself at my expense.

"Um, Paul. I'm not sure—"

"Before you decide, it's just two friends hanging out. We both might be here over the summer and we aren't seeing anyone. What do you say?"

He's right. I'm not even allowed to contact N at the number he gave me.

Reluctantly, "Okay. Sure. Why not? On one condition." We stop in front of the library and he waits for my terms. "Not until after my last exam on Thursday. What about Friday—lunch?"

His smile is infectious as he nods in agreement. "Great, I'll message you with the details after the weekend. I'll probably see you around, but if I don't, good luck on your last exam."

I say my thanks and turn to run up the steps, taking them two at a time. I'm a few minutes early so I can eat my lunch before my shift starts.

As I open the doors to the library, I feel a guilty pang hit me. I know nothing about N. He's probably forgotten all about me, but deep down, I feel bad for agreeing to see Paul even if we are going out as friends.

I don't know anything about N, other than he is hot and his smile melts my brain. I know he's confident just by talking to him and he has money; how much or where it comes from, I don't know. The money is actually a negative. I rarely fit in with those crowds. It took Nina and I almost a half a year to get to know each other. When I first met her, she was all about possessions and the next big thing and it just wasn't me, but spending some time with her through the year, I realized it is a front she puts on to keep people away.

It wasn't until I found her crying on her birthday because her own parents forgot about her that I began to learn more about her and now we are pretty much inseparable. I realized I was too quick to judge those who had money and I've been working on being better.

I just had such bad experiences when my father became ill. Vultures descended on his business and his home with only dollar signs in their sights and it left a bad taste in my mouth but Nina and our friends have been the exception to my rule.

Even Paul offered to help me get a job at his family's resort if I wanted and the guy could probably just go somewhere and sit on a beach all summer if he felt like it.

But then there is N. Both times I met him, he gave me more money than I needed and that makes me uncomfortable. Thinking about it now, maybe he thinks I'm the poor girl who can be bought and the thought doesn't sit right with me.

Besides, I just met the guy yesterday. It's not like we have a long term commitment. At the rate I'm going, if he gave me one letter to his name each week and depending how long it is, I might know what it is in a couple of months.

I can't live my life based on what might happen. I learned long ago that the best laid plans often have huge potholes just below the surface.

9

NOAH

"Thanks for suggesting the gym instead of dinner. The last thing I needed after court today was a juicy steak and a cold beer. Who knew what I really needed was to get my ass kicked over and over again at racquetball?" My sarcasm rolls out of me as I rub my sore muscles. Joshua rolls his eyes as he joins me on the seat and gulps his water.

"Sorry about that." Joshua half laughs. "I had too much energy after seeing that guy in court today. He just glared at Emilia the whole time." He takes his anger out on his racquet as he tries to jam it into his bag.

Today was a particularly rough day. Emilia was required on the stand and Brent made it extremely awkward for everyone. She was kind of a badass though. She didn't falter and she spoke clearly and with strength. Joshua was also able to sit fairly still in his seat while the cross examination dragged on.

"Yah, I saw him. He's just wasting time now. Even the judge looked bored when he carried on about how he's the real victim. Go through the motions, right?" I remind him and he nods.

"It just sucks that it has to happen—for Emilia." He mutters and I sense he's getting wound up again.

"It does, but she's strong." Another nod. "Speaking of, are you both still going to Ravenous this week?"

"No, I gave her some tasks to work on and I want to talk to her a little more about it before we go. She's having dinner with Lexa tonight to ask her some questions. I think there is some kind of new member event in a couple of weeks and we'll go then to support the club and ease her into it. You should join us. There may be some new faces." I nod but don't answer.

Now that I've met Hazel, I feel like some things are more up in the air. If we move forward, going without her wouldn't be an option and it might be too soon to go with her. Hell, I don't even know for sure if this is something she would like to consider.

"What's on your mind?" Joshua asks and I realize he's already stood up and gathered his equipment.

"Huh? Oh." I don't make a move to stand and Joshua stays still, waiting. "What if I told you I might have met someone?"

"*Might have?* You don't know if you did?" I've amused him and now he's just mocking me.

"Well, I met someone, but it's early."

"I see. Where did you meet her?" He drops his bag and sits back down.

"At a coffee shop last week."

"She was just having coffee and you started talking to her?"

"No, she was serving it. She actually ended up spilling a

tray of coffee all over me." Joshua stares at me in silence before speaking.

There it is. He knows she was working there. I don't expect it makes a difference to Joshua. We both worked hard for the money we've earned and we know where we came from.

"So that was on Thursday then?" He asks.

"How did you know?"

"When I called you back to my office you were wearing a different suit than earlier." He replies with an air of cockiness around him. Someone is proud of his sleuthing skills.

"Aren't you a smarty pants?" He laughs at my response and I'm happy he is forgetting about our draining day in court.

"Why did she spill coffee on you? You make that good of an impression on her?" More chuckles.

"Fuck off. We collided when she was trying to serve our table."

"Well then, tell me about her."

"Her name is Hazel and she's 26. She goes to college and, from what I can tell, she's also working at least two jobs. She is different from a lot of people I know. I can't explain it. She's just—well she's extremely trusting for one."

"Anything else?" He lowers his voice as he lifts his brows and I know what he's getting at.

"I haven't gotten that far yet but it's promising. She responds positively to some of the comments I've made but I don't think she has any experience with the lifestyle."

"Interesting. So where did you leave it at?"

"She has exams, I told her I would contact her when she was done. I don't want to put a lot on her. I'm going to message her on Monday after all the exams at the college are over."

"That sounds like a good idea. Why do you think she is too trusting?"

"She has this way about her. It's small things. She doesn't lock her phone, she offered me a lot of information about herself. Maybe she's just naive. There's this innocence about her that makes me want to..." I trail off. I can't put my finger on how she makes me feel.

"Protect her?" Joshua finishes my sentence and I shrug. That's exactly what it is. She makes me want to take her and protect her. "Maybe it's just you she trusts."

"Maybe. Like I said, it's still early. With the amount of information she gave about herself, the first page of a Google search gave me enough info on her. She's taking veterinary sciences at the college. Good grades. I didn't dig deeper. I prefer to learn everything else from her."

"Why her?"

I raise my eyebrows at Joshua, asking for more information, and he expands on his question.

"What is it about her that has your attention? You don't usually like someone this quickly and by the looks of you, she's already under your skin and in your head." Unzipping his bag, he reaches for his water bottle and takes another sip.

"I don't know. She's raw and real. It's weird but I enjoyed how she spoke to me. She has an attitude but the way she listens when I tell her to do something just grabs at me. I don't know if it's going to go anywhere but I know I'm curious to find out. Does that make sense?"

"You know my history with Emilia. Of course that makes sense. So then you'll wait until she's done her exams?"

"Yes. We have court this week and I have a dinner

meeting with some new prospects on Saturday. It turns out Drakus Properties is going through a bit of an upheaval and we may be able to pinch a couple of their top sales guys. I'm just finalizing those details so I'm busy anyway."

"Nice job, Wilde." He only uses my last name when he's really impressed. Standing, he repeats his motion to leave. "I look forward to hearing more about, well, everything."

Next Monday, I'll message Hazel and ask to see her. It wasn't my intention to go without her knowing my name for long and I want to clear that up and get to know her a little better, then I'll tell her everything else.

I just hope I can wait until Monday.

10

HAZEL

*B*etween work and studying, this week has flown by while mentally crushing me as it passes. N hasn't messaged me at all since his driver dropped me off and I would be lying if I said I wasn't disappointed.

Still, I can't let it consume me. Today was my final exam and dropping my pen down on the table after I wrote my last word felt pretty amazing.

That is it. My whole year all wrapped up and now I wait to hear where I placed.

The TA caught my attention on my way out, handing me a message to stop in to my prof's office before leaving and I made my way across the campus easily as most of the students have already cleared out.

"You asked to see me?" I knock on the open door and Mr. Harris looks up from his writing.

"Yes. Thank you for dropping in, Hazel." Pointing his finger at the chair in front of his desk, I drop my bag and take a seat.

"You're welcome. Is everything okay with my work?" My worries get the better of me.

He smiles at my question and I realize I must look concerned. "They are better than okay. The results for last week's exam won't be out until tomorrow but I can tell you, you are at the top of your class." I find myself taking a deep breath. "That isn't why I asked to meet with you, though."

"Oh."

"Do you have a job lined up for the summer?"

"Not really. I had three jobs but I'm losing hours over the summer. Why?"

"Well, this is highly unusual, but it does happen. Do you remember our conversation earlier this year when you asked about the possibility of finding an apprenticeship or internship in place of some of your course load?"

I nod. I remember all of it. I was looking for a way to combine my work with education so I'm not constantly burning myself out. But there just wasn't anything available.

"Well, a wildlife rehabilitation facility just beyond the town limits contacted us yesterday. Apparently, they received some type of a financial grant to allow them to hire through an apprenticeship program and they are interested in a student from our veterinary sciences department. The job would continue through the next school year. I thought this might be of interest to you."

"Would it interfere with my courses next year?"

"Technically, we can list it as an internship credit. When school starts up, you'll be required to check in and you'll be given the course outline and materials, but you will not participate in any group projects, labs or be required to physically attend any course on campus. You would still be required to write any exams and tests that count to your final grade though."

I ask a few more questions and everything sounds like a perfect fit for me.

"This sounds too good to be true. How do I apply?" I open my bag and pull out a pen and pad to take notes.

"That's the thing. They specifically asked for you. They reviewed our class list and you are consistently at the top and they are only interested in meeting with you. If all goes well, the position is yours. I told them I would talk to you today and then set up an appointment for you to go down if you were interested. How does tomorrow afternoon sound?"

I feel my eyes blink a few times as I consider his words. Nina was right, all of my effort is starting to pay off.

"It sounds—great. Yes. Thank you."

"Wonderful. It also allows us to take on one additional student in the course next year. I'll make those arrangements when I get notification you've been placed in apprenticeship status. I'll contact them to set up a time and I'll be in touch. Congratulations, Miss Masters. This is an amazing opportunity." He writes a note on a piece of paper then, tearing it off, hands it to me and I glance to see the name and address of the sanctuary. Before I can say thank you again, a knock at the door cuts off my train of thought.

I recognize the student from one of my classes. Judging by the stressed look on his face, he needs to talk to the professor more than I do right now and I quickly gather my things and leave them alone.

I pull out my phone to message Nina as I make my way across the empty campus to our dorms.

Hazel: You won't believe what just happened.

Nina: N finally messaged you?

Hazel: No. :(
Hazel: I got a lead on a job.

Nina: Are you crazy?
Nina: You have enough of those.

Hazel: Well, you're right about that.
Hazel: But this is a job that will let me quit all of my other jobs, and it is in my field.

Nina: Are you serious?
Nina: Hazy, that's wonderful.
Nina: But what about school?

Hazel: It's an apprenticeship and it is approved by my professors.
Hazel: I get credit to work.

Nina: WHAT?
Nina: That is amazing.
Nina: Wait. Do you have to move off campus?

Hazel: I asked and they said no because I'm still a student.

Hazel: Instead of going to school, I'll just go to work.

Hazel: It pays really well, too.

Hazel: I can look for a cheap car to get me out there.

Nina: This is insane.

Nina: I'm so happy for you.

Nina: What's the job?

Hazel: It's a rescue and rehabilitation organization. I'll be working outside with wildlife. I have a meeting with them tomorrow.

Nina: I'm at our place for a bit, just finishing packing for my visit home. I can help you pick out an outfit for your meeting.

Hazel: Great. Almost there.

I turn the corner and our residence comes into view as I type my last message.

I can't believe my luck. Finding a job in my field when I was just about to call the search off for the summer. Now I can do what I love and get credit for it next year.

Once I know the time of the interview, I'll message Paul and confirm our lunch tomorrow.

Nina is dancing around the apartment, pulling clothes out of drawers and matching them to items in her closet when I open the door.

"How about this one?" She meets me in our living room, holding up a fancy number that almost looks like a prom dress and I drop my bags on our sofa and shoot her an incredulous look.

"Nina, I'm meeting about a job with wildlife, not accepting an Academy Award." I laugh.

"Fair enough. I'm just so excited for you." Beaming, she turns and makes her way to her room, tossing the dress on her bed and I wander over to dig through the mountain of clothes she managed to pull out in the five minutes it took me to get home.

"Thanks. Me, too."

"Are you sure you'll be okay here for the next few weeks? I'm going to miss you so much."

"Don't worry about me. I'll be fine. If it goes well tomorrow, I'll have this new job to get used to. I'll have to look for a car and put in my resignation at the club and I won't return to the library in the fall. I'll be sad to leave, but having something regular will be awesome. You'll be back before you know it." I know Nina is dreading her trip back home to see her parents. "And some of the group are still around."

"Oh, who? I thought everyone was taking off."

"Well, I guess Paul is the only one I know. I forgot to tell you, we are going out to lunch tomorrow. He asked me out."

"Like on a date?" She drops the clothes in her hands and sits down, waiting for the details.

"That's what I said. Yeah, it's a friend date. It's just lunch." I shrug then pull out a light sweater from the pile. This would probably be a great fit for the interview.

"Oh, look at you. A new job, a new guy." She raises her brow.

"We're just getting to know each other." Nina makes a humming noise at my answer. "What?"

"Hazy, you know the guy's been into you since the beginning of this year, right?"

"What? No. What?"

Nodding, "That guy has been asking about you for months. I didn't say anything because I know how hard you've been working and this has been a killer year for you. I know your funds were running low and you were trying to keep up. But now you have some time to breathe, right?" I consider her comment and agree. "And Paul seems like just the thing to distract you from that N guy."

"Ugh. Don't bring him up." I was just getting him out of my system.

"Still nothing?"

"Not a word. The guy tells me to go home and study, then nothing. I'm so far off his radar, he probably forgot about me the next morning." Placing her hand on mine, she taps a few times.

"You can always text the number in your phone." I pause as she offers the suggestion.

I can't do that.

"No way. Besides, I deleted it a couple of days ago." I wince as I confess and she looks shocked.

"You what?"

"Having it there messed with my head. It was too tempting. So I deleted everything and now I couldn't get in touch with him even if I wanted to." I shrug and wince at my answer. I'm sure Nina thinks I'm crazy. I almost texted him three times and having his information in my phone only served as a reminder that he isn't contacting me and it began to weigh on me.

"Wow. Hazy. You're kind of fierce."

"You think?" I smile. Fierce has never been a word I would use to describe myself. "Let's hope this hellion lands that apprenticeship tomorrow. For all I know, they could have approached a few schools. I could be walking into an interview."

"You sure you don't want this dress then? It's backless." She holds up a little sparkly red number and attempts a sultry wink but her giggle gives her away.

"Funny." I laugh and hold the sweater I like across my chest and she clasps her hands and smiles in agreement.

"You'll do great, Hazy. I'm running around for most of the day tomorrow. Will you text me when you're done?"

"You'll be the first person who knows."

"Great. And we're still on for group drinks on Saturday before I have to head home?"

"I wouldn't miss it for the world."

11

HAZEL

"Thanks again for meeting me for lunch a little early." I smile at Paul. I'm lucky I have my interview this afternoon or I would have been very underdressed for this restaurant.

The moment I stepped into the room, my sweater felt like it was both two sizes too big and too small. Paul seemed happy with his choice of places and I imagine he's trying to make a good impression, but this just isn't me.

"I don't mind. I'm glad you could make it. That's crazy about your interview. Apprenticeships are hard to come by around here." He finishes his veal and I look down at my salad.

I'm nervous about my meeting this afternoon and a large meal will only make it worse. Also, the prices on the menu were intimidating and I won't order something extravagant just because someone else is paying.

"They are. I guess I was in the right place." He smiles at my answer and I go for a question of my own. "Nina tells me you're in your final year of Business but this is your first year here. Where did you go before?"

"I was at Stanford. It wasn't my thing. I wanted to be closer to home and the prestige of the degree isn't necessary for what I plan on doing so I transferred back here. What about you? Why did you choose this college?"

"It's a solid, well-respected program in its field and it is close to my family. Kind of the same as you, I guess. It's perfect for what I want to do." As I answer, Paul looks down to his meal and I take a second to check him out.

Paul is clean cut and good looking. I've seen girls around us watch him when we are all out together and he's been nothing but kind to me. I'm sure many of those girls would kill to be sitting here with him right now. So why don't I feel anything more than a friendly fondness for him?

I barely had any time with N and it looks like I won't see him again, but I still felt more of a connection with him than I do with Paul and that should be enough of a sign that I don't want anything more than his friendship and I almost feel sad. It would be easier if I felt something more for him.

What the hell is wrong with me?

"So you're staying around then? That's great news."

"Fingers crossed, I still have to meet with them this afternoon."

"I have a feeling you'll do great. Are your parents sad they won't see you this summer?"

"My mom is okay. I'm going to try to get a few days off and go see her near the end of our break. My dad passed away a few years ago." I always hate this part in the conversation. When someone finds out you've lost a loved one. It's always awkward.

"Oh, damn. I'm sorry, Hazel."

"It's fine. You didn't know."

Our conversation lulls while we finish our last few bites. I've found comfort in the silence others find so uncomfortable.

"Are we still going out tomorrow?" Paul quickly changes the subject and I don't mind.

"We are. It'll be nice to have a last dinner before everyone leaves for the summer."

"Do you know what time we're meeting up?" I knit my brows trying to remember if we had agreed on a time.

"I'm not sure. I'll message Nina." Flipping my phone over, I turn it on and send the text as the waitress drops the bill at the table."

"I'm going to use the washroom before we leave. Watch my stuff?" I stand and Paul rises with me then sits back down, scanning the bill and pulling out his wallet.

Leaving my bag and phone at the table, I make my way to the side washrooms and take my time. I'm not good in formal situations and sitting there, quietly, at the table while he paid the bill would have felt too awkward.

I earn my fair share of glances as I wash my hands in slow motion then make my way back to the table, happy that Paul appears to be getting ready to leave. Tuning my phone over, I check to make sure I'm still on schedule to catch the bus to my interview and we make our way out to his car.

"I had a really great time today, Hazel. We should get together again when you have time." My mind is shifting to my meeting this afternoon and I don't have it in me to discuss our friendship right now so I smile and tell him I enjoyed our lunch and next time is on me.

In truth, It'll be nice to have a friend around this

summer. With Nina gone for most of it and my possible job, I have no one else to do anything with.

I still can't wrap my head around my meeting today. My professor was right, it wasn't an interview as much as it was an icebreaker. Shanna, the organization's head told me, they received a private grant for the purpose of hiring an apprentice and they jumped at the chance.

The sanctuary is a little piece of heaven and I felt like I was dreaming during my tour. I can't believe I get to spend my days here next year, working hands on and getting credit instead of going to class.

Making my way out here on a bus proved to be harder than I thought it would and I ended up calling a cab to drive me the last 20 minutes out. Luckily that will be changing soon, too.

After the interview, I decided against catching a bus to the club and stayed in the cab for the whole ride back. This gave me the extra time I needed to message Nina without any distractions.

Hazel: Nina. I got the job.

Nina: OMG. Congrats!!!
Nina: Tell me everything!

Hazel: Well, I start one week of training on Monday. My last shift at the club is tonight, then I was getting laid off for the

summer so it all works out. I just need to work out shifts at the coffee house.

Nina: So you get to have a bit of a summer before you start. You said you were buying a car?

Hazel: It turns out they have an old company car I can use if I don't mind their logo on the side and I just pay for the gas I use.

Nina: Hazy, that's wonderful.

Hazel: It is. I can start saving for things now.
Hazel: I don't even remember what that feels like anymore.

Nina: Oh, girl. I'm really happy for you. Lots to celebrate this weekend. We still on for tomorrow?

Hazel: Yes. Working my last shift tonight then I'm off until next week.
Hazel: I've gotta go. I'm at Echo. Will you be home after my shift?

Nina: I will but I'll be asleep, I have a lot

**to do tomorrow before I leave but we'll
have time tomorrow night.
Nina: How was your date?**

**Hazel: I'll tell you about it tomorrow. I'll
be quiet when I get in.**

The taxi stops in front of The Echo Club and I don't
have enough time before my shift starts to explain my *date*
with Paul. I'm not even completely sure of anything
myself yet.

Now that my meeting is out of the way, I can think more
about it tonight and have a better idea of how I'm going to
approach him in the morning.

12

HAZEL

"*I* thought you told everyone to be here around nine." Checking my watch, we've been here for about half an hour and it's only 8:30.

The place is laid back and relaxed; a different scene from my date with Paul and the perfect place for our last get together before everyone leaves for the summer. Suits mix with casual dress easily and the dimmer lighting allows for a more private feeling.

"Oh, I did. I just want you to myself for an hour. We've both been busy and we haven't had our girl time. These last few weeks have been crazy." Nina says as the waiter pours our wine and leaves the bottle between us.

"I'm going to miss you." I take a long look at my friend. I don't know how I would have gotten through my workload this year without her.

"Me, too. You know, you're my first friend I am actually going to miss. I mean, I came here for school and I never even felt like messaging any of my high school friends. I'm legit messaging you every day." Her promise makes me smile. It feels nice to know I have someone, other than my mother, checking in on me.

"Well, I'll be here and I'll be messaging you back, constantly." I hold my pinky up and she links hers with mine in a promise.

"Okay so spill. Tell me about your date with Paul."

"It was fun. I'm glad I went, but I don't feel anything romantic for him." I confess with a shrug.

"Oh, really?"

"Is that weird? I mean, he's attractive and nice and funny, but he feels like a friend to me. I guess I'll have to talk with him about it."

"Aww. I'm sorry. I thought you'd be good together. I don't know a lot about him, but he seems cool."

"Maybe, but I don't feel it right now. I'm hoping we can hang out a bit more over the summer to see if I feel differently, but don't you think I'd feel something small if there was even a chance?"

Nina considers my question before answering. "You're probably right. And if you talk to him sooner, you can keep your friendship intact."

"That's what I was thinking." I agree, taking a sip of my wine when my phone vibrates on the table.

Unknown number: Good evening.

"Who's that?"

"Hmm. Looks like a wrong number. Doesn't matter. It's girl time." I respond and hold my glass up, clinking it with Nina's.

"I like the sound of that. I'm going to order some appies. Cassie has shit-taste in food. Well, except for that Sake. That was really good." She giggles. "Oh, hey, how did your bosses take the news?"

"They were fine with it, mostly because summer gets a little quiet near campus. The library is closed for the summer and I took my name off the library list for the fall. The Echo Club operates on a skeleton crew so I don't have a job until the fall anyway. The only thing is the coffee shop. They aren't sure if they can keep me on now. I should know in a week or so."

"Wow, you've been busy. You don't even get any time off before you start your new job."

"I don't mind so much. I'd just be sitting around missing you." I wink.

"You're making me wish I was staying here with you." Nina looks genuinely regretful and I'm not sure if it's because she wants to spend time with me or avoid her family.

"You'll have fun." I try to convince her with a smile.

"Yes, but it gets old, fast. I go home. My parents throw their expensive parties. I show up, I smile, people who want some of my family's money talk at me. I nod, I leave. My friends are all about appearance and being popular. I hate it. I wish my parents had time for me one on one, but they don't. I get more out of my time here with you."

"I never told you this before, but I'm happy they put us together. In our room." Nina smiles at my confession.

"You're the realest thing in my life, Hazy. I'm happy, too."

The silent buzzing of my phone catches my attention again.

Unknown number: I've been thinking about you.

"Do you need to get that?" Nina asks as I reread the message.

"No. I think it's a wrong number. If they message again, I'll let them know." I look up and catch our group out of the corner of my eyes as I answer. "Oh look, everyone is here."

Cassie waves and makes her way around the tables to our own followed by Paul and a couple other friends. One by one everyone claims an empty seat but Paul keeps moving around the table and, placing his hands on my shoulders, leans into my space.

Thinking fast, I lean back and hold my hands out in a hug gesture and it takes him a second before he recovers and returns my friendly hug before walking to the empty chair.

"I see you guys started without us." Paul clears his throat and says in Nina's direction as he takes the last seat.

"We did. I wanted her to myself for a bit before I left." She answers, refilling our glasses as Cassie reaches for a menu.

"Aw. You guys are so cute. Hey, Hazy. Maybe I can room with you next year." Cassie looks up from the food choices and winks telling me she's joking but Nina isn't having any of it.

"Cassie, I know we are friends, but I will cut you. There are only two things I am possessive about. One is cake. I think we all know what the other one is." The table laughs at her response as she continues, "Besides, you'll just corrupt our little Hazy."

Cassie nods, "This is true. I don't have a body like this so

I can sit at home by myself. Speaking of which, anyone notice the older guy checking this table out? He's hella hot."

I realize I'm going to miss this banter as I laugh along with our table and glance across the lounge.

My breathing feels forced and a lump forms in my throat as my eyes focus on the man everyone is now looking at; the handsome stranger who looks up and stares right back at the table and not just the table.

N is looking straight at me.

At once, all of my senses become heightened and I feel out of place as I watch N talk with the other two men at his table while taking the occasional glance in my direction.

Oh, he definitely sees me. My heart thuds into my chest at the thought. I can't even tell Nina that it's him right now. Not in front of Paul. I haven't told him I just want to be friends yet. And part of me wants to keep this to myself.

I want to keep N to myself.

As everyone at the table takes turns glancing up at the stranger, my phone vibrates in my hands.

Unknown number: I gave you two rules, Miss Masters.

Hazel: Pardon?

Unknown number: I've been sitting here for 45 minutes watching you ignore my messages when my rule was to not leave me waiting.

"Shit." Muttering under my breath, I'm instantly on guard when Nina startles at my voice.

"What's wrong?" She looks concerned and I scramble to cover for myself.

"Oh, sorry. I just remembered I forgot to tell my boss something. I'm just going to send off a text, I'll be right back. Order some food, I'm fine with whatever." Waving my phone, I excuse myself and hightail it down the hall to the washroom before texting N back.

Hazel: I didn't know it was you.

N: How did you not know it was me?

I pause for half a minute, staring at my phone. I don't know how to respond. He put all of his information in my phone and I deleted it.

N: I'm waiting...

Hazel: I deleted your number.

N: Interesting.
N: Tell me then, are you not interested in considering an arrangement?

Hazel: I am but you didn't message. I thought you forgot about me. I felt stupid.

N: Did you tell your friends about me just now?

Hazel: No.

N: Hmmm. I'd like to speak to you, outside for a moment.

Hazel: I can meet you out front in two minutes.

N: You'll meet me out back. In one.

13

HAZEL

You'll meet me out back, in one.

His challenge sends shivers down my spine. Stepping out of the washroom, I turn toward the back entrance and quietly open the door leading into the alley and away from everyone at the table.

I hear my breath in my head as seconds feel like minutes. For a moment, I consider chickening out and going back inside but I can't bring myself to walk in the direction of the door. I won't pass this up. Instead I pace, wringing my hands together until the creak of the door stops me from moving.

There he stands in the alley only six feet away from me. He's completely still yet I feel the force of a storm whip through the air around us and I will myself to maintain eye contact when all I want to do is find something to hide behind.

"Give me your phone, Hazel." He takes a slow step toward me, reaching out his hand and I look down to my own, clutching it tight in my sweaty palm.

"You told me never to give my phone to strangers." My courage fades fast as he takes another step.

"Your cheeky attempt to cover for the fact that you ignored one of my rules is not earning you any points, Miss Masters. I won't ask again." He chides and I break eye contact.

"Fine, here. I said I was sorry." Handing him the phone, I watch as he adds his information back in.

"Oh, in fact, my dear, you have not yet said you are sorry. And that's because you aren't. But you will be." His words carry intrigue and my mouth goes dry at the thought of how sorry he could possibly make me feel. Handing my phone back, "You should lock your phone, Hazel. Anyone can access it. It isn't safe."

I feel my face heat up at his concern. "Um, thank you."

"Turn around and place your palms on the wall, Hazel."

"Why?" The question is extraneous. I think I know why he wants me up against the wall but I need him to spell it out.

"You will come to understand that once I decide you have a punishment owed, you will not be in a position to question me. Your only responsibility is to accept it and comply." He waits passively for me to consider his response and I want more information.

"I don't understand." In truth, I don't understand. Not on a personal level. I've never had anyone treat me this way and I've never felt my heart beating so hard.

"I think on some level, you do. There is something deep inside of you that understands what I am offering or you would have already left me out here and gone back inside to your friends." I look at the closed door. He's right. All I have to do is put one foot in front of the other and leave him out here, but I won't. I'm drawn to him and I want to follow this path to see where it leads.

"That's what I don't understand." My stomach flutters as I admit my inexperience.

N's eyes soften as he takes another step toward me and I welcome his proximity.

"It's just the two of us here. Be honest with yourself. Do you like the way I speak to you?"

"I—think so." My voice is quiet, almost a whisper. My admission is more for myself than him.

"Why?" His tone matches my own as he lowers his voice.

"I don't know. I think about it all of the time. I've thought about you since we first spoke. It's so different from…" I allow my words to linger as I contemplate what I'm saying.

" … from the way you've been treated?" He finishes my thought.

"Yes."

"And you respond to it? To me?"

"Yes." I nod as I answer.

"Tell me, Hazel. Why did you delete my information?" He looks hurt and I want to tell him everything. I don't want to hide from him and I don't want to hide from myself.

"I couldn't stop thinking about you. We've barely said anything to each other and I can't stop replaying it over and over in my head. I was confused. The temptation to message you was too much and I was hurt because you didn't message me." His lips press together in a thin line at my answer.

"I understand, I've been thinking about you." I feel light at the thought I crossed his mind, too.

"Then why didn't you message me?" I feel my own hurt come out with my words.

"I've been busy on a couple of urgent business projects. I

told you I would give you your time for your school. I was going to contact you on Monday but I saw you here tonight."

"Oh." Now that he says it, I realize I acted prematurely. I should have given him more time. I shouldn't have entertained the thoughts I did.

"Is that Paul? Your... friend?" N tilts his head in the direction of the back door to the restaurant.

"Yes, he's just my friend."

"You should tell him that."

I can't stop the grin spreading across my face. "Careful, jealousy isn't a good look for you." I speak his words back to him and he offers me a hungry smirk in return.

"Touché. Which reminds me, your failure to follow my rules and your temerity have earned you a punishment. Palms on the wall, I'm going to spank you."

"WHAT?" The air around me feels thick and my world freezes. I don't even know what *temerity* means but I get the feeling asking right now isn't going to help my defence.

"Tsk, tsk, tsk. You know how I feel about that word." He isn't even attempting to hide his enjoyment.

"I beg your pardon." I correct myself.

"Better." He waits for my answer.

"But what do you mean? You want to spank me?" I wasn't ready for his candor and I feel myself start to blink excessively.

"Correction. I *am going to* spank you, Miss Masters. And we need to make this quick, your friends will be missing you." His eyes stay on me and I feel exposed. I forgot about my friends.

Images of them finding me being spanked in an alley freeze me in place.

"I don't think I can—" I answer, my breathing becoming deeper.

"I'm telling you, you will, Miss Masters. Palms—wall—Do it without another word and I won't take down your pants." I almost choke on the thought that I might be standing here with my ass bared to a stranger in the alleyway.

I'm more surprised that the thought excites me. It's now I notice that N is still standing still, watching me. I'm not being forced into this, he is waiting for my consent. He's waiting for me to place myself on the wall.

While he's controlling this moment, he's waiting for me to hand over the power to control the narrative of our relationship. He said it himself; I can leave. But in doing so I would be telling him I am not interested in this, and that would be a lie.

I stare at him for a tense minute then turn to the side and walk over to the cold brick of the building. I feel every moment, every sensation, as I lift my hands, spread my fingers and make contact with the rough stone siding as his scent closes in on me and he touches me, intimately, for the first time.

In these few seconds, I feel our connection change. There is no flirting; we're no longer dancing around each other. This is my consent. I've made myself vulnerable and placed myself in his hands and we have both accepted this new, unspoken dynamic.

"Very good." His fingers trail up the back of my thigh, over my clothes and lightly glide over the curve of my ass. Leaning his body against me, his breath hot on my neck. "Why am I spanking you, Hazel?" Everything outside of us fades away. His question makes my body tense in anticipation.

"B—because I didn't answer my phone." I turn my face from his to the wall.

The first spank switches something on inside of me. The dark alley lights up and my senses swirl together as my chest swells into my throat. I've never felt so right as his open hand lands on my ass as he starts listing all of my infractions.

"For disobeying my rule and not responding promptly when I saw you were not busy."

Smack

My chest feels tight as the impact of his palm jolts through me.

"For deleting my number."

Smack

Nerve endings ignite, sending mixed signals all over my body and I have to force myself not to clench my thighs together in response.

"And this is for your relaxed attitude toward your obedience to me, also known as your *temerity*." I can almost feel him smile to himself.

Taking his last swing, I feel the cool breeze fill the space he leaves as he steps back from me and I miss his contact immediately as tears fill my eyes.

"Are you okay, Baby?" His gentle voice and pet name make me suck in a breath and I open my mouth to answer when only a squeak tumbles out so I nod instead.

I feel my body hesitate before I take my hands off the wall and tuck them into my chest as I turn to face him. As much as I try to make eye contact, I can't; and, in the end I give in and lower my head, taking a half step toward him, searching for comfort. His hands are warm as they travel up my arms, then he pulls me in and wraps himself around me in a reassuring embrace.

It's a conflicting sensation, seeking comfort in the hands that punish and a mountain of confusion fills me. The reality of my situation hits me at the same time. My friends are still inside and I just let a stranger spank me in a back alley during dinner.

His fingers feel gentle running along my cheek, cupping my chin and pulling my attention up to him.

"Is there anything you want to say?" His eyes bounce around my face as he speaks.

I close my eyes, searching my thoughts before meeting his gaze to say the first thing on my mind. "I—I'm sorry I disobeyed your rule and deleted your contact information and I apologize for my attitude about it."

"I accept your apology. I understand this is new for you. I'm willing to show leniency toward your inexperience, but you will still face punishment and the severity will grow. Some will end with you in tears. But trust me, you'll come to crave discipline. There is a need in you to find balance." His tone is comforting.

This doesn't make sense but there is something else I want to say. I squirm in his arms as he follows my lead and releases me from his hold. "I want to say thank you?"

"You're saying that like it's a question." His smile barely registers but I'm sure I've amused him.

"It just doesn't make sense. Why am I thanking you for doing that?"

"Because I gave you what you needed." His answer is both so simple and so complex. "You were very good for me, Hazel. Tell me how you feel."

The question catches me off guard. I feel our time

passing. If I don't get back inside, someone will come looking for me.

"I... I don't know. I feel... confused and a little tired. I need to process this." I mean, I still don't know the guy's name and it doesn't seem like now is a good time to ask.

"That's understandable. That was only four strikes. I can honestly say, this will be the lightest punishment you will ever receive I wish I had more time with you. Your friends will be missing you and I need to get back to my table." We both know we are running out of time. "I'm here for you if you need me. If you are feeling off, just head to the washroom and text me. If you leave the restaurant, I'll assume you are okay and I will contact you shortly. And, Hazel?"

"Yes?"

"Don't leave me waiting next time."

"I... I won't."

He smiles and nods his head toward the door, allowing me to leave first. I turn and pull the heavy door open, making my way into the hall. As I pass the washroom, Paul steps into the hall from the restaurant and I jump.

"Oh, hey. We were wondering where you were."

"You startled me. I'm just heading back."

"Did you get in touch with your boss?" He asks his question but my mind is focused on the door to the alley.

"About what?" I respond and he looks confused. I remember, too late about my little lie. "Oh right. Yes. Everything is okay."

The door to the alley groans on its hinges and we both look to see N enter and glance between us before turning into the men's washroom and Paul looks back at me and I attempt to walk back to the group before he steps in front of me.

"Listen, about earlier. I thought we had a great date."

I wish I had a better place to handle this conversation but I can't go back to our group with Paul thinking we are more than friends.

"I had a great time. I enjoy your company, Paul. But I just don't think we are a good fit for anything beyond friends." He straightens up at my response but doesn't back away and I stay still, hoping N doesn't come out of the washroom to this.

"Oh, okay."

"I value your friendship, Paul and wanted to talk to you about it early so I don't damage what we have." As I clarify, he takes a step out of my space.

"I appreciate that, but I think you're making a mistake. Luckily, I have the summer to try to change your mind... as your friend, of course."

I'm not sure where he's going with this but I decide to let it go. "We should get back to the group."

I don't wait for his reply. I lead the way and notice our table is now covered in appetizers and drinks. As I slide into my seat, I wince. How could I have forgotten I was just spanked. I feel my cheeks warm all over again at the reminder.

I have a dark little secret. No one here knows what just happened to me and I feel a surge of excitement at the thought. This is unlike me.

Lifting the plate in front of me, I choose a few random appetizers. It doesn't matter what I've chosen, I'm not sure I could eat anything right now with everything that just happened.

"Oh look, he's back." Cassie attempts to whisper but falls short and the table looks at N's group as he sits back down with the two other men.

I can't hold my attention on the table for long before I find myself retreating inward in embarrassment. Everyone at the table is looking over, everyone except Paul. I watch him out of the corner of my eyes as he watches me carefully and I wonder if he knows something is up.

"Man, I'd like to get my hands on him." Cassie says as everyone's attention returns to our own space.

"Oh?" I aim for aloof as I pick up a chicken wing and stuff it into my face to hide any guilty look I might have.

"Yeah, I mean just look at him. He's hot in a mature kind of way." She defends her initial assessment and I realize I have about four years on everyone at the table. I suddenly feel old

"Really? Are you straight up telling me it has nothing to do with his money, Cass?" Nina's question surprises me.

"Well, that doesn't hurt either."

"Wait. You guys know who that is?" I blurt out the question and Paul looks up from his plate.

"Hazy, everyone here knows who he is. That's Noah Wilde. He's one of the top guys at Connor Realty. He was invited to our marketing class for a series of lectures. I mean, not like anyone here actually heard what he was saying. That smile could strip paint." Nina giggles and Cassie agrees.

"He could strip something else..." Cassie laughs and the table joins in as I begin to feel a little protective. I look over to the table and catch his gaze as he looks in the direction of our laughter.

"Oh, wow. I didn't know." I take a sip of my wine to wash down the lump in my throat.

Well, at least he's not a criminal, I think to myself. But he does have a lot of money and that isn't something I ever considered I would go for, especially after everything.

But he isn't like everyone else. There's something different and tempting about him that isn't letting me go.

I know his name. Somehow this doesn't feel right.

Glancing back to his table, I wonder what is going through N's mind, then silently chastise myself. Look at me. I now know his first and last name and I won't let myself say it. I'm still calling him N. Maybe he was right. Maybe I understand more than I realize.

I haven't earned his name, yet.

But I want to.

14

NOAH

*T*he laughter from Hazel's group catches my attention and I take a quick glance to let her know I see her when the other faces around the table casually attempt to look away.

I recognize a couple of her friends from a series of lectures I was invited to participate in at the college earlier this year. If they remember me, then it's only a matter of time before she knows my name.

I don't mind. I want to hear her say my name almost as much as I want to hear her laugh.

"Let's get to the bottom line. Drakus is a great company and a solid competitor, but it's no secret, recent changes have made things difficult for a lot of its staff. I'm going to go out on a limb and say *present company included* or you would have both passed at my request for a meeting." As I speak, I watch over one of the guys shoulders and, one by one, her table glances over again. Everyone except for her and I still feel my fingers tingle at the contact from earlier.

"Working at Drakus has been very rewarding but I think

I speak for the both of us—", the second gentleman at the table nods in agreement as he continues, "—when I say we are interested in hearing what you have to say."

While these negotiations are far from over, I offer them a broad scope of Connor Realty and how they could fit into the company without sharing too much of our business plans. Having senior sales experience like these two would quickly replace the gap Brent and Sean left. After a while, our conversation turns personal as we get into sports and current events. My sales pitch is over. They have some things to consider and I'll need to talk to Joshua about next steps before we come to the table with a serious offer.

As we shoot the shit, I look back to the occasional glance my way. Hazel is talking with the other women at the table, but it isn't her I notice. Her friend Paul keeps looking over at her and shifting his gaze back to my group and he doesn't look happy. It was the same look he shot me when I came in from the alley.

I'm not sure he knows anything is going on between Hazel and I but he sure recognizes the competition. His glare at her is predatory, territorial. I know because I feel the same.

"Tell me about your current sales team. We know Connor Realty also went through a setback recently." Clive asks as I turn my focus back to my meeting.

After going through our numbers and recalculating the sales Brent and Sean stole from their own team, it turns out we have a couple of staff we severely under recognized. While Brent and Sean were good at their jobs, two other salespeople quickly rose to the surface.

"It was a blow, but it's in the hands of the courts so I can't discuss much of it. Our sales team is resilient. They are focused and they are an amazing group. We would be happy to count you among them."

"And Rosalyn Murphy? How is she?" Maynard asks, catching me off guard.

"She's one of our top sales people. How do you know Rosalyn?" She's Emilia's best friend and those closest to her call her Rosie but I won't use the nickname with Maynard since he hasn't used it.

"She's been a thorn in May's side for a while. The top three biggest sales he lost last year went to her." Clive laughs at his buddy's misfortune as Maynard takes a drink.

"I see. She is tenacious." I chuckle.

After the sales numbers were recalculated to show the accurate sales, Rosie rose to the top of our sales team.

"That she is." Maynard mutters his reply to himself and I sense an undertone of something else in his voice.

I've seen Maynard once outside of our business related functions. It was at a newcomer evening at Ravenous about a year ago but I haven't seen him since which doesn't mean much. Many show up because they are curious or want to meet more people in their community. Some stay, others don't come back for many reasons. It could be that it isn't for them after all or they prefer to keep their private life private, or they didn't find what they were looking for—or they did.

"So tell me Noah, when will we hear more about our possibilities with Connor Realty?" Maynard catches himself and switches back to business quickly.

"Give me some time to talk with Joshua. He will definitely want to sit down with you to discuss everything in more detail. I'll contact both of you this week if that's acceptable." I offer and both men nod as the waiter brings me the bill.

As we leave, I make a point of not looking at Hazel's table. I sense she's chosen not to tell anyone about me yet and I don't want to confirm Paul's suspicions by stealing a glance. It's up to her to share with her own group as I shared with Joshua and I'll let that unfold at a pace she's comfortable with.

Once we're outside, we shake hands and separate toward our own vehicles. I had Marcus park at the far end of the parking lot. As I near the vehicle, he steps out and opens the back door.

"Where to, Mr. Wilde?" I stop and look around as he asks. We are far enough removed from the building but I still have a good view of the front door.

"Nowhere just yet, Marcus. I need to make some calls." I get into the car and grab for my notepad to write down some information about my meeting before leaving a short message for Joshua about my conversation with Maynard and Clive.

Having two seasoned sales managers like them on our team will go a long way in keeping our own momentum going and it would ease a lot of my workload at the office. I make a note to check Rosalyn's sales files. She seems to have made an impression on one of the guys and I think her role within our team needs to be reconsidered. She is definitely one of our best sales assets at the moment and I don't want to lose her like Drakus is about to lose their top two sales guys.

I have a couple of other calls to make but they can wait a day. Marcus sits in the front seat, waiting for a destination but I'm not ready to leave yet. I know where I want to go right now, I want to take a stroll down that back alley and relive my earlier time with Hazel.

Stretching out my fingers in my lap I play our

conversation over and over in my mind. Her hitched breaths, small gasps for air as my palm made the connection against her ass. The rosy flush in her cheeks and her wide eyes. Everything is better than I had ever thought it would be.

I've scened before but a connection, this connection, has never been there. In hindsight, the alley wasn't a good time for it. I should have waited until I could provide more care and comfort for her at the very least. I should check on her even though I said I'd leave it until tomorrow.

Movement at the front of the restaurant catches my attention. The first two people walk out and I know instantly, it's Hazel's group. She follows behind with one of her girlfriends and Paul walks quietly behind them. That guy doesn't sit right with me.

Everyone loiters in the lot for a few minutes before splitting into smaller groups and I watch her get into a car with one of her girlfriends. I wait until they've driven away before sending her a message.

Noah: I noticed you leaving and wanted to see how you are feeling.

I see the dots as she begins typing her reply almost instantly and it pleases me to see she's following her rules.

Hazel: I thought you left already.

Noah: I did. My meeting was done. I stayed behind in the parking lot making some phone calls. I wanted to be here in

case you needed me after our time in the
alley.

**Hazel: That was very kind of you. I'm
feeling good. Really good :)**

**Noah: I take care of what is mine, Miss
Masters.**

Hazel: And I am... yours?

Noah: Yes. You are.
Noah: Are you going home?

**Hazel: No, we are going out to a late
movie.**

Noah: Everyone?

Hazel: Yes, all of us.

I want to caution her about Paul but stop short. I could
be overreacting because of my feelings for her and she's with
all of her friends. I change the topic to get the thought out of
my head.

**Noah: Judging by the looks on your
friend's faces, I assume you know who I
am now?**

Hazel: Yes.

Noah: Who am I?

Hazel: You are N.

Wow. Now it's my turn to suck in a breath of air. I read and reread her response, my lips stretching into a wicked grin. She is definitely the one I want.

Noah: That's my VERY good girl.
Noah: Tell me, Hazel, did you enjoy my hands on you earlier?

Hazel: Yes.

Noah: Were you relieved when I stopped spanking you?

Hazel: No.

Noah: And why is that?

Hazel: I wanted more.
Hazel: I don't know what else there is, but I felt
Hazel: I don't know how I felt.
Hazel: It's strange to type but you make me want more even though I don't know what 'more' is.

I have to say there is something to be said for communicating by text. Sometimes sitting with our own thoughts and without having to look at the person we're talking about, can build a lot of confidence and opening up becomes easier. I look forward to the day when she speaks directly to me like this.

Noah: Thank you for your honesty.

Hazel: Why did you do that?
Hazel: In public?

Noah: Spank you?

Hazel: Yes.

Noah: Because you earned it.
Noah: You've been earning that since the moment I met you.
Noah: You've earned more than what I gave you in the alley.
Noah: Do you agree?

I'm pushing her a bit, but I want to leave her with some things to think about.

Hazel: Yes.

Noah: I thought some of your friends recognized me and wanted some time alone with you before you found out who I was.

Hazel: I understand.

Noah: Does this change anything between us?

Hazel: No. You make me feel like you can see me. Another me, I didn't even know was in here.

Noah: It isn't another you, it is the complete you, I see.

Hazel: I never thought of looking at it like that.

Noah: I'm glad I could offer that point of view. I want to show you more about yourself, Hazel.

Hazel: I want that, too.

Noah: Very well. Enjoy your time with your friends. You may message me if you need. Otherwise, I will contact you tomorrow. Good night, Hazel.

Hazel: Good night, N.

She's left me with a lot to think about as well. I'm not dealing with someone who is knowledgeable in my lifestyle.

Little rules and a small spanking in a private alley is mild. I can't rush anything with her.

I need to move at her pace and we need to set some initial guidelines. No matter how much of a fit she is for me, she needs to feel safe as she explores herself and that will mean holding back some aspects of myself until the time is right.

"Take me home, Marcus. Thank you." The car pulls out of the lot as I go over our text conversation.

While I will take my time, this is one journey I am looking forward to. I'm excited at the prospect of being the one to guide her and share in her experiences and I'm looking forward to seeing her again.

15

HAZEL

*M*y room in our dorm looks like a bomb went off. Dresses, tops and pants drape over the bed and dresser and, suddenly, I don't like any of my clothes. I changed my outfit three times and I'm still not sure I made the right choice.

My appearance has never been an issue for me. I haven't been on many dates recently but dressing for them was never something I obsessed over.

Tonight is different. N is different and I find myself thinking about his reaction to me. I want my choices to please him and nothing I own seems to fit right.

To add to this fashion disaster, Nina is on a flight home to her family now. We woke early Sunday morning so I could drive her to the airport. I wish I had gotten his text before she left, I could have asked for her advice.

N: I would like to see you tonight. I will have Marcus pick you up at 5 if you are available.

I glance at the message on my phone again. No matter how many times I read it, I am no closer to knowing where I am going or what we are doing but I answered him almost instantly to tell him I was available.

I should have just asked him what we were doing but somehow knowing the answer might be worse.

Every other time we've seen each other, it hasn't been planned. I almost prefer it that way in comparison to fretting all day about every detail, which is exactly what I'm doing right now.

The knock at the door startles me and I jump off of the mountain of clothes and head for the door, checking the time on the microwave as I pass by.

4:45.

N's driver is early but it doesn't matter, I'm ready to go. If I stayed here much longer it would just mean another wardrobe change.

"Hi, Hazel." The contrast of Paul's voice when I was expecting Marcus causes me to pause.

"Oh, hi Paul. I wasn't expecting you." As I speak, his eyes drop down the length of my body. I'm not exactly dressed for a night of staying in and I fidget with the front of my sundress as it suddenly feels like it's too short.

"I know. I was driving by and thought I'd drop in and say good luck on your first day tomorrow." He points at my outfit, "Um, am I interrupting something?" As he asks the question, his eyes leave me and move into my room.

"What?" I peek down at my outfit. "Oh. Yes. I'm going out for a bit."

"Oh, I hope I'm not keeping you. Do you have a few minutes to chat?" As he asks, I look into our kitchen at the clock on the microwave. I have about 10 minutes but it's not enough time to invite him in.

"Just a couple. What's up?" I stay in my spot, blocking any entrance and he stays put.

"Is Nina around?" He glances over my shoulder and into our little apartment.

"I thought you knew she caught an early flight this morning. That was why we couldn't stay out after the movie." I was pretty sure Paul was standing right beside me when I said all of this last night.

"Oh, right. Now that sounds familiar." His sentence stops abruptly and he takes a long stare at me before continuing. "Well, you must be excited about your new job."

"I am. First day tomorrow. It's a week of training but I can't wait to just get out there. It'll be better than serving coffee all day." I laugh a little awkwardly and he takes the cue and smiles in agreement. "Are you working at your dad's resort then?"

"Yeah. It'll be pretty easy stuff." As he answers, he combs his fingers through his hair. "Hey, maybe we can get together later this week and talk about our new jobs."

"As friends." I confirm and he nods. "I'll give you a call and let you know my schedule."

"Oh, sure. So where are you heading out to?" He tries to tone down his question but I'm not entirely convinced he's on the same friend wavelength I'm on and I glance back at the clock once more.

"Um, Miss Masters?" Both of us startle and look in the direction of the voice.

"Oh hi, Marcus." I reply as N's driver comes up to stand a few feet away from us. Paul stays still beside me and I catch him giving Marcus a solid look over as I reach into the apartment and grab my things.

"Sorry I'm early. I can wait at the car if you need a couple of minutes." His eyes shift from me to Paul and back with a casual smile.

"No, I'm ready now. Paul, thank you for dropping by. I've got to get going." I spin and lock the door behind me not bothering to introduce the two to each other and neither seems interested in meeting anyway.

"No problem. Good luck at work tomorrow." Paul stretches out his arm allowing us to go first and I say my goodbyes as he takes a step in the opposite direction. Waving us off, he pulls out his phone to make a call.

Marcus walks one step in front of me while we leave my building and we make small talk about how quiet the campus has gotten since school ended.

"I apologize for interrupting, Miss Masters." Marcus says as he approaches his car, opening the back door for me and I pause before getting in.

"Nothing to apologize for." I smile, "Please call me Hazel, Marcus." Then I lean in and lower my voice. "I'm not really fancy like that. It makes me uncomfortable."

It isn't until Marcus leans in to whisper back that I realize I didn't need to be so secretive and I duck my head and escape to the back seat to avoid embarrassing myself further. As the door shuts, I look out the back window and see Paul standing on the steps watching as Marcus returns to the driver's seat and pulls away, thankful for the tinted windows hiding me from his view.

"Are we going far?"

"It's about twenty minutes this time of day. Would you like to know where we are going, Miss Masters? I am permitted to tell you." I sense a smile in his voice. To some extent, he must be aware of who N is. I mean, I'm the only one still calling him N.

"Oh um," I straighten in my seat trying to decide if I do, in fact, want to know. "No, that is okay, Marcus. I trust N's judgement." I'm not sure I sound convincing enough.

"Very well, Miss—" I clear my throat, reminding him how to address me. "—Hazel."

As the minutes go on, my curiosity begins to get the better of me. "I mean. It's not as though I'm being taken anywhere unsafe." I half snort the ridiculous thought out.

"If you say so." Marcus responds, leaving me with nothing to go on and I get the feeling he is enjoying himself.

He's going to make me ask.

More minutes tick by and I find myself looking around every time the car slows down. We're getting further into the city but it isn't downtown. Rather it seems like we are sticking to the edges as we near the waterfront.

"I hear it's going to be a little chilly this evening. Maybe I should have dressed warmer?" My sentence sounds more like a question now. It really is hard to just sit back and trust in someone else. I've spent the last eight years being the one others trust. This is different.

"I think you'll be fine, Hazel." I catch Marcus's eyes in the rear view mirror and they look like they are squinting. He must be smiling now and I cross my arms in defiance.

Another couple of minutes drag on before I break. "Okay, fine. Where are we going?" I hear him chuckle from the front seat before he answers.

"I am taking you to his place. He's making you dinner and I hope you're hungry. He is an excellent cook." Huh, that wasn't the answer I was expecting but now I know, it is actually the perfect place to be. I think I'm relieved we aren't going out. I'm not sure I could handle any more fancy restaurants and I get the feeling that, no matter how dressy or casual I am, N will be okay with it. I sink into the backseat and watch as we pass each building, no longer worried about the destination.

We've been driving for almost the full 20 minutes before the little thought enters my head.

Maybe he isn't taking you out in public because he's embarrassed. My hands reflexively stretch across my lap as I look at the thin fabric. The dress is a brand name but I bought it at a second hand store. It was such a great find. Nina didn't stop talking about it for a week when I first brought it home.

I felt like a million bucks the first time I tried it on but now, I suddenly feel like the three dollars and fifty cents I paid for it.

No. The little voice in my head shoots my thoughts down. I'm projecting this onto him and he doesn't deserve that. These are my own insecurities. This is my own baggage.

Before I am able to wage war with myself any longer, the car comes to a stop and Marcus turns the engine off. I feel disoriented. I wasn't paying attention and now I don't know where I am. I stupidly spent the last five minutes looking down at my lap.

A warm breeze pushes its way into the backseat as Marcus opens the door and reaches his hand in to help me out and my eyes travel up the height of the four-story building as I steady myself on the sidewalk out front. A quick glance up and down the street tells me we are in a bit of a trendy area. I notice a couple of restaurants and a few other quaint stores tucked away.

Taking a couple of steps toward the door we are parked in front of, my confidence picks up as Marcus follows behind me.

I pull on the handle but it doesn't open and Marcus excuses himself and reaches around in front of me with a plastic card and swipes it over a reader. The sharp click tells me it's time to pull and the door opens.

The area is inviting with four doors leading up to the lift. With each step closer to the elevator, I realize N isn't on the first floor.

Pushing the button, the arrow pointing up turns green and I listen to the gears groan as it brings the elevator down to us.

"This is where I'll leave you, Hazel." He begins as the bell dings and we wait for the doors to open.

"Oh, um. Which floor is his?"

"Well, technically, all of them are. But he lives on the top floor." He answers, reaching out to hold the door open for me.

"Oh. Thank you, Marcus." I step in and he reaches around me, swiping his card again before I push the number four and he releases his hold on the door as we say our goodnights before the elevator shuts completely.

As each number takes its turn lighting up, I feel butterflies begin to stir deep inside of me. How does just the thought of him have this effect on me? I know his whole name, yet I haven't been able to bring myself to do one single search on the guy.

I feel like I'm waiting for something before I go looking for information on him. Permission, maybe? He arouses something inside of me I don't understand, but I'm not afraid. When he talks to me like he does, I feel overcome with a need to relinquish myself to him and I feel right in doing that.

As the top floor lights up and the ding of the bell announces my arrival, I realize I forgot to ask what his apartment number is but I quickly realize it isn't necessary as I step into a small area opening into what I think is all of N's home.

Unlike the main floor, this level seems to be one giant open space. I could fit at least six of my dorm rooms on this floor. The sounds of a sliding door calls my attention toward the back of the building and I watch as N comes in carrying a tray.

The moment he sees me he smiles and I know, without a doubt, I'd follow that smile anywhere tonight.

16

NOAH

My phone vibrates as I close the lid to the barbecue; perfect timing.

Marcus: She's on her way up. Message when you need me.

I thought long and hard about where to take Hazel today. For the first time, we are seeing each other on purpose.

A date.

The innocence in the thought of seeing her like this makes me impatient. I glance through the balcony window to take a last minute mental checklist of everything I've prepared in the kitchen. I haven't entertained guests here for a long time.

I had considered taking Hazel out but I want the chance to get to know her without distractions. I don't want to make any assumptions about what she likes and, if I'm being honest with myself, I don't want any interruptions. I can serve her here just as easily on my own.

It's a nice evening and the deck has a beautiful view of the street below. Happy hour has started although not many make the trip down here on a Sunday night. The crowd is more subdued tonight with mostly the locals coming out to enjoy the neighborhood so it's an entirely different vibe. This is my favorite night of the week because I get all of the benefits of the music playing in the streets below without the constant stream of people.

I see the light above the elevator light up from where I'm standing on the deck before the doors open and I stand still waiting for her to enter.

She takes a tentative step into the room then freezes as she looks at the elevator doors closing behind her, unsure if she should stay or not and the sight of her makes me smile. Pocketing my phone, I pick up the plate with our food and make my way back inside.

At the sound of the door, she squares her body in my direction and fiddles with her bag. The first time we bumped into each other, her hair was wavy and last night it was straight. Now, her hair bounces softly with just the slightest curl near the tips.

I watch as she smiles and drops her gaze down to my feet; I'm barefoot and she slips her sandals off and places her bag on a counter near the elevator.

"Thank you for coming. You look beautiful." Her hands retreat to her stomach and she flattens her dress against her body as I speak.

"Oh, um, it's a Givenchy." She suddenly looks uncomfortable. I smile as she offers the information. I don't know a lot about fashion. I buy what I like but I get the feeling she's trying to tell me it's worth something.

So there is an obstacle with her and money. I'm not sure yet what exactly it is so I stare for a quiet moment before she chooses to fill the uncomfortable silence with more information. I watch her shoulders slump a bit as she confesses, "I, um, bought it at a second hand store."

So her issue with money is that she is worried that I value brand names and prestige. Well, that I can work with.

"I'm not interested in that, Hazel. I'm interested in you. It has nothing to do with what you're wearing; it has to do with who you are. Now I gave you a compliment. You look beautiful." I stand still with the distance between us waiting for her to figure out what I want from her.

Her eyes bounce around the space between us before snapping back to my own and she answers again. Tilting her head, her hair falls forward, framing her face. "Thank you, N."

I place the plate on the counter and close the distance between us.

"That's my good girl, Hazel." I brush the hair away from her big eyes. This was what I wanted to do when I first saw her in the coffee shop.

Pulling her attention back up to mine, I twirl the soft strands of her hair around my fingers and I notice I've matched the rhythm of her deep breaths with my own. I don't think she realizes it yet, but her lips have parted, just enough to kiss and I lean forward, watching as her eyes close for me in acceptance before I meet her soft lips with my own.

The kiss is simple, almost chaste and I pull back to examine her reaction when I hear the softest protest whimper out of her, urging me to continue—and I do.

Snaking my fingers into her hair, I slide my hand to the base of her skull, holding her still. Her eyes shoot open, searching mine and I feel her body relax in my grip. The tension between us is tangible and heavy and I push back into her lips for another taste.

Everything she does drives me to her. Every taste, every smile. Her hand travels up just below my ribcage, hesitantly clutching onto my shirt and the slightest graze of her fingertips against my skin through the fabric makes me want to skip dinner and go straight to dessert.

As if sensing my own greed, I release my hand from her hair and step back. She offers me a shy smile as she tucks some stray strands of her hair behind her ear and I watch her face warm with a beautiful blush.

As if remembering where she is, she shakes her head and looks further into my apartment.

"Your place is amazing. I bet you can see pretty far from up here." She speaks as her fingers fumble along the buttons of her jacket.

"Keep your jacket on and I'll show you." I step back and curl my finger, calling her to follow and she treads softly behind me. I make a stop in the kitchen to offer her something to drink.

She looks around the countertops for a hint at what I might have and I wait for her to ask. I enjoy the awkward silences between us. Those little moments when she is too shy to be bold and I sense she is waiting for me to take the lead with her again which I can't wait to begin doing.

"Wings?" She lands on the plate I have on the counter and she almost looks excited.

"Yes. We are having chicken wings and salad with my own dressing. They can wait a few minutes. Can I get you a beer, I also have wine." I already know how she's going to answer by the way her face lights up as I list her options.

"I'd love a beer." I reach into the fridge to grab two and she continues offering me more of an insight into herself. "I like wine, too. It just sometimes gives me a headache and I have my new job in the morning."

"Right. Tell me, will you be handling hot beverages at your new job?" I wink as I twist the cap off and hand her a bottle. She laughs and I finally get to hear what her happiness sounds like; I love it.

"Funny. No. It's in my field of study. I'm interning at a wildlife rescue center just outside the city." She shrugs like it's no big deal, but I sense it is.

"Is it the one in Penner County?" She nods as I ask the question so I ask a follow up. "Do all of the students get internships?" She shakes her head.

"As far as I know, I'm the only one. I think it's pretty rare, actually." She takes her first sip and hurries to suck back the head on the beer as it rushes up the neck, successfully stopping it before she spills.

I walk to the back, sliding the glass door to the patio open and ushering her through. "Well, congratulations then. You must be doing very well to have achieved that."

"Oh I don't know about that—" I stop her, raising my eyebrows at her response and she catches on quickly, "—I mean, I am. Thank you, N."

"Please, call me Noah." Her little gasp of air tells me I've made her happy and as we sit together on the couch, I see her smiling.

I sense she hasn't used my name yet. Not even to herself. I can tell by the way she's preparing herself to say it now. Her lips move in silence as she practices it once in her head before answering. "Thank you—Noah." She can't hide her eagerness from me.

"We should go inside. Dinner's ready." She looks over her shoulder, then back at me.

"Um, do you think maybe we could eat out here? I don't mind casual and it's still nice out. I mean if that is okay? I just—my place doesn't have a balcony and this is really nice." Her hesitance is adorable.

I'm all for casual and I like that she is more laid back when it comes to relaxing and I pat her leg, silently telling her to stay put while I gather our food.

As we nibble on our dinner, I ask her about her courses and she shares information about her family. Some mysteries are answered as she tells me about her father's battle with cancer and how she started her post-secondary education late. I get a better sense of her issues surrounding money as she tells me about her father's business.

I tell her about my family. I'm the second youngest of four. She met my younger sister, Paige and I tell her about my older brother and sister.

"Marcus told me you own this whole building. You're the landlord then?" She asks, reaching for a mug of hot chocolate I brought out with dessert.

"Not really." Her brows scrunch up at my answer so I elaborate. "It's a bit of a story."

She pretends to check the invisible watch on her wrist. "Oh look at that. I have time." She says with a smile.

"My family is not wealthy by any means. We've always gotten by but it wasn't until I went to work at my job that I began to accumulate the money I have." She nods her head as I tell my story. She understands where I'm coming from. "Anyway, my grandmother was living in this building and, back then, it was falling apart. The landlord wasn't fixing anything and they were months away from having the place condemned. She had been living here for years after her husband, my grandpa, passed away and her rent was grandfathered at a really low rate. The landlord threatened her and told her she would have to break the lease and sign on at the higher rate if she wanted anything fixed."

"That's awful. Who does that?" Her question is genuine. I think on a deep level, Hazel really believes in the good in people first.

"Well, he did." I answer.

"What happened?"

I pause for a moment before starting. "This isn't going to make me look good but I called the city on him. I said I was a concerned neighbor and listed all of the things wrong with the building then suggested they do an inspection on the rooms of the most elderly and grandfathered tenants. A week later, the guy was served with so many infractions and health code violations, it would probably drain his savings just to get started." I take a breath to let her process just how much of an asshole I can be when you threaten the ones I love. "Then I called him up and offered to buy the place from him at an extremely low rate."

"Oh." She suddenly looks like I've struck a nerve.

"Are you okay?"

"Well, it just sounds like what the businessmen did to my dad. They knew he was sick and his competitors began taking his clients until he couldn't even make enough to open his office for the day. He was dying and he had no other choice." I see the moral war waging inside her head and I realize I've hit the main vein of her issues with money... and possibly with me.

"Hazel, what those men did to your father was despicable. I would never, never take advantage of anyone without absolute cause. I hope you'll understand that. The man I took this building from was not a good man. I heard horrible stories from the tenants about him. Failing to keep my grandmother safe is just at the top of my list. He solicited some of the younger female tenants for sex in exchange for rent when they were short or went through a rough patch. If this was just about getting a building, I would have offered him fair market value for it."

"What happened to the tenants?" She changes the subject, looking for a silver lining and I'm more than happy to provide her one.

"Well the building did need major repairs. The two floors with the most damage were the third floor and this one. I offered the tenants a buyout for their rooms. I could only keep about a third of them while I fixed the rooms that were in need of the most repairs."

"Is that normal? To buy someone out of an apartment?"

"No. It's unheard of actually but I couldn't just kick these people out on the street. The money I saved from offering fair market value to the old landlord went to the tenants that wanted the buyout. And most of them did. For the ones who stayed, I gave them a reduced rent rate for the neighborhood. I fixed my grandmother's room up first and she lived on the second floor rent free until she passed away a little over a year ago. My older sister moved into another room on the second floor for a bit, also rent free, but then she met her husband and they bought a house with the money she saved. There is no one on the third floor right now and I haven't rented them out yet. In all honesty, as people move out, I haven't been renting them. I have a couple of tenants on the first and second floors. You've already met one of them," I see her going through the possibilities in her head. The list is short. "It's Marcus."

"Your driver lives with you?"

"No. He has his own place on the main floor. I offered it to him a couple of months ago. I use his car a lot and he mentioned he was looking for a place to live. He was asking what neighborhoods he should look at because I work in realty. I told him about my place."

"Oh. That was nice of you."

"Well, it was a bit selfish. Marcus is an ex-marine and I like having him around. He provides a good level of security for the building and I am his main client so he doesn't need to go far. I pay him his rate as a driver and he lives rent free in exchange for being present around the building now and then. We've had some issues at our work recently so it's an added layer of security."

"Wow. That is a bit of a story." She looks overwhelmed and the air is cooling off so I decide to move the conversation inside to ask a couple of questions of my own.

Hazel's body shivers and I stand, holding out my hand to her and leaving our plates and cups. Her cool fingers slide into mine and she allows me to lead her inside to the couch.

"There is something I want to say. I hope you know you could have asked me my name at any time and I would have told you. It's important you know you can ask or talk to me about anything." I want to make sure she understands she has rights to anything she wants to know.

She listens intently as I speak, nodding her head. "I, um, liked how you talked to me." She loses eye contact for a second.

Her obvious display of vulnerability gives me pause and

I've been holding myself back. There is something else I need to know before we move forward. "I'm going to ask you something and I am only curious. I don't mean to offend you." She bobs her head again and I continue, "Are you a virgin?"

17

NOAH

"*A*re you a virgin?"
The smile on Hazel's face freezes while the emotion behind it falls away.

"Tell me about your sexual history." I try to reword my question and she shifts on the couch beside me.

I don't want to command our situation until I know what she has experienced and, for the first time in a long time, I feel the rhythmic thudding of my heart beat as I wait for her reply.

This is the difference between finding someone to play with and finding someone to care for. I'm invested in her. It's still new, but there's something inside of me that is already preparing to claim her as mine in all ways.

Emotionally, I want to wrap her in bubble wrap; mentally, I want to own her thoughts and physically, I want to sate her needs while I glean what I crave from her.

But before I can do all of that, I need to know what I'm working with.

"I'm not a—um—virgin." Whispering the last word, she's unsure of herself.

I move a couple of inches toward her and place my hand on hers. "There's no wrong answer, Hazel. We're getting to know each other." She smiles as I prompt, "Tell me more."

"I was 18 when, um, it was my first time. He was my boyfriend. We only did it a few times. We had plans to go to college together but—uh—that didn't work out." She stops and shrugs like it's no big deal but I sense, at the time, it was. "He met someone else a few months later."

I give her hand a squeeze. Everyone before me is irrelevant to me and soon it will become unimportant to her as well. "I'm sorry, Hazel. And after him? I'd like to know more."

She takes a breath as if to answer, then stops herself and scans my face before starting again.

"Well, um, that was it." Shrugging again, her eyes leave mine. She looks at my neck, my shirt, my hand on hers, but no more eye contact. I stay silent for a moment, giving her time to decide if she wants to add anything further and after a quiet minute, she does, "It's just that, when my dad got sick, my mom didn't handle it well in the beginning. I kind of had to take care of both of them and I—um—I didn't really go out."

She stops as though a realization hits her and I suddenly feel like I've stumbled onto a part of her she doesn't let anyone see.

"So you were taking care of two parents then? That's a lot for a teenager to take on. Who took care of you?" As I speak, I already sense her defences going up.

"It wasn't like that. I mean I just didn't go out a lot so I didn't really meet anyone and all of my friends went away to school and met new friends. Then, when I started college—well, I couldn't mess up my only chance." She's rambling excuses for what I think she feels is a response I don't like.

Nothing could be further from the truth. With every new thing I learn about her, I want to know more. She has a history, but she still has so much to explore. She's been hurt, but not to the point where she guards herself against new experiences.

She sacrificed a lot of herself to take care of the people she loved the most. To her, she was just doing what had to be done. When, in reality, she set aside her younger years that should have been hers to squander away on setting out on her own, making mistakes and meeting new people. She grew up faster than any of her friends around her had to, and she knows the value of her education and the second chance she has now.

I search her for clues on how to proceed when I see her wringing her fingers together and playing with the hem on her dress.

"Do I make you nervous, Hazel?" Her hands stop fidgeting at my question.

"Um, I don't know if *nervous* is the right word." Her eyes lift as high as my mouth so I make a point of dragging my teeth along my lip before continuing.

"What word would you use?"

Licking her lips, "I—I'm not sure. I like the way you talk to me. It feels like..."

"Like I'm taking care of you?" I offer and she coyly nods her head. "I want to take care of you, Hazel." I lower my voice and let the suggestion hang in the air between us and now I'm the one watching her bite her lower lip.

I want to bite her lip. I've been restraining myself all

night. Since she first stepped off the elevator and I gave her that one little kiss, I've wanted nothing more than to take another and another from her soft lips.

"I—I want that." Barely above a whisper, she finds her courage and meets my eyes.

"There are so many things I want to show you." Whispering, I muse to myself but her eagerness gets the better of herself.

"Like what?" Impatience wraps around her question.

"Let's start with patience." I wink. "I'll give us both everything we need—in time. Stand up." Reaching out my hand, I take hers as her legs shift and she rises, allowing me to place her where I choose.

I move her to stand a foot in front of me, between my legs and I wait. It takes a few seconds before she settles, deferring to me to take the lead.

I take my time to look at her, examining every inch as my eyes travel up her body. Her shin has a bruise on it. It isn't noticeable so it is either fading or she doesn't bruise easily. I'll find out, in time, which it is.

My fingers start low on her legs, trailing over her bruise on her lower calf and then rising slowly as she stays still, waiting for me.

"Do you like it when I take charge of you, Hazel?" I ask, keeping my eyes on her legs as my fingers continue their journey upward.

"Yes." Her soft voice hitches as she answers.

Her skin is hot against my cool fingers and I notice her fist her hands as I slide across her skin. She's nervous whether she thinks she is or not. Her body is telling me everything I need to know.

Her dress is a wrap around, but me untying it and

removing it by myself is no fun. I want her to participate in her surrender.

"Lift your dress." My command is short and I keep watching her fingers as they settle when I speak. It must be the silent tension causing her unease.

Her hands travel down to the hem of her summer dress and she watches me as she hesitantly lifts it upward, slowing just as it gets to the very top of her thighs.

"Higher." I urge, she complies. "Stop there." I command and she obeys, suspending the hem of her dress at waist level. Her white cotton panties are exposed to me and I move my attention back to my fingers on her legs, trailing them over her knee.

Her body settles as I speak and I'm guessing the more I stay silent, the more uncomfortable she will become. I take my time moving over her supple thighs, squeezing them gently as I go and offering a couple of light pinches to her leg. I already know I'm going to enjoy playing with her.

Images of everything I want to do with her flood my mind. I want to tear this designer dress away and wrap her in rope. A designer shibari dress of my own to adorn her body, leaving breathtaking marks when removed, claiming all of her as mine.

"Red." I announce to no one in particular as I remain focused on exploring her body.

"What?" She asks and I suddenly feel heat surge through my veins as I pinch the fleshy inside of her thigh, pulling a yelp from her as I rap my fingers over the tender area a few times. Looking up at her, demanding her attention, I wait expressionless. "I, um, mean... pardon me?"

"Good girl." I feel my cheeks twitch with a hint of a smile as I offer her praise before moving my eyes back down and sliding my finger over her panties until I find the warmth I was searching for and she stifles a moan. As I rub back and forth over the thin white cotton I feel a slight movement in her hips. I make eye contact again. "I'm giving you a word, it's called a safe word. It is a word you can say if you ever become uncomfortable or wish for me to stop anything I am doing. It is usually a universal safe word, meaning others around you, in my—our lifestyle, will know you are asking for something to cease if you use it. It isn't to be used lightly as it will end everything that was to happen during a particular moment and I will not restart once it's used. You may say *stop*, if you simply want to ask a question or need a moment and *go* to continue. *Red* is your safe word. Do you understand?" I stop moving my fingers to wait for her response.

"I understand." Whispering she continues to watch my eyes, her cheeks flushed a pretty pink hue.

Without another word, I move my hand to her side, hooking it into the seam of her panties and trail my other hand up to rest on her hip. She takes a deep breath and forces a swallow down, remaining still with her dress lifted up as she continues to expose herself to me.

Hooking my fingers on my second hand, I let gravity take my arms down, taking her panties with them and as they fall, I watch her...watching me.

For someone who is trying to teach patience, my own is chipping away at my sanity. Maintaining control over myself, I force my eyes to stay put when all I want to do is drop them to everything I've just uncovered but I would be missing out if I did because the look on her face is precious.

Her wet lips part slightly and she swallows every few

seconds. Her mouth must be watering at the thought of relinquishing herself to me.

Abandoning her panties to rest, taut between her knees, I watch as her cheeks blush while my hand moves back to its intended target. The moment I touch her mound she whimpers and shifts in place.

Moving my free hand around the back of her thigh, I adjust her back to the position she was in and hold her steady as I advance, sliding my finger into her folds. She's become my precious, mysterious toy and right now I want to learn everything about how to play with her properly. What touch grants me what sound? Does she like pain? Will she like being restrained, gagged...plugged? How far can I go before she unravels for me?

I'm not sure if this will ease or agitate her nerves but I shift my eyes and my attention to her pussy. She's trying hard to stay still for me but I can tell the rubbing is having an effect on her as her hips twitch when my touch hits a sensitive spot and I commit everything to memory.

"Is there anything you want to ask me?" Casually, without lifting my gaze, I continue to watch my fingers explore her body.

"Uh, ummm..." She takes a long pause before asking, "Um, are *you* a virgin?"

18

HAZEL

"*A*re *you* a virgin?" I regret the words as soon as they come out of my mouth.

I have this awkward habit of saying ridiculously stupid things when I am clearly out of my league.

There is no possible way this guy has never had sex before. I mean, I had to practically draw my first boyfriend a map to all of my bits and this guy is moving around like he owns the place and I can't believe that was the question I asked.

But now what I regret more than my words is the obvious cringe on my face as Noah's eyes travel up my body to meet my own.

I have to give the guy credit, as I watch his gaze move up, the look on his face makes me feel like he is treating it like a legitimate question. He's giving me the respect of seriously considering it but it all changes when his eyes land on my face and the crazy grimace I now feel plastered across my features.

In an instant, his sincerity turns predatory. He knows I can be a smart-ass and he's been dying to punish me for it.

"Would you like to repeat your question, Hazel?" He challenges, dark seduction laces his tone.

"N—not really." My bravado shrinks away under his stare and the pressure from his fingers increases as he makes his strokes longer. My legs tremble but he holds me still with his other hand.

Out of the corner of my eye, I notice my white knuckles as I clench my dress so tight in my grip to keep myself still for him and one hand has already begun to shake. I can't stop the feeling building in me and if he doesn't stop soon, I'm going to have an orgasm and I'm not sure I'm supposed to since he said we were working on patience.

A groan falls freely from my lips and he doesn't relent, working me closer and closer to the edge and a calm trance approaches me. With a wicked grin, he slows and I feel myself wanting to protest but after my stellar question, I decide to keep my mouth shut and I'm rewarded as he slips a finger deep inside me and I involuntarily and very shamefully bow my body forward, silently begging him to take anything he wants.

I've never experienced this level of pleasure before. Even when I touched myself, nothing has ever come close to this consuming need growing inside of me from a place I didn't know existed.

"P—p—please." My plea dribbles out of my mouth and I'm moments away from grinding my own hips down on him when he abruptly pulls his hand back and stands up in front of me, keenly watching my reaction and I try to keep myself calm although I desperately miss his touch. I already know I'm failing miserably by the triumphant look on his face.

My punishment has started.

I've passed the point where I was able to maintain any type of composure over myself. Since he spanked me in the alley, I've wanted to feel that energy flow through me again. From the moment he spoke to me, authority and confidence in his voice, I've wanted to know what being with him would feel like.

"That's a smart mouth you've got there." Raising his eyebrows and smirking he looks like he's expecting a response.

"I—" I have no idea what I was about to say but my words are cut off as he pushes his fingers into my mouth and my tongue tingles at the foreign taste.

"Sshhh. Taste yourself." Whispering deeply, he urges and I feel my eyes go wide. I've never tasted myself before and I'm doing it in front of him. "Go ahead. Suck yourself off my fingers." His instruction hits me hard and I greedily begin to suck everything I can from him as he pushes his free hand between my legs. Leaning in, he whispers into my ear. "I was looking forward to tasting you first but this is so much better." His free fingers slide easily back into my opening and my stomach clenches as I continue to hold my dress up for him and whimper around his fingers.

Removing his hand from my core, I watch as he lifts his other hand to his lips as I continue to swirl my tongue around his fingers and I groan against his hand as he opens his mouth to taste me.

I've never done anything like this before. I don't even think I've read about anything like this before. I mentally agree with myself that I need to increase my reading level to more of an advanced rating when he snaps me out of my thoughts by pulling his fingers out of both of our mouths and my lips suddenly feel puffy.

"You're a smart girl, Miss Masters. I think you can learn two lessons at once. I'm going to add humility to that list." Before I consider where he is going with his plans, I feel a tug at my waist and my dress loosens itself from my body and opens. "You may let go now." He commands and I feel a dull ache in my knuckles as I release my hold and drop my hands to my side waiting for his instructions.

Raising his hand to the base of my neck, he inches his fingers into my hair then fists his hand before tugging a couple of times to demonstrate the control he has over my body.

"I like you like this; compliant, eager and under my guidance." Another brief pull stings my scalp before he wraps his free arm around my waist as he steps backward to the couch and sits down, taking me with him and settling me in his lap.

I move to curl up against him but he stops me, pushing me onto my back and exposing my front to him. With his hand still in my hair, his other moves to my dress, further pushing it open and revealing my mismatched bra to both of us and I wonder if this is what he means when he says he wants to teach me humility. My thought is discarded as he speaks again.

"Play with yourself." Lifting my leg up and out as he demands, I feel the air hit the wetness coating my entrance.

"What?" If I wasn't already lying across his lap I would have fallen over. Then I realize my mistake. "I mean—oww". The swift tap against my sensitive area before I am able to finish my sentence startles me and I reach a hand across my mound to cover myself and he raises a brow. Quickly recoiling my hand away, I try again. "I beg your pardon." I remember him telling me he was fond of that phrase and his satisfied smile tells me I've earned some good points in his book.

"I want to watch you masturbate, Hazel." He says matter of factly like we are discussing the weather.

"I—I'm not sure I—" I stumble over my words as my situation sinks into me. I'm laying in his lap with my legs spread wide and if that wasn't sobering enough, he lifts his hand and rests it on top of my mound as his fingers begin to comb through the small patch of pubic hair I have. I've never felt more intimate with another human being and I suddenly feel docile.

"You have touched yourself before?" He questions and I nod as much as I can with his hand in my hair. I don't think I have any voice left. "Show me." His eyes look hungry and I tentatively move my hand over his.

We stare for a long minute before he pulls his hand out from underneath mine and, placing it back on top of my own, he guides my fingers lower and onto the nub of my clit. Placing pressure on top, he rubs my hand, pushing it onto a sensitive spot and my eyes stay glued to his face.

A gentle tug on my hair focuses my attention where he wants it to go and I look down to my fingers as he releases my hand and adjusts my leg wider as he watches everything I do.

Slowly, I run my fingers around my swollen area, trying to find the spots I usually focus on when I'm alone, then I slide over my labia and further down, searching for the entrance he claimed so easily. No matter where I touch, it doesn't hold a candle to what he made me feel earlier and I sense my own efforts become frenzied.

As though my body is rejecting my own touch for his,

nothing I do brings any relief. I move my stare up to his own, silently pleading for him to take over.

"I—it's not enough." I mumble, embarrassed by my shortcomings. "I need—" I stop myself.

Focusing all of his attention on me, he provides no assistance. "Tell me what you need, Hazel." He coaxes with a low voice that could lull me to sleep if I wasn't so wound up.

"I need you to touch me—please." My lips quiver as I beg.

"Have you been able to bring yourself to orgasm while playing with yourself before?" He asks calmly, concern all over his face.

"Yes, but I— it wasn't like— how did you?" My fingers continue their pathetic attempts and I feel a lump form in my throat.

"How did I bring you so close—so quickly?" He fills in my blanks and I nod while a frustrated whimper escapes me.

As if rattling the gate to my cage, he clenches his hand tighter in my hair and the sharp pain releases some of the energy that has been spreading inside of me. As it flows out of me in a moan, I feel my legs spread wider, but he isn't touching me, I'm spreading my legs for him.

"You instinctively respond to my control. It calms you and frees you." As he speaks, he replaces my fingers on my clit with his own and I feel a weight leave me as I pull my other leg up and out, displaying everything to him and he lets out a groan of his own. "You are so beautiful like this, Hazel. Offering yourself to me."

Before he is done with his sentence I already feel my stomach tightening like it did before and I slide my hands over my legs spreading myself as wide as I can, greedily displaying myself to him. I've never been this brazen before.

"Look at you, showing yourself to me." He taunts and all I can offer him is a whimper as I hold myself open for him. "Do you like this? Giving yourself to me? Allowing me to take control of your pleasure and pain?"

My head nods desperately at his question, pulling his fist tight against my scalp, and I'm rewarded with a carnal smile as he continues to find sensitive spot after sensitive spot.

Swiveling my head, my attention moves from his face to his hand and I watch him move across my sex possessively. My limbs feel heavy as I sink out of my head and into his actions and I feel as though I could float away. My hips begin to jerk on their own accord as I gasp and moan under his hands.

I steal a glance to his eyes and he is still looking at me. The whole time he touches me, he doesn't once move his eyes to watch what he's doing. Instead he fixates on my reactions; examining my every response, mentally recording my every weakness and I feel a hot tear roll down my cheek as I turn my attention back to his fingers.

Am I crying?

Just as I feel the final stretch to my orgasm approach, he removes his hands and grabs my leg closest to him, pulling me wide and releasing my own hand.

"Please me. Be my good girl and make yourself cum for me, Miss Masters." He ends his command by gripping my hair tighter and, this time, keeping my focus on his face and I don't hesitate.

I know exactly where he made me feel good and I'm inspired. Spurred on by my need to make him proud of me, my hips jerk instantly as I find my spot and begin to rub with purpose. He's ordered me to play with myself; his toy, and something foreign takes over.

His eyes jump around my face, no doubt committing everything to memory. Every gasp, every twitch belongs to him and he is taking everything as I give it. I want him to take control. I feel like I'm spiralling yet he is holding me tight. As much as my entire body wants to fly away, I know he won't let me fall, then I feel it.

"I... I'm g—gonna," I choke on my words as my body takes over and carries me closer to the edge all because Noah wishes it.

"Not until I say so." Noah's voice is harsh, seizing my attention.

"Wh—"

"Don't stop, keep going but you will not come. And you don't want to find out what happens if you say 'what' to me right now." His expression darkens and his eyes are all I see as I attempt to ease my fingers away from my sensitive area. "Do not let up on yourself, Miss Masters, or I will take over and fighting against an orgasm with me in control is next to impossible."

"Pleeeaase..." I beg, then pinch my lips together in a long moan as I return to the intensity I had. "Please let me."

"Let you what?" He asks.

"Please, let me come." Bucking my hips, I blink the tears out of my eyes. I'm definitely crying now.

I continue on, waging war with myself. I'm pulling myself toward an orgasm I can't have and my head begins spinning with contradiction. I'm about to outwardly start bawling when his face softens and he leans close to my ear, whispering.

"Please me. Show me who you belong to and come for

me, my perfect little doll." His lips on my forehead are a gentle contrast to the room spinning around us and I feel the tension in my body release at his name for me.

I am his doll, displayed as he wants me and here for him. The thought pushes me over and I feel my back arch as I wail out my orgasm. Before I remove my fingers from my nub, he covers my hand with his own and slides my hand down further toward my opening. As waves of aftershocks hit me, I meekly allow him to push one of my fingers inside of me along with one of his own before removing our hands and pulling mine to his lips.

My body spasms in his grasp as I feel the bumps of his tongue glide over my sapped hand and his own finger traces along my lip, searching for entry. Licking my taste off, he pulls our hands out and searches my face before crashing his lips to my own and I sink into a sated void as he pulls the sides of my dress across my body and finally allows me to curl up in his arms.

After what feels like five minutes of blissful silence as he plays with my hair, he shifts on his hip and pulls out his phone to check the time with me.

Marcus: We have a problem.

I see the unread message pop up on the screen as it turns on and Noah reads it along with me before I quickly try to turn away. It wasn't my intention to read it but it was short and it was hard not to.

Noah opens his phone and taps the screen before setting his attention back on me.

"Everything okay?" I ask.

"I'm sure it is. I should get you home soon. You have an

early day and I don't want to keep you up late but I would like to talk to you for awhile before you leave tonight. About this." He gestures between us and I see the glow of his screen.

Turning his phone a little away from me, I try to watch his face for clues but he offers none.

"It looks like one of the tires on the car was slashed while we were all inside. I'm sure it's nothing to worry about. We are dealing with a bit of a legal mess at work right now—disgruntled employee situation. It could also just be random. Marcus is changing the tire before we go down and take you home. I guess we have that time to chat now." He winks but there is something behind his expression that tells me his work problems might be a bit bigger than he is letting on.

19

HAZEL

"I still don't know how you got her to come to you so quickly." Shanna shakes her head as she gently sets the raccoon back in her cage.

"I think my peanut butter and jam sandwich had a lot to do with it." I laugh, dangling the half-eaten, torn apart pieces of bread between my fingers.

"I would agree with you, but Jeff was in there for 20 minutes trying with a tin of tuna and you go waltzing in there and get her in less than a minute." Closing the gate to the cage, she turns and picks up her clipboard. "I chatted with the team earlier; you have a way with the animals." Writing a note on her paper, she smiles.

"Sometimes I think I understand animals better than people." I shrug. "Besides, yesterday I spent a lot of the day with her working on her rehabilitation. She probably just remembered me." I toss the sandwich into the trash bin as my stomach growls.

"Well, whatever it is, you are a great addition to our team, Hazel. I can't tell you how lucky we are that we got

138 | RUN WILDE

this extra funding to bring you on." Shanna's writing picks up and it looks like she's signing her name on the sheet in her hands then she looks back up. "That's it. Your week of training is done. Don't tell anyone but you know more about the animals here than most of our casual staff. You are now our permanent apprentice. Let me just photocopy this for your records and I'll send a copy to your professor so they can proceed on their end."

I knew this week was just a formality but hearing it's all signed off, eases my anxiety. Now I am here for at least the next year and my professors can fill my spot at the school with another body.

The salary is enough to live on and it's good because I found out yesterday a couple of us have been laid off at the coffee shop for the next couple of months, effective immediately since our hours weren't full time.

Not wanting to hover, I wait outside of the manager's office as Shanna gathers my papers when I see a familiar car pull into the parking area. Paul jumps out of the driver's seat and rushes to the passenger side, then pulls out something wrapped in cloth and heads for the front door.

It's near the end of our day and everyone except Shanna, the night staff and I are around and I meet Paul at the front desk and he looks worried as I hear a high-pitched squeal come from the fabric.

"I saw this guy at the side of the road." Unwrapping what looks like Paul's school hoodie, an adult rabbit writhes in pain and his screaming alerts everyone. The door to the office opens in unison with our back door and Shanna and Jeff flank either side of me as we do a quick examination while Paul watches silently, concern etched into his features.

"Did you see what happened to him?" Jeff asks, taking the lead and Paul shakes his head.

"No, I was driving home from work and I saw it on the side of the road. I didn't think anything of it but then I saw it move as I got closer. Is it going to be okay, Hazel?" Worried, he looks at me and I feel Shanna's eyes on me as Jeff continues to examine the rabbit. "I remember you saying the name of this place when we were talking about your new job and I brought it here. Can you help it?" His worry for the animal is endearing and, her silent question answered, Shanna gets back to work.

"Jeff?" Shanna asks, prompting for an initial diagnosis.

"Initial scan makes me think he'll live. His right, hind leg looks broken though. I'll get him in the back and start him on some fluids and painkillers." Jeff doesn't wait for permission. Pulling out a basket with one of our own blankets in it, he takes the rabbit from Paul's sweatshirt and transfers him in, then sets the basket on a cart we use to move the animals around so we don't drop them.

"I'm going to assist Jeff until he is sedated. Hazel, can you take the information from your friend?" I nod at Shanna's question, reaching under the desk and pulling out our inpatient questionnaire.

"Are you okay, Paul?" I ask before I get started. He looks pale, no doubt from sitting in the car with the rabbit while it made those high-pitched screams.

"Um, yeah. Just shaken up, I guess. This has been the worst day." He looks light on his feet as he answers so I point to the chairs to the side and move around the counter to join him in sitting down.

"I can't imagine. The bunny is in good hands. The people here are amazing. Can you fill in all of your own details at the top? It'll save time." I hand him the clipboard and he sets to work, filling in all of the boxes before I take it back and look at the list of questions to ask.

"You said you saw it on the side of the road? Where was this and what time?" I draw a small circle, willing ink to flow into my pen then hold the pen still, ready to take down his information.

"It must have been about 25 minutes up the highway, heading back into town so it was about half an hour ago. Driving felt like hours with the rabbit crying like it did." My attention on the questionnaire, I write down his answer and ask another without looking up.

"Was anyone else there? Another driver or anyone who might have stopped as well who saw anything?" I see him shake his head out of the corner of my eye.

"No, everyone just kept going."

"Was there anything else in the area that looked out of place? Other animals, anything?"

"Nothing. I'm sorry I didn't see anything else. When I saw it, it was all alone. I thought it was just roadkill at first, then it flopped over and tried to stand. Then I stopped." He chokes on his words as he recalls what happened.

"Hey. It's okay. The fact the bunny is alert and making those noises is a good thing. He's in the back with help now." I reach out to touch his palm and he quickly grabs my hand.

"Thanks. I'm a bit out of sorts. Don't tell the gang about this, okay? I'm kind of embarrassed. I must look awful." I find myself shaking my head as he speaks.

"I won't say a word. I promise. It's okay to be worried about something so helpless. I'll make sure to call you next week when I get back into work and check on him. Until then, he will be well taken care of." He continues to hold my hand while I comfort him.

"Thank you, Hazel. I was already having a rough day. I have to admit, I miss our friends. I have my job for the summer, but there's no one to go out with to socialize. I'm starting to feel like a shut in. And on top of that, I had two tickets to the outdoor jazz festival tonight, but the girl I wanted to go with just cancelled on me. Now this. It's just a lot, you know?" I've never seen this side of Paul before. I'm not sure if any of our friends have.

"I'm so sorry, Paul. That is a bad day." As I comfort him, I begin to realize that I also miss our friends. I'd probably be going out with Nina for dinner tonight. As it is, Noah said he had a busy week with work and a legal issue he is handling and we've barely texted since our crazy night together at his place.

"Hey, what are you doing tonight?" Paul's question catches me off guard. "Maybe we could go to the festival together—as friends, I know. I don't want my tickets to go to waste and I've been looking forward to going out tonight all week. If you're not busy, I'd love to hang out. I'd like to ask you more questions about the rabbit anyway." He suggests.

I did say we could be friends and Noah hasn't contacted me to make any plans yet. Besides, I have all weekend to see him and Paul looks absolutely defeated.

"You know what? I miss our friends, too. Nina and I text everyday and she keeps telling me how she misses it here. I can meet you there. I have a car now." Paul's face lights up as I answer and he bounces up.

"That would be fun. If you haven't eaten, I'm buying dinner. They'll have some awesome food trucks there. They always do." The color comes back to his face and my stomach grumbles at the loss of my PB&J once more.

"That sounds great. Do I have time to get ready?" I ask and Paul checks his phone.

"It'll be tight. How about this, I'll pick you up at your place and we can take one car. Then you can have a little more time to get ready and I'll go home and pick up the blankets to sit on." He offers.

I could use the extra minutes as I fear I must smell like a raccoon and a few other animals all rolled up into one.

"Sounds good. I'm going to clock out and say good night here and head home. Text me when you're on your way?" I ask, hoping to get a little warning.

"Sure." He spins on his heel and waves as he rushes out to his car.

Clutching the clipboard to my body, I make my way into the back room and the bunny is already resting peacefully while Shanna and Jeff prepare their area.

"How does it look?" I ask, setting the paperwork by Jeff's work area and he picks it up, glancing over the answers quickly before mumbling to himself.

"Just by looking at it, I'm sure he has a broken leg. If your friend found it on the side of the road, it looks like it got hit by a car. It couldn't have happened too long before he found him though because an animal cry like that would have attracted any predators in the area. His breathing sounds fine but we won't know until we take x-rays if there is internal damage. There are no abrasions or blood on him so it looks like the impact was solely on the hind leg. He almost made it across the road." Jeff stays focused on his work area. Setting my notes down, he opens and closes a few drawers before finding the tools he needs then he looks up to the both of us.

"I'm good here. Shanna, it's always nice to see you but I've got this. Really, it's Friday night. Go home, enjoy your night for me. I'll take good care of *Bugs* here" He winks at both of us.

"Thank you, Jeff. Good luck and you have the list of staff on call tonight if you need." Shanna says and Jeff starts waving us out the door.

"Well, that was an interesting last day of training for you. Sorry about your sandwich." Shanna smiles then continues, "I have to shut my stuff down and email this letter to your professor before I go. Have a good weekend, Hazel." She's already half in her office as she finishes speaking and I say good night while I gather my bag and head for the car with our logo on it.

The car is a little beater and it runs a bit rough but it'll do. I've gotten some fun stares from people as I drive onto campus but I don't care in the least. I can't wait to show it to Nina when she gets back. She's going to cackle at the sight of it.

Just as I get into my room, my phone vibrates and I feel my stomach drop. Paul can't already be heading over here. That's not a lot of time to get ready.

Noah: Good evening. How was work?

Hazel: Eventful, I'm officially done my review. I'm an apprentice.

Noah: Congratulations. Can we celebrate tonight?

Hazel: I can't. I'm going to a Jazz festival with Paul.

I wait a minute for his reply, but none come. I'm wasting time standing here so I make my way to the bathroom, stripping my clothes as I go. I really do smell like a wild animal. Turning on the shower, I pull my hair on top of my head in a bun and step under the warm water. I won't have time to dry my hair but I can wash all of this dirt off of me.

Three minutes later and I'm out, toweled off and heading into my room. I grab a pair of jeans and a casual top, then make my way back to the bathroom to let my hair down and do my makeup when my phone buzzes.

Paul: Leaving now. There in 10

Hazel: Great. I'll be out front.

Remembering we will be out into the evening, I make my way back to my room, gathering my work clothes as I go and tossing them in the laundry basket before pulling a sweater out of the closet as my phone buzzes again.

Noah: You're going out with Paul?
Noah: Will anyone else be with you?

Hazel: It's a long story. It's just us.
Hazel: He's still my friend.

Noah: Does he know that?

Hazel: Yes. He was at my work and we were talking about how we missed our group of friends.

Noah: Why was he at your work, Hazel?

Hazel: It's a long story. He's going to be here in five minutes. Can I tell you later? I've missed you this week.

Noah: I've missed you, too, Doll.

I suddenly feel light-headed at his nickname for me and now I wish I wasn't going anywhere tonight.

Noah: I'd like to see you after the festival. Can you spend the night at my place?

Oh hell yes, my inner voice screams before I catch myself. I don't want to ask Paul to drop me off at Noah's place. And I want to show Noah more of my life.

Hazel: Can you spend the night at my place instead?

20

NOAH

*T*his week has been a flurry of activity at work and none of it has been productive. Our legal case against one of our employees should have been open and shut but Brent Davis has been prolonging his inevitable.

Our other defendant, Sean, has come out with some information against him but Brent's lawyer quickly shut it down by exposing a drinking problem and attacking his character on the stand.

Then there was an anonymous tip sent to the business reporter of our local newspaper about Brent being unfairly targeted because Emilia was back in town and she simply didn't like him because he refused her advances in high school.

I've been working overtime with Joshua, Emilia and our team of lawyers just to stay on top of everything Brent keeps piling on. It's just a matter of time but the week has been a bit rough.

I haven't even mentioned my slashed tire to Joshua

because it could just be a random event and I know the knowledge would send him off the deep end.

But now, it's Friday and even justice takes a break.

I wasn't sure if I'd be working late so I didn't want to get Hazel's hopes of seeing each other up only to cancel and now, staring at my phone screen, I realize I should have messaged her sooner.

She has a date with Paul. I don't care that she doesn't think it's a date. I'm pretty sure he does no matter what she says.

Noah: Of course. I'd love to see your place.

Hazel: Great. I'll message when we are heading there. It shouldn't be later than 11pm.

Noah: Enjoy the music.

It would be over three and a half hours before I heard from her again and those hours felt like an eternity. Waging war with myself, I was tempted to take in a jazz festival of my own but decided against it.

The park where the festival was taking place was public and the event was very popular. There would be crowds everywhere.

And I trust Hazel. Everything is new between us, but I trust her. I just don't trust him.

Her last message came a little after 10pm.

Hazel: We're leaving now. I'll be home in about 30 minutes.

That was 35 minutes ago and, as I wait in the car in front of her apartment, I can't help but continue to check my phone for an update when two bright lights pull into the lot in front of us and Marcus shields his eyes.

I wait for the lights to turn off as they glare into our car but they don't. The passenger side opens and someone steps out. I can't quite make them out so I step out of the car on my own to see Hazel as she notices me at the same time and waves, all smiles. Marcus exits the car and stands quietly beside the driver's door, waiting for my prompt.

As Hazel waves, the driver's side opens and the headlights finally dim. Paul gets out of the car with a sly smirk on his face and crosses in front of the vehicle to talk to Hazel. I can't make out the conversation from this distance and, before she can get away, he pulls her into a tight hug.

In an instant, my entire body tightens and I want to tear him off of her when I notice her hug him back and a piece of my heart hurts at the sight but I stay still, unaffected.

The hug goes on a little too long for friends and, just before they pull apart, I see his head move up in my direction.

This is for my benefit.

I really don't like this guy and I have no reason other than him attempting to claim something that is already mine.

I should have messaged her earlier.

For the first time in a long time, I understand my friend Joshua. I once told him to show patience when he had to handle the boyfriend of the woman he loved. I now see how absolutely ridiculous my advice was.

Maintaining control when someone is standing right in front of you, blatantly trying to claim someone you already have is infuriating. I'm standing still because I trust Hazel. I'm also standing still because I fear if I take even the smallest step, I will wander over there and take what is mine right in front of him and that could cost me Hazel's trust in me.

She's already closed half the distance between us before I realize the embrace has ended and Paul is opening his door and getting back into his car when she reaches me.

"It's good to see you." My smile feels a little forced. It is good to have her with me now but I'm not happy with the current situation.

"I'm glad you could come over. It's good to see you, too." As she answers, I lean into her and pull a leaf out of her hair. My mind goes to all of the worst places, thinking about how a leaf could have ended up on her head.

"What was that about?" My chin lifts in Paul's direction. I know I sound jealous but I don't care.

"Oh, he had a rough day. He needed a friend to hang out with. He was just saying thank you." I could take her answer at face value but Paul's car is still sitting there watching us. He's mocking me and I can't let it go.

"It seemed a bit long for a friendly hug." I question. I'm not challenging her personally, I'm taking issue with the way she perceives their relationship.

She takes a moment before answering and I'm happy she does. I want her to question him and consider her actions around him.

"He knows we're just friends." She shrugs, defending him and I feel my will step over my breaking point.

"Really?" I push.

She takes a deep breath to answer but I don't give her the chance. Stepping into her, I dominate her space and wrap my arm around her to grab the same fistful of hair I had her in when she played with herself for me. As I tighten my fingers to the hold I want, she sucks in a deep breath of air and her eyes bulge as she instantly deflates in my grasp, waiting for my lead.

I can't help the carnal surge coursing through me as I lean in and push my lips against hers, my tongue immediately pushing through her lips to taste her as I take the kiss I've been craving all week.

Wrapping my free hand around her, I grab the ass I'm going to be spanking soon and squeeze her into me and she offers no fight, only a deep guttural moan as her hands grip my sides, pulling me in.

I don't stop, I don't open my eyes and I don't look for Paul because this is entirely for my benefit. The fact that he has to sit there and bear witness to Hazel's choice just makes her taste that much sweeter.

There is no doubt who she belongs to now and he can accept his place and be her friend or he can leave her alone but I won't tolerate any further displays like the one that just happened.

The squeal of tires against pavement catches my attention and I open my eyes as Hazel lazily opens hers and looks at me. I don't think she's realized Paul is peeling out of the parking lot yet. Half a second later, her body startles at the screech of his tires as he takes a sharp turn and catches her attention and she sees what I've seen all along.

He does have feelings for her.

"You didn't have to do that in front of him. Did you kiss me because of Paul?" She asks, raising a brow.

"No, I kissed you because you are mine and I've wanted this all week. Don't question me, Hazel. You seem to think the guy just wants to be your friend. I proved in less than a minute, you are wrong. He needed a visual reminder." Clutching hair tighter, I wait for the little spark flickering inside her to subside and I continue, "You belong to me, Doll. Or do you wish to deny that?"

"N-no. I don't deny that." She lowers her tone. "I'm yours." A silent void lingers between us while I hold her steady. I want her words to sink into her own psyche. "I'm sorry, Noah. You're right. I will handle him differently from now on. Nina is back in town in a few weeks. I'll make sure we are always with our friends." She places a hand on my chest, pulling at my shirt and I settle slightly at her touch.

I want to tell her she is never to see him again but it isn't fair to her as it seems they have the same friends in common and I don't want to be the possessive boyfriend that breaks up friendships.

"While I appreciate that, until your friends return, I want you to notify me when your schedule changes and be prepared that I might have an objection." I'm adding to her list and the look on her face tells me, she knows it.

"You mean you want to track me and tell me what to do?" She attempts to clarify and I slowly shake my head.

"No, Hazel. You are to tell me if anything changes. Like if you are going to go out with anyone, or your daily routine changes. I can't take care of you if I don't know what is going on. I think you'll find I am very understanding, but I don't trust your friend." I loosen my grip but maintain my hold on her and she stays still in my arms.

"I understand, Noah. Thank you for watching out for me." At her response, I release her and she takes a step back.

"How did he come to be at your work today?" I ask as Marcus continues to stand by and I'm aware he can hear everything which is fine by me. It'll save me time notifying him later.

"Oh, he found a rabbit hurt on the side of the road and brought it to the facility. We got to talking and he said how much he missed our friends and how upsetting the situation with the bunny was. His date stood him up for the festival tonight and he asked if I would go with him—as friends. I should have texted you before I answered him. I just thought you were busy and we'd see each other this weekend." She looks regretful.

"I see." I'm not convinced he's this innocent. Maybe I'm being over-protective but everything sounds a little too convenient for my liking.

"He did ask tonight if he could come by next week and see the rabbit. I told him it was fine and said I'd text when I knew more. Is that okay?" Tentatively she adds this piece of information.

"Make sure you set up a time for the visit ahead of time. Only when others will be present and with you. Do you understand?" Her expression is unreadable.

"I understand. I'll make sure one of our technicians is with us and I'll keep it short." She offers and I nod my agreement.

"I'm going to talk to Marcus and gather my things, I'll meet you at the door." I smile casually and she offers a grin in return then walks around me and up the steps to the front of her building.

"Can you stick around for about half an hour? Just make sure the guy doesn't circle back. Then you're free to go. I'll message you in the morning unless I need you sooner." I speak as I grab my bag from the back seat.

"Sure thing. Listen—that kid—" Marcus lowers his voice from Hazel and points in the direction where Hazel was dropped off.

"Paul?" I confirm and he nods before continuing.

"Yes. He was at Hazel's apartment when I dropped in to pick her up last Sunday. He was only in the hallway but I got the impression she didn't expect him. He didn't acknowledge me, just looked put out that I interrupted their conversation." He offers.

"He's going to be put out a lot from now on. Thank you for letting me know, Marcus." I respond and, in the back of my mind, I realize Hazel never mentioned that to me either.

She's too trusting and she's too kind and these are things I'll have to gently break her of before someone takes advantage of her down the road.

Waving myself off from Marcus, I turn to find Hazel waiting patiently by her front door.

"So, what do you want to do tonight?" She asks and her face is already flush with a rosy hue.

"It's been a long week and I've been aching for this time with you. Off the top of my head, I can think of a few things, Doll." I imagine I'm a little intimidating right now. I feel hungry, starving for a taste of her. The bag I'm carrying brushes against my leg, reminding me of its contents. "Let's get you up to your room, get your clothes off and take it from there. I have something I want to show you."

21

HAZEL

*W*e hit a landing in the stairwell and I turn to ascend the last flight of stairs when I look back over my shoulder and catch the sinful look in Noah's eyes. His intensity catches me by surprise and I trip over my own foot as my body involuntarily reacts to his predacious stare.

Foreign feelings surge into me and my world tilts as I feel the shift in my balance. Sidestepping to shorten the distance between us, Noah slips his hand around my waist before I fall and pushes me back against the wall to steady me without dropping his bag.

"Thank you." I'm almost out of breath and I'm not sure if it's because I almost face planted onto the concrete steps or because he now has his body pushed up, flush against mine, pinning me to the wall behind me.

I hear someone giggle before I realize the flighty sound came out of me and it's affecting him in a way that is making my head spin as I feel him grind his hips into my midsection.

Nope, that's me, too. I'm brazenly and rather impulsively

grinding my hips into him while he stays still, pinning me to the wall. What is happening to me?

"Patience. Unless you want me to take you right here." He threatens, then scans my face for a response before continuing. "Tell me, during the summer months, what are the chances of someone taking the stairs this late at night and seeing just how dirty my little doll is?" He nudges his nose into the crook of my neck as he growls his question against my ear before his hips push me back into the concrete with the same amount of force as my own and my eyes roll up to the ceiling.

I'd never considered myself to be this bold but his words are taking over and my panties feel wet against my core. As if reading my mind, his hips thrust up, against my jeans and I groan at the friction, drawing a smile from his lips.

"It looks like I might have a little exhibitionist on my hands, literally." Dropping his bag and reaching behind me, he grips my ass, lifting me and coaxing my legs to wrap around him and I gladly follow as he continues, "Tell me, do you like the thought of being naked and spread while I fuck you here? Where anyone can see how desperate you are for me?"

Everything he says touches something inside of me. As if walking down a corridor filled with locked doors, his words hold the keys to every one of them and I'm being led into a more obscure part of myself. Images of my legs spread wide and Noah fucking me where we could be caught wage war and make me light-headed. Do I really want someone to watch me like this? Is it just the thought turning me on? I would die if Nina saw this side of me. But I want Noah to see it.

"I don't know." Confusion takes hold. There are some

parts of me I don't understand and I've never considered. I'm afraid to say I do because what if I don't or I embarrass myself? And I'm afraid to deny it and close the door on learning more about myself.

"I think it's something worth exploring, Doll. But not here and not right now." Relief surges through me but I'm not sure if it's because he's saving me from a public display or because he's hinted at the promise of showing me more another time. "Let's get you to your room." Kissing my forehead, he releases my legs and gathers his things before allowing me to lead him up the stairs to my floor.

It takes half a minute to steady myself and Noah stands silently beside me, examining my moves and offering me the time I need to compose myself. This little act in itself makes me feel safe around him.

Stopping in front of my room, I unlock the door and take a step back, catching his attention. I see it written in his features, my actions have intrigued him. It's my place, but I want him to enter in front of me. I want him to lead me. I want to follow him.

He only takes a few steps into the living room before stopping where the light from the hall ends and I reach in to turn on the light switch before he continues his way into the middle of our living area, dropping his bag in front of the couch while looking around.

"You have a beautiful home, Hazel." Turning slowly, he scans the living area before asking, "Other than the books on the shelf, how much of this room belongs to you?" His eyes continue to examine everything around him.

"Less than five percent, but not zero." I answer with a smile on my face.

We don't have a lot of stuff and I love Nina's style. I also don't have any extra money to buy my own decorations right now. The furniture is provided and we keep the room fairly clean and simple.

"Interesting. So by my calculations, you have about one thing in this room that is yours... other than some of the books." He states and I nod to confirm before he cuts me off. "Wait, don't tell me." He circles the perimeter of the room slowly looking at every picture and trinket and occasionally glancing back to see if he's close and I keep my features impassive.

"Well, everything here has a beautiful fun style, but if I was a betting man, I'd go with the item that matches your personality, Miss Masters." Smiling, he runs his fingers along our books, then lifts his hand to the shelf above them. "Something with character—something complex." Tapping his fingers on the plain wooden box on the shelf. "This is yours."

"How did you—" I don't think I'm hiding the amount of shock on my face.

"It's a puzzle box. It reminds me of you." He says, picking it up to inspect it further. "On the outside it looks unassuming, but it is actually complex, and full of intrigue. And that's before I even get to the treasure that awaits on the inside." Winking, he answers as his fingers tentatively slide along the smooth edges, searching for all of its hidden secrets.

My mouth waters at his words. I'm not sure he's talking about my keepsake anymore and I clear the lump out of my throat before replying.

"My parents bought it for me when I graduated high school. I had it in my room but Nina loves trying to open it so I left it out here. She's been dying to see what my parents put inside it. Can I get you something to drink?" I ask, opening myself a bottle of water.

"I'll have water as well. Thank you, Hazel. So you don't know what your parents put in it?" He asks and I bark out a laugh.

"I solved it during my first summer, eight years ago. It drives my roommate mad but she loves trying to figure it out, so I didn't have the heart to tell her. I opened it a year ago and put two candy necklaces in it and a twenty for a bottle of wine, just in case she ever opens it." I can't help but giggle. Every time I watch Nina, face contorted, trying to figure out the box, I have to sit silently, but now I can laugh about it and it feels good.

I see my story has amused Noah. His smile shines through his eyes. Accepting the bottle of water, he places the box back on the shelf and sits down on the couch, patting the area beside him and I join him.

"Sneaky. What was in it?" His curiosity is genuine.

"They wrote me a letter and gave me a necklace that belonged to my grandmother. Both are at my mom's for safekeeping. The locks on these rooms are flimsy." As I answer, I watch his brows scrunch together as he glances over his shoulder at the inside of my door.

"They are simple locks." He grumbles.

"We don't keep anything of real value here anyway." As I speak, he looks almost incredulous.

"Hazel, you are valuable." Goosebumps creep along my arms under my shirt.

"Thank you," I say, then change the topic. His declaration feels foreign. It is welcome, but I'm not used to it. "Um, what did you want to show me?"

Noah carefully scans my face before he responds and I

feel as though he's torn between answering me and discussing my building's poor security.

Reaching his arm to the side table to set his bottle down, he settles back in place.

"Curious little girl, see for yourself. It's in the bag." His roguish smile stretches across his entire face as he offers me a wink and my attention moves to the bag on the floor in front of us.

I stay in my place for a long moment then place my water bottle on my own side table before returning to my position. The weight of Noah's stare settles on me, but it isn't a burden. I feel as though I'm being inspected as much as I'm examining the mysterious bag, sitting closed in front of me. I get the feeling once I open the zipper, something will change and I become excited at the thought.

Wriggling my hips to the edge of the couch, I reach for the bag and it is heavier than Noah made it out to be. I feel his presence beside me as I grab the zipper and feel each click over the metal teeth as it opens revealing—

"Rope?" Pulling the pliable, smooth link from the bag. "Are you going to kidnap me?" I hold the coil loosely in my hand, running my fingers along its worn length as I ask and it's Noah's turn to laugh.

"It's a special kind of rope. It is something I am interested in. Have you ever heard of Kinbaku?" Slowly shaking my head, I feel like an outsider and he attempts to clarify. "How about Shibari? Rope bondage?"

"Like tying someone up?" I clarify.

"Yes, but a little more intricate. Can I show you some pictures of what I mean?" Noah asks, holding up his phone and I nod.

Now I'm curious. I think I've seen some photos of what

he is describing. At least, I hope it is the same thing because what I remember was stunning. Nina wanted to check out a sex expo last year and she showed me a pamphlet. A woman had rope wrapped around her entire body and she was suspended and the image took my breath away. It turns out, tickets were sold out for the event and I was disappointed because I had my heart set on learning more about whatever it was.

Pulling me out of my memory, Noah places his phone in my empty hand and I examine the image. It is a different position but it is definitely the same style I saw before. The woman is lying flat and rope wraps around most of her body, securing her almost like a mummy.

"That's amazing." My eyes stay glued on the photo as I follow every strand around her body.

"What do you imagine being tied like that feels like?" He asks quietly.

"I think it would be comforting to be wrapped tight like that, like a big blanket." I answer, making eye contact and he smiles.

Swiping his finger across the screen to another photo, I feel his eyes move back to me again. "And this one?"

I take my time looking at the picture. The woman in the image is also lying down but her arms are tied away from her body and her legs are bound, spread wide and attached to whatever she is on.

She is open and vulnerable at the hands of anyone else who is there with her and I feel a shiver run down my spine.

"I think I would feel very exposed and maybe helpless?" My voice rises at the end of my sentence making it sound like a question.

"I think you would feel helpless if you hadn't chosen to

surrender yourself." I nod my head as he speaks then he leans in to me, dropping his voice to a whisper.

"Imagine, giving yourself to the person who did this. Have you ever wanted to let go; let someone else take care of you, let everything that weighs you down just float away?" His questions land in a dark part of my heart and I feel mesmerized by his words and the smooth ridges of the rope in my hand. The pads on my fingers have become highly sensitive, each little bump in the rope tickles as the threads graze my skin, sending shivers deep into my core.

Have I ever wanted to let go?

During the pain of watching my father deteriorate and my mother lose pieces of herself. From picking up so many jobs just to keep us under a roof and listening to my mother's sobs late at night when she thought I was sleeping. From being dumped by text and forced to see all of my friends move on without me, not one of them ever checking up on me. From putting myself through college, working three jobs and watching the world pass me by...

"Yes." I answer under my breath and catch a desperate sob before it escapes me. Then, mustering my courage, I ask, "Are you going to do that for me?" I hear the hopeful undertone in my words.

"I will, in time." His smile is soft, comforting and I drop my eyes back to the rope in my hands as he takes his phone back.

"This feels amazing. It bends so easily. I've never seen rope like this." I run my fingers along the length, memorizing each bump and dip. It bends and twists without effort and wraps around my hand as if it has a life of its own.

"This is a different kind of rope. It's called jute rope and this one here has been conditioned to feel this way." He places his hands over mine, holding me in place around the threads.

"Um, what did you mean by *in time*." A sense of urgency consumes my thoughts.

"Patience, Doll." His satisfied smile draws me in and settles the storm building inside of me. "As a matter of fact, I'll take great pleasure in teaching you patience when I've got you bound on my bed, *in good time*." A sultry wink ends his sentence.

I'm beginning to get the impression I'm not as good at this patience thing as I thought I was since Noah keeps saying the word over and over again. As a matter of fact, the more he says it, the more impatient I feel myself become.

"But..." My rebuttal is cut short as he moves his hand from mine and slides it up my leg toward the apex of my thighs and I realize how heated I've become at something so simple as our conversation.

"The process of binding you, slowly removing your own free will and restricting your movement bit by bit is a process, a journey we will travel together. There are nerves in your body we both need to be aware of to avoid damage, there are discussions we need to have. I'm not just going to tie you to the bed, Hazel. I'm going to educate you, bind you to my will and claim every delicious drop of your surrender. Then I'm going to take what you've accepted is mine to take. All. In. Good. Time." The heavy thud of my heart beat and my throaty breath is the only thing keeping his words company as I sit here, stunned and blinking rapidly at him.

I'm pretty sure it's my turn to speak, but I have nothing. Suddenly the room feels stuffy. Reaching a hand to my face, I expect him to gently caress my cheek, but he doesn't. Placing two fingers under my chin, he lifts and, as my teeth click shut, I realize I've been staring at him slack-jawed while he spoke all of those steamy words that I really wish I could remember.

"So you're only *showing* me the ropes tonight? We're not going to...?" Lifting the rope in suggestion, I know I sound sullen. I feel my body slump in defeat. How can he show me this only to take it away?

With purpose, his hand moves, cupping between my legs on top of my pants and clenching gently, I bow forward, relaxing my grip on the rope and letting it fall into his hands as my head rests in his neck and I moan for him. I'm so wound up from this new information, I feel my own wetness soak into my jeans as he rubs between my legs.

Moving his fingers back up to my chin, he draws my attention to him. His wolfish grin returns to his face as he licks his lips. "I didn't say that, Doll."

22

NOAH

"So you're only showing me the ropes tonight?" My lips curl up at her play on words, but once my eyes meet Hazel's, I know she didn't mean it as a joke. Her wide eyes and fallen face tell me she's disappointed.

I had no expectations when I packed the rope tonight, I merely wanted to give her a glimpse of what I was interested in. I was curious to see her reaction. The new member event at Ravenous is coming up soon and I wasn't sure if I should introduce Hazel to more so early in our relationship, but she is clearly ready to explore.

When I asked if she ever wanted to let go, I saw the answer in her eyes before she even spoke. Her body relaxed into mine in understanding.

She's spent her adult years taking care of everyone around her and working to keep her head above water so she can claim back the life she wanted before her family fell on hard times. A sweet submissive taking control and caring for everyone else while her own needs and self care got pushed to the side.

I don't answer her question right away. Instead, I reach over to her, desperate for contact. I don't hesitate, moving my hand between her legs, I settle on the place I want to be and cup my palm over her mound through her jeans. The expression falls from her face, replaced with a heady desire and she leans further into me as she releases the rope into my hands, the smooth texture pulling me in and I instantly know what I want to do with her tonight.

Lifting her face to meet mine, the slight part of her lips tug at my restraint, threatening to unravel my control bit by bit. She's right here with me, I'm not leading her, I'm not guiding her or pushing her. We're descending into this together.

"I didn't say that, Doll." I feel hungry, starving to get started.

Swallowing a lump in her throat, her breath comes out in heavy pants as she stills, waiting for my lead. She likes it when I call her *Doll*; when I objectify her as my property. She also responds when I call her *Baby*; I sense it comforts her. Both terms fill a different need for her.

"Stand up and take off your clothes. Keep your panties on." She stands up and faces me, her arms moving across her midsection to gather her sweater in her hands. "it is up to you if you would like to keep your bra on but you'll enjoy this more if you take it off." I lean back on her couch, watching every little move she makes.

Her eyes dart from mine to her hands as she removes her clothes, letting them fall to the floor beside her until only her underwear remains and she shuffles in her stance, considering my suggestion.

Her eyes drift down my body until she gets to my lap before she freezes, first licking her lip, then biting it. I'm hard; this is what she does to me. I know she can see me and I know I'm smiling. I can't help it.

Without a word, she reaches both hands behind her, unclasping her bra and rolling her shoulders forward to shift the straps down her arms. I'm sure she set the bra down but once my eyes land on the curve of her breasts, I stay fixated on her pert nipples, watching them slowly stiffen under my gaze.

"Come down to the floor. Get in a comfortable seated position." She lowers herself to the area rug on my command and I rise as she crosses her legs, placing her hands on her lap.

Moving back to her door, I turn the cheap lock then remove my shoes and socks before making my way back to her as I pull my shirt off over my head. Her inexperience makes her an open book and her expressions are easy to read. I know she is affected by the sight of me. Her eyes are wide and her mouth has dropped open again and I don't think she's realized it.

Dropping the rope, I lower myself to the floor behind her, spreading my legs around her and lining my front to her back. One gentle kiss to her shoulder is all I'll allow myself before I draw my fingers over her soft skin, watching as goosebumps appear.

"I am going to use the rope on you tonight, but I'm not going to bind your wrists or tie you down." As I speak, her body doesn't move. I know she's confused. It's a common misconception that Shibari is just tying someone to the bed. "Trust me, you will enjoy yourself." I feel my lips stretch wide at my guarantee.

Wrapping my hands around her shoulders, I slowly pull her back to rest on my chest, opening her front up to me and her arms fall limply over my thighs. Cupping my hand over one breast, she fits perfectly and I draw my fingers around her areola, pinching her nipples softly as I whisper into her ear.

"It's just us, Hazel. I want you to relax and concentrate on the sensation. *Red* is still your safe word but now, if you have a question or need a moment, you'll say *yellow* then *green* to continue. Like traffic lights. Do you understand?" I play with her pebbled nipples, waiting for her response.

"I—yes." Her voice catches in her throat.

"You're my good girl." She whimpers at my praise. "But just to be clear, stop and go no longer work. What do you say if you need a moment?" I caress her ear with my lip as she clears her throat.

"Yellow."

"And what if you want to stop everything for the night?"

"Red."

"Very good." My fingers trail down, searching for her centre and she uncrosses her legs, propping her feet against the floor, habitually opening herself for me and I can't help a groan of my own as my fingers skim over her panties, finding a telltale wetness between her legs.

Tilting her head to the side with one hand, I drop my head to her neck, licking a trail from her collar bone up to her jawline and I feel her little fingers dig into my legs as my other hand remains on the thin fabric that is hiding her sex from me.

Her body is strung tight with anticipation and I'm not going to release her just yet. Against my own desire, I remove my hand from the cloth of her panties and sit her up straight, drawing a quiet protest from her that makes me smile.

"Patience." I unravel the rope and run it over her skin.

She arches and bows, following the sensation from the threads and I begin to move with her, slowly as if dancing to a song only the two of us can hear. "Stand up." She pauses only for a second before standing and I rise with her. "Stay here." I drop the rope by her feet and leave her in the living room as I make my way down the hallway to a free-standing full length mirror I noticed when I first looked around her place.

Carrying it back to the living room, I prop it up and face it to her, reflecting her naked form back to her. She watches me but keeps silent as I move around behind her to make sure she can see everything I want her to see, then I step up behind her, possessively massaging her breast while my eyes stay locked on hers through the mirror and I notice her chest rise and fall more prominently as her breathing deepens.

"Are you ready, Baby?" She nods toward our reflection.

"You can be as quiet as you want while I tie you, but right now, I need to hear you tell me you are ready?"

"Oh, sorry. I'm ready." Her voice is deceptively raspy. She's more than ready, I chuckle to myself at the thought.

Picking up the rope, I decide to start with a basic chest harness. Doubling the strands together, I start by hooking the rope through itself around her midsection and allow the soft rope to flow against her skin as she watches me work behind her through the mirror.

Every move, every twist and tie is slow and it is intentional and she watches with rapt attention, every now and then catching my eyes in our reflection and smiling meekly.

I adjust everything I do, checking that I am wrapping her properly and the tension is only tight enough for what I need and I feel myself slip into my own space as I work, mesmerized by the movement of the rope and the place it claims along her skin.

Shifting myself around to her front, I work near her sternum, framing her breasts and I feel her eyes on mine even though I'm focused on my task at hand. I steal a glance at her and she smiles when we make eye contact before I shift around her so she can see herself in the mirror and she sucks in a deep breath as her eyes round at the sight of her chest bound, her hardened nipples evident.

Staring at her unmarked flesh, my mouth waters and I drop my head down to suck her nipple into my mouth, biting it indulgently before releasing her and licking away the ache, then I return to my rope.

I take my time finishing off the harness with a tied handle that I plan on using soon. Then look over her shoulder into the mirror before catching her attention.

"This is a chest harness. You have full movement of your entire body if you need. I could extend it and bind your hands, arms and even legs, but this is where I want to stop tonight. What do you think?" The anticipation makes it hard to breathe as I wait for her response. Her eyes are wide as she silently examines her body through her reflection.

"It—it's beautiful." She answers as she tries to turn to her side so she can see my work at the back. "Can—um—can we do more?" Instead of looking at me through the mirror, she turns herself to face me, eyes pleading.

"We will, Baby. I promise, but not tonight. This is my limit for our first time, but I'm not done with you." Spinning her back to look at herself, I continue, "Tell me how this makes you feel."

"I—I don't know if I can explain it, but I feel amazing."

Lifting her hand, she trails her fingers along the ropes wrapped around her midsection.

"Shibari isn't necessarily a sexual act. To some, it's comforting, to others it's an art, and to some, it can be erotic. I find it to be a combination. I'm going to ask you the same question again. Tell me how this makes you feel."

"Oh." Realization dawns in her eyes and her cheeks burn crimson, answering my question. "I—uh—I feel like it's a combination, too."

Taking a step into her until my chest is flush with her back, I trace my fingers over the rope. "While your hands are not tied, I forbid you to touch yourself. Would you like me to touch you, Doll?" Purposely using the name I reserve to play with her, I'm telling her where we are about to go with this if she chooses.

"Yes." There is no hesitation. She almost makes it sound like a demand and I lower us to the floor, back into the position we were in earlier, but now we are facing the mirror.

"Watch yourself." I speak low, my lips against her ear.

Her legs are closed and tucked to her side as I begin rolling her hard nipples between my fingers as I kiss along her neck.

"There are so many things I want to show you, Hazel. I can tie you up in different ways. I can spread you wide, make you vulnerable, or I can cocoon you and make you feel secure." Leaning her body back against mine, I move my hand over her panties and rub a long line over the fabric and she pushes her legs wide, propping them up like before.

Her moan is music to my ears as I slide my fingers under the seam of her panties, pulling the fabric to the side and exposing her to our reflection. "Tell me, Hazel. What do you want me to do to you?" I feel the vibration in my voice as my tone turns into a growl against her ear and I don't wait for her to respond as I slide a finger deep into her slick entrance.

Her head rolls back, lifelessly on my shoulder as she releases a moan and I quickly add a second at her entrance as she grinds her hips forward and tightens her warm walls around my fingers, asking for more. "Tell me, Hazel. What do you want?"

"I... ohhhh..." Her words come out in whimpers as she continues to buck against my hand.

"Come on, Hazel. Use your words." I taunt, applying just enough pressure to keep her wanting more without letting her come completely undone. "I won't ask again. Tell me what you need."

23

HAZEL

*T*ell *me what you need.* Noah's words pierce my mind. It isn't a question. It's a demand. And it's one I can't ignore as I watch myself shamelessly humping my hips onto his hand as he slides his fingers in and out of me, my release just beyond my grasp.

"I need you." It's a confession of sorts; a realization that I need everything Noah is offering me. I focused so much on being the one in control when I was only holding on all of these years.

I can't stop staring at these ropes wrapped tightly around my body, binding me to him. With each wrap, I sank deeper into this space I'm now in. The ropes are both soft and unforgiving. Holding me close while setting me free. Catching my breasts bounce as I arch my back, I had forgotten I took my bra off. This is how transfixed I am on him.

I'm unable to restrain the moans escaping me each time

he hits a sensitive spot and he hasn't responded to me yet. He stays still, touching me with his eyes fixated on mine.

That's because I didn't answer his question, I realize.

"I—" Being tied like this sends my thoughts into a tailspin. There is something I want and need, I've been curious since we met but can I put it into words? I feel my face heat up at the thought of asking for such a thing.

"We can sit here like this all night but I guarantee, not being able to come will lose its appeal fast. I won't say it again." His whisper is gruff against my ear and I close my eyes, focused on the sensation and hoping it will grant me the courage to say—

"I need to taste you. I want to touch you." His fingers pause for a split second and I open my eyes to see the surprise on his face before his wolfish smile takes over.

He wasn't expecting that. Maybe he thought I just wanted him to make me come again. I want that, too but right now, I want to please him for doing this for me. For tying me up like this and showing me this side of myself.

Clearing his throat, Noah rises without saying anything and I worry I might have said the wrong thing. Taking a few steps in front of me, he lowers his head to look down at me.

"Slide your panties off and get on your knees." He commands and my heart thuds to life as I quickly close my legs and pull them down before swiveling my legs to the side and rising on my knees, resting my ass on my heels while I maintain eye contact.

A nervous wave hits me as I realize I don't have a lot of experience to back up what I just asked for and I swallow a hard lump in my throat.

I wonder if he senses my anxiety as his hand reaches out,

combing through the hairs on my head and brushing along my cheek before he runs his thumb over my parted lips.

"You're perfect." He mutters low to himself but the room is so quiet I make it out.

Unbuttoning the top button to his pants, he returns to his position, one hand brushing through my hair as he looks at me, waiting.

He's waiting for me to be brave; to take what I need and I feel my arms vibrate with anticipation as I raise my hands to unzip his pants and remove them from him. As my fingers fumble he grants me the small mercy of helping me get them off and as I pull down his boxer briefs, his cock springs to life and I can't stop the nervous yelp I make at the sight of him.

My experience is limited and, in that time, I've never seen anything like this. I know I must be gawking at him, I can't help it. My last personal experience with the male anatomy was a long time ago. I realize everyone grew up without me and, sexually, I'm an awkward teenager stuck in a woman's body.

Craning my neck to look at his face, his blue eyes reflect a hunger that I feel and it rattles me.

"Hazel, if you're not sure, we don't have to—" He speaks slowly and I think he's mistaken my hesitance for reluctance.

"I want to." I cut him off. "I just... um... don't have... I don't want to disappoint you." The concern in his brows releases as he crouches down to my level and it isn't lost on me, his cock is still just out there. I wish I had his confidence.

"You will never disappoint me, Baby. As long as you are being open and truthful to both me and yourself."

I don't know if he was going to say anything else because I place my hands on either side of his face and push my lips onto his, silently begging for him to kiss me and his tongue bursts into my mouth, claiming everything as his.

I desperately suck in a deep breath of air and the ropes tighten against my skin, reminding me I am his and my desire consumes my nerves.

Reaching for his hard length, I break the kiss and he rises, keeping his hands on my face, watching me. I decide to leave my insecurity behind as I touch and explore him as I want. Groaning, he drops his head back as a droplet forms at his tip and I extend my tongue to taste him.

"That's— " His thought is cut off by another deep moan and his fingers comb into my hair, spurring me to continue and I do, wrapping my lips around him and swirling my tongue over his head.

"Play with yourself." My hand instinctively moves between my legs at his command, searching for my own sensitive areas as I hum my pleasure around his cock and his fingers tighten in my hair, urging me to continue.

Glancing up, my eyes meet his. His face painted in lust ignites a heat deep inside of me. I drop my hand from his shaft and stop moving my head as I relax my throat as much as I can and he takes my cue to lead.

Slowly at first, he pulls back, speaking only to direct me, then his thrusts become steady and deeper as his hands control my movement, giving him the pleasure I want him to have. I can't close my eyes, I can't stop looking at his face as he comes undone and my fingers continue to rub my clit and I moan around him, occasionally choking. He watches me intently, his eyes glazing over as he adjusts his thrusts to accommodate me before his hands fist up at the side of my head and he stills inside of me.

He was so close.

I continue to control my breathing as I wait for him to move and, after a few seconds, he pulls out, dropping himself back to my level and studying my face. My lips tingle at the loss of him.

"You're full of surprises, Doll. How do you feel?" Brushing my hair off my forehead, his face only inches away from my own.

"My lips feel puffy." I answer.

Stellar, Hazy, I think to myself. Of all of the sexy things I probably could have said, this was none of them.

"You look stunning. Keep touching yourself." My fingers pick back up as he leans in for a much more gentle kiss than last time and he pinches my nipple between his fingers. The small sensation of pain immediately increases the pleasure I feel and I think he senses my arousal as he moves to my other nipple, repeating his move.

"Do you enjoy pleasing me, Baby?" Shifting to my side, he removes my hand and continues to rub from my clit to my pussy, spreading my wetness around.

Something out of the corner catches my eyes and, as I shift my attention forward, I realize my reflection is in full view.

A different version of me has emerged. The rope surrounds my body, comforting me and my knees are spread wide, offering everything to him as my hips buck in response to his touch. The contrast shocks me. I considered myself reserved. I'm sure some of my friends would say I was a prude, but with Noah, I feel free.

"Yes." I draw out my answer as my body bows forward following the fingers he's pushing inside of me.

"Look at yourself and tell me what you need me to do to you, Doll." His husky tone sucks me out of the room we are in and places me squarely in a space where it is only the two of us.

The woman in the mirror is who I always fantasized I would be. Her hair is messed up, gasping for breath and she is surrendering control and Noah sees all of me. I've never felt more protected.

"I need you to—um—be with me, Noah. I want to feel you." I rasp my answer. I don't want him to be gentle. I want to know what it feels like to be taken by him, to be owned by him.

"I am with you, Doll. I want to hear you say it." His tone challenges me, it urges me to show my base self to him.

"I want you to fuck me." Goosebumps tickle across my hot skin at my brazenness.

"Hands on the floor, bend over, put your forehead on the carpet." His fingers don't stop teasing me, his words are direct and I love it. I obey immediately.

Shifting behind me, he draws his free hand along the rope, then tickles his fingers over my ass without removing his other hand from my core and I unabashedly grind my hips onto his fingers.

"Patience." The all too familiar word startles me almost as much as the smack to my ass and my conflicting sensitivities coil together as I try to stay still. "That's better. Lift your ass higher."

The next two spanks are more forgiving and I lift my ass as high as I can for him as I moan into the carpet. Pleasure takes over and my head spins as I feel him move around behind me, spreading my wetness from my nub past my entrance and he continues on. I've never been touched there and I steady my hands in the threads of the rug.

"Did your ex ever touch you here?" His voice is low as

his one hand focuses on my susceptive clit, his finger tapping on my back hole.

"N—no." I have a slight worry my answer will start something but I trust Noah not to go too far, and I have my safe word.

Red, lingers in my mind but I don't say it.

"It's okay. Relax, I won't take you here tonight." He settles my fears.

I take a full breath and let my stress go as he continues to touch me, circling my tight ring and pushing a finger a little into my entrance while increasing his pressure on my clit, alternating between rubbing and inserting a finger into me, hitting a spot deep inside before pulling his hands away.

I want to argue. I want to beg him to keep going but his order rattles around in my head.

Patience.

Before the silence becomes unbearable, he reaches into his bag before moving behind me. My heart hammers into my chest as I hear the sound of a condom wrapper and the stretch of latex and I wait, listening to the rustling sound behind me. Before I look back, I feel the head of his cock push up against my entrance and I can't help but picture his length as he slides into me before pulling back and thrusting in again, the taste of him still on my lips.

The feeling overwhelms me and my arms fall limp from the floor to my sides as he takes control. Everything feels better when he takes the lead and I let go.

"Fuck, Hazel. You're so good for me." He growls as he continues his onslaught and I feel the strands tighten around my body. He seems to have a hold on the rope somehow and the intensity of being tied by him hits me all over again.

A few deep thrusts and I feel a little tinge, a tickle

forming around my sex as my stomach flutters and I feel myself tighten around him.

"Noah, I think—"

"I know, Doll. I feel you. I want to hear you when you come. Show me you belong to me." Growling, he doesn't slow, there is no reprieve from the edge we are barreling toward.

I feel my walls begin to spasm around him and his fingers slide up the back of my neck and fist my hair at the base of my skull.

I open my eyes from the shock as I watch the whorish sight looking back from the mirror. I'm on my knees, allowing myself to be taken so fiercely and the wanton expression on my face is unrecognizable. Noah continues his onslaught. He has a grip on my ropes and he's reining me in as he fucks me and I'm watching myself surrender to him.

I am his.

I scream out my release as I watch myself shatter around him and he follows me over the ledge as he throws back his head and growls out his orgasm.

I attempt to steady myself on my hands and knees, but my arms are shaking from the adrenaline and I lean forward to rest my upper body on the carpet when I feel him wrap an arm around my waist, lowering us together as he pulls himself out of me and spoons me on the floor in the middle of my apartment.

As the tension leaves my body, I feel exhausted and I stir when I feel him kiss the top of my head as he brushes his fingers through my hair.

"You are incredible, Baby. How do you feel? Anything hurt?" His voice is low, soothing.

"Um... no, I'm okay. That was—intense." I feel his breath in my hair as he chuckles at my answer.

"That description is accurate." He chuckles.

I attempt to roll over so I can look at him but the knot tied at my back digs in and I wince. Catching me, he lifts me up to sitting with him and checks me out.

"You're okay, but I want to get you out of these ropes and show you something else." He stands up and reaches a hand out to help me rise.

I feel a little apprehensive. I don't know if I can handle *something else* tonight but I trust him and follow his lead closer to the mirror.

Placing me directly in front of myself, he goes to work tugging on the rope behind me. It takes a minute before I feel the release of the first tie and he unwraps me, reversing everything he did when he first bound me.

As I watch the ropes fall away, I can't help the shock escaping my body in a gasp.

He's marked my body with the pressure of each tie and it looks beautiful. He's all over me.

Fixated on my reflection, I trace my fingers gingerly along each indent afraid, if I touch them too hard, they'll disappear.

When the last tie falls to the floor, the warmth of his body leans against mine, sending goosebumps across my skin. His cock pressing against my lower back as he joins me, his fingers touching all of the places that he's claimed.

"I—I love it." I'm hypnotized by the lines wrapping around me, securing me and cradling my breasts.

"Enjoy it now. I eased off on the tension of the ties. I didn't want to injure you so these marks will be gone when we wake up in the morning." I feel a sense of loss already. I want to see these on me for longer than that.

I meet his eyes in the mirror and he's smirking at me. I wonder for a moment if he can read my thoughts.

"Don't worry, Doll. I'll spank you good and hard at some point and those marks will stay with you for awhile. Knowing you, you'll earn that soon enough." He winks confirming my suspicion, he's reading my mind. "Come on. Let's go to bed. I want to take care of you before you fall asleep.

While he wraps himself around me, we talk about his interest in Shibari and I ask some questions, always getting a full answer. Then our conversation shifts to a place he goes to with a friend of his now and then.

I had only heard of sex clubs and I didn't think they were popular, but he tells me this one is membership-based. He studies my face as he talks about it and I wonder if he is trying to see if it is something I find worrisome. I ask more questions and he answers every one, then he stops talking and I feel the events of the day catch up to me. I welcome the haze of exhaustion, knowing that these marks won't be here in the morning.

I can't seem to get close enough to him and I wrap my arm over his midsection, nestling my face into his chest. He continues to talk to me even though my answers have turned into murmurs as a calm wave pulls me under.

Before I close my eyes to fall asleep, he lifts my chin. "They are having a newcomer event at Ravenous in a week. I want you to meet some of my friends. I'd like you to attend with me."

24

HAZEL

Nina: I can't believe I'm missing out on all of this.
Nina: You're making me want to get on a plane and come home NOW, Hazy.

Hazel: Haha. I miss you so much.

Nina: You know, Cassie is going to shit a brick when she finds out you're with Noah Wilde.
Nina: I think she might just hate you for real.
Nina: I want to be there when you tell her!!!
Nina: Just let me have that, okay?

Hazel: I don't want to tell everyone yet if that's okay.

Nina: Any reason?

Hazel: It's just very new and we're getting to know each other.
Hazel: We spent the whole weekend together between my place and his. It was really nice.

Nina: You didn't do it in my bed did you? Dirty girl!!! LOL!

Hazel: OMG, Nina. NO!

Nina: I'm just kidding. I won't say a thing.

Hazel: Thanks.
Hazel: How about you? What's going on with your family?

Nina: Ugh. I'd prefer to just talk about you.
Nina: Every couple of days it's the same thing. Posh party, everyone looking down their noses at everyone else. No one gets my jokes. My parents are too busy to spend time with me. I miss laughing with you.

Hazel: It's only a few weeks longer.

Nina: Seriously, Hazy. I wish you were here.
Nina: You'd hate it. We could be miserable together.
Nina: I swear, if I wasn't screwing Dad's head of security, it would be a total wash.

Hazel: Wait... WHAT?

Nina: I told you about him. He's like 10 years older than me or something like that.
Nina: He's always around, in my business.
Nina: We had a run in a few days ago and it was the best sex I've ever had.
Nina: He's bossy. I like that.

Hazel: I know the type.

Nina: We so need to catch up.
Nina: So tell me more about this sex club.

Hazel: I don't know too much.
Hazel: They are having a new member event on Friday. He wants to introduce me to some of his friends.
Hazel: I'm getting nervous. It's only a couple of days away. I told him I'd think about going.

Nina: Oh. It's getting serious.

Hazel: I wouldn't mind if it was. I'm interested to see what his friends are like.
Hazel: But then what if I'm just crazy awkward?
Hazel: What if I stand out too much?

Nina: You'll fit right in. I'm sure it'll be fine.
Nina: GO!!! Feel free to raid my closet.
Nina: I keep my sluttiest clothes on the left side ;)

Hazel: I just might do that. I've gotta go.
Hazel: Dinner is over.

*P*acking up my sandwich, I get up from my little blanket and head toward the main building of the wildlife sanctuary. We have a lunch room, but on nice days, I love being outside as much as I can.

This is my first evening shift so Shanna scheduled herself on to show me what needs to be done overnight.

When I come back into the main office, Paul is there and he and Shanna look deep in conversation but they stop talking as soon as they see me and Paul smiles.

"Hey. I thought I'd drop in before your shift ends to check in on the rabbit." He steps closer to me but doesn't go in for a hug and I'm grateful.

"I'm on night shift today. Learning the ropes." I nod at Shanna and she picks up the conversation.

"I was just looking at the chart a few minutes ago." She pauses for a moment, looking between us as she considers her words before continuing with a smile that looks a little off. "It looks like he will make a full recovery. He was lucky you came along before a predator got him." Shanna says, all smiles, and I wonder what they were talking about earlier.

"That's great. Thank you for helping him." His mood lightens even more. "Hazel, do you have a second?" He steps away from our trio telling me he wants to talk alone and Shanna takes the hint, excusing herself and giving me a few minutes before we begin my night training.

"What's up, Paul?" The humid air from outside hits me again as I open the door and begin walking slowly to Paul's car.

I know Noah doesn't want me spending time with him outside of our friends and I respect his wishes.

"I had a lot of fun at the festival and I was wondering if you'd like to catch a movie this week?" I stop as he finishes his question.

"Um, this week isn't good for me. Nina is back in a few weeks. Maybe we could get together then?" I offer and he hesitates before speaking again.

"Are you seeing that guy?" He sounds hurt and I feel a pang of guilt hit me.

"I am." I answer, hoping he'll drop it.

"He's the guy from the restaurant. Were you seeing him then, too. When we went on our date?" Now I realize what this looks like to him. He thinks I've been seeing them at the same time.

"No, Paul. I had met him just before then but we hadn't gone out yet."

"I see. Is that why we can't hang out together?"

"Partly. I have a busy few weeks here. Nina will be back before we know it though. Maybe we can all get together." I suggest.

"Maybe. You know, I don't like that he tells you what to do, Hazel. I appreciate our friendship. I hope you'll reconsider. You have my number if you're ever bored or need to talk." He slips his keys into the door and pauses. "You're such a special person, Hazel. I hope he values you."

Without waiting for my response, he slides into the driver's seat and starts his car.

I step back to wave him off before returning to the office with his words in my head.

I know Noah values me; he tells me all of the time. How he speaks to me during sex and some of our more intimate times together is different and separate from how we value each other all of the time. It's like an added layer.

"Is your—uh—friend gone?" Shanna asks as we both step into the main room at the same time.

"He is. Is everything okay?" I ask.

"Oh, it is. I just wasn't sure how much I should tell your friend about the rabbit. He was so torn up over it when he brought him in, I wasn't sure if I should add to it. That rabbit was lucky your friend found it in time."

"Why do you say that?" She opens the file and I join her at the admitting desk to look at it.

"It looks like the bunny wasn't wild. It happens now and then and it isn't the best part of our job. A lot of people get pets thinking they can handle them but end up hurting them or abandoning them outside of city limits when something goes wrong. This rabbit belonged to someone." She starts, pointing at the x-rays and I see instantly what she is getting at.

"The break doesn't look natural. It looks like he came from an abusive owner." She nods as I speak my thoughts out loud.

"It does. He probably just missed whoever tossed him out on the road. Your friend was so shaken when he brought him in, I didn't think I should mention it."

"It was probably the right decision. He talked for most of the night about it. What will happen with the rabbit when he recovers?" When I worked for my father in his clinic, he never let me deal with those situations.

A lot of our conversation at the festival was about the chance of recovery. I guess sitting in a car with a rabbit squealing will shake anyone. Paul is a lot more sensitive than I imagined he was.

I guess it's a side he doesn't show too often around his friends and I feel bad I turned him away tonight when he wanted to hang out.

"We have some programs to have him placed with a more suitable permanent owner." Closing the file she taps it on the counter and holds it into her chest.

"That's good then. I can't wait to learn about them."

"Well, now is as good of a time as any then. Why don't you put your blanket away and we'll get started."

I spend the next few hours going through our overnight and emergency procedures. When Shanna takes a break, I look around our intranet and get myself familiar with how it is laid out.

Only one call comes in from a local farmer who reports a wounded Elk on his property. Shanna takes the call hesitantly, then takes her time packing up our gear. She puts me in charge of gathering the medical supplies and tranquilizers in case we need to knock the big animal out and call for backup transportation.

When I get outside, she's got our truck ready to go, but she isn't in a hurry and it confuses me. She spends the drive going over possible scenarios and what our procedures are as she hands me a piece of paper on a clipboard.

"This is our initial assessment. We fill it out to report the call and our follow up. It's different then the drop-off sheets we use. You can fill in the information we have at the top and we'll add the details once we are on site." I take it and jot down the few bits of information we know between each other and she pulls up to the ranch just as I finish writing.

As we step out, I make my way to the back of the truck, sling the medical bag over my shoulder and grab the tranq gun just in case. It isn't loaded and the safety latch is on so I let it hang on a clip at my side before joining Shanna as she walks up to the porch.

As I round the bushes, I see a woman rocking in a chair and we make eye contact. She seems a little surprised to see us.

"Dammit, did he go callin' you again?" She asks, rather perturbed and Shanna instantly nods her head, confusing me.

"He sure did, Mabel. Said he spotted a wounded elk. What was it this time?" She stops at the steps and puts her hands on her hips.

"I'm sorry, Sugar. I asked him if he called anyone and he said he di'int. He's passed out upstairs now. It was just our dog. Came back after a few days being gone. Scared the living shit outta him. For a 200 pound grown-assed man, that dumbass has the highest-pitched scream." She shakes her head before she continues and Shanna starts laughing. "You didn't have to come all of the way out here, Honey."

Shanna waves her hand at Mabel as though it isn't a problem. "It was good for us. This is Hazel. I'm training her at the sanctuary. It was a good chance to show her our procedures before she gets thrown into something serious." Mabel stops rocking at the introduction and I wave.

"Well, I Iazel. It's good to meet you. I see you brought the tranquilizers." She leans to the side, eyeing my gun as it dangles and I nod. "I swear, he's going to call you ladies one too many times and I'm going to take that gun and shoot him with it myself."

All three of us burst out laughing at the thought and Shanna wipes a tear from her face before speaking.

"Like I said, it was good training for us or I would have just called you back for confirmation before driving out here. We should be getting back to our animals." She takes a step back and Mabel rises to say good night.

"It was nice to meet you, Hazel. In your description, you can just write that the asshat doesn't know the difference between a 50 pound barking dog and a 500 pound wounded elk. Even if it was beneficial, I still apologize." I smile and say goodbye, following Shanna back to the vehicle and securing everything in the back.

When I join her in the truck, she is already handing me the clipboard. "I would have told you earlier, but I thought this would be a great hands on experience. I'll still get you to write out a little assessment and we'll treat it as such. I'll show you how to complete the reports once we get back to the office, we just won't file it away." I look at her for understanding and she keeps talking, "Mabel and Stu lost their only son years ago. He was in the military, stationed in the Middle East. It hit them hard, and he's had some benders over the years, usually when important dates come up like missed birthdays or the day he passed." She pauses again and her compassion comes out. "I just don't think they should be reported or fined for making these calls when it takes us only a few minutes to call Mabel back and confirm."

I nod in agreement. "I guess on a regular night, I'd just call Mabel back then?"

"Yes, I have her number with our contacts. I'll show you that and give you more of a rundown on our locals once I show you how the overnight reporting works." She turns the key and the truck starts up taking us back to the office as she tells me some crazy stories about Stu's previous calls.

Since I'm training, we stay up a little later than we normally would and it's almost three in the morning when we make our way to the small cots in a back room.

It's nothing fancy, just a place to sleep on site in case there is an emergency or one of the animals has a problem. Normally one person stays overnight, but since I'm also learning opening procedures as well, Shanna needs to be here with me.

While she is busy brushing her teeth, I pull out my phone to a couple of messages. The first is from Paul, apologizing for coming by unannounced and hoping his presence today didn't damage our friendship and I feel bad again for shutting him down.

The second is from Nina, telling me, again, that I should take a walk on the wild side. Those were her exact words. Maybe I do need to relax and trust in someone to show me new things.

Noah didn't text. I knew he wouldn't. He knows I was working tonight and he asked me to message when I was done. For someone who comes across as possessive, he sure gives me the space I need to do my things.

Hazel: Training is done. We're getting ready to go to sleep.

Noah: We?

Hazel: Shanna and I. We have cots in the back.

Noah: Hmmmm.

Hazel: What?

Noah: You're putting all kinds of images in my head, Doll.
Noah: I'd like some time with you alone on one of those cots all the way out there where only the animals can hear you scream.

Hazel: You're making me blush.

Noah: Good.
Noah: You're up late.

Hazel: There was lots to go over. I'm exhausted.
Hazel: You're up late, too.

Noah: No, I was sleeping. I turned my
volume on. I wanted to be able to say good
night to you.

Hazel: You didn't have to do that.

Noah: I know. I wanted to.
Noah: Get some sleep, Baby.

Hazel: Oh, I almost forgot.
Hazel: I want to go with you on Friday
night.

25

NOAH

*T*he mood around the office has been lighter since both sides presented their closing remarks in court yesterday. Our lawyers are confident it's going to be an easy win, everyone is.

Hearing from Hazel early this morning just before she fell asleep at work was the icing on the cake.

Checking my watch, it's early afternoon and she's probably just getting home from her double shift. I know she'll be tired so I decided to use my time tonight to get some extra things done at work today.

"You can go right in." Faye smiles as soon as she sees me and I only stop to knock before letting myself into his office.

"Hey, Stranger." I take a seat in front of Joshua's desk, unbuttoning my jacket and leaning back.

"Don't get me started. I can't believe this mess is pretty much over. I need a drink." He won't follow through with his statement. I know he has a sales meeting shortly that he doesn't want to be tipsy for. "So what do you need?"

In Joshua's defence, most of us enter his office because we need something from him.

"Just a chat this time. I have good news." I pause, knowing full-well his Type A personality is going nuts.

"And?" He finally says impatiently after a half-minute of silence and I chuckle.

"I'll meet you at Ravenous tomorrow. Hazel will be joining me."

His eyes light up and he smiles, which is rare for a Thursday. "That's great news. So things are going well then?" He pushes his paperwork to the side and loosens his tie.

"They are. I just wanted to give you a little notice...um... both of you." I wait for Joshua to catch on to what I'm saying and he nods, staring at me in a trance until realization hits and he startles.

"Oh, shit. Yes. Thank you. I didn't even think about that." He picks up the phone and asks the person on the other end to come to his office. Placing the receiver down he's all smiles. "I almost forgot. We've been working on certain protocols and respectful obedience for Ravenous. I feel like I'd be setting her up for failure if I didn't share this with her. Thanks, Noah. So we get to meet Hazel then?"

"Yes. I told her I had some friends I wanted her to meet. She's new to all of it but she is interested and she's been receptive to everything I've shared with her. I understand there are some beginner presentations happening. They may be helpful." Joshua nods as I speak.

"There are. Actually Emilia and I will be doing one of the presentations. It's on the basics of discipline. I just confirmed it with Alexandra. Emilia has a punishment coming." His sly smile gives him away.

"So you're spanking her as a punishment while giving a Ted Talk on how not to hurt your sub?" I chuckle and he huffs out his humour with me as the door opens.

"Not exactly. Our little Emilia here has come to crave a certain amount of pain. Spanking, in and of itself, isn't an effective punishment anymore." His attention drifts from me over my shoulder as he continues. "Care to tell Noah what your punishment is tomorrow night, Emilia?"

I follow Joshua's attention to his partner in all things and she smiles sheepishly as she approaches the other chair at Joshua's desk. She is always so professionally put together. Today her hair is pulled back into a loose bun and she's wearing a form fitting blouse with a pencil skirt.

"Hi, Noah." Her cheeks are flushed and I nod. "Um, it's the public spanking. In front of people, that is my punishment."

"Interesting." I know I'm grinning like an idiot, I don't care.

Joshua will be spanking Emilia in front of everyone at Ravenous. This is actually perfect because I know Hazel has an interest in public acts. I'm just not sure if it is as a voyeur or as a participant yet so this will serve a dual purpose.

"Clothed?" I ask and Joshua immediately cuts in.

"Yes." If it was possible for my grin to get any wider at Joshua's possessiveness, it just did. My cheeks are starting to hurt.

"I'll be wearing my bra and underwear." Emilia clarifies and I snort out loud.

"Get your chuckles in now, Jackass. I have it on good authority that Alexandra might be asking you to step in for a basic rope session. Her rigger cancelled on her this morning." My face falls, but only a bit.

For a second, I automatically imagine having Hazel on stage with me, but it's too soon for that. When I told her there are things we need to go over, most of it is safety stuff as well as emotional support. I make the mental decision to help only if she has an experienced bondage model on hand and Hazel is okay with it.

"Um, I'm not complaining but I've got a conference call in 10 minutes. Did you need me?" Emilia looks between us and Joshua straightens.

"Right. Sorry, Ems. It turns out Noah has met someone and she'll be coming with him to Ravenous tomorrow night. We wanted to tell you now because we know how you get when—" He doesn't get to finish.

"Really? Noah, I'm so happy for you. Tell me about her. What's her name?" I open my mouth to answer but she's already onto the next question. "Where did you meet? What's she like? What is she wearing tomorrow night? This is so exciting. Does she—"

"Baby!" Joshua lowers his voice and Emilia immediately stops talking as her eyes go wide. "I was talking and you cut me off—again." His smile is etched across his face as though he's caught his prey in a trap.

She opens her mouth to object but Joshua raises his hand and continues speaking.

"I'll remind you, this is why you are getting punished in front of everyone tomorrow night in the first place. Cut me off one more time, and you'll be taking your punishment in front of everyone with a vibrating butt plug up your ass." As soon as he puts the possibility on the table, Emilia's submissive side makes an appearance as her eyes round and her soft blush travels across her entire face.

She is extremely good at hiding those things about herself, but Joshua has an even better gift at exposing her.

"I apologize. It's a bad habit of mine. I get excited." She looks between us, then settles on Joshua, giving him serious sad eyes. "But will I get to ask all of my questions? Do I get to talk to her tomorrow?"

Joshua contemplates her question. "Show me you can be my good girl and listen while we are at Ravenous; and that includes, no talking unless I allow. Then we can leave an hour early and grab a slice of dessert from that place you like and Noah can ask Hazel if she'd like to join us." He waits for her response and she wriggles in her seat, pausing a moment to make sure he's stopped talking this time.

"I like her name," she says to me before turning her attention back, "Yes, Joshua. I can do that." He clears his throat and she corrects herself, "I will do that. Thank you. I've got to get to my call." She stands, smiling and gives a slight wave and we watch her go.

"You have no idea how happy you've made her." He says as the door closes. "She's been lonely for another friend in the lifestyle. I think she's going to tell Rosie soon, she just wants to wrap her own head around everything so she can answer any questions she might have."

"I understand that. I think it will be good for Hazel, too. Emilia and her are closer in age than she is with her school friends. Anyway, I need to get back to my desk. I'll text you about tomorrow night." I stand and turn to go as Joshua slides his stack of papers back in front of him.

Now that the courts are pretty much done, both of them should have more time over the next few weeks to talk and I can always make a dinner date at my place so they can get to know Hazel better.

My phone vibrates in my pocket just as I close my office door and the feeling that hits me when I see it is Hazel can only be described as giddy.

Noah: Hey, Baby. I was just thinking about you. Did you just get home?

Hazel: Yes. I'm exhausted. I'm going to try to stay up for a few hours then go to bed early. How is work?

Noah: I think that's a good idea.
Noah: It's steady today. I'm going to work a little late.

Hazel: I want to tell you, Paul stopped by yesterday afternoon to check on the rabbit he brought in.

I feel my lips thin into a grimace as I read her words. I really don't like that guy. Before I can think of a response, I see the flashing dots on the screen and I'm glad she's still typing.

Hazel: He was only there for about 15 minutes. I told him about you and Shanna was there.

Noah: Can I ask why you never mentioned this last night before you went to sleep?

Hazel: I'll be honest, I forgot. He was here a short time and I was overwhelmed with all of my training.

Hazel: He did ask me to hang out, but I told him no and I told him about you. I do feel a bit bad. He is my friend.

Noah: You have a beautiful heart, Hazel.

Noah: Thank you for telling me. I trust you.

I just don't trust him. But I did say she could see him to give him an update. Now he knows she's taken. It's on the table and he can be her friend and support her or he can keep pushing and deal with me.

Noah: Can you come over to my place right from work tomorrow? I'll make you dinner here and you can bring anything you need and have a shower over here.

Hazel: I'd love that. I have a couple of outfits that I can borrow from my roommate and I wanted your opinion.

Noah: Why do you want my opinion, Hazel?

Hazel: Because I feel better knowing you approve.

I smile at her response. I'm happy she likes dressing for me because I picked her up something to wear for tomorrow night on my lunch break that I think she'll look absolutely amazing in but I'm willing to see what she has as well.

Noah: Will you be taking a shower before bed?

Hazel: Yes, why?

Noah: After you're done washing your hair, I want you to touch yourself.

Noah: Play with yourself until you come.
Noah: Then text me when you are done and tell me about it.

She's still new to everything and I want her to feel confident being open with me about some things, especially if I'm taking her to Ravenous tomorrow night.

Hazel: I will.

Noah: That's my good little Doll. Do you own a vibrator?

Hazel: No. I always thought maybe Nina would hear it.

Noah: Have you ever used a vibrator?

I watch the three dots on the screen as she takes a moment longer to respond and I know she was thinking about what to say when I get a one-word response that doesn't warrant the amount of time she took to type it.

Hazel: No.

Noah: We'll fix that tomorrow.
Noah: Message me when you are done with your shower.

Hazel: I will, Noah.
Hazel: Thank you.

26

HAZEL

"You look like you're about to skip town." Noah chuckles as he meets me at his elevator.

Glancing down at my over-sized duffel bag and backpack at my feet, I try to hide my smile but fail. I probably could have narrowed my clothing choices down a bit.

"I think I got carried away." I sheepishly shrug and he laughs, settling my nerves as he reaches for the large bag and carries it inside to the couch.

"Well, let's see what you've got in here, Baby." He steps back a foot to allow me to open the zipper as he continues, "Are you hungry?"

My stomach tightens at his question. I was okay until the end of my shift, then my nerves began to wreak havoc.

"I—I don't know if I can eat." I stop mid-zip and straighten to look at him.

I don't want to make any mistakes but my stomach is fluttering like crazy. I don't know what to expect and I'm out of my league. My mind has been flooding itself with pictures of what I can only imagine a sex club looks like and I'm terrified I'm going to embarrass Noah with everything I don't know.

"Are you nervous?" Noah's expression is soft, concerned, and I nod.

"I don't want to do something wrong." The thought of disappointing him almost brings tears to my eyes but the feeling eases when he takes a step closer to me, gathering my hand in his own, his smile never leaving his face.

"Hazel, you can't possibly do anything wrong. I understand your apprehension. I've been nervous all day."

"What?" His revelation shocks me and I forget myself as the corner of his lips wickedly widen.

"You know how I feel about that word, Doll." Taking a strand of my hair between his fingers, twirling it gently. My anxious energy begins to morph into something else, something darker as I focus on him.

"I'm sorry. You've been nervous? You?" I feel my eyes widen at my question.

"Yes, me. You're meeting my friends, remember? I'm showing you the parts of myself and my lifestyle I don't openly share with just anyone. What if you reject me after I expose all of those parts of me?"

Silence settles into the room around us as I consider his stake in all of this. How did this not occur to me? I glance up to meet his eyes and he stays still, giving me time to process his questions.

My heart is already deep into this. I haven't completely admitted my feelings to myself, but I know I already want to be with Noah. I'm falling for him hard and fast and that's why I'm nervous. I was so scared I was still being assessed, I didn't consider he could feel the same about me.

"I—I never thought about it like that. I was worried I'd do something stupid and you wouldn't want me. What if your friends don't like me? What if I talk when I'm not supposed to, tonight?"

"Then you'll fit right in with my friend's sub." He releases a small chuckle then gives me more information. "They're working on that very thing." He winks then sits on the couch, tugging me down to join him. "First of all, my friends will love you. You have a kind heart, Hazel. You wear who you are on your sleeve and they will see what I see in you. I thought you might be a bit anxious, so I made a light snack. There is food at the club and we can leave to get something to eat if you need. Nothing is set in stone tonight, okay?" His hand squeezes my own and I realize he is still holding me.

"I understand. Thank you." I answer and he stands, moving quickly across his apartment to pick up a plate from the kitchen before returning and placing it on the table in front of us.

"Good. We do need to eat something though. Even if it is small. Deal?" He reaches forward, picking a strawberry up and eating it himself before nudging his head for me to join him.

"Deal." I answer, gathering a few pieces of fruit for myself.

"Eat a bit more and I'll tell you about the club if you'd like." I nod and pick some cheese off the platter as he starts to talk.

Over the next half an hour, I listen with rapt attention as he tells me about his friends and the club. It turns out that, while he has gone to the club and participated in some events, he has never brought anyone into the club as his guest and my anxiety turns into excitement at the thought.

"There is one thing about tonight we need to discuss before we get there. There will be a series of demonstrations from some of the members there. Joshua and Emilia will be doing a session on discipline. I've been asked if I would do a basic intro to rigging. It's the rope tying I showed you the other night." I feel my cheeks warm at his words and I'm already excited but I'm not sure if I can get up in front of everyone. "I told the owner I would only do it if she had an experienced bondage model on hand and you were okay with it." His words hit me and my expression must show it as he quickly lifts my chin back to his face. "Hey, they had a rigger, but he had to cancel. He has an emergency with his work but his partner can make it. I want nothing more than to do this with you, but there are a lot of things you and I need to discuss before I put you in that situation. I won't risk hurting you. There are check ins and cues we need to learn together and I won't put you in front of anyone until I know you feel mentally and physically comfortable."

I nod absentmindedly as he continues, "Remember I told you rope bondage for me is many things?" Nodding, I latch onto the memory of his words and he continues, "For me, it is only sexual when I do it with you. That being said, I won't do it at all if you feel uncomfortable in any way."

The tickle of his finger drawing circles on my palm catches my attention.

"I appreciate your concern for me. I'm sad I can't do that with you tonight, but a part of me is really curious to watch you do it to someone else. Does that make sense? I mean, I don't want to *watch* you do it with someone else, but I loved every moment when you did it to me and I want to be able to step back and watch you work, um, without zoning out." My smile meets his. "I'm okay if you do it. Thank you for asking me."

"I'll let Lexa know then." I crinkle my forehead at the name. "Alexandra Loren. She's the owner of the club and a friend of mine." Releasing my hand, he slowly stands, pulling me back up with him. "Now, let's take a look at the—extensive—wardrobe you've brought for tonight, then we're going to take a shower."

"We?" My excitement returns.

"Of course. I still need to punish you for saying *what*, then fuck the nerves out of you and we're running out of time. So we're slaying a whole lot of birds with one stone...or shower." The hunger in his smile makes my stomach clench in on itself as I release the most out of place giggle. "Take your clothes off." He chases my courage away with only four little words as he waits for my compliance.

Unzipping my pants, I slide them down with my panties in one quick push and pull my shirt over my head as I stand back up. I'll probably need to work on my sexy factor for next time. I slip my arms behind my back to remove my bra. The straps fall over my shoulders and I don't bother to catch it as it falls.

I feel the air compress between us as he steps forward, taking my breasts in his hands and running his thumbs over my nipples as they harden under his touch. "I have plans for these later, Doll." He winks. "Now show me what you've got here."

Moving my hands quickly to the duffel bag, I pull out the largest pieces. I have one of my own nighties in here and a few of Nina's dresses. Below those items lies every piece of sexy underwear I own. At least it's my version of sexy.

His fingers trail over everything I pull out. Lifting some pieces to inspect them more closely. Setting some aside in one pile and creating a second pile off to the side and I'm not sure which pile he doesn't like yet.

"And you'll feel comfortable in all of these?" He asks, holding up Nina's most indecent dress. On further inspection, I'm not so sure it is a dress and I notice, a little too late, it's missing the fabric that would normally cover my chest as I cover my mouth to hide my snort.

"I didn't get a good look at that one, sorry. These are my roommate's. I just quickly grabbed them and—" Noah raises his hand, cutting me off and takes the rest of the clothes from me, placing them back in the bag.

"I got you something I would like you to consider wearing tonight. Would you like to see it?"

"Yes." I almost blurt out a loud *thank-you-for-saving-me* as relief floods into me with the deep breath I just took.

Spinning in his spot, he reaches across the table and it's just now I notice the box on the other side. Tugging at the ribbon, it isn't lost on me the box isn't very big. I pull up the edge and it opens, hanging on one side almost like a book and the black fabric inside mesmerizes me.

"It's see through." I run my fingers along the soft fibers as I speak.

"Only in some spots." Noah reaches into the box, lifting the mini dress out so I can see the whole thing. "Your front and ass are covered and your breasts are hidden. It's revealing, but at the same time, it hides everything. I thought it would be a comfortable choice for your first time there." He speaks as he shows me both sides of the little dress.

Sure enough, it will hide everything and the fabric is stretchy so it should fit rather nicely.

"I like this better than what I brought over." I answer quietly. "Thank you. And thank you for trying to make me feel comfortable."

"I'll always look out for you, Baby. Now, speaking of which, I owe you a punishment." His wolfish eyes, slide down my naked body and my stupid thought is out before I can stop myself—again.

"I'm not sure how owing me a punishment is looking out for me." I think out loud.

"You'll see how it is soon enough, Doll. Now, go to the bathroom and run the shower. I'm about to introduce you to your first vibrator."

27

NOAH

*S*team escapes through the thin crack in the bathroom door as I make my way down the hall closer to Hazel, weighing this toy in my palm.

My cheeks stretch wide as I remind myself Hazel has never used a vibrator before. I can't contain the energy surging through my veins; a combination of desire and unabashed exhilaration.

Hazel is my perfect match and I'm about to make her dance and sing for me, then I'll make her beg.

Stopping one step away from the bathroom, I tug off my shirt before silently pushing the door to walk inside, wearing only my pants.

She jumps in her spot as I enter, her tits bouncing a couple of times. "I wasn't sure if I should get in." Her fingers fidget at her sides as she waits for my instruction.

"Good girl. Stay there for one moment." I put my back to her, and turn on the faucet in the sink to clean the toy once more, then step into her space and raise my free hand to her nipples, capturing one between my thumb and pointer finger. As I slowly squeeze, I feel her pert nipple stiffen under my touch.

Replacing my fingers with my teeth, I nibble as she moans, arching her back for me and moving her hands up to my arms to brace herself and I allow it. My same hand moves purposely down, over her stomach and between her legs over a small patch of soft hair.

Her nails pinch my arms as I push her folds aside, sliding my finger easily along her slick sex searching for her most sensitive areas and her body shifts as she opens her legs wider for me, urging me to continue and I take full advantage.

Shifting the object in my hand, I angle it, sliding it deep inside of her as she pauses, confused. Kissing her gently on her forehead, I offer her some space to stand and inspect herself.

Her eyes bulge as the tips of her fingers make contact and her lips round together as if she's actually about to say *what* to me again.

"It's a vibrator, this is one you wear. No one needs to hold it. There's a part inside of you, and the outside part is nestled nice and tight against your clit. Do you want to know what it feels like, Baby?"

Hazel opens and shuts her mouth a few times before deciding a small nod is the best answer and I reach into my pocket to pull out the little remote.

The instant I press the button, she groans out her surprise and lurches forward, digging her fingers into my arms once more, but this is different than before. The need etched across her face is more intense as her eyes widen in surprise.

"I can't tell you what watching your first time with a

vibrator deep in your pussy is doing to me, Doll." My voice is low, barely contained and I cup my hand over the vibrator, pushing it further against her and her moans draw together in a beautiful song as her hips sway into me, searching for more.

Fisting my hand into the hair at the base of her neck, I pull her closer, my hand firmly covering the vibrator as it hums into her. Angling her head up to meet my face, my composure wanes as my need to control her takes over. She allows me one delicious whimper before losing her composure, granting me a rare glimpse, I know, no one else gets to see.

Her lips twitch as I grind the toy against her body.

"H-how is this a p-punishment?" Her words dribble out of her as her body jerks on its own accord. "Wh... I think I'm going t—"

Clicking the remote she forgot I was holding, I answer her question with a devious grin.

"Um, it stopped." Her wide-eyed innocence makes me want to hold her and never let her go back out into the real world again.

"You were asking me a question." I steer her back to our conversation.

"Uh. Um, oh I asked how is this a pun—ohhhhhh." Realization dawns in her pretty eyes and she offers me a shy smile. "Oh no."

"Oh yes, Doll." I hold up the remote with a wink. "Now get in the shower. We're going to play a game." I reach into my pants and pull out the rest of the items I need as she turns and gingerly steps under the hot water.

Dropping my pants, I palm the remote and join her, trailing a finger over her bare body as the water pours down.

Turning my palm up, I open my hand to give her a look at what I was hiding.

"Pennies." The questions are written all over her face.

"Yes. We're going to play a little game before I punish you. You'll place a penny under each finger and hold them up against the wall. I have 10 pennies for your fingers and thumbs."

We shift around each other and I help place each one until all of the coins are secured between her fingers and the wall of the shower. Her arms are stretched out and a little higher than her head and her face is frozen in concentration.

"Now, I am going to spank you, but you've been so good for me so I want to let you choose how many spanks you'll receive. And, if you take them like my good little girl, I'll keep the vibrator on during your punishment." Leaning into her ear, I lower my voice. "Do you have any questions?"

"What happens if I choose zero spankings?" Her eyes blink rapidly through the spray.

"Cute, but you'll be choosing your number differently. You'll get one for each penny you drop." I watch as she considers my answer before I see her fingers tense.

I scan her face and make eye contact before examining all of the pennies held between her fingers and the wall and I look back, catching a confident smirk from my mischievous little toy.

Game on.

Leaning into her once more, I murmur, "You didn't think I'd take it easy on you, did you?" As I ask my devious question, I click the remote for the vibrator and turn it to its highest setting. Her head drops back as her body zings to life to greet its welcome onslaught and her hands struggle to stay in their spot.

One by one the pennies clink to the floor of the shower as she fights to hold her connection before pushing her body against the wall in an effort to maintain control over the few pennies she has left.

Turning off the vibrator, I lean down and pick up the coins she couldn't hang onto while she groans out the loss of sensation between her legs.

"Tsk, tsk, tsk. Seven. Someone likes their new sex toy. Very good. Here's something a little more manageable." I lower the setting on the vibrator to a soft hum before dropping all of the pennies on the floor and stepping to her side. "Bend forward, palms back on the wall."

She listens instantly, the occasional mewl flowing freely from her lips.

"Why are you being punished, Baby?" I ask as I pull my hand back in preparation of my first strike.

"I said *what*." My palm connects with the fleshiest part of her ass as she says the word and she squeaks out her shock.

This isn't as fun as her first spanking. This is me guiding her into her place. Each smack will be harder than the last and the first one was no picnic.

"Say that word again, Baby." Reaching between her legs to push the vibrator closer to her sensitive spot, I taunt her.

"What." My free hand comes down over her sit bone and she tries to lurch forward but my hand over her pussy holds her in place.

"Say it again." I demand.

"What." Her voice breaks on the word and I spank her again.

"Again." I challenge her.

"Wh-what." I connect again, the sound of my palm on

her ass echoes off the tiled walls and I'm beginning to feel the sting in my palm so I know she's feeling it on her ass.

I don't even ask her to repeat herself. Instead I wait.

"What?" It sounds more like a question and it doesn't matter. I spank her a fifth time.

"What." This time it sounds forced and I wonder what is registering with her more; the bite of my strike or the shame of being disciplined; spanked like a little girl in my arms and I really hope it's the latter.

This time, she doesn't return to her spot for her final smack and I immediately turn the vibrator off. Her body freezes; she remembers the deal. It stays on if she takes her punishment, and I wait under the hot water for her decision.

Shifting her body, she pushes herself bottom back from the wall and arches her ass upward.

"What." Her voice is calm, confident and most importantly, shameless and I'm proud of her for exposing herself to me.

I turn the vibrator on at a higher speed and swing my palm one final time, landing an equal amount of pressure as the last and she releases a satisfied moan into the shower.

Standing her upright and spinning her to face me, I reach down between her legs, running my hand along the toy and her arousal coats my fingers.

"It feels so... fuuu...um, please." She whispers the last word out, her eyes unfocused.

Without another thought, I wrap my arms around her waist, lifting her up and against the tiled wall, allowing the water to rain over us and her legs wrap tightly around my waist.

I pause, knowing full well the vibrator is still chipping away at her resolve; and slowly remove it from her, hitting all of her sensitive areas on its way out and her body twitches and grinds on its own.

"Mmmm. I love the sounds you make for me, Doll." I growl my words low against her ear as my fingers squeeze her punished ass. Sliding my fingers toward her entrance, I drop my head to kiss and nibble along her neck and her hands grip around my arms. It isn't lost on me she's angling her hips, opening herself for me, but she isn't asking for anything.

She knows this is my time and I will go at my pace; which, at the moment, is about to start to pick up.

"You're lucky I don't have all night." My warning earns a sweet moan from her as I guide myself to her entrance, her sounds urging me to ease both of our aches, and I don't hesitate.

Her head drops against the tile, her eyes rising to the ceiling before closing as the wails of her pleasure echoes off the walls and I waste no time settling into her as my pace starts out strong. The effects of her discipline and the vibrator won't take long to push her over the edge.

Water sprays everywhere and I close my eyes to concentrate on the feel of her slick walls, milking my cock as I slip away on the mewling sounds of her moans begging for release.

Her thighs vibrate around my waist as I continue to fuck into her, alerting me she's close and I feel my body tighten in response. I'm not far behind.

"Look at me." I command and her eyes blink rapidly through the water. I want her to watch as we fall apart in each other's arms. When she walks through the front doors at Ravenous tonight, I want there to be no doubt in her mind who she belongs to. "Come." I demand.

Her features falter as her eyes widen. I know she was trying to hold out but there will be none of that when I determine it is time. For a moment she looks doubtful, but her body is already listening to me even though her mind is playing catch up and her legs grip tight as her body begins to shake around me and her cry sounds like a song as her orgasm takes her over.

Her embrace tightens around me as I feel my own end approach and I suddenly realize my mistake.

We haven't discussed birth control. How could I have been so stupid?

My entire body tenses and I feel her freeze as she scans my face for explanation. Taking a deep breath; I pull myself out, releasing her legs to the floor.

"I'm sorry. We didn't talk about—" Her hand on my erection shuts my brain off.

Without any prompting, Hazel drops to her knees, wrapping her soft lips around my cock and sucking as far down to the base as she can. I'm snapped out of my haze when I feel her fingers on my own as she raises my hands, placing them on either side of her head.

She's asking me to take control and my fingers grip tight as I raise and lower her along my length. Her mouth suctions me in and her tongue licks greedily in all of the right spots as I feel my balls tighten once more.

I meet her eyes as she stares up at me and I lose myself to her.

"Fuck, Doll." I grind out through gritted teeth as I give her everything I have and her tongue slows as she works to swallow it down. The tension of my orgasm recedes as she finishes and stands to meet me.

"Um. I am on birth control. I appreciate you worrying

about me though. That meant a lot to me that you would try to stop like that." Her voice is timid.

I turn off the shower and stand in the silence with her, taking every inch of her in for a long minute and she allows me my time before I lean in to claim her mouth in a kiss. Her body relaxes into my arms as she grants me access to all of her.

"How's your ass?" Breaking the silence, I attempt to pull our conversation back to a playful tone and she dips her head with an impish smile.

"It tingles." She giggles as I turn the shower back on, surprising her.

"Good. Get used to it." Punctuating my promise with a wink, I guide her head under the shower then reach for the shampoo. "Has anyone ever washed your hair before, Baby?"

"Other than a hairdresser?" She asks and I nod. "No."

"Good. Get used to that, too." I answer, squeezing some shampoo onto my hand.

28

HAZEL

*R*avenous is nothing like I pictured it in my head. After our shower, Noah dried my hair and watched as I dressed. Having his eyes on me while I went about each task made me feel secure. My stomach tightened when he smiled approvingly; I found comfort in his appreciation.

The dress fit like a second skin. It stretched around my body and hugged me when I moved.

I was nervous about the car ride to the club as Marcus would be driving us but I found out quickly, nerves were not necessary. Marcus was a perfect gentleman. He treated me as he always did, offering me a smile and some light conversation as though it was a normal day.

Noah told me about protocol in the club and how different members have different interests and rules so I wouldn't get offended if someone didn't look up to greet me. He told me how the members mark their claims with collars, leashes or bracelets and offered me the choice of a collar and leash for the evening.

For most, that meant the sub was owned and not available for conversation with anyone. Since Noah was going to be on stage for a bit during the evening, this would prevent someone from wandering over to try to talk to me.

Apparently, one of his friends, Joshua, doesn't take kindly to those who don't follow club rules so it would save us all the trouble and should keep anyone away from me which I appreciate. While Noah and I are exploring this new dimension of mine, I'm not interested in talking to anyone else about it right now.

As Noah's, I am to sit quietly by his side until I am spoken to and Noah nods that I can speak. A month ago, I would have found the thought of this preposterous. Now, I'm thankful for the mental and physical timeout. This gives me time to process. His world is new to me and my anxiety left me as soon as I realized I don't have to talk to anyone. This collar grants me Noah's protection and care, I think to myself as I reach up to touch the metal clasp holding the short leash in place.

"Don't touch, Baby. You're doing fine." His lips tickle my shoulder from the back as he slides my coat down my arms before handing everything to the woman behind the counter. "Everyone has to check their bags and coats here. They'll keep everything secure." He looks at my hand and I follow his eyes to my phone.

"Oh, right. Sorry." I answer immediately then catch myself before putting my hand over my mouth. I'm not supposed to talk so I mouth the word *sorry* with an awkward wince which makes him laugh out loud.

His features soften before he leans in to kiss my cheek before whispering, "Starting—now." Winking, he opens my handbag and I drop the phone in.

"Mr. Wilde, your party is already seated. Raif will show you to your table." The woman speaks to Noah but smiles at me and I smile back.

"Thank you, Reva. Is Alexandra here tonight?" He checks out the room while asking his question.

"She is. Just finishing up some work in the back. I'll make sure to tell her to say *hello* when she comes out." She smiles between us again.

Saying his thanks, Noah gently handles me by my upper arm and I let him guide me as the man standing behind Reva leads us to our table. Lounge music plays just below the level of the voices in the club and I hear snippets of conversations from all over.

I told Noah earlier that I was afraid I would show my surprise at seeing new things and I didn't want to offend anyone so he told me to keep my eyes focused forward or down and to look directly at him if I wanted to speak and so far this is working.

We stop at a table off to the side from the stage and closer to the back and the couple seated stop their quiet conversation. The woman immediately looks down, but I see the pupils in her eyes lift to look at Noah and I as the man stands.

"Noah, we're glad you could make it tonight." As the man speaks, I sense his eyes are on me for a moment, then he shifts to follow my line of sight down to the woman who is still sitting.

"Sorry we're late. Joshua, I'd like to introduce you to Hazel Masters. Hazel, this is Joshua Darkly and Emilia Connor." Joshua extends his hand to mine and on impulse, I reach out to him before stopping myself and looking at Noah who grins and nods his head for me to continue and I shake his hand.

I can't control the smile across my face.

"So, you're the one we've been hearing about. It is nice to finally meet you. This is Emilia Connor," he introduces me before turning to the woman, "you may introduce yourself."

The woman freezes for a moment, absorbing his words before taking a deep breath and lifting her eyes to meet mine fully.

"It is so nice to meet you, Hazel." Her smile stretches across her entire face.

"It's nice to meet you, too, Emilia, Joshua." I answer and Emilia sighs before Joshua clears his throat and she returns her eyes down.

As Joshua turns his attention to Noah, I take another look at Emilia. She's dressed in less than I am but she looks comfortable. Her hair is pulled back in a braid that runs down her back.

Lifting one hand, she tickles her fingers over a beautiful collar around her neck. It isn't like the one I have on. Hers looks more custom. The leather is dark and worn and the clasp and lock at the back is a hammered metal. She lifts her head just enough to give me a defiant wink and a smile and I wink back.

I like her already.

Noah takes a seat on the couch and pats the spot beside him for me to join him and I feel my tension begin to fade as I sink into the sofa and Noah orders us both a club soda and lime.

The lights in the room are dimmed but I am able to see almost all of the way across the club. Everyone is so different from each other. Some are fully clothed, a few are completely bare. Most are seated on the seats and some are kneeling on the floor beside what I assume is their Dominant.

"There you are." An impeccably dressed woman stops in front of the table and she exchanges a smile with Emilia before addressing the men. "I can't tell you both how much I appreciate your help with the presentations tonight. We've got quite the packed house. There's lots of new interest." As she speaks, her eyes circle the table and land on me. "Speaking of new interest—I'm Alexandra", reaching her hand out to me.

I don't fall for it a second time. A quick glance to Noah and a nod then I shake her hand and introduce myself before looking back down and I can't help but worry that I'm being rude, but I remind myself that my actions are in respect to Noah, not in disrespect to Alexandra. The thought makes me smile to myself.

"Joshua, the stage is yours. There's no set time limit but try not to go over 30 minutes. Announce that Noah is next when you have about five minutes left so he can get ready backstage. Reva will meet you back there when it's time." Both men nod in understanding and Alexandra excuses herself.

"Well, Love, it's time." Joshua says, turning to make eye contact with Emilia. "I wish I could say this is going to hurt me more than it's going to hurt you, but I'm going to thoroughly enjoy myself." He runs a finger down her arm and I see her move with a shiver.

I'd probably faint if Noah said that to me right now.

He stands, excusing them and they make their way to the stage to get ready. The first few tables nearest the stage quiet but the rest of the club hasn't noticed yet.

"What do you think so far?" Noah takes a glass from the waiter and hands it to me before taking his own.

"This is pretty cool. Your friends are great." I say, taking a sip and the bubbles in the club soda tickle my nose.

"I'm happy to hear that. I already know everyone likes you." Noah leans back in the seat, crossing his calf over his knee and watches the stage so I decide to join him in spectating.

Joshua and Emilia are together, looking at the bench in the middle of the stage and they are deep in conversation. Before I can ask Noah what they might be talking about, Joshua waves off to the side of the stage and Alexandra walks out, introducing herself as the owner of Ravenous.

She spends a minute welcoming old members and new guests, then introduces Noah's friends and Joshua speaks into his headset and begins talking about discipline as the lights dim further.

My eyes fall mostly on Emilia. She looks nervous, but I see her settle every time Joshua makes a physical connection with her, either by placing a hand on her back or petting her head. I imagine that is how I feel when Noah caresses me.

I learn more about domination and punishment in 15 minutes than I knew in my whole life and a new door begins to open for me. When Joshua spoke of his love for Emilia and how they both contribute to her discipline, I felt a connection to their story. While I get the impression they are both still very private about their lives, the knowledge they both shared was valuable.

As Joshua announces Noah's spot, I see Reva slip behind the curtain at the back and Noah leans over to give me a chaste kiss before whispering in my ear. "I just need to talk to Reva before we go out about limits, communication, and the like. Stay here, no one will approach you with the collar. Joshua and Emilia will be back shortly. They may just need to regroup backstage after that scene. You good?"

"I'm good. I can't wait to see you." I answer, and it's the truth. I have no jealousy in me at all.

I sit up straight, listening to Joshua say his final words as he helps Emilia up. Noah told me this punishment was real for her and I can tell by the new expression on her face that the message was received.

The room fills with applause as they disappear behind the curtain and I wait with butterflies to see Noah make his way on the stage. Reva walks out first and Noah begins speaking as soon as he gets on stage.

His voice captures me and my stomach knots in excitement as I see the ropes in his hand. I feel a rustling beside me as the couch bows. I glance to see if Joshua and Emilia have returned so quickly and the blood drains out of my head.

"Wow, Hazel. I never thought you'd be in a place like this."

"P—Paul? Wh—what are you doing here?" My head spins as I try to fit my two worlds into the same space.

"I'm here with my friends. We heard about the open member night and thought we'd drop by for some laughs," his eyes rake over my little outfit and this is the first time tonight I don't feel comfortable in it, "and here you are in a dog collar."

"It's not a dog collar. I'm here with friends, Paul." I say as I glance to the stage and notice Noah is still at the front. He probably can't see past the first table with those bright lights on him.

"Friends? Is that so? I was your *friend*, Hazel." He bites back.

"Paul, this is different. I'm here with Noah." He laughs at my words catching the attention of a couple at the table in front of us.

"So he makes you sit here wearing a dog collar and watch him on stage with another woman?" He reaches for Noah's drink like it's his own.

"It's not like that." I answer weakly, trying hard not to draw attention to myself and embarrass Noah. If Joshua and Emilia would just come back, he'd leave me alone.

"I would have treated you so much better than this." His disdain pours out with his words.

"Please, Paul. Just go."

"No, see, you don't get to tell me what to do. You're the one wearing the dog collar, sitting here like a little slut."

The table in front of us turns around and I see the man wave to catch security's attention out of the corner of my eyes. I can't take this anymore. I don't want to cause a scene for Noah and the only way to not be an embarrassment is to leave the room. I stand abruptly to leave but before I take a step away, a harsh pull around my neck sends me crashing to the floor and I take some of the drinks on the table down with me.

Shaking, I look up to see a Paul I've never seen before and he's holding the end of my leash. His eyes are wild and I can feel the hate on him.

"I'm holding the leash. You're my dog now, Bitch." He towers over me and the men at the table in front of me stand and I hear Noah's voice stop talking.

"LEAVE ME ALONE, PAUL." Panicked, I yell and I hear a crash and feedback through the speakers as he tugs hard at my leash a second time, pulling me up to meet his eyes.

"Fine, you don't want me to treat you right then I'm taking it all away. That apprenticeship at the sanctuary was my doing. It was my gift to you and this is how you treat me. I'm pulling the funding. Now you'll have to go home for the summer." His sneer reaches his eyes and my world crashes down.

"You can't do that. I gave up my spot in class at school for this. Another student already has it. I can't complete my course if I don't have the internship." I plead, hoping the Paul I knew was in there somewhere and I realize he was never the Paul I knew. "Why are you doing this?" Tears coat my eyes as two large men in suits step between us just as Noah reaches our growing group and his eyes land on Paul.

"GET AWAY FROM HER." Noah's threat carries weight. I feel it and it rattles me to my core and so does Joshua as he steps in close, holding Noah back while he tries to reach for Paul.

I take a couple of deep breaths but I feel like no air is getting to my lungs and I reach my fingers up to my throat and the collar stops me cold. The men around me are all talking over each other and the hostility is building. My fingers trail down my leash and suddenly I feel bad.

Not guilty, bad. But Dirty. I feel ashamed.

Do I look like a dog? The thought makes me suck in a deep breath, but it isn't enough. I feel my next breath wheeze down my throat and the collar feels like it has started tightening on itself.

My fingers fidget desperately along the leather around my neck, searching for a clasp to loosen its grip.

I hear a woman's voice but the club looks like it has gotten darker.

"Baby? Baby, you're safe. It's Noah. Hazel, you're safe. They're escorting him out of the club. You're okay." I feel Noah near me, but I don't think I believe him.

I am very far from *okay* right now.

29

NOAH

I begin my segment with a brief outline of what Shibari is and where it originated as Reva settles herself on stage. I know she would rather be doing this with her partner and in all truth, I would rather have Hazel on stage with me but it isn't possible until I know how she will react to being completely bound.

Because I am not Reva's Dominant, we've both agreed, she would wear a skin tight white bodysuit to cover her and to show off the ropes across her body. I decide to talk about the most basic tie techniques and Reva offers me her arm to start with a column tie.

I talk as I work and I settle into a comfortable pace as I list some of the first dos and don'ts to rope bondage.

Reva senses something is off before I do and her head jerks up and to the side of the stage.

Then the sound of glass dropping on the floor and a commotion in close proximity to our table startles me and I stop talking as I make out the shadows of people standing a few tables back.

"LEAVE ME ALONE, PAUL." Even the slightest chance the distressed voice is Hazel's propels me off the stage and I tear off the headset before my feet hit the ground.

The table in front of ours is standing and two of the security guys have just joined the commotion as I see one removing the end of her leash—from Paul's hands.

What the hell is he doing here?

Hazel's eyes are wide and she looks terrified. He has no right to her and my entire being wants to rip him apart. I don't care if my membership gets revoked for this.

Hazel should feel safe and I failed her.

"GET AWAY FROM HER." Both Hazel and Paul startle at my words and only Paul's shock recovers into a sleazy sneer as I attempt to lunge at the bastard but I feel someone hold me back before Joshua moves to my front and steps between us.

I knew he wasn't who he pretended to be but it saddens me that this is how Hazel has to find out. She was so nervous about tonight and now this. In front of my friends at a sex club no less.

Paul just laughs and glares at Hazel who looks lost as I see her reach for her collar and I want to go to her but Lexa has joined her security team and I see her talking to a couple of the gentlemen from the table in front of us and I don't want to cause more chaos so I stay still for a moment before she quickly joins our group.

"Did this man assault you?" Alexandra asks, narrowing her eyes on Paul, but Hazel doesn't respond and the tension inside of me changes to worry. She looks traumatized.

"I was just leaving. Hazel, call me when you want to discuss a new arrangement." Paul struggles to get out of Raif's grip but he isn't having any of it.

"Who's name did you put down as reference?" Alexandra directs her question to Paul and I wait for the answer but he offers none before she addresses her security detail. "Gather his things from the front and take him to the side room. We'll sort this out there. I want to see his entry sheet."

The two bouncers flank each side of Paul and escort him toward the front of the club and Lexa takes a step to Hazel.

As our attention shifts back to Hazel, I notice her breathing has become sharp and she looks like she can't get enough air in. Both of her hands are now on her collar and her fingers are fidgeting along the outside.

"Baby? Baby, you're safe. It's Noah. Hazel, you're safe. They're escorting him out of the club. You're okay." Rapidly blinking her eyes at my words, tears roll over her cheeks.

"I'm so sorry this hap—" As Alexandra attempts to comfort Hazel, I touch her arm and she recoils from me.

"Take it off." Her fingers become frantic, almost digging at the collar around her neck and I feel my fight drain out of me as she leans into me, begging, "Please. I can't breathe." She whispers.

I move fast and drop the collar to the floor and open my arms, offering her sanctuary without forcing my comfort on her and she takes it, sobbing into my shirt.

Joshua looks worried and he says something to Lexa. She nods before turning and motioning for the table beside us to take their seats.

"Follow me." Joshua's voice is low as he spins in place and walks toward the stage and I trail with Hazel under my arm, protecting her from the world around her.

As we near the stage, I see a solemn Emilia waiting for Joshua. Her eyes are wide and she's been crying as well. At once, it hits me, Emilia went through almost this very thing at the hands of Brent not long ago. Joshua quickly opens his arms to her and she tucks herself in as they walk toward the back door together.

I want to kill Paul for what he's done.

"I—I'm sorry." Hazel says into my shirt. She's so quiet, I almost think she didn't mean for me to hear her and I stop to lift her eyes to mine to make sure she knows it isn't her who should be sorry before I continue to follow Joshua and Emilia into the back area.

When we were last back here, Emilia had run away from Joshua and their situation had come to a head.

The moment the heavy door closes behind us, the sound fades to a distant murmur and a door opening draws our attention as Reva joins us. She's still in her bodysuit but she managed to grab a robe to tie around her.

I watch Hazel lower her eyes to the floor. While the lights are not bright, they are lighter than the room out front and I struggle to adjust to the glare.

"Alexandra will be back shortly. She is handling the situation up front and asked me to get you settled." She raises her hands to the individual rooms and Joshua instantly leads Emilia to the one with the number 4 on it.

As he passes, he speaks in a lowered voice. "I need to take care of Emilia. We have some unfinished business in this room. I'll meet you out here shortly." I nod.

"You can take any room you want." Reva offers and I move us to the second room. My patience is wearing thin and I need to provide care for Hazel.

I reach to the wall inside the door, hoping to lower the light in the room and find a dimmer switch.

"Have a seat on the couch." My blood pumps through

my veins at a record pace and I make a concentrated effort to keep my voice calm even though I want nothing more than to head out front and strangle Paul. There is something more important to take care of.

"Where are you going?" The fear behind Hazel's question makes me weak.

"Just right here." I point to the open closet beside me. "I'm getting you a robe." She nods and sits herself down as I join her, draping the cloth around her.

"I ruined your talk." She speaks as though she's just realized her worst nightmare came true. She was worried she wouldn't fit in. She was worried she would embarrass me.

"Let me be very clear. None of this is your fault. You were perfect tonight. Neither of us could have seen this coming." I hold her attention to my own as I speak.

"It's just—I—he—" Her eyes swell with tears and I pull her into a hug to stop her thought process. Playing with her hair, I kiss the top of her head and her arms stretch around my waist. "Why did he do that?" She pleads for an answer that will make this make sense.

Her question is naive which is a beautiful reflection of her kindness. He did this because he is a monster. His facade would have held if she'd only loved him back but she doesn't and he doesn't care about her. He cares about what he can have and what he can't.

"Baby, can you tell me what happened?" She stays, wrapped around me for a minute longer while she takes deep breaths before sitting up beside me.

"I was just sitting there, watching you. I was so excited. You were really good up there." She smiles and I return her warmth then raise my eyebrows, asking her to continue. "I thought your friends came back and I looked over and it was

him. There was something different about him, it scared me."
Her forehead creases with concern.

"Did he say what he was doing here?" I attempt to lead
her into leaving her emotions behind for a bit.

"He said he was there with friends. They came for a
laugh." She shrinks into her body as though she's ashamed.

"Then what happened?"

"I think I asked him to leave and he called me—um a
name." She has a habit of not looking me in the eyes when
she feels shame which is exactly what she is doing now.

"What did he call you?"

"He said you put a collar on me and made me watch you
with another woman like a dog. Then he called me a slut."

A migraine-sized sharp pain shoots through my skull as
she recounts what happened. I'm going to kill him.

"Is that when I got there with security?" I ask with hope
behind my words that this was all she had to endure.

"No."

There's more? How long did I leave her to this
nightmare?

"Then what happened?" I try to keep my tone even and
gentle.

"People were starting to look and I thought if I could just
find a women's bathroom, then I could hide out and not
cause a scene. I stood up to leave and he pulled me to the
ground by the leash and he told me I was his dog. Then he
called me a bitch and that's when I yelled at him." A loud
ringing in my ears freezes me in place as the image of Hazel
being assaulted while under my protection stabs at my very
soul and I feel as though I've slipped into a dark void.

"Noah, you're scaring me. Are you okay?" Her fingers
wrapping around my hand shock me back to our little room.

I've never experienced rage. In my whole life, I've never felt like I could actually kill someone, but the fury seething through me at this moment tells me I am capable of it.

"I'm okay, Baby. But none of this is okay and none of this is your fault. You need to know that. No one here thinks it is. We are all only concerned for you. And that's when we all got there." I don't ask it as a question as I know we were alerted after she raised her voice.

"Oh, Noah, I think I'm going to be sick." She starts to sob in her hands and I suddenly feel like I've missed something.

"You're okay now." I take a stab in the dark at comforting her and she raises her blotchy tear-soaked face to mine.

"No. Before you got there he told me he was the one who gave the grant to the wildlife sanctuary and he was taking it away so I would have to go home this summer, but they already filled my class spot next year. I won't be able to finish school when I wanted. I don't know what to do." She cradles her face as I pull her into me.

Now Paul's final words telling Hazel to call him make sense. He thinks he's won by holding the internship over her head. He's trying to buy her.

He bought her internship knowing it would keep her here with him over the summer and hoping it would buy him her appreciation. I feel sick at the depths Paul is willing to sink to take her against her will.

"Is that why you wanted the collar off?"

"I can't explain that. I loved having it on at first. It felt safe. I felt safe, but then I couldn't breathe and I didn't want it to touch me. But then I felt bad because you put it on me." She's confused by her reaction and I understand why.

"Baby, I want you to lay down on the couch." I slide myself off the sofa and onto the floor beside her and she doesn't let go of me, but follows my lead, placing her head on the cushion at the top. I get myself comfortable and run my fingers through her hair, pulling a soft moan from her lips.

"Close your eyes and listen to my words. If you fall asleep, it's okay. If you open your eyes and I'm not here," her body tenses at the thought, "I'm just outside the door talking to Joshua. No one will enter this room without me present. Okay, Baby?"

"Kay." I can tell the difference when Hazel tries to relax and when she is actually relaxed and right now, it is the former.

"When Paul pulled you down by the leash, it was no longer my leash. He turned it into an albatross around your neck. He tried to punish you and he tried to force his own will on you. You rejected the collar he tried to give you without your consent. You were right to want it off." I pause for a minute to allow her to process my explanation and I feel her body soften in agreement.

"Hazel, I'm proud of how you handled yourself tonight. I should never have agreed to do the presentation. I should have never left you alone even for a minute. I'm so sorry I wasn't there for you." Her hand covers mine.

"Neither of us expected this. I don't want you to feel guilty." Her words comfort me but I do feel a tinge of regret. I nod as she speaks. We are both trying to claim a certain amount of guilt for what happened but the truth is, it isn't either of ours to declare. It is all Paul's.

"You're right." I watch her eyes open and close slower than before. Tonight is catching up to her. "Close your eyes and rest. I want to talk to Joshua and Lexa for a moment. We'll call your work in the morning and meet with your boss. I'm sure we can sort something out."

I sit quietly, combing my fingers through her hair until her breathing evens out and I stand to lay a blanket over her before lowering the lights a little more.

Hazel was stronger than all of us tonight and what Paul did to her is unforgivable. As much as I didn't like the guy, I never imagined something as vile as this.

As I watch her drift off, I hear a door shut in the area outside and I slip out of the room to learn more about what is going on so I can deal with Paul myself.

30

NOAH

I step into the main area at the same time as Joshua leaves his room without Emilia and see Alexandra pacing before us, concern set deep into her features as Reva waits off to the side.

"Lexa. What do you know?" I don't mean to direct my short tone toward her but I can't stop my curt words.

"Noah. I'm so sorry this happened. You have to know, security moved as fast as they could once they were alerted of an issue."

I don't have time for this. I got there just behind Raif and the other guy. I know they moved fast. I want information.

"Alerted of an issue? He assaulted her and called her his dog, Lexa. What. Do. You. Know?" I ask a second time as quietly as I can through gritted teeth and Joshua steps closer to us.

"Hey, Noah. Lexa's here to help. Let's step away from the doors and talk this out." It isn't lost on me that Joshua is the new voice of reason here as he points to the chairs across the room and it is still close enough to Hazel's door.

"I want to see him." I have to try. I already know the answer. Company procedures won't allow it.

"You know I can't allow that on company property. We have everything we need from him and since Hazel didn't speak up in pressing charges, he was removed from the premises. If she chooses to do so at a later date, everything we have is available to her. Come and sit for a moment and I will tell you what I know." Alexandra takes a few steps and sits in a chair beside the couch and I follow.

"I reviewed Paul's entry sheet and it's a bit concerning. I've got a couple of calls in." She shifts in her seat.

Everyone entering Ravenous must fill in an entry sheet. It's a general information sheet with ID, contact information, health alerts, an emergency number as well as a reference name. The name of someone who is a member who can vouch for their entry.

"Who was his reference?" Joshua asks, clearly one step ahead of me.

"That's the thing. He wrote down Timothy Davenfield as his reference." She pauses and Joshua and I exchange a glance.

"How does he know Mr. Davenfield?" I ask.

We've always called Timothy, Mr. Davenfield because he is a large client at Connor Realty. Joshua has had his fair share of run-ins with his overbearing daughter, Tawny, over the years.

"Well, I'm guessing by Paul's last name, there is a familial connection." Lexa answers.

"His name is Paul Davenfield?" I ask, incredulously.

"Yes. Before you ask, I have a request in to Mr. Davenfield for a meeting to discuss the situation." She offers, attempting to pacify me.

"And what about his friends? Did they all list Mr. Davenfield?" I ask and Lexa looks a little confused before regaining her composure.

"What friends?" She asks looking between Joshua and I.

"He told Hazel he was here with his friends tonight." As I answer, Lexa slowly shakes her head.

"He was alone. I confirmed it with our cameras and security at the front. He came alone and he left alone." I sense Joshua lean back in his seat in silence as I consider the lie he told Hazel.

Does this mean, if he came alone, his purpose for being there wasn't coincidence and he targeted Hazel? He had no way of knowing she'd be at the club tonight unless he followed her to my place then followed us to Ravenous after waiting for us for over two hours while we got ready.

I find the scenario highly unlikely as Marcus would have noticed someone following us if that was the case. It is literally what he is trained to do.

"Is she okay?" All eyes move to the door where Emilia now stands, fully dressed and Joshua jumps to his feet and moves gingerly to her dragging his fingers through his hair.

"Hey, Ems. How are you? Do you want to join us?" He stretches out his hand toward our group and she takes his place on the couch.

"I'm fine, really." She smiles at us while Joshua slides in beside her, scooping her hand in his own. "How is Hazel?"

"She's resting. She was looking forward to meeting you both tonight." I'm trying hard not to make this conversation about me wanting to destroy Paul.

"She seems really nice. Maybe we can get together after all of this sometime." As she makes her suggestion, she looks at Joshua who nods in agreement and pats her lap.

"I think she'd like that but we have some things to deal with first." I answer Emilia before turning my attention to Joshua. "It turns out, the internship she took at the wildlife sanctuary was Paul's doing and he threatened to pull it all tonight."

Emilia sucks her shock in a deep breath and I continue, "That isn't the worst of it. She was going to work her internship as credit for her in-class attendance next year and the college gave away her seat to another student already so she won't be able to graduate when she wants to."

"What an asshole." Joshua answers and Emilia nods fiercely in agreement as Joshua continues, "Why don't you just cover the donation?"

"I'm not sure that's a good decision. While Paul did it to own her, I don't want her to have any thought at all that she would be indebted to me like that. It's—complicated, but I don't want to give the impression that I am throwing my money at her. It wouldn't be received well."

We all sit in an uncomfortable silence before Emilia speaks up. "Well, it's settled then."

"What's settled?" Joshua slows his voice down.

"I'd like to take over the donation." She deadpans.

"What?" I go against my rule using the word and it sounds like I'm speaking in stereo when I realize Joshua just said the same thing.

"I'm sure we can work something out. After Connor Realty's current legal matters, supporting a locally owned not-for-profit would be a good business decision that could help shine some positive publicity on the company. Don't you agree, Partner." She looks to Joshua to make her case. "Of course, I could oversee the funding. It would keep everything above board where no one can question the motives behind our good will. It will also take the donation off the table so decisions made between the both of you carry no financial consequence."

"We'll need to see some numbers and discuss this further, but I think we can look at that—Partner." Joshua answers back and I'm in shock.

"You guys haven't even had a chance to really talk to Hazel yet. Why are you doing this for her?" They both look at me like I just asked the dumbest question.

"Noah, you've been nothing but a great friend—to both of us. It's clear she means more than just *something* to you and you are like family, which makes her like family-to-be." Emilia's answer catches me off guard. "Besides, I've always wanted a sister." She shrugs and Joshua chuckles.

"Look, I understand how helpless she felt tonight. I felt that recently and it is a very lonely and terrifying feeling. She shouldn't have to worry about her work and school on top of that." She turns to Joshua, "We should get going soon. They probably want to get out of here and be alone."

Joshua nods and Emilia makes her way into the room she came from before returning with a bag and Joshua stands to join her.

"We'll take a rain check on dessert. You okay, Man?"

"As good as can be expected." I answer Joshua. "Lexa, can you have our things brought back here? I'll text Marcus and have him bring the car around back."

Lexa and Reva follow Joshua and Emilia out the doors leading back into the main area and I wait until the door closes again before going to the room Hazel is resting in.

Her heavy breath is the only sound I hear as I steal a minute to take her in and allow her presence to calm me.

She has no idea how deeply she is already ingrained into

the fabric of my soul; how much she is a part of my life and how important she is to me.

It's my turn to kneel and I lower myself in front of the couch where she's sleeping and remove some hair that has fallen into her face as she stirs.

"Hey, Baby." I smile as her eyes flutter open and it takes her a moment before the pain from earlier registers and I wish I could have captured her in the moment where she had forgotten.

"Did I sleep long?" She sits herself up and I take a seat in the space she left.

"Not long. I'm having our things brought back to us. You can change in here and we'll head out the back. I'm taking you to my place for the night."

She nods, "I'd like that." Standing, she stretches her arms out and looks around the room. "This room is so nice. What is it used for?"

After everything Hazel has learned this evening, I don't have the heart to properly explain how these rooms are private rooms used mostly for people who wish to sell themselves like Emilia once did. It's a conversation for another time and that part isn't my story to tell.

"They are often used for private functions." I offer and she shrugs, taking my simple answer at face value. "Hazel, can I ask you a question?"

"Sure." She answers Alexandra knocks on the open door and enters with our belongings.

"Hi, Hazel. I just want to say how sorry I am. This is not how we operate and I want to assure you, the person in question has been dealt with and is no longer permitted back. I spoke to Noah, but wanted to let you know, if you wish to press charges, you have the full support of myself, my staff and I'm sure the other witnesses who were here tonight."

I watch Hazel carefully as she listens to Lexa before meekly smiling.

"Thank you. I appreciate that but I'm not going to press charges."

"Are you sure, Baby?" I ask, standing to meet her and she nods.

"Very well. I'll leave you two to get ready. The back door is open when you're ready. Raif is watching it." Lexa leaves quickly. She can be very perceptive to cues and knowing when people want privacy is her strength.

"May I ask why you are set against pressing charges?" I try again and she shrugs.

"I don't want to make a big deal out of it. He could be kicked out of school or arrested. We still have the same friends." Her excuses run out of steam while I wait patiently for her to reach the real reason. She pauses briefly and I get the sense she wants to say more so I grant her the awkward silence to do so. "I don't want to have to explain—this." She points to her dress then motions around the room.

I can't argue with that. I'm just introducing her to this lifestyle. If she made a police report, she would have to explain where she was, then go through the questions where they ask her about what she was wearing and everything else that would paint an unfavorable picture of her. I can't ask her to stand up for herself when she is still getting to know herself. I can only support her.

"I understand, Baby." She looks surprised at my words. I think she expected resistance from me. "We will talk about ways to keep you safe though and I will not tolerate him coming anywhere near you again. Am I understood?" She quickly nods to answer my question.

"Was that what you wanted to ask me? Before Alexandra came in?"

"No. I was just wondering if you told Paul you were coming to Ravenous?" She's already shaking her head.

"I didn't. I only told my roommate, and before you ask, I know she wouldn't tell anyone."

I accept her response and hand her bag over to her, turning my back so she can get dressed into her casual clothes. I know I've seen everything already but she needs to feel protected right now. "I want to get you home and into my bed so I can properly take care of you. Then we'll figure everything else out tomorrow."

I hear her rummage through her bag as she changes and I am left to my thoughts.

So the question still remains. How did Paul know Hazel was at Ravenous?

I need to figure this out to stop any future chance encounters and keep him away from her for good. My mind reviews tonight's events and I feel my anger spark anew.

"Hazel, one last thing. I'm going to need Paul's number tomorrow. He and I need to have a little talk."

31

HAZEL

*N*o matter what happens, life always goes on; with or without us.

I learned that lesson when my father got sick and my mother fell apart. She managed to keep it together for a while, but as he deteriorated, she began to step back from herself, and from me. She put all of her strength and attention into helping dad get better, then the day came when we were told that there was nothing else to be done.

There were no more trials to apply for, no new things to try, and his cancer had become stronger than any treatment. We were now merely passengers being pulled along, forced to watch helplessly as my dad was slowly taken from us.

He was given a time frame.

That was the same day my mother mentally packed it in. We had no support system in place. It was just us. They were both only children who had an only child and I was done school and ready to go into the world on my own.

She was done.

Knowing the one you love is leaving no matter what you

do, no matter how loud you scream and how much you love, takes something from you that can't be replaced.

She stopped going out, she stopped getting up, she stopped eating.

During that time, I had become lost in my own pain so it took me a couple of weeks to realize that I was alone and it was up to me to keep both of us moving along with life because I didn't want to lose her as well.

And this is why I'm in Noah's kitchen at four in the morning, looking for a spatula.

I got knocked down last night. We all get knocked down. But if I stay down, I become lost and life leaves me behind.

"Baby, it's still dark out and I smell burnt toast. Do I need an ambulance?" Noah rubs his eyes from across the room, startling me. The guy is like a ninja in the dark.

"Oh, shoot. Sorry about that. Our toaster at the dorm is old and we have to turn it way up to get it to work. I'll try again." I open the door to the waste and toss the blackened slices of bread in the garbage.

"I'm not complaining." He speaks as he joins me, pushing buttons on his coffee maker and I'm grateful because I have no idea how to use something so fancy. "The last time I woke up to the smell of bacon being made for me, I lived with my parents. But, um, shouldn't you be sleeping? Preferably naked and wrapped around my body?" His smile is light but I hear the concern in his voice.

"I couldn't sleep." I try to make my shrug look inconsequential, like it's no big deal. "I guess I'm a morning person." I answer and he stays still, monitoring me while his fingers tap on the countertop.

The truth is, I am tired. I know I am. But I can't close my eyes. I feel like I got knocked back and I need to catch up. I feel like I need to push myself forward until I fall back into step with my life.

When I think about what happened last night, my memories hit me in a combination of vivid detail and blurry thoughts.

After Noah and I arrived here, we went straight to his room. I probably should have been hungry because we didn't have dinner but the knots in my stomach wouldn't allow me to eat so he put one of his t-shirts on me and got me ready to sleep before wrapping his arms around me, pulling my head into his bare chest as we talked.

It's the same lithe chiseled chest I can't take my eyes off of as he turns his attention back to the coffee maker. His bottoms hang off his hips, exposing his muscled torso and I lethargically graze my eyes over his form as I—

Searing pain registers, pushing me back from the stove as I instinctively grip one hand in the other and Noah rushes over to me, guiding me toward the sink.

"Shit, Hazel. Are you alright?" The alarm in his tone confuses me as I hear the water rush out of the tap and he angles my hand under the water.

"Yeah. I—Ow. OWWW!" I growl, looking back over my shoulder, trying to piece together what just happened as another stinging sensation registers.

"Just hold still, Baby." His eyes meet mine and I must look confused because his tone shifts. "Hazel, listen to me. I think you are still very tired. You just put your hand right on the stove you were cooking on. The cold water will stop the burn from going deeper."

Turning my palm over under the water, I watch as my fingers tremble and take a deep breath, trying to calm my body's reaction.

"I—I don't see a burn. I think I'm okay." Removing my hand from the water, I examine my palm and it looks a little red, but otherwise it's normal but I feel an invisible ache. Noah runs his fingers over the skin on my hand and I wince to myself a bit but I don't show it.

"Hazel, I think your hand will be fine but I think you're far from it. Talk to me." I know he means well but I feel a little suffocated.

"We talked last night. Look, I'm fine. Let's eat." Noah doesn't move. For seconds that feel like minutes, he examines me and it takes every ounce of strength I have not to crumble before he agrees, opening the drawer to the utensils and grabbing our plates.

I follow him to the heavy wood dining table, checking my hand out behind his back before plastering on a smile while we settle at the table and dig into our bacon and eggs.

As he cuts into his first egg, I feel myself picking up my pace as I am overcome by hunger. A combination of not eating a meal since lunch yesterday and wanting to keep my mouth occupied so we don't have to talk has me shovelling my breakfast down as Noah steals the odd glance in my direction.

I know he senses something is off which drives me to try harder to show him everything is normal. As I speed up, he slows down, drawing out his meal and my fingers fidget around my empty plate, adjusting my fork and spreading out my napkin on the table until I get an idea.

"I'll get started on these dishes." Standing, I smile

Before I slide my chair back his fingers circle my wrist, catching my attention.

"No. Please, sit." He feeds himself another piece of egg

with his free hand and chews as he watches me closely. His expression is unreadable.

"It's no trouble." I say half-heartedly but don't move. His tone is already telling me I won't be going anywhere right now.

"Sit down, Hazel. I said *please* as a courtesy. It isn't optional." His tone becomes domineering and I feel vulnerable. It's the kind of tone that would make me wet under different circumstances but right now, I wish I was invisible.

I'm wound tight, wrapped in layers of protection and I'm not even sure what I'm trying to keep hidden far below my surface.

"Sure. How's your breakfast?" I make an attempt at directing the conversation.

"Why were you making breakfast before the sun rose this morning?" He asks his own question as though he never heard mine and it catches me off guard.

"I already told you." I remind him with a smile.

"I know what you told me. Now I want to hear the real reason." His eyes bounce between my own, as if he's searching for an answer and I feel another layer being taken away.

"I don't know what you mean." I smile but it's disingenuous. I feel the trepidation bristling under my feeble surface. One wrong move and he's going to topple my house of cards over and I've never resigned myself to chaos before.

Picking up his last piece of bacon in his fingers, he takes bite after bite, chewing it until it is all gone while he watches me in silence and I have an eerie feeling he is deciding how to approach me as well. Suddenly, I feel like prey and I begin looking for the trap.

"Paul assaulted you last night." Indifferently, he speaks his words as though he's telling me what he saw on the news and I feel a flash of anger.

"I know." I snap at him but he doesn't react. He doesn't escalate the conversation and I lose my courage, dropping my eyes down to my empty plate and deciding to move my fork into a different position as I feel another layer dissolve under his stare.

"Hazel, I think you're exhausted. Let's go back to bed. We'll sleep in and take it easy later." He's trying a different approach. He's feeling me out, learning me and I don't want that right now.

Right now I need to keep moving. I'll bounce back. I always do. I just need some time and space to push this down.

"I'm going to clean up a little. Why don't you go back to bed and I'll join you in a bit." I offer hoping his agreeable tone will last until I can get him back to sleep.

"It wasn't a suggestion, Baby. Let's go." The clank of his knife on the porcelain plate sounds louder than it should and it pierces my eardrums.

"I'm not tired." I respond evenly. I'm proud of my tone but it isn't lost on me, I'm not making eye contact.

"I won't tell you again. Get up and get into bed." Even as he speaks, the need for sleep creeps into my body. I know I'm tired but if he would just give me a few hours and a cup of that coffee neither of us has touched, I know I will put it behind me.

"No." Now I make eye contact. He doesn't look mad; he looks concerned and that sets me off even more. It means he knows I'm struggling and he won't let me do this alone.

The thing is, I've always done this alone. This is new for

me and I don't know how to navigate fixing myself with someone else.

"Fair enough. I want you to remember, we could have done this differently, Hazel. It didn't have to be difficult for either of us." My brows knit together as he speaks. He's not making any sense. How is this difficult for him? He's not the one Paul harassed last night.

"What—" The air pushes out of my lungs as he lunges out of his chair, lifting me along with him and the rest of my sentence comes out in a squeak.

The plate in front of me is shoved away and my upper body is placed on top of the table in its place as I hear the porcelain break apart on the floor.

It takes me a second too long to take action and he's already positioned his weight behind me and stretched my arms away from my center so I can no longer use them to push myself up.

"You know how I feel about that word, Doll." Leaning over my body he whispers gravely into my ear and his pet name tugs at me causing me to pause.

"I—I'm sorry. You're right. I'm tired. Let's go to sleep." I speak quickly as my heart thuds into my ribs and against the table I am spread across.

"Oh, we will. But I'm going to take care of you first, Baby." His words offer me comfort but I know his next actions won't be so gentle and I feel a rush of anticipation. "Tell me, why are you being punished?"

"I said the word *what*."

"No." He responds cooly.

"What?"

"Well now I'm just going to add it on. Tell me, why *else* are you being punished?"

"I—I don't know." I answer. I don't want to guess at five things and have five new things added to my slate. "Why?"

His cold chuckle behind me sends goosebumps across my arms. "Maybe you can figure it out while I punish you then."

"Why are you up so early?" As he asks, he slides his shirt I'm wearing up, exposing my cotton panties and I blurt out the first thing that hits me.

"I couldn't sleep." I wince as I answer, bracing myself for his first smack but it doesn't come. He must have accepted some truth in there and he asks another.

"Why couldn't you sleep?" His fingers slide along the seam of my panties just under the elastic.

"I'm just not tired." The band to my underwear snaps against my skin as he withdraws his hand and smacks me hard across my ass before muttering to himself.

"This won't do." With one hand, he yanks my cotton undies down to the middle of my thighs and spanks me again as I cry out and he continues, "You're exhausted Hazel. Your body is falling asleep on itself. Why won't you lay down?"

"I don't know what you want from me." I plead to indifferent ears as his palm lands again.

"Stay put." The anger in his words grounds me in place and I don't dare move; I won't even lift my head as he walks into the kitchen, opening a drawer before returning to his place. I wait for a question to come and it hits me. I haven't answered his last question when I feel a sharp sting across my ass and I jerk at the difference in pain.

"Ow. What was that?" My eyes swell with tears of their own accord.

"It's a wooden spoon, Hazel. If you think you didn't like

that, just answer another question wrong. Why are you avoiding me?"

"What? No wait—" I don't catch myself in time and the contact with the spoon hurts even more as I jerk forward against the table. I'm sure I'll have some bruises on the front of my thighs soon.

"The pain from a wooden spoon is nothing compared to me punishing you over a spot I've already reddened. What are you afraid of?" His threat grounds me to my core. My mind spins and tears roll freely over my cheeks and onto the table.

"I'm not afraid of anything." I feel challenged and I shake uncontrollably from the inside out. Layer upon layer are being stripped from me and I don't know how to hold myself together.

Noah offers no response as the spoon hits across my sit bone and I begin sobbing.

"Last chance, Baby. Why are you making breakfast in my kitchen at four in the morning when you should be sleeping?" I feel his arm pull back from me.

He already knows I'm going to fight him and I feel a weight expand inside of my heart. I don't want to fight him. I shouldn't have pushed him away. I need him. For the first time in my adult life, I need someone and I'm scared. I'm terrified that if I give him this power, he will reject it. He'll reject me and I will fall apart.

I'm scared so I did what I always do. I run away and attempt to fix me by myself before coming back with yet another layer built on top of all of the others.

The realization makes me sob out my response. "I don't want life to go on without me this time."

The only sounds I hear are coming from me in the form

of a big ugly cry. The confession has released me from my tension, unraveling my fear and letting my anxiety go. I have no choice but to welcome the chaos that comes with opening myself up to Noah completely and hoping he'll know how to nurture me.

32

NOAH

"*I* don't want life to go on without me this time." After she says the words, the tension leaves her as her arms go slack and her body deflates. Her sobs control her limbs as she stays in her place on the table, showing me another dimension of her.

Her fear.

I'm not talking about superficial fears; the ones we say we have because something makes us uncomfortable. This is darker. Those surreptitious terrors that hide, even from the one to whom they belong because they consume everything when brought into the light.

From the small amount of information she has shared with me, I believe I know where this stems from, but I don't know why.

"Where is this coming from?" I ask, placing the spoon on the table.

She takes a moment of silence and I allow it. She hiccups in her sobs while I run my fingers through her hair, I know she enjoys the feeling and her breathing begins to slow.

After a minute, I prompt her to answer. I won't give her mind the chance to shut me out. I don't want to go through all of this again to bring her back to this space. Lightly, I run my fingers along the curve of her ass and she murmurs her discomfort but I won't ease up. I'll keep her in this position until I know what I'm dealing with.

"I—I feel like I'm—I feel like I'm losing my second chance. I can't let it happen." Her cheek is still resting against the table. I'm not ready to lift her up to face me yet and she is making no effort to stand. "I thought I lost my best life before; when my dad got sick and I gave up almost everything. But now, there's you and my dream job and I wouldn't give any of this up and I feel like I can't stop or I'll lose it all over again."

Her fear is losing her life with me? The answer almost knocks me over.

"... and I'm afraid because everything is so new. We just started—um—dating and I have always been on my own and I don't know how to fix this."

I probably should let her continue but I can't. Not when there is the smallest chance she doesn't understand her place. Lifting her to stand, I face her to me and look into her bloodshot eyes.

"Hazel, we aren't *dating*. You are mine. This isn't a trial run. I need you to know this relationship is permanent; it's set in stone. Do you understand?" I search her eyes and notice the tears line her lids.

She opens her mouth to answer then swallows her words as she blinks, pushing her salty sadness down her face and I move us to the couch, watching her wince as she gently sits her self down beside me.

"It's just that, I'm new here and I'm learning how we work. I mean, the sex is great, but—"

I can't help it, I bark a laugh at her simplicity causing her to stop her crying as she watches me quizzically.

"But you aren't sure if that is all there is between us, for me? Because if all it is is sex, then why would I stick around to take care of you when you need me?" Her lip trembles at my question and she nods.

"Baby, I want all of you. What we have, what I want to have with you isn't just about us letting go sexually. I want you to give me everything. I want to show you your fears only hold power over you when you hide them away from me. We are stronger together. I'm asking you to give me some of that power so I can help you manage them. You don't need to worry that your life is going on without you because I'm right here with you. I won't allow you to be left behind ever again. Together we are going to go at our own pace, life will need to catch up to us. It's not the other way around."

Blinking rapidly, she stares at me dumbfounded for a long minute. Without warning, she lunges into my arms before tensing in shock.

"Ow, sorry. I forgot about my ass." Her declaration instantly eases the strain in the room as she pushes herself onto her knees on the floor, taking a position to stop the pain.

A strand of her hair has become stuck in her dried tears on her cheek and I lean forward to brush it away. "You need to learn when and how to surrender to me. It isn't a weakness and it isn't just sexual. You need to learn how to navigate within our new dynamic. You can't fight your demons by fighting me."

"That's why you punished me? It was a different kind of

submission and I was fighting it. You were trying to show me how painful it is to reject what I need... and I'm not talking about my ass; I'm talking about my emotional epiphany which hurt even worse." Kneeling, staring up at me as understanding dawns on her, she is the most beautiful thing I've ever seen.

"More painful, yes but also it was more detrimental to you. You can't handle these setbacks by going on like nothing happened. You may be fine for a while but eventually those pieces of us that aren't properly healed turn into jagged shards and begin slicing away at us from the inside out. Then, before you know it, you're frying eggs in someone else's kitchen, in the dark."

She looks at me to see if I'm still being serious and I am, but I give her a smile to show her her punishment is over. "Come here, Baby."

I help her stand, then pull her into my lap, cradling her in my arms, careful not to put too much contact on her bottom.

"Tell me more about what happened when your father became sick. You said it was just you and your mom?" I ask as she settles her head on my shoulder.

"For awhile, yes. Then it was just me. I think that's where this comes from."

"I don't understand. Where did your mom go?" I ask as her fingers draw a picture along my chest and it feels nice to have her contact.

"She didn't go anywhere. I told you I kind of took care of both of them but I didn't really say how bad it got. I didn't tell you everything. I didn't want you to think badly of..." Her voice hitches I lift her eyes to my own, taking in the blotches of red across her cheeks.

"Hazel, I would never think badly of you." I pull her in for a hug but her hand shoots between us.

"No. Not me. My mom." I allow her to push me away as she continues, "You need to know she isn't a bad person. She just hit her breaking point and we had no one else but each other. Then I was alone. It was like standing on a broken down platform watching the train that carried my old life as it left for good."

"I'm confused. Tell me what your mother did." I urge her to put her head back down. I've learned she is more open to sharing when she doesn't have to look me directly in the eye.

"No. It's not what she did. But to tell you the story, I have to include it and it doesn't make her look good. It's just important to me that you see her with that understanding because she is important to me and—you are—important to me." I smile into her hair. It's what I want to be to her.

"My dad was given a time frame and, as it came closer, she just couldn't handle not having him. She gave up on herself. She just turned herself off to avoid the pain. When I realized what was happening, I had no choice but to take care of both of them. It got to the point where I had to remind her to shower so she would feel better and I started doing the grocery shopping, then the cleaning, then paying the bills and rent. I thought, as long as we kept moving along, we wouldn't get left behind. We would take the bus to the hospital and visit with Dad. I'd leave them for a bit and get groceries for the day, then we'd catch the bus back home. I'd make her a meal then set her in front of the TV and go to work. I'd come home and get her into bed, then go to my second job. I'd get home and sleep for a few hours, then we did it all over again."

"How long?"

"Pardon me?" Her choice of words makes me smile.

"How long did this go on for?"

"Well, my dad began to show some improvement and we were able to get him back home with us after a couple of months. Mom was great at taking care of him, but she still didn't take care of herself. Every bit of strength went into helping him beat his diagnosis. Before I knew it, two years had gone by. Then one day, she snapped. It's almost like her breaking point had a breaking point of its own and I woke up to find her making breakfast and doing laundry. She still took care of dad, but it was like she found her way back to herself, and me, and began preparing for a life without him."

I play with her hair as I consider her story.

"And you're scared if you don't keep pushing ahead that life will go on without you again."

She cranes her head back, looking me straight in the eyes. "Not just life, but you. You are becoming my life and I don't know how to handle that. I didn't know how to say it because I don't want you to think I'm a clingy stalker. We're still new. And now I think I have to go to my mom's for the summer and find a new job. I have to start over again. I can't believe he did that to me just because I didn't want to date him. He was my friend. I will lose my spot in the program because of him."

It takes a lot of effort to stop my hands from clenching tight into fists as she speaks about Paul. The memory of his disgusting sneer last night as he tried to force himself on Hazel makes me sick.

I know his type. He's had money around him all of his life and he lacks the emotional empathy to understand the damage of his actions. Everything is a commodity and Hazel is no different to him. His threat confirms it. The weasel believes she would actually be grateful to him for what he's done to her.

And maybe she would have. A chill runs up my spine at the thought. If I wasn't here, he could have forced her hand and backed her into a corner. I don't know her friends well enough to say they would help her and it doesn't sound like her or her mother have built up enough savings. Before I found her, she had invested everything into finishing her program at school and starting out on a life of her own.

He could have easily inserted himself and manipulated her before she realized what was happening.

"He was never your friend, Hazel."

"You're right. I know this." Watching her learn this lesson breaks my heart.

She's right; we are still new. I'm trying to build a deep trust between us and this deception from Paul will hit her hard and I hope she doesn't begin to question all of the faith she has placed in those around her because of it. But she's wrong where she thinks it is only up to her to fix it.

"As for everything else, we will face it—together—after we get some sleep." I finish my sentence with a kiss on her forehead before something catches my eye. "Well, there is one silver lining to being up so early in the morning. Follow me. I want to show you something." I stand to leave, speaking my warning over my shoulder. "And if you even think about clearing those dishes, I'll tie you to the bed until dinner."

The image of Hazel tied to my bed stirs a plethora of filthy thoughts as I walk to my bedroom. There will be many opportunities to play out each one, but not right now. I just finished telling Hazel our relationship isn't just about sex and I need to follow our conversation up with actions.

"WOW. This is beautiful." Hazel lifts her hand to block the bright sunrise from her eyes.

"It is. I lived on this floor for almost a year before I started construction on the rooms. Everything is placed purposefully. I put the bedroom on this side so I could see the sunrise when I woke up and built the outside deck so I could sit and watch the sunset." As I speak, Hazel walks to the full length windows to look out across the downtown buildings in the distance.

"But wouldn't this wake you up even when you wanted to sleep in?"

"And that's why I had the blinds installed, too." I answer, removing my pants and waiting for Hazel to turn around. "Take off the shirt, Baby."

She spins in place and my girl's poker face is gone. I love how she doesn't restrict her expressions around me.

"Oh. Well..." I let her entertain her unspoken thoughts for a moment.

"Hey. Eyes up here, perv." I point to my own eyes and her face floods with the crimson color of embarrassment before I chuckle. "I'm just kidding. I'm totally looking at your tits."

For the first time since yesterday, she laughs her unrestrained laugh and I know she's going to bounce back. We just need a little bit of time and some more discussion.

I crawl onto my side of the bed and stay on top of the sheets while she joins me on the empty side, laying on her back. Turning on my side, I prop my head up in my hand.

"Can I ask you something?" She asks as I begin to draw imaginary lines across her bare torso.

"Of course."

"Earlier, you said I chose to do it the difficult way. What

was the easy way?" My fingers swirl around her nipple until it perks into a peak before I move to her neck.

"Well, this would have been the easy way. I would have played with your hair and drawn on you while we talked and I would have gotten the same answers out of you. Just in a more pleasurable way." I continue to draw in silence while she thinks about my answer.

"So then, the hard way just ends up leading to the easy way... anyway?"

"Pretty much." I smile. "But sometimes the hard way is necessary."

"How so?"

My eyes follow my fingers as they cover every inch of Hazel's front from her lips down to her panties and she lays still for me, enjoying the sensation as I change my motions. Surprising her with the odd pinch of her nipple to my nails along the underside of her breasts.

"I know your response wasn't easy. I saw your tears. It was a painful truth to share with me and to admit to yourself as well. How did you feel after?" My hands don't stop, slowly caressing her and I watch her eyes open with more effort each time she blinks.

"I felt—lighter. Tired."

"You needed the release that only the hard way would provide."

"How did you know I needed that?" She attempts to draw a line with her own fingers up my arm, but I gently place her arm back on the bed. I'm the one taking care of her tonight.

"You told me." She lifts a questioning brow at me and I clarify, "Not with your words. I'm learning to read you."

"And what do I need right now?" She attempts a sultry

look but falls a little on the cute awkward side and I stretch out to meet her lips with my own in a kiss before I answer her.

"You need sleep, my little sexpot. Same thing we started with. Now close your eyes, feel the sun's rays on your body and follow my fingers until you drift off. I'll be right here when you wake up."

She obeys me easily this time as her eyes close and don't reopen. I watch her chest as her breathing evens out and the smile fades into deep sleep before clicking the button on my side table. As the blinds close out the morning's rays, I find a comfortable spot as close to Hazel as I can get before I shut out the morning and drift off beside her.

33

HAZEL

"*A*re you sure you don't want me to go inside with you?" Noah asks a fourth time as Marcus pulls into the wildlife sanctuary.

After my punishment in Noah's kitchen yesterday morning, I woke up at some point in the early afternoon on Saturday and we spent the day just as he said we would. We watched a movie; there was a lot of talking and I sat and watched as he made a fancy pasta dish for dinner. He laughed every time I tried to say the name of the noodle so I just resorted to calling it the twisty pasta dish.

Even though I slept an additional eight hours that day, I was still tired when the sun set so Noah ran a bath and joined me, washing my hair and body before drawing two orgasms out of me as I sloshed around the warm bubbles in the tub.

After that, I barely remember my head hitting the pillow, but I do remember his arms wrapped tightly around me and his fresh scent mixed with his minty mouthwash as I took my last deep breath before dozing off.

I got a call a little before 10 this morning from Shanna asking me to meet her later today at the office and my stomach sank. Paul must have gone through with his threat. I made no attempt to get in touch after Friday night and he pulled the funding. There isn't anything else it could be. Today is supposed to be my day off.

I handled myself calmly, then had another good cry after I hung up and Noah sat with me through everything telling me that, if our hearts are in the right place, things have a way of working themselves out. I believe him...to an extent.

I'm happy we are together. I'm more confident in our connection than I was before, but it's still a punch to the face that I will need to reapply to my program and finish a year behind my classmates when I had worked so hard to graduate at the top of my class next year.

"I'm sure. I know you're with me, Noah. We're in this together. And that is giving me the strength I need to take this as it comes. I need to do this meeting on my own—but not alone." I make sure to include the distinction between the two and he gives my hand a squeeze.

"We're out here if you need." My door opens and I get out, meeting Marcus's kind eyes.

I'm pretty sure Noah filled him in on what happened. I can tell by the way he handled himself around me this afternoon when Noah invited him up for lunch. It wasn't overly obvious but there was a protective undertone in the way we interacted, he felt almost big brotherly. Well, I guess if my brother was some ex-navy undercover seal marine spy, or whatever he is. He wasn't very forthcoming with those answers and I noticed the topic being changed on me when I asked. The only answer I got out of him was a half-joking, '*If*

I told you, I'd have to kill you. Then Noah would kill me. So I'm doing all of us a favor.'

It's just before dinner and the center is quiet when I step inside. Judging by the cars in the lot, only employees are on site right now.

"I'm in my office." Shanna raises her voice, waving her hand at me and I make my way around the counter into the back, closing the door behind me as she hangs up the phone.

Shanna looks frazzled. Before she speaks, she takes a deep breath as though she's trying to breathe the stress out of her. "Whooo, what a day."

I smile. "Crazy? You wanted to see me?"

"Yes. Um, I don't know how to say this so I'm just going to start from the top. I got a call this morning informing me the funding for your internship fell through." Her hands skim over her desk, shuffling papers around.

"Oh. So what happens now?" I ask, waiting to hear what I know is coming. I'm half-tempted to tell her I will do the internship for free. I'll work pro-bono. I wonder to myself if I can even do that. I could get my shift at the coffee shop and club back in the fall.

"Well, like I said, it's been crazy. Nothing happens now." Her hand settles on a folder and she pulls it in front of herself, opening it.

"I don't understand."

"Oh Hazel, this was killing me for most of the day. I didn't want to lose you. But The Lord works in mysterious ways and two hours ago, we received a call from a different foundation wanting to match the donation we just lost." She finishes and looks at me eagerly. I'm sure she's expecting me to jump up and high five her but I can't bring myself to move. I just nod my head, letting all of this information sink in.

This internship sounded too good to be true the first time and I should have known it was. The chances that some psychic investor just decided to call up this not-for-profit to make a donation that matches one that just *fell through* is preposterous.

"Uh huh." Is all I answer as Shanna snaps out of her excitement and sizes me up.

"Wait. Is there something I should know about?" She asks, looking between me and the open folder in her hand.

"Yes. I found out the person who made the initial donation had ulterior motives. I turned his offer to date down and he pulled the funding." Her eyes bulge out of her head.

"What? I knew that guy was no good. I just had a feeling."

"You knew it was Paul who made the donation?" I ask in shock.

"Well, not at first. We had the donation marked down as coming from Davenfield Industries and Paul Davenfield was the one who signed the deposit check and papers. It wasn't until I saw his name on the animal surrender report and matched the signatures from when he dropped off the rabbit that I put it together and asked him about it when he was here. He asked me not to say anything and that he preferred it be anonymous."

I remember them talking and stopping abruptly when I came into the room the last time he was here.

"Does this new benefactor wish to be anonymous as well?" I ask.

Shanna glances at the paper in front of them before answering. "No, actually they said they wish to be completely transparent. The name of the foundation is CR Cares, it's a charitable division of Connor Realty."

I feel my nodding continue well after she is done speaking. Noah works at Connor Realty. I wish he would have talked to me about this first. I feel a little set back that he did this without discussion when he's been pushing for us to be more open with each other.

"There is a request here though. Since the donation is coming in after we already have an intern in place, they've requested to meet with you to go over your school transcripts and do an informal greeting so they can register it correctly as a donation and satisfy their auditors."

"I see." I half roll my eyes. I can just imagine what an *interview* with Noah is going to be like. "And when should I meet with Mr. Wilde?"

"Ummm..." Shanna flips a few pages before responding. "I don't have a Mr. Wilde listed here. It says you are to meet with Emilia Connor and she has requested to see you just before lunch tomorrow. I know you are scheduled to work tomorrow, but we can handle it here. I think it would be a good idea to get it done so your internship isn't set back. Can I confirm the meeting?"

"Oh—uh—yes, please. This is great news." I switch to a happy expression and Shanna doesn't skip a beat as she writes something down on the paper.

"Great. I'm so happy this worked out. We are lucky to have you here." She catches herself and her expression changes to concern. "You said Paul withdrew the funding because you wouldn't—what—be his girlfriend?" I'm already nodding as she asks the question.

"That is the short version of it." I don't really want to share my personal business here so I don't add anything further.

"Well, what a stupid shit. Don't you worry about him. It's best he isn't able to hold this over you anymore then."

I release a deep breath. I am happy he can't hold this over me but now Connor Realty is involved and I need to get back to Noah to find out more because I don't feel entirely free.

"Shanna, my ride is waiting for me outside. Do you have the information for the meeting or should I pick it up when I get in to work in the morning?" As I ask, she stands up and I follow her lead.

"Oh, Sugar. Sleep in and go to your meeting first. It's downtown in an office. You can't go in there dressed like this." She gestures to her attire and I laugh. "Just come in after. Here's the information."

She hands me a sticky note and steps around the desk to give me a motherly hug before I say my goodbyes and make my way back to Noah and Marcus.

The men don't hear me approach them at first. Their backs are to me and Noah is pointing at something off between the trees as they talk. Once I step onto the gravel of the parking lot, it doesn't take them long to hear the gravel crunch under my steps.

"Mr. Wilde." I speak cautiously, a smile stretching across my lips.

He pauses for only a moment before straightening, matching my grin with a sly one of his own.

"Miss Masters."

Marcus circles the front of the car to open my door but I stop him. "Marcus, I'd like to speak to Noah for a minute before we head back into town." I look to Noah for approval and he nods so I continue, "Can we take a short walk? There's a nice path this way that leads to one of our remote work sheds." I stretch out my hand toward the worn trail that disappears into the bushes.

I watch as the men exchange a glance before Noah shrugs and nods. Marcus moves back to the front of the car, facing me and the direction we are about to walk in as Noah joins me, offering me his elbow and I hook my arm through his as we walk into the woods.

We walk for a couple of minutes in silence, listening to the birds and the wind in the trees before I decide to speak.

"Did you cover the donation for my internship?" I've learned there is no beating around the bush with Noah.

"I'll be honest. It was my first thought. It crushed me, when you told me he tried to buy you like that." The reminder of what started all of this silences me as he speaks. "Watching you as you slept at Ravenous, I wanted to fix it and make it all better. But I knew I wouldn't be fixing anything. I would be putting myself in his place. I don't want you to be obliged to me in any way other than because it's what we both want."

"But I know the donation came from CR Cares." He smiles. He looks relieved.

"I meant what I said. If the donation didn't come, we would have figured something out. I was upset and told Joshua, my friend I introduced you to, about it. His partner overheard us and she had mentioned the possibility. You met her as well that night. We haven't had the chance to talk about it yet. I was going to set up a time to discuss the option with her this week once we knew for sure your internship was falling through."

"I don't know what to say." Stepping over some exposed roots in our path, I lead the way through a narrow section of the forest and he follows close behind.

"Well, tell me what happened." He asks, and I know by his question, he really doesn't have anything to do with this donation.

"The donation was recovered. Emilia signed the paperwork and the internship is secure. It all happened just a couple of hours ago." The path widens and he joins my side looking a little shocked.

"That happened fast."

"I'll say. Noah—your friends—I can't thank them enough —and you. I would have lost so much."

He doesn't hesitate, draping his arm around my shoulder, he pulls me closer to his body as we walk and I see the red roof of the shed come into view.

"Now isn't it better when we just talk about things. There's something to be said for taking the easy way although, I have to admit, I wouldn't mind bending you over out here and spanking the defiance out of you." I laugh under my breath as we stop in front of the wooden building and I open the doors.

The building needs a lot of repairs and we've been maintaining it the best we can but its creaks show its age.

"I work out here a lot. There's a stream outside the windows in the back." I point through the screened in windows across the room and he walks to take a look. "We have some feeders out here. Some animals are released right on site and their first feeding grounds are out here. We have a bunch of feeders along the water. See?" I point in a couple of spots and he looks around as a sparrow lands on one of the feeders halfway up a tree.

"Wow. Hazel. This is beautiful. I can see why you like it."

"Thanks. I really am happy when I'm here. Um, I have a

meeting with Emilia Connor this week to finalize the funding. Do you think she would like it if I offered her a tour of the sanctuary? I mean, as part of the donation interview?"

"So it isn't Joshua Darkly who signed as the benefactor?" He asks, a smirk on his lips.

"No. Is that a problem?" He laughs at my question.

"It's only a problem for Emilia." His words sound foreboding but something in his expression tells me it's all okay. "I think you should invite her out for a tour. It would be beneficial for both of you."

I nod. It's set then. I feel a tinge of excitement at my meeting tomorrow. I'm happy to continue on without feeling indebted to someone but there's more. Before everything fell apart at Ravenous, I had the feeling that I wanted to get to know Emilia. That we would be friends. I remember, I was so nervous but then she winked at me. It was a small gesture but it meant a lot to me and I'm happy to get the chance to talk to her again.

34

NOAH

"*T*he place looks a lot different when the lights are on." I observe as Joshua and I wait patiently in the same seats we occupied on Friday night.

The lack of music and bright lights this early make Ravenous look like an abandoned building at 10 in the morning.

"Not nearly as much fun." Joshua remarks, unbuttoning his jacket. "How is Hazel?"

"She's doing well, considering." I wave my hand around the room, indicating the mess from just a few days ago and he nods. "And how is Emilia?"

"The same. I had forgotten how strong she is. No, *forgotten* is the wrong word. I take her strength for granted sometimes. We both have our things we're working on. Her first defence is a strong offence and I need to remember that instead of just reacting with my own show of force." He answers, staring at his untouched mug of coffee sitting on the table.

I push down my urge to rib him about his epiphany.

Joshua is not one to admit things lightly so, when he does, I've learned to know when to joke around and when to listen.

My friend's own growth, since finding Emilia, has been phenomenal. From what he's shared with me, he and his father were extremely close before he died and I sometimes wonder if he closed himself off after his loss. He chooses who he opens himself up to and, to most outsiders, he comes across as a real asshole...which is great for business at times, but not beneficial for personal relationships.

He's lucky Emilia sees beyond his defences. Although since her, he's been slowly lowering his guard and I don't think he is even aware.

The sound of the back door opening followed by the sharp clack of heels against the floor, stops me from responding to Joshua as he leans over to take a sip of his coffee.

"Joshua, Noah, thank you for meeting me here at this time. Getting three businessmen together for an emergency meeting isn't easy." Alexandra spins a chair and sits down in front of us as one of her security guards adds two more beside her before walking toward the front of the club. "Raif will let Mr. Davenfield in when he arrives."

"You okay, Lexa." Joshua asks and I notice her face temporarily soften before she takes a deep breath.

"I'm good. Thanks." She sets a ring of keys on the table and adjusts her jacket before leaning back in her seat. "Just the situation. We haven't had something like this happen in awhile. Everything went by the book—it's just been a busy weekend." She answers Joshua then turns to me. "I want to talk to you a little more about your sub. Maybe for a few minutes after the meeting?" She asks as I hear movement in the front room and I nod my response as I watch Raif walk in, followed by Timothy. Paul trails a little behind them, looking around the room.

Alexandra stands to meet them and Timothy quickly smiles, reaching out to take her hand.

Around here, Lexa is queen. This is her house and membership here is a privilege, one that can be taken away quickly. While we don't conduct business at the club, many top level connections can be made and we all know how valuable our access is for more than the obvious reason.

"Mr. Davenfield, thank you for meeting with me here. You know Mr. Darkly and Mr. Wilde." She becomes formal and succinct and we stand to shake his hand while Paul hangs back, taking the seat farthest away from us, sitting slightly behind Timothy.

I make a point of looking directly at him and I notice his shiner. His eyes stare right through me, his hostility barely contained; but to his credit he shuts up. I'll have to ask Alexandra if he earned his black eye at the club. Judging by how he cowers to Timothy, it's my guess he got it by embarrassing the Davenfield name and dragging him, personally, down with him.

We sit quietly while Alexandra speaks, only Paul looks around the room, unwilling to give her the respect she deserves. Yes, we could have called a meeting at our office, but this isn't a business matter. The transgression happened on club grounds and dealing with the situation, without Alexandra would be taken as disrespectful as it was her business that has been affected by what unfolded.

We are all to blame. All four of us, but taking a quick glance at the other men around the table, only three of us are taking any accountability. For my part, I should have refrained and allowed the security team and Alexandra to control Paul. While I was within my rights to defend myself and Hazel, they were present and club rules dictate they handle any disruptions. Joshua isn't really to blame but it was our table that was involved and he had spoken for the table that night, so he is here. Even Mr. Davenfield is taking his share of the responsibility and it wasn't his choice that his name was added as a reference, but he is still here to shoulder what is his.

The only one who is looking around, rolling his eyes and staring at me like I'm entirely responsible for everything that has gone wrong for him is Paul. And the blame is mostly his to carry, but he's already decided not to.

"My boy used my name to gain access on Friday night without my permission." As Timothy speaks, Paul touches his eye. "As I understood the situation, he saw his friend here and attempted to approach her not fully understanding club protocols."

"He didn't just approach her. He assaulted her." I speak as steadily as I can, not wanting to hurt my standing with Ravenous or Lexa.

"I was upset." Paul barks back. "We were dating and seeing her here at the club, surprised me. She—"

I won't let him finish with lies. "My girlfriend." I correct him.

Paul looks like he wants to lunge at me but he stays seated as he continues. "*She* shouldn't play people like that. I donated to the place where she worked so I could help her get a job and she played me."

I want to fight back for Hazel but Joshua's hand on my arm catches me. Paul is trying to bait me into fighting. He's trying to drag me down to his level because that is the only place he has a chance of coming out as the victim.

Timothy nods, pacifying his son and Alexandra looks at me, silently urging me to speak my piece because she knows what really happened.

"That isn't accurate, Mr. Davenfield." I catch his attention and Paul looks like he wants to murder me. "I spoke to Hazel and, when she rejected your son's offer to date, he pulled the funding. As a matter of fact, as of right now, all of the charitable funding from your organization has been pulled back." Timothy's eyes bulge out of his head at my words. Without a doubt, without question, I can tell he instantly believes my claim.

"Well?" Staring Paul down, Timothy offers no other words.

"It's—I—She deserved—", he stutters.

"Enough. This is unacceptable. Mr. Wilde, I deeply apologize for the way my son acted while my name was used to permit his entry. I will gladly reinstate the entire donation. This is not how we do business." He speaks to me, but his words look like a dire warning to his son and I imagine he'll probably have a second black eye to match the first one soon enough.

"While your offer is more than generous, Mr. Davenfield, the donation has been settled and I think it is best for all parties if this particular donation remains outside of your foundation." Timothy nods as I speak and Paul continues to glare at me, now knowing he hasn't set Hazel back one bit.

"I agree with you there and thank you for bringing this to my attention. It appears I need to reassess the signing

280 | RUN WILDE

authority I grant on some things around the office." He warns over his shoulder.

"Where's Hazel? Is she hiding in the back?" Paul's question shocks everyone and Timothy looks like he wants to strangle him.

"Hazel isn't here." Alexandra injects catching Paul's attention.

He turns his phone over in his hand. I assume he's checking the time before he speaks.

"Of course she is. I know she's here." His eyes dart around the room and I look to Joshua, sure that my confusion matches the look on his face.

"Paul, that's enough. We are here to listen to Ms. Loren and apologize for our part on Friday night at *her* club."

Paul opens his mouth to object but Timothy swivels his entire body in his seat to square off with his son and he quickly backs down. "I—I'm sorry about your club, Ms. Loren." His words don't match the anger on his face but Lexa nods curtly.

"I want to thank all of you for meeting me here on such short notice. In light of everything and unless anything else needs to be discussed, I am willing to maintain all three of your memberships here at Ravenous if you so choose. However, Paul will not be permitted on the premises and this decision is final and permanent." To her credit, Alexandra looks everyone in the eyes as she speaks and all three of us nod in silence as Paul simply looks at the ground.

"Gentlemen, I have some business to attend to and you are welcome to stay for a while to speak, respectfully. Raif will get you a coffee, Mr. Davenfield and he is here if you need anything further." We all stand as she rises to leave and Joshua and I take our seat again.

"Wait for me in the car." Timothy turns to Paul and he looks like he is going to ask a question when he raises his hand. "I won't say it again, Boy."

As Mr. Davenfield sits back down to our table, I see Raif bringing out a cup that matches the ones Joshua and I have and I reach across to take a sip of my lukewarm coffee. As Paul leaves, he keeps glaring over his shoulder at us but I no longer look directly at him.

"Joshua, Noah, I can't apologize enough for what happened. I wish I was here that night. I would never have allowed him entrance. He doesn't belong here." He nods at Raif and takes his coffee.

I feel on edge. I don't know what I expected from today but this doesn't feel final. The way he spoke about Hazel wasn't accurate. I don't believe for a second she led him on. What matters though is if he is lying or if he really believes what he said.

It also disturbs me how he was sure she was here. What if she was? What would he have said to her? I don't think an apology is anywhere in his mind. Listening to him today, I think he actually believes he is the victim.

"In all of our dealings, I didn't know you had a son, Timothy." Joshua changes the subject and I'm thankful he is here.

Timothy relaxes at the use of his first name. Joshua has separated our business and pleasure dealings and the small talk is resetting our environment.

"He doesn't really seem interested in the family business. He was closer to his mother before the divorce. He took it hard when she moved away and left both of them here. She isn't really around at all." He looks like he wants to say something else but pauses to take another drink. "We don't have a lot in common."

Joshua continues his small talk for another 15 minutes while I jump in occasionally until the tension is gone. Timothy leaves before we do and Joshua hangs back for another five minutes talking to Raif about the club to give the Davenfields a chance to drive away.

I'm thankful I don't need to see Paul again as I've finally calmed down enough to focus on what is important.

"Raif, thank Alexandra for her time today for us and let her know I'll call her later. Noah and I need to get back to the office." Raif nods and we walk to Joshua's car as his driver opens the door for us.

This is unusual for me. Normally it is me who is watching over Joshua and talking him down, but today he stepped up and managed a level head while I had to compose myself.

"Thank you. For—in there." I break the silence after a few minutes.

"Of course. How many times have you covered for me? I'm sure Kyle would have left this city in a body bag instead of on a plane if it wasn't for you." His tone is light and I look up to a smirk as I shake my head. We really changed spots today. "Besides, nothing can knock me out of the good mood I'm in today. I had a great weekend with Emilia after Friday night. We did a lot of talking and we're really good."

"That's great news. I forgot to say thank you. Hazel is over the moon that Connor Realty made the donation to save her internship." I pause, scanning his face with a stupid grin on my own. I'm waiting to see if my hunch is right.

"The donation?" His tone evens out and I am able to read him like a book.

"Yes." I feel my own voice begin to rise as I try to contain my humor. "Hazel is meeting with the CR Cares benefactor as we speak to finalize the application."

"Let me guess," He releases a deep breath shaking his head in mock frustration, "the benefactor is..."

"Yep." I finally laugh out loud. Now is the time to taunt him.

35

HAZEL

"*M*iss Masters is here to see you." I follow the woman into the office and step out from behind her.

"Thank you, Faye." Stepping around her desk, she reaches her hand out, smiling at me and I feel my cheeks blush as I remember the last time we met. "It's really good to see you again." Her eyes scan to the door as it closes before she continues, "Can I call you Hazel?"

I nod. I would feel better if she did. Formalities make me uncomfortable and I can't imagine she is much older than me.

"Good. Let's see." She extends her hand, offering me a seat and I set my bag down behind the chair before we both sit down. "I've already sorted the paperwork out with the wildlife sanctuary and I sent the updated files through to your professor this morning. We have a standard questionnaire here that will go in the donation file in case we are audited." She opens a file, pulling out a sheet and grabbing a pen. "Do you have your transcripts? If not, it's okay, I can request them from your professor."

I'm already unzipping my bag and digging through my work clothes for the papers before she finishes speaking. "Here they are. My professor gave them to me in case the wildlife center wanted a copy." She takes the sheets from me and spins in her seat, running them through a desk copier before handing them back.

"Okay, great. So I filled in most of the details; names, contact information, etcetera. The rest is a little bit of background on you in relation to your internship, what the donation goes toward and how your position will benefit the not-for-profit." Her eyes scan the paper while she speaks.

"Well, I was thinking of asking if you wanted to come out for a tour—um—to look around the place. Do you think that would help answer those questions?" She stares at me for a long moment before answering.

"Oh my gosh! Yes, I would love to." The genuine excitement on her face instantly relaxes me. "I mean..." She clears her throat, attempting to pull herself back to business. "I'm sure I could, I think. I'll just check with our foundation to make sure that is acceptable." She types a note quickly and clicks a button before turning her attention back to me.

"Is everything okay?" I ask and she pauses, a devious smile forming along her lips.

"Oh yes. It's—ugh—okay. Can I tell you something?" I nod. "I just got signing authority on our CR Cares account a couple of weeks ago. This is my first donation and I'm kind of really excited about it." Her enthusiasm is contagious and I smile with her but I get the feeling we are now partners in crime.

"I wanted to say, I really appreciate your donation but I need to be honest with you, too." Her smile fades for a moment as I continue, "Noah said something along the lines that he thinks you might be in trouble because of it." I leave my sentence at that and her smile returns after a few seconds.

"I think I might be. I should have gotten Joshua's official approval first so I'll probably lose my signing privileges for a while and—well, you know the guys. I'm sure there's also a punishment in there somewhere." Her eyes seem to smile at the thought. "But I know Mr. Darkly and this donation was going to happen anyway."

"May I ask, then, why not just have him make the decision?" The corner of her mouth twitches and she gives me the same wink she gave me at Ravenous.

"What's the fun in that?" She asks and we both stare at each other in silence before giggling at the situation. "Besides, they both know I wouldn't stay away from you for long. I mean, I have been dying to meet more people like...well...me. Seriously though. It'll be fine. What's important is that the donation got made. It's a good cause, too. I love animals." She closes the file before leaning back in her seat. "I am really glad you and Noah found each other."

I smile and drop my eyes to her desk. Being a part of Noah's life like this and talking to his friend as I am his makes me feel like I belong in my skin.

Glancing at her phone, "It's almost lunch and the guys should be back from their meeting shortly. Do you want to stick around and chat for a bit? No more business talk." She looks hopeful and I reach into my bag, grabbing my phone to check the time.

"Is something wrong?" Emilia's words draw my attention up to her.

"Um, no. I just realized I must have grabbed Noah's phone by mistake. I think he has mine. I'd love to stick around, I'll need to swap phones with him anyway before I head out to work."

She jumps up at my answer as I toss it into my bag. "Great. Let's sit on the couch. It's less stuffy. Now tell me how you met Noah."

"He was in the coffee shop where I was working. I accidentally spilled a tray of coffee all over him." She covers her mouth to hide a snicker. "It's all still really new for me." I admit.

Outside of Noah, I have no one to talk to about what I am experiencing so I find myself treading lightly.

"You know, I'm still new to Joshua's lifestyle and I don't really have any friends that know this side of me. I have one really good friend, but I don't know exactly how or when to bring it up so...if you ever want to just talk about anything, maybe you could consider talking to me." Emilia's face is soft yet serious and I could almost cry at her kindness.

"Thank you. I just might. I have a good friend I kind of hinted it to but I haven't really told her. I appreciate your offer."

We exchange a smile before I hear voices just outside the door before it opens.

"Mr. Darkly, she's in a—" The receptionist doesn't finish her futile sentence as Joshua walks in, followed by Noah in his fitted suit and I feel my throat constrict at the sight of him.

"Thank you, Faye, but we are expected." He says kindly, first looking at Emilia's desk, then spinning on his heels to find us sitting across the office on the couch.

As the door closes behind them, Joshua narrows his

sights on Emilia and I follow his stare to see her smiling defiantly back at him.

"My dear, Noah just told me the oddest thing on our way back here." His voice sounds predatory and I shiver. I can't imagine what this is doing to Emilia.

"Oh, is that so?" Her voice wavers but she holds her ground and Joshua's grin stretches further.

"Oh yes, that is so. You see he told me that, after I had said we would discuss a certain—donation—," his eyes jump to me for effect and I stay still as he continues, "at another time, that you went ahead and made the donation on your own on our company's behalf. And I told him that you wouldn't dare do that because you are my good girl." I'm pretty sure I just heard Emilia swallow a lump in her throat beside me. "And you are my good girl, aren't you, Emilia?"

I catch Noah grinning behind him and he flashes me a carnal wink of his own as Emilia and I stay seated on the couch waiting for them to pounce.

"I, well, I—" The tone is light but I get the impression Emilia didn't expect to be dealt with in front of us. Joshua raises his hand, cutting her off.

"The choice is simple, Emilia. Right now, you are either my good girl, or my bad girl." I keep my eyes on Noah as they speak and he looks happy with my decision to sit still.

"Bad." Emilia whispers before standing and flattening out the front of her skirt. "I would just like to say that some things are totally worth their punishment." She smiles at me and I grin back to let her know I agree.

My eyes shift back to Noah before I notice his raised brow as he watches our little rebellious coup and I humble my happy expression.

"I would also like to point out this was a business

meeting and we agreed there will be no public punishments in front of business...um...people." Emilia points to me as she challenges Joshua and I hear Noah snicker behind him.

I get the impression that, as much as these guys enjoy holding dominance, they equally revel in being challenged.

"Your case is weak, Emilia. But I will allow it. Just know that I have the rest of the day to plan a more—fitting— punishment and I can not wait to get you home, my love." At his promise, he crosses the room and she stands, lifting her chin to him as he places a gentle kiss on her lips as though nothing just happened before stepping back from her and facing me.

"Hazel, it is nice to see you again and under better circumstances this time." Extending his hand, a smile on his face. "I trust you both sorted everything out here?" He glances between us and Emilia answers him before asking if she can visit my work for a tour and he says it is allowed.

"Do you think we could do the tour on Wednesday? I have most of the afternoon free." I nod as she asks.

"I'm pretty sure it works for me. We have a team workshop on Tuesday and I'm off on Thursday and Friday so Wednesday should be good. Can I email you, or?" I ask and she steps around Joshua, grabbing a pen off her desk and reaching for a business card.

"You can text me. For anything. I wrote my cell number on the back." I slide the card into my bag and lift it over my shoulder as Noah joins me placing his hand at my lower back.

"Joshua and I were just going to see if Emilia wanted to go across the street for lunch. Can you join us before you have to get back?" His eyes stare at my lips and I'm dying to kiss him but I'm not sure if it's a good time.

"I'd love to but I've already been gone for the morning. Before I forget though, I think you have my phone." I dig my hand into my bag.

"Um, I don't think so. I've got mine right here." Holding up the same black case as my own, he turns it on. "Wait, huh, how about that. I'm going to have to get you a different case for yours." Holding it out to me, I take his phone and return the one I had.

Joshua and Emilia leave the office to offer us some privacy as I say my goodbyes and Noah steps into my space as we swap our phones back, lifting my chin and licking along my bottom lip. My breath escapes me faster than I can breathe it back in.

"I know you enjoyed the way he spoke to her, Baby." He whispers in my ear. Now it's my turn to swallow the growing lump in my throat. "Come with me."

We step into the main area and he walks up to Joshua as Emilia is putting on her coat.

"I'll meet you down there in a bit. Order me a burger?" Joshua nods then leads Emilia to the elevator as we follow behind them.

Everyone is silent while we wait for the lift to arrive and I keep my eyes forward on the door as I feel my heart thump into my chest.

A couple of employees step out, leaving the four of us to an empty elevator as Joshua presses the button for the main floor and Noah presses the level below us. I take a quick side glance at Emilia and, as the doors ding and open, I think I see her mouth the words *have fun* and she winks again before I am whisked off the elevator and down the hall into an office.

"Good afternoon, Mrs. Townsley. Enjoy your lunch."

Noah says with a finality that anyone would pick up on as we head straight through the doors with his name on them.

And all at once, he becomes extremely composed. He stands me on my own and steps back, taking me in before locking the door to his office and stepping around his desk.

"You need a place to change before work. Here you go." I look around the office and fully expect him to turn his back as he did before, but he doesn't.

I could turn myself to the side and hide myself away. I know that would prompt him to give me some privacy but I don't want any right now and we both know it. He saw my reaction to Joshua and Emilia's conversation. I can't deny my need to surrender has become a driving force. I feel like it calls to me now and I lift my hands, my fingers trembling to my top to undo the buttons before sliding the soft fabric down my arms.

I slowly unzip my skirt and it falls away on its own before I step out of the heels I borrowed from Nina's closet.

"You are beautiful...and you're mine." He leans further back in his seat, showing me the bulge of his admiration without shame.

It isn't a question so I don't answer. Instead I feel a surge of confidence rush through me as I walk around his desk, kneeling in front of him and reaching for the button on his pants. It releases easily and so does his zipper and I bite my lip as I pull them down before licking the tip of his already hard length as he drops his head back against his chair with a moan.

"Am I though, really?" I ask in my brattiest voice, remembering how much Emilia enjoyed taunting Joshua and Noah narrows his eyes on me.

"Oh, Baby. Do you not feel loved?" He asks a simple question.

Loved.

The word hits me and I pause. I've been loved by my parents and I've felt a strong love between friends, but love in the deepest sense? I've never felt loved like this until now.

I open my mouth to answer, but the air is pushed out of me as he lifts me, before I am spun and deposited on top of his desk, his hand in the middle of my back, holding me against the wood.

"Ssshh, Baby. I'm going to show you a love you never knew existed." My breath catches in my throat as he spanks my bottom without warning before returning to my ear in a whisper. "Keep it down, Doll. You don't know if my receptionist left for lunch. She usually eats at her desk so you're going to need to be a good and quiet little girl for me." He spanks me a second time before I settle, feeling the cool air hit my slick warmth as he slides my panties to the side and my head spins against his desk.

Before I gather any of my senses, the tip of his erection presses between my legs and I groan openly into the wooden surface.

"That's my good little doll." His voice drops and I can't help pushing my own hips back, offering myself to him.

Without hesitation, he slides in and we moan in unison as my hands come up to the desk to brace myself against the onslaught I desperately hope will come, and it does.

My head spins at the thought I am being used over his desk while his secretary might be enjoying her lunch just outside his doors and it takes everything inside of me not to scream as he angles himself deeper inside of me. His fingers dig into my hips and I hope they leave bruises all over me so I can enjoy them for days as I continue to ride everything he gives me.

I feel as though I'm falling apart around him as I lift my leg across his desk, spreading myself further open; desperately offering everything I have and he continues to fuck into me, sliding one hand over my mouth to silence me and I roll my eyes into my head, allowing him to take complete control.

The image hits me as fast as my orgasm does. I am entirely his to do with as he pleases and he is taking me over his desk at lunch, enjoying my body fully. My stomach tightens as I clench tight around his length and I groan into his hand as I come, my body shaking underneath him as he thrusts a few more times before coming and stilling over me as we lay across the top of his workspace gasping for breath in unison.

I lay in a moment of silence, feeling the pulse of his cock before he sits back in his seat, taking me with him and cradling me in his lap.

After a few minutes of listening to his breathing, his voice brings me back to reality. "Are you sure you won't join us for lunch?"

I laugh in his arms, "I really have to get to work." I move to stand and pull my work clothes out of my bag.

"Watching you get off on authority makes me hard. I know you're working a little later tonight and I have a dinner meeting on Tuesday, but I want to see you Wednesday after work. Text me when you are on your way home. I'll have Marcus bring you to me. You'll be staying over since you don't work on Thursday." He joins me standing as his lips claim my own and his arm slips around my waist pulling me into him, almost lifting me off the ground. "I needed that, Doll. Come, I'll walk you out."

"Do you think she heard me?"I ask sheepishly.

"Who?" He asks as though he really doesn't know.

"Your receptionist." Flustered, I whisper.

"Oh, Susan. She had a dentist appointment. I gave her the rest of the day off. She left right after we saw her." He laughs as he sizes me up and I feel my face flood red in embarrassment before I look to the ground.

"Don't do that." He stops moving in front of me.

"Pardon?" He smiles at the proper use of my words.

"Good girl, but don't ever hide your face from me. I love every part of you. Your humor, your fear..." Dropping his voice, he steps closer to me "...your shame. I own it all. Don't ever hide it from me, Baby. All of you belongs to me."

36

NOAH

"You left your burger at the restaurant." The paper bag hitting my desk startles me out of my thoughts as Joshua unbuttons his jacket and takes the seat across from my desk. "Oh wait, you never showed up for lunch." He leans back in his seat, sniffing the air like an animal catching the scent of its prey. "It smells like sex in here."

I take a deep breath to try to smell what he's smelling before I catch Joshua's smug smirk.

"Asshole."

"You know it." He chuckles.

"Thanks for bringing lunch back." I don't wait for his permission to open the bag before unwrapping my cold burger and taking a bite.

"Looks like you worked up an appetite." He stays seated in front of me.

I continue to chew, refusing to acknowledge his unasked question as my eyes land on the tipped over pencil holder on my desk and my thoughts drift back to Hazel's body stretched out underneath me. Her body surrendered itself to me, her slender fingers knocking my pens over as she stretched her arms, searching for something to brace herself against while I took her in my office. The sounds of her moans as I covered her mouth still sing in my head.

The thought of that alone clouds my resolve and I'm thankful we don't work together or I'd be calling her back in her for the remainder of the afternoon. I don't know how Joshua and Emilia concentrate working so close to each other.

Clearing his throat while he taps his knee, Joshua yanks me out of my daydream. He pauses for a moment before speaking as he mulls something over in his head.

"You know, Emilia really likes her." He offers to take the conversation in a more serious direction and I bite.

"Yeah, Hazel likes Emilia, too. I think they are good people for each other." I take another bite as Joshua nods.

"Did you tell her about your meeting this morning?"

"She knew I was going to the club to discuss what happened on Friday night. She had asked if she could come along and apologize for herself but I told her the house rules and she understood." Joshua nods at my answer.

At Ravenous, only the responsible parties are required to show up. While she was the target, she had not provoked her part in the situation or made anything worse. Simply trying to remove oneself from a dangerous circumstance is not a transgression. I was responsible for her and my actions toward Paul on Ravenous grounds, Joshua was responsible for the table and Timothy was responsible for his guest. As such, we are the ones required to redress the balance.

"Did she know Paul was there?" He watches me carefully.

"I didn't say he would be, because we didn't know he was there until they showed up together. I'm going to mention it when we have more time. I want to prepare her for Paul's view of what happened. It just wasn't a good time today."

"What the hell was he going on about? He was so adamant Hazel was hiding in the back room. I mean, she isn't my sub and I wanted to pummel the guy." I attempt to contain my smile as he becomes outraged on my behalf while rambling on. "I say this, fully knowing I've done some stupid shit in my life, but that guy seems a little unhinged. Are you worried about him?" Crossing his ankle over his knee, Joshua continues to tap his pants with his finger.

"I won't admit this to Hazel, but—yeah—I do think there's something off. She knows enough to stay away from him, especially now. I'm hoping she'll just slip off his radar now that his father is involved. I've already spoken to Marcus about him so she's secure."

"When she's with you...but she's not always with you." I tense up at Joshua's words and he shifts forward in his seat. "Look, I'm not trying to scare you but you're my friend and if something happens to her then something happens to you and I won't sit back and just let it happen. You know I'm not wired like that." The expression on Joshua's face betrays his bravado. He's concerned for me.

I watched him gut himself when everything about Emilia finally came to light. Years of pushing her away only to learn she had been taken advantage of when he was too swept up in his own anger and abandonment issues to notice; it almost crushed him.

Since then, his loyalty to those he loves has only become more intense.

"I know. I've been trying to decide what to do about that. I can't turn her into a prisoner under me in order to free her from him. I've already told her I am installing a better lock on her door and she didn't fight me in the slightest so that's a start. I'll feel it out and see how it's going."

He shrugs and I know him well enough to know he's not going to push it further right now. "I heard back from Lexa. Paul didn't get that black eye at the club. She checked the cameras with Raif and Helix, he was the one outside the door. Paul left without any further altercations. It happened off Ravenous property."

I shrug back. The information isn't that important to me.

Swallowing my last bite I slide the paper bag into the trash and point at my phone. "Time to get back to work."

"Oh good. I'm still in the right place then." Joshua smirks again as he continues, "Dinner tomorrow night?"

I open my drawer to pull out the folder with all of the information I need. "Right. I've got the paperwork here. We're meeting Maynard and Clive at The Plaza at seven. They want to hear hard numbers so we should sit down and discuss our salary ceiling and other perks that will be on the table so we don't look like we're just treading water."

"How do you feel about it?"

"I get the impression their relationship with Drakus is coming to an end. They're looking for some of the freedoms they had before the company restructured and I think Connor Realty is more in line with their goals now." He raises his brows, nodding his head.

I know this makes him happy. It would strengthen our sales team and release me to assist Joshua on higher level projects and it would ease some of the pressure our newer sales staff are under and we want to keep our employees satisfied with their jobs before we lose them like Drakus is about to.

"Great. It's set then. I'm actually looking forward to this meeting. Thanks for setting it up." I nod as Joshua stands, buttoning up his jacket.

"And everything is good with Emilia?" I ask before he leaves.

"Of course. Why do you ask?" Joshua raises his eyebrows and I smile. Now it's my turn to lean back in my seat.

"The donation." I remind him.

"Oh, yes. Dammit. Now I'm not going to be able to concentrate at all this afternoon. That's another meeting I'm looking forward to." I feel the desire behind his words and I understand his anticipation.

"I can't thank you both enough for doing that—for the both of us."

As if another thought hits him, he steps back to his chair, taking his seat again. "I agree with what you said at Ravenous on Friday night." I lift my brows in confusion. Most of the evening was a blur and Joshua fills in the blanks, "About not wanting to buy her with a donation like Paul did. I really thought that was a good decision on your part, as much as I know you wanted to help her."

He pauses for a long minute before extending his thought, "It's just that, you know I messed up a lot of things before Emilia and I finally talked. Don't get me wrong, I still would have bought her because she had no other choice but after it was all over, I did have some moments of regret for how we went about finding each other. It wasn't until I released her from her obligation to me that we both realized we were never an obligation to each other in the first place. We both hid our hearts behind the false security of wills and contracts instead of just facing our fears together. By removing the contract, we removed the resentment that lingered with it. What I'm trying to say is, I was always going to allow the donation."

"Wow. That's pretty deep for a Monday afternoon, Darkly." He grins and stands, chuckling at my words.

"Yeah, well. Don't get used to it...and, I'm serious, Wilde. It smells like sex in here. Get yourself a scented candle or some essential oily shit." I laugh out loud, flipping him my middle finger and he turns, waving his own back at me as he leaves.

The door to my office closes and my smile fades. Something doesn't sit right with me. Joshua doesn't show his concern lightly and if he noticed Paul's brand of crazy during the meeting then I need to listen to his warning.

Opening my desk drawer, I exchange my file folder for my phone.

Noah: Move up the new door lock for Hazel. She'll be with me on Wednesday evening. Can you install it then and bring the keys to my place?

Marcus: Sure thing. Everything okay?

Noah: I'm sure it is. Just being careful.
Noah: One more thing, remember how you ran information on a guy for me a few months ago for Joshua?

Marcus: Kyle Gershaw?

Noah: Yes. Can you do it again?

Marcus: Paul?

Noah: Yes. It's Paul Davenfield. And I'm pretty sure this is his real name. Attends school with Hazel but his classes are more business. His father is Timothy Davenfield but I don't want any information on him. We do business with him.

Marcus: Understood. Anything in particular?

Noah: No. Just interesting events over the last five years or so. Thanks. The guy really rubs me the wrong way.

Marcus: On it.

37

HAZEL

*S*ince Monday, I have been looking forward to today for two reasons.

The first reason just pulled into the parking lot.

"I've got this, Georgia." I call over my shoulder to our part time volunteer and she turns her attention back to the computer screen.

Today is the perfect day to be outside and the grounds behind the facility have so many interesting spaces.

"Good afternoon." I greet Emilia as she steps out of the backseat of her car. It isn't lost on me she has a driver as well and I look down at my work shirt and khakis, brushing away some dirt.

"Hi, Hazel. Wow! This is a nice place. You're making me question my career choices. I could work out here all day." I perk up at the comment and the sight of her attire. The collar she wore at Ravenous is gone. In its place sits a beautiful chain wrapped loosely around her neck and attached with a little silver lock. She's dressed down in jeans and an old pair of Vans as she takes a few steps toward me before turning to speak to the man standing at her car.

"I'll be about an hour..." Then looking at me, she seems to change her mind. Turning back, she corrects herself, "... or two. Do you want to grab lunch and I'll text you when I'm ready?" Her driver nods, shutting her door and Emilia hooks her hand in my arm, spinning me back toward the building I just came out of. "Now, where were we?"

"I was thinking of starting inside. Our main building is where we do most of our work and we can show you the animals on site." Walking through the front doors, I introduce Emilia to two of our part time staff. Then Jeff, our resident vet joins us for a bit and takes us on a tour of our back area, showing her the animals we are currently working with.

I shared Shanna's regrets that she couldn't be here this afternoon and Jeff talked about our charitable goals and forecast, no doubt touching on every one of Shanna's speaking points. Emilia was graceful and polite but I could sense the numbers didn't matter as much to her as the animals did. She perked up each time Jeff brought out a new animal, making cooing noises and kissy faces at each one.

We moved into the storage area as Jeff talked about the medicine, tranquilizers and other stock we keep on hand and I could see Emilia was fading fast.

"Could I take Ms. Connor outside and show her around the grounds a bit? If that's okay with you?" I ask and Jeff looks relieved as he shoos us away with his arms.

I point to the back door and Emilia steps through it as I turn to say thanks to Jeff for his help.

"No problem. Giving these tours is my least favorite thing about this place. That Paul guy asked so many stupid questions on his tour." His eyes go to the door Emilia just walked out of, then back to me. "Shanna told me what happened. I'm really sorry."

I didn't realize Paul came for a tour. It must have been just before I saw him at Ravenous. I smile to ease his concern and thank him again as I join Emilia outside, brushing the memory of Paul to the side.

We look at each other for a moment and I get the feeling she wants to drop the business talk as much as I want to.

"If it makes you feel any better, Jeff tells me the tours are painful for him, too." I smile and she breathes out a chuckle as I continue, "How about I take you down some of the trails we have out here? We can chat...about anything." I wink and she visibly releases her shoulders clasping her hands in front of her.

"I would love that. Where should we start?" Her eyes look around and I point off to my right, deciding to take her to the same place I showed Noah on Sunday.

"How about we start with the questions on your donation sheet, if you remember them. I'd hate for you to leave here and not have the answers you need."

As we walk along the path through the trees, Emilia starts by asking me how I got into animal sciences to begin with. I tell her about my dad and his clinic and how I've always grown up around animals.

She listens quietly as I share his illness and I find out she recently lost her own father to a heart attack and we walk together in silence for a few minutes before she speaks her thought out loud.

"It's why I came back here, you know?" Her voice surprises me and I look at her for more information. "I was in school on the other side of the country and, if I'm being honest with myself, I wasn't coming back. Then he passed and everything in my life changed."

"And you met Joshua." I offer to lighten the mood and she huffs out a bitter breath.

"I already knew Joshua. I'd known him for years. He was the reason I left in the first place." She answers matter-of-factly.

"Oh, I didn't know." I have no idea where to go with this so I just start walking.

After half a minute, Emilia offers more of her story. "Joshua is one of the best things to ever happen to me. It just took a lot of hurt to get us to that point. He comes across as gruff and demanding but he has his reasons for it and I happen to respond to him and I love him; all of him, even his weaknesses he tries hard to work on. I love the person I am when he challenges me to reach a higher standard and I get off on the praise and rewards as well as his discipline."

"Why are you telling me this?" I stop for a moment, not sure of how to proceed but Emilia keeps walking so I pick my pace back up.

"I saw you on Friday night. Do you ever watch a person and instantly know what they are feeling because you see yourself in them?" She glances at me and I smile. "I'm going to go out on a limb and say I think you are new to the feelings that come with this certain lifestyle. I see the curiosity written all over your face. I'm kind of new as well." She talks while we walk, keeping her eyes on the ground to avoid the roots and rocks jutting above the ground. "I used to think there was something wrong with me. In my daily life, I've always been strong and confident but I struggled to be that around Joshua. I had darker fantasies and I never shared them with anyone. Joshua made me feel safe to the point where I could just let myself go and I came to understand we all just want different things; our needs are just different, not wrong. And I saw that in you. But I also saw that guy try to push you back down and I think it's because he knows he could never give you what you need. And that is why he tried to force you to change into something he could handle. Wow! Look at me overstepping everywhere." She winces at herself.

"My very long point is, don't let anyone else dictate who you are. Their actions and reactions are who they are. It isn't who you are. And I think you're great—and I'm pretty sure Noah does, too." Her smile is infectious.

There is a lot of truth in everything she said. On Friday, I wanted the collar off because of what Paul did, but I remember feeling a flash of shame based on what he said to me that night. I had felt instantly embarrassed and I allowed his words to become my reality.

"Well, that's a lot to absorb." I smile.

"Yeah. I'm sorry about that. I don't get to talk about this type of stuff very often. Usually, it's just me thinking about things or talking to Joshua but the conversation is different because he's...you know. Maybe I should start journaling."

I laugh as she speaks, catching her attention and her brows knit up in confusion. "I really like you, Emilia. I think we are a lot alike, too. We're at our first stop." I point at the same shed I showed Noah a few days earlier.

Our conversation turns back to the center and some of the past wildlife we've rescued and treated. Emilia helps me replenish all of the feeders near the water and I check on a couple of bug traps we placed in the area before we move on to one of our other sites and Emilia tells me about her cottage and the garden she planted there with her father when she was younger.

There isn't a lot to see at our second stop but I show her the equipment we use when we've released some of the rehabilitated birds back into the wild.

A quick glance at my phone tells me we are getting close to the two hour mark and I should get back to cover for Georgia's end of shift. As we walk toward the facility, I stop at an area I know she'll enjoy.

"Are those raspberries?" She asks, her eyes going wide.

"They are. Shanna told me they planted a couple of bushes out here years ago and it turned into this monstrosity." I point to the field.

"They really spread out. Do we have time to eat some?" She asks, already reaching her hand out to the closest bush.

"Of course. It's actually the birds that grew this field out. They'd eat the berries then poop out the seeds all over the place, and this is what happened. Sometimes, I come out here and eat until I'm almost sick. I love raspberries." I snicker.

"Me, too." She grins, showing me her raspberry ruby-tinged lips.

By the time we both get back to the main parking lot, Emilia's driver is already waiting for us.

"I had the best time today. I'm tempted to make another donation so I can have another tour tomorrow." We laugh as we near the car.

"I'm glad you came out today but I don't think Jeff would like that very much." We giggle together at my answer and I can't tell if my stomach hurts from laughing or too many raspberries.

Emilia stops at her open door, turning back to me.

"Joshua isn't perfect." She starts talking and her driver immediately steps back to excuse himself from our conversation. "And neither am I. What is perfect is how we fit together. He isn't for everyone, but he is for me. And I see that with you and Noah. I have to go, but text me. I mean to get together; like hang out, okay?"

"I will." I answer then let her get into the car. I wave as the car pulls out with her words still stuck in my head.

I worry that I am too inexperienced for Noah, but maybe my lack of understanding along with my curiosity and willingness to learn more is exactly what he's looking for. I get the feeling that it isn't the destination Noah seeks but rather the anticipation and experience of the journey.

When I think about Friday night, I did let Paul get to me. I let his words get past my armor and they shouldn't have because he doesn't matter to me, Noah does.

Speaking of which, I spin on my heels and almost skip back to the office because the second reason I have been excited for today to finally get here, is meeting me at his place in a couple of hours.

38

NOAH

"*I* thought we were staying in tonight." Hazel greets me at her door wearing the sleek black dress I sent over last night.

"Well, I thought about it and, trust me when I say, seeing you in this makes me want to steal you away to my place and not let you go for a few days." I attempt to wink flirtatiously, but inside, I'm telling the absolute truth.

Her cheeks stretch wide in a smile as she looks down at herself. "Thank you. And thank you, for this. It's so soft." Running her fingers down her torso, I imagine the silhouette of her naked curves and I can't wait to see that fabric in a pile on my floor later.

She reaches inside her room to gather her overnight bag and I take it from her, slinging it over my shoulder and extending my hand in wait. Turning to fasten her old lock one last time, she spins, glancing at my palm before offering me her key.

"So where are we going then?" I sense hesitation in her

voice as my hand drops to the small of her back, guiding her down the hall and out to my car.

"Does it matter?" I question directly.

Excitement flashes across her face but, to her credit, she settles herself quickly. Her reticence is adorable and alluring.

I find myself suddenly starving but it isn't a hunger for food. It's a greedy desire to jump beyond all of our formalities, all of our communication, all of our questions and discussions and have her stripped bare and bound to my bed; waiting for my lead, needy for my touch, begging for the sweet mercy of her release.

Before she settles into the backseat, she turns to answer.

"No. I guess it doesn't matter." Her words are humble; her tone, ambivalent.

"Well then, I'm not telling you." I respond pointedly and she pauses a moment to absorb my obnoxious retort before exchanging a glance with Marcus and he simply shrugs in reply.

I hand Marcus her key and he pockets it with a nod and a smirk, before I join her in the back seat. Marcus is aware of my interests and we share an affection for dominance.

"If you are ever curious about anything, you only need to ask, Baby." I nudge. I want her to feel comfortable asking me a question without worrying about scaring me off. Communication is essential and I get the impression Hazel has gotten a little too comfortable keeping things to herself. She needs to learn to speak her mind around me or I see many punishments in her future.

"I trust you." She smiles.

It's not enough for me. I know she trusts me to a certain extent, but she isn't at the point where her trust is absolute. Time to taunt her into using her big girl words.

"Lean forward." I order as Marcus pulls into traffic and we head back toward my neighborhood.

Without pause, she braces either hand on the seat beside her thighs and bends forward. I reach behind her, unzipping her dress down to her waist and pushing it forward off her arms.

"Sit back." Now she pauses.

She knows when she returns to her position, the top of her dress will be in her lap. Her fingers tighten into the leather of the seat.

"I won't say it again."

"But Marcus will see..." She whispers so quietly as though she's attempting to make it sound like she didn't just defy me and I feel my cock swell against my pants.

"Challenge me and Marcus will watch as I bend you over the front of this car and spank you. Don't worry about him; his eyes are on the road." She nods her head quickly, returning to her upright position and the top half of her dress covers her thighs in a fluid heap.

"Remove your bra. Put it in your bag. You don't need it anymore tonight." To her credit, her head stays put but she side eyes me, swallowing hard.

Pulling her hands out of the sleeves around her wrists, she reaches behind her, unclasping the black lace bra and unzipping her bag. Her breasts free, her hands swiftly return to the sleeves of her dress, attempting to pull it back on.

"Not yet." She stills when my hand halts her own and she relaxes her body, her eyes shifting between me and the rear view mirror in the front. "He won't look at you, Hazel. It's just us. This is much better." My eyes drift down to her front as her nipples slowly swell under my attention.

Giving into my need to feel the convex of her breast, I

run my hand over the milky white skin around the outside of her areola as I watch her tips stiffen further. As we move through traffic, her eyes stay on me and her breathing has quickened; I can only imagine the sensitivity is building within her.

"I have something for you." I can't contain the deep rasp of my avidity.

"Wh-what?" Her head lolls forward slightly, lost in my touch.

"Oh, Doll." I tsk. "That word gets you into so much delicious trouble with me." I punctuate my warning with a pinch to her nipple and she arches her back, surprising me with her fervor.

Pinching her lips together with a whimper she murmurs an apology and I return my focus back to the lesson at hand.

Leaning into her, I command her space as my lips open around her chest and she moans deeply. Her reserve seems to have left her because, while Marcus isn't watching, I can guarantee he still has his ears and I grin wickedly against her as my tongue licks over her hardened nipples.

Replacing the pinch of my fingers, my teeth bite down gingerly, eliciting another moan and her fingers comb into my hair. Moving my attention to her other breast, I wet her tip and end with a nibble before pulling away. The gentle tug of her fingers urge me to continue but this is my show tonight and she will move at my pace.

As if slapped with reality, her eyes round as she slips out of her lust-filled haze and her eyes travel once more to the front seat. To further push her, I speak to Marcus.

"How many more minutes?" I ask, putting enough space between us to watch as the cool air sinks into the spots I made warm with my tongue just moments before.

"About five minutes." He answers without looking back.

I focus my attention back on Hazel, watching as she scrambles to control her breathing. She follows my lead so well; I can't help my pleased smile. Pulling the little items out of my pocket, I reach across to her bare breasts, her hands resting in her lap and her eyes are on me.

Pinching her nipple between my fingers one last time, I place a small metal clip on each and her attention drops to her chest.

"What are these?" She lifts one hand to touch herself, but I ease it back down.

"These are the jewelry version of nipple clamps. They aren't as restrictive." The metal wraps around her nipple, offering tension without pain and a jeweled bead hangs an inch down from each one. "They will arouse you and provide some stimulation every time you move tonight and the thought of you with these on under your dress will drive me crazy. Especially where we're going. You can put the top of your dress back on. We're almost there." The insinuation hanging between us, I smile wolfishly at her, licking my lips for effect and she makes herself smaller beside me.

She's taking the bait. It's just a matter of time now before she decides to communicate with me. Biting her lower lip, her eyes dart around to the buildings surrounding us.

"Okay. Where are we going? It matters to me." She gently sets her dress against her body as her eyes plead with me for an answer and it is one I would have gladly given had she just stood her ground in the first place.

"There's this really trendy lounge that just opened up; extremely high end. I know a lot of influential people who are going to be there tonight. Some politicians, a couple of celebrities, but mostly businessmen and their wives." I wink and she pales. I almost feel bad for joking around with her.

"Oh." She plasters a smile on her face but she looks like she's going to hyperventilate any time now. I know the pomp and circumstance of our city's elite doesn't intrigue her.

"Relax." I slide my hand under her dress and settle on her knee as Marcus pulls up to the curb. Her head whips around trying to locate the restaurant and I assume she's mentally preparing herself. "This is it." I point out my window and her brows scrunch together in confusion. "I was joking. This is one of the pubs in my area. Super low key, tucked away. They make a great burger and the batter on their fish is delicious." I wait for her to catch up and she glances back down at her outfit, then my own.

"Are we over-dressed?"

"Ah, Doll, you can never be too over—or under-dressed for me." I wink and she finally smiles and relaxes at my answer. Marcus opens the door and I offer my hand to help her stand as we walk into the little restaurant.

I reserved a small table out of the way for our dinner tonight and, as we settle in, I get right to the point of looking over our menus and ordering because I want some privacy. Hazel picks up the menu, scanning the options before closing it quickly, catching my attention.

"The battered fish sounds like something I'd like to try."

"You won't be disappointed." I smile at her as the waiter approaches to take our drink order. I save him time by ordering us two tap beers and two of the house fish and chips before we regain our privacy and I ease back into my seat.

"I like it here. It's really cozy." Hazel leans out of our little alcove to look further into the restaurant.

"I sometimes come here to work at night when I'm

brainstorming projects for work. I'm glad you like it." I watch her take in everything she can, her nose lifts as she catches the scent of something delicious wafting out from the kitchen before licking her lips.

"I'm not complaining. But I thought we were having dinner at your place." She sits back as the waiter returns with our drinks.

"We have to talk about some things and I wanted to do it in a place where I wouldn't get distracted." I answer.

"But out in public; isn't this distracting?" She waves her arm around indicating the ambiance.

"Not that kind of distraction, Baby. I want to discuss exploring our dynamic and I have a few questions. Based on some of your answers, I don't want to jump ahead of myself and fuck you on my living room floor until we've discussed everything we need to." She coughs on her gulp of beer but manages to keep everything down.

Bringing her fingers to her lips, she clears her throat. "Oh."

"And being out in public—" I leave the suggestion hanging.

"—keeps you on your own figurative leash." She answers, winking back at me like a little smartass and I have an insane urge to push her over the table and make her come until she's drowning in her need and begging me to stop.

And this is *exactly* why we are in public.

As we eat, I tell her more about Ravenous. I had wanted to show her around after my demonstration to ease her into what she could expect should we ever attend again. There were some more private rooms and events happening in other areas and I had Lexa's approval to take her on a tour, but we never got that far so instead I described them all to her while we enjoyed our dinner.

"And you have some questions for me?" She asks, pushing her plate back and reaching for her beer.

"Yes. It's important we communicate everything between us. If you have a question, ask it. If you have a concern, share it. Everything, Hazel." My tone is serious and she follows my lead, placing her glass on the table, leaning back, waiting for me to start.

"We've already discovered you enjoy bondage and, most likely, restraint. I want to talk about that a little more on the drive back to my place. For now, tell me what you fantasize about." I decide to lead with a simple question, taking a gulp of my beer and as I look back up to meet her eyes, I'm hit with the thought that maybe only I consider it an easy question.

"I never really thought about it. Um, okay, give me a second." Her fingers fidget on the table and she glances around as though her answer is hidden somewhere in the room before she speaks. "I fantasize about what we do."

I smile, feeling an awkwardness to our conversation.

"I fantasize about that, too, Baby. Go on. What about before we met?" Her lips form a circle and her eyes go back to searching.

"I—I didn't really... Okay, well maybe stuff like..." Her sentence trails off on a breath of frustration.

"This is where we communicate. You can tell me you've got nothing. It's my role to guide you when this happens. But I can't help you if you don't tell me. Do you understand, Baby?" She sheepishly nods.

"Maybe you could tell me what *you* fantasize about." She suggests and I slide her closer to me in the booth.

"Of course. Since meeting you, my fantasies have all involved you. I imagine testing out your tolerance and enjoyment of pain. The look your face makes when your eyes roll back into your head as you welcome my smacks on your ass sets me off. I wonder how you would enjoy feeling the same thing, but on your breasts, your pussy or your inner thighs." I casually watch her as I speak to make sure I'm not going too fast and I notice her dress move as she squeezes her thighs together so I share more.

"I fantasize about tying you down and bringing you to the brink of orgasm, then punishing you until the edge is gone before bringing you back until your sweet voice begs me to take you and fuck you as I want. I fantasize about your tears. Those times you shed them; not because you were in pain but because you accept, on a deep level, that you ache for it." I stop talking a full minute before she realizes it and I take the time to examine her. She is swallowing a lot more and I imagine her mouth is watering at her increased arousal.

"Oh, um, those are good fantasies." She smiles. "Mind if I steal them from you?"

I smile back. She's deflecting.

"Let's move on to triggers."

"Triggers?"

"Yes. Hazel, outside of your inexperience, there is another reason I didn't do my bondage demonstration with you at Ravenous and it's because we haven't discussed triggers. A trigger is an event; it could be a word, a smell, a situation or any combination of things that could *trigger* a past trauma or memory. If I were to put you in front of everyone without knowing anything about you, I could potentially do severe harm to you." Her eyes are wide at my explanation. This hadn't crossed her mind at all.

"You can table this to discuss with me later, or you can answer. I will start by pointing out your fear of your life being derailed and needing to start over again. Being abandoned by your friends and your boyfriend hit you harder than you realized. Knowing that, it is important for me to always show you that I am right here with you. I mean, I am. But it's important I remind you of that. So that being said, is there anything else you can think of that we may need to explore together?"

"Wow. This is a discussion." She takes a deep breath and swallows another gulp of her beer before reaching for her cold fries.

"You're stalling." She attempts an incredulous expression at my observation and I'm not having it. "When I talk about something that is a bit deeper for you, you stall. How are those cold fries?" I raise my eyebrows and she stops chewing, swallowing it down and I continue, "When you don't want to face something, you are standoffish then combative; and when you want to deflect because you are excited or aroused but you don't know how to handle it, you are a smartass so I'm waiting for the response you're going to choose to use." I lean back, offering her the floor.

She opens her mouth to say something before shutting it in contemplation. Then she opens her mouth a second time before snapping her pouty lips shut and slouching her shoulders.

"I do do that." She confesses before letting my discovery sink in. "Huh!"

She ponders the question a little further before answering. "No, I don't believe there is anything before my father got sick that I would consider a trauma. Losing him and almost losing my mom is the single worst thing that happened." Reaching my arm to her, I pull her back into me, speaking into her hair.

"And we will talk through that another time or any time if you ever want to."

Straightening up in her seat, "I'm not trying to deflect, but what else do you want to know?"

"Just some basics, I will share I am not into blood or water sports." The skin on her forehead lifts with her silent question and I can't control my laughter. "I'm not talking about water skiing. It's what it's called when, um..." Her innocence is contagious and I don't know how to tell her about this so I just look at my crotch like the 12 year old I apparently am.

"Oh. OHHH! Okay, no. I don't like that." She giggles nervously into the last sip of her beer and I laugh with her.

"I'm almost done." Hazel can't hide the breath of relief she just exhaled at my words. "Humiliation, voyeurism and exhibitionism."

"Oh, is that all?" She rolls her eyes, then catches herself. "Sorry. I was being a smartass there, wasn't I?"

"You're learning." I wink. I could ask her to describe herself but she struggles with the words because of her lack of experience so I'm going to spell it out for her and just get her opinion. "I get the sense you enjoy being called *Doll*. I think you love the thought of being my toy and the images of being used it conjures." I brush my fingers over her nipple, reminding her of the piece of jewelry she has hanging from it before whispering in her ear. "I think you crave my words when I tell you all of the dirty things I'm going to make you do. When I speak directly to the place where your shame thinks it's safe. When I pull it out and play with it while I play with you."

I sit back catching her attention before continuing and her eyes look glossy, "But I don't think you want to be humiliated anywhere else, or degraded. Am I correct in that thought?"

"Yes." She answers quickly, not even needing a moment to clear her throat.

"Good girl." She smiles; I already know she seeks my praise. "As for voyeurism and exhibitionism, I think that is something we are going to slowly explore together, without fully immersing ourselves into public view. Are you open to discovering more about that?"

"Yes." Another short but confident response.

The timing of the waiter with the bill is impeccable and I drop some cash on the table before motioning for Hazel to get ready to leave. Our night together is still young and I have so much more for her planned.

We step out into the evening and Hazel shivers under my touch, goosebumps forming over her arms. Pulling my jacket off, I drape it over her shoulders.

"Do you ever get the feeling you are being watched?" She asks. "I feel a little, um, naked after our talk."

She's talking about her vulnerability and I realize my decision to have this discussion in public was the right one.

"Doll, this is nothing. Once I get you home tonight, you will be very very naked and every part of you will belong to me."

39

HAZEL

*M*y head has been swimming with an intense yearning for almost an hour. When Noah talks to me, I feel seen, all of my truths exposed. His questions open doors I never knew existed. When he holds me accountable, I feel possessed.

I'm so inexperienced that his questions alone have me glowing with a fervent need for his touch. I like to think I'm maintaining an outward calm but inside, my desire is feral. It claws at my modesty, mocking my diffidence.

I know I've become flushed, I can barely handle a steady breath and a warm wave hits my cheeks as his hand settles on my lower back, guiding me into the back seat of his car.

I'm thankful Marcus isn't looking directly at me but then I realize he is probably respectfully granting me privacy by averting his attention while I'm in this state. Shame floods me at the realization he must know how affected I am.

Noah, however, doesn't relent. As promised, he talks about bondage and restraint; asking me to share more about how I felt when he first wrapped his rope around me. Every word I speak unravels the control I mistakenly thought I had over myself and I become his, giving him my power with every honest answer.

"I want to mark you, Baby. I want you to look at yourself and see the physical manifestation of my ownership on your body tomorrow." My heart takes flight as he speaks. I want to be his. "It won't be a permanent mark, something small, gone in a few days, but I want to see myself on your body when we wake up tomorrow morning."

I don't say a word. I can't. My need is too strong and I nod and mumble out what I hope he takes as consent as I fist my hand into his shirt at his waist. My mind flashes to how visceral the marks from his rope sunk into my psyche. I'm wound up so tight and I'm ready to snap.

Placing a box on my lap he nuzzles his nose into my neck, whispering, "Open."

Grateful for the temporary distraction, my fingers feel around the lid for a weak place to lift the box open while I bounce my attention between the mystery item and his eager smile. Lifting a felt bag, I pull at the drawstrings, exposing a bright pink, curved vibrator.

I barely feel Noah remove the box and bag from my lap, dropping them to the floor before drawing his fingers in little circles on my thigh.

"Thank you." I whisper without taking my eyes off of the thing.

"Remove your underwear, Miss Masters." Comes the order and I feel myself hold onto my breath as I hear my heartbeat thump between my ears.

I take the smallest of moments to gather myself and reach my fingers up underneath my dress to pull them down my legs, letting them pool on the floor around my ankles.

"I'll remind you, you have safe words, always." I nod and he leaves it at that, pinching the fleshy part inside my thighs before continuing, "Now turn it on and fuck yourself for me."

I know I should just do as I'm told but it's hard to let go of a morality that dictated my actions up until this point. I yearn for more though. I ache for those little moments of truth when he sets me free to explore myself and grow.

My eyes drift to the back of Marcus's head. He's in the car with us. He hasn't looked back once, but the knowledge that there is someone else here bearing witness to my descent makes this feel more tangible.

"I won't say it again, Doll." Noah leans down, stepping one of my feet out of my panties. "Slide your hips down to the edge of the seat." With a hard swallow, I obey and his fingers slide up my thighs, seeking entrance into the heat of my core. "You're already wet." His eyes search mine before settling on the little item in my hand.

I can't take my eyes off him, his features are set, determined. Lifting the vibrator I examine it to find it's on button and he removes his finger before lifting it to his lips, tasting me on his tongue and I feel like the backseat of the car is a little low on oxygen.

"You're going to fuck yourself with this until you come. It's your choice how quiet or loud you want to be." The insinuation that Marcus is still in the car with us settles on me. "I have no shame where you are considered, Miss Masters. I would prefer to hear you scream your surrender, but that is your choice. What isn't your choice is your orgasm. You will finish before we arrive home, or you won't come at all tonight. Do I make myself clear?"

I feel as though a trap door just broke open below me,

but I'm not falling. Instead, I'm suspended here, caught in his strict demands and I have no words to answer him. Well, at least none that aren't cheeky so I just nod and press the button on the tip of the vibrator and a low buzz fills our space.

A predatory smile consumes his lips and he leans back, pulling me near him while his fingers pull my dress up to my hips, revealing my trimmed mound. His lips near my ear, I hear him suck in a breath as his fingers comb over my pubic area.

"Spread your legs." I haven't started yet and I already feel a mounting pressure pushing me forward as I lift my feet off the floor and his arm reaches out, pulling my thigh across his lap.

As I open myself to him, I notice my panties dangling off my ankle and the sight of it hanging there makes me whimper.

"I love you like this. Revealing yourself to me. You're my good little toy, aren't you?" His voice is low, mesmerizing. My arms feel like they are about to float away on me.

"Yes." My answer comes out on a raspy breath.

"Then say it." He challenges.

"I'm your good little toy." My words moan out of me as I use one hand to open my lips, placing the vibrator directly on my clit.

"Good girl." His praise lands like a drug. "Look at you exposing yourself like this." My hips grind up to meet the dildo as I slide it closer to my entrance.

Flagrantly, I move my free hand along my labia, touching and showing myself to him further. I need his eyes on me; watching him examine me with lust in his eyes drives me to offer him more. His attention liberates me; his approval makes me feel powerful.

The toy moves into me with a deep groan and I barely register his fingers combing through my hair as he soothes me. "Such a good girl." He murmurs against my head as I pull my hand out and push the vibrator back in, unable to tear my attention away from watching myself as my own hips move around, searching for release.

My eyes flutter and my head spins as I continue to thrust the toy in and out of me. My frenzied state is a direct contrast to Noah's composure. Like a tether, he suspends me in limbo then his words make me soar.

"You're loud, Doll. *Everyone* can hear how much you enjoy fucking yourself for me." The knowledge Marcus can hear my sounds and knows what I am doing sinks me deep into space and I groan as Noah keeps his touch gentle. "Do you like being my dirty girl?"

"Yes." It's a simple answer but I draw the word out in a plea.

"Then say it." He growls deep into my ear.

"I love being dirty for you. I love fucking myself for you." The wet sounds of the vibrator sliding inside of me echo in the back seat as I feel a deep tingle ignite.

I know I can be quiet. I know I'm allowed but my shame has left me. I want anyone near me to know I am Noah's. I belong to him and this is what I want with every inch of my being. My moans turn into wails as I lewdly plunge the dildo as deep as I can, delirious on the thought of pleasing Noah.

"We're almost home, Doll." He taunts, meeting my eyes. "Are you going to come? Show me you're my sweet little slut. I want to hear you cry my name as you come for me. Go ahead, tell Marcus who you belong to, Baby."

Out of the corner of my eye, I see my lacy underwear, still hanging onto my foot as it dangles and jerks around with my movements and Noah pinches my nipple through my dress, reminding me of the clips on my breasts.

My body implodes on itself. Arching my back, the vibrations hit a sensitive spot at the same time he challenges me to publicly declare my place and everything inside of me unlocks and snaps wide open. "Yes, yes, yes, YES, YES—NOAH!" I wail into the car. "I'M YOURS!" Clenching his shirt in my hand, my hips convulse and grind on their own. I struggle to catch my breath as my pussy contracts with each new wave of release and my body collapses in on itself as my fight is slowly replaced by sated exhaustion.

Everything around us becomes soft and fuzzy as I feel myself remove the vibrator. At least I think I'm the one pulling it out. Strong arms wrap around my body, lifting me closer to Noah's scent.

"Give us a few." I hear Noah say as my eyes focus on our surroundings and I recognize the front of Noah's building before Marcus pulls back into traffic and Noah kisses the top of my head before brushing his fingers over my forehead.

"You have no idea how perfect you are. His lips move against my hair as he speaks and I keep my head against his chest listening to his beating heart. "Watching you like this, lost in yourself... You are beautiful, Hazel."

I don't answer him. Noah has taught me that some things don't need an answer and instead I allow his words to wrap themselves around my heart. We ride in silence for a few minutes before he speaks again.

"How do you feel, Baby?" He raises his hand as he asks, catching Marcus's attention in the mirror and I notice Marcus nod once as I sit up.

"I feel good. Um, I'm not sure how to answer that." I shrug and he smiles.

"Thank you for your honesty. Your answer is fine." He slides my dress down and leans forward, hooking his fingers in my underwear and removing them from my foot before they disappear from my sight. "I'm asking to see if you need some time or if I can take you up to my place now and continue. I'm not done with you yet, Miss Masters."

The thought of what just happened being an appetizer makes me giggle nervously before I cough to hide my restlessness. "No. I'm okay to go up."

The car comes to a stop in front of Noah's building and he reaches down, gathering my bag and placing the vibrator back in the box it came in before Marcus opens the door.

As I step out of the car, I catch a glimpse of Marcus's face before I glance away, too chicken to look him in the eye. I feel goosebumps prickle down my arms.

He knows what I did. The thought doesn't scare me as much as I thought it would.

"I've got it from here. Thank you. Have a good night." I watch out of the corner of my eye as Marcus bows his head as Noah speaks before quietly leaving and he makes the smallest look in my direction before turning to get back in the car.

He didn't say anything to me. He just left. As if reading my mind, Noah circles his arm around my shoulders.

"He didn't speak to you because he felt you needed some time. Learning who you are and what you enjoy can take its toll and you need space to work through things. You haven't changed his perception of you at all. He's just letting you speak at your own pace. I thought you should know that." He says matter-of-factly.

I guess if I'm being honest with myself, he's right. I feel fine with everything that happened but I do need to reflect. "Have I changed *your* perception of me?" My voice is feeble. I don't think I could handle knowing he thought less of me.

"I know who you are, Hazel." He turns me to face him, steadying me in his arms. "I see you. I've always seen you. This is about you seeing yourself. The question should be, have you changed your own perception of you?"

I have no words. This discovery isn't about how others would perceive me, it's about how I look at myself. The fact that anyone else does or doesn't accept who I am carries no weight. Who I am is a reflection of what I love and value regardless of whether anyone else agrees with me.

"I—I guess I have. But I think it is more of an evolution in my view. Does that make sense?" I hope I don't sound like an amateur.

"Yes. It makes sense, Hazel. Come now, I'm taking you upstairs. I still need to mark that delicious body of yours." Stepping toward the door, he reaches out for the handle before stopping and turning to me, a more serious expression crosses his face before he speaks again.

"Tell me, have you ever had a hickey?"

40

NOAH

"You mean like a high school hickey?" Hazel stops mid-step at my question, but I continue to lead her into the elevator and up to my place.

Her wide-eyed confusion makes me laugh. She has no idea how refreshing her raw innocence is.

"Yes." The elevator opens with a ding and I nudge her in, pressing her against the back as I trail my fingers to her neck. "I'm going to give you a hickey here." I graze the sensitive skin along her lower neck, just above her clavicle before continuing, "It'll match the hickey I'm going to give you— here." Dropping my free hand between us, I dip under the hem of her dress and circle near the fleshy apex of her thighs.

Her breathing intensifies and I don't think she realizes she's pushing her body into my hands, offering herself to me again.

The thought of seeing the purpled mark on her tomorrow makes me feel protective, and the knowledge it'll reflect the one between her legs makes me feel possessive.

"I—I don't think I've ever had one. I tried to give myself one on my arm when I was a kid. Does that count?"

"No, it doesn't. I get another first from you then." I smile into the kiss I place on her forehead and the ding welcomes us home.

"So, um. After all of the questions—uh, what are we going to do tonight?"

"I'm going to take care of you, Baby." I drop her bag on the couch and her doe-eyes follow me around the room and into the kitchen as I get her a glass of water. "Here." I leave the command to drink it off the end of my sentence and she takes it and drinks it anyway, handing the glass back with a smile, waiting for my lead. I fill the glass again before tilting my head toward the bedroom and she follows behind me.

Setting the cup on the nightstand, "Take off your dress." Her eyes reflexively go to the windows spanning my entire room but she doesn't hesitate. While her attention remains on whatever is on the outside looking in, she twists her arms behind her, unzipping the dress in an impressive fashion, and lets the fabric drop to the floor around her feet exactly as I fantasized about.

Her hands move slowly, covering any spots visible between her and the window before turning her body to face me so only I can see her.

"How does it make you feel knowing that a stranger could see you like this?" I probe.

"I—I don't know. I guess my first thought is what if someone recorded it. I wouldn't like that."

"Fair enough. And what if it wasn't recorded, only enjoyed by someone who wants to participate? Admiring the curves of your body, enjoying how your face contorts and your voice pitches when entirely gratified? Can you place yourself in that moment?" I stalk over to her, but keep my touch to myself. "Imagine drowning in your lust, whorish with need. That moment when I take your body and you push aside all sense in desperate search of your release. Tell me, how did it feel to submit yourself to me while Marcus listened from the front seat?"

My own need blazes to life as Hazel ponders my question. I already know her answer. I saw how compliant and reconciled she became as she pushed herself into submission while I watched and Marcus listened.

"I felt unfettered. Like I shed everything and just existed." Her body settles at her answer. She's releasing the tension she first felt when she stripped in front of the open window.

The truth is, I already know no one can see in right now. Our room is dark. If I turned on the lights, then the neighbors across the way could catch a glimpse from this angle, but all I would have to do is close one of the curtains to block this side of the room.

I sense her body enjoys the thought she might be seen even if her head is unsure. But until her mind catches up to those pert nipples that are standing erect, I'll put her at ease.

"No one can see you right now. That doesn't mean you should go waltzing all over the room though." I wink. "And whatever you do, don't turn on the lights yet." Her breath sighs out of her, releasing her relief. "Come, let's get ready for bed."

"Wha—Uh, ugh. I thought we were going to—" Her objections flow fast.

"Oh, we are." I promise. "This is a process. I want you on that bed, arms and legs spread. I'm going to taste you, mark you and fuck you. Then I'm going to take care of you. I'm going to bathe you and lay with you and we are going to talk until you fall asleep."

"I thought we were going to do the things you asked me about." I adore that she looks genuinely devastated.

"I need time to process your answers so I can prepare something fitting. I do have a space to play in but not tonight. Tonight is about you and I can take better care of you here. Now, get your little ass on my bed and wait for me. I have a day planned for us tomorrow and you're mine until the sun comes up on Friday—unless I decide to extend it."

In a flash of excitement, Hazel bounds onto the bed, bouncing a couple of times before settling down and stilling herself as she tries to wait patiently.

I close the blind I need before turning on the lights and removing my clothes making no effort to conceal my visible reaction to her. Her eyes land on my erection before quickly snapping up to the ceiling and I can't hide my smirk. I could get drunk on how easily I affect her.

As I round the bed, her limbs fidget and I consider tying her to the headboard before deciding against it. There will be enough of that tomorrow night. Tonight is about touching and feeling.

Tapping the inside of her ankle with my fingers, I crawl on the bed as she spreads herself open for me granting me space to settle between her legs. Resting my chest on her thighs, I drop my head to kiss her lower belly and her hands comb through my hair.

"No touching."

"P-pardon?" I feel a tinge of disappointment that she didn't say *what*.

"No touching me until I fuck you. If you want something to do with your hands, your nipples need pinching." I can't tell who is getting off on my words more right now. "Come whenever you want, Baby."

Without waiting for her reply, I drop my mouth to the place I've wanted to be since I picked her up tonight and her hips push up to meet my tongue as she moans. I feel her hands hover around my head for a brief moment before I open my eyes to catch her balling her palms into fists before hesitantly placing them over the soft curve of her breasts.

Switching my tongue for my fingers, I begin to kiss at her inner thigh while she writhes under me. This is where I'll mark her.

Pushing her leg up and out I hold her open with my free hand, exposing more of her to me and getting her ready. Her body twists on itself as I pick up the pressure, alternating between sucking her sensitive bud and sliding my fingers inside of her, curling at a spot that makes her hips buck into my face.

"I feel you squeezing my fingers. Are you going to come for me?" She groans at my question.

"Yyyesss." She sings.

I growl against her pussy as her entire body tenses and I switch my attention to the inside of her leg as my fingers continue to fuck her through her orgasm.

Latching my lips onto her trembling thigh, I suck hard as she arches her body, pushing her head back into the bed, riding into her abyss. Her hands stay on her nipples, pinching and pulling them as every aftershock rattles around before leaving her spent underneath me.

"That's your first mark." Running my fingers over her bruised flesh I watch the fascination in her eyes as she stares at her hickey. Her fingers join mine as we silently caress the physical mark of my claim.

The need to sink myself deep inside of her is more powerful than my restraint and I shift up the bed, moving her other leg up and out before pushing myself against her pussy. I still have enough discipline to pause, giving Hazel a chance to adjust but she doesn't seem to want the reprieve. Her fingers slide around my hips, nails digging into my ass as she pulls me into her and I waste no time thrusting forward to a shared moan.

"Fuck, Hazel. I'll never have enough of you." Feeling her tight warmth hugging my length sends me into an alternate reality. The sight of the hickey forming on her thigh sets me into a primal headspace and my rhythm increases as her hands grip my cheeks.

"That's it, Doll. Give me everything." I growl into her ear at the thought of her nails marking me as hers.

Her head lolls back, exposing her breasts to me as she arches against the bed and I know I'm pushing her over the edge as I feel my own end spiral toward me. Reaching my hand around her hip, I probe my finger close to her bottom, circling the ring of her ass before gently intruding into her tight muscle.

"Hhhholy. I'm..." I rock harder into her and the remainder of her sentence comes out without sound as she chokes out the words *coming again* before spasming around my cock as I suction my lips around the skin at her neck and continue to thrust into her as her hands grasp at me, taking every sensation.

I could draw this out and fuck her all night but the sight of her body thrashing through its orgasm begs me to join her and I accede. Jerking my hips forward one final time, I shudder my release as I lower my weight onto her, before rolling onto my side and taking her with me.

And there we rest in the sweaty, glistening heap of heavy breathing we've become. Her arm rests limply over my torso, her head tucked into my chest; and I feel the very definition of euphoric.

"What are you thinking, Baby?" I lift my hand to brush through her hair and she nuzzles her face into my neck.

"I'm thinking if you tell me this is just the start of tonight, I might have to say *uncle*." I huff into the strands of her hair. "Oh, sorry. I was being a smartass."

"No, I like your humor. Don't apologize. I just won't allow it at times but I'll always let you know when that is. Don't stop being you."

"Okay, but I was only half-joking about what comes next. You've tired me out." She leans back with a smile.

"Good. That's what I was going for. As for what's next, I'm going to talk you into taking a hot bath with me, then crawling naked into bed. I want to stare at the marks I gave you while we fall asleep."

"That sounds perfect." She shifts to get up but I pull her back, running my fingers over her hickeys.

"What are you doing tomorrow?"

"Well, I don't work until Saturday so I was going to go shopping. Maybe buy some new clothes. Why?"

"Meet me for lunch. There's a nice restaurant near my work. I'll see if Joshua and Emilia can join us." She sits upright, placing her hand on my chest.

"Really? I would love that."

"I can't make any promises but I'll ask. Now, you need some cleaning, Dirty Girl, and I can't wait to show you your new marks."

41

HAZEL

I could get used to waking up in Noah's bed after a night like we just had. He had completely exhausted everything in me to the point I didn't hear him leave for work this morning.

I woke up in a dreamlike haze, naked and spread out across his bed like a starfish. The sun warmed my skin and my first instinct was to close my eyes and stay there until Noah found me and used me all over again.

Rolling over, I found the note he left me beside the bed, held down by a single flower I recognized from one of the planters on his deck.

Baby,

Sleep in and enjoy your day off. I've made you a plate in the fridge. My place is yours. When you're ready, Marcus's number is on the table near the elevator. Text him and he'll take you wherever you want to go

*today. He knows where to bring you for lunch. I can't
wait to see you.*

PS. Drink your water.

His note was something so simple but I felt giddy at the
thought of it. I felt kept and cared for. The weight I carried
on my shoulders was no longer just mine and I felt more
powerful because of it.

I had become a creature of habit and waking up here felt
foreign at first. My dorm room had a bustle about it in the
morning. During the school year, a steady stream of students
meant no one was sleeping in and the isolated location of
Noah's place way up on the fourth floor made me feel like I
was on a retreat.

Making my way into the kitchen, I pulled the fruit
platter out of the fridge, placed it on the counter, then
opened the doors to the deck and the sounds of the cars
below flooded into the room. The thought of having a
morning coffee out there with Noah made me grin like a fool.

Normally when I was at my place, I would get up, make
coffee and have a shower before checking my calendar and
packing myself up for my classes and jobs for the day.

I felt like I was on vacation.

Nina: Hey. You there?
Nina: Message me when you get this.

I hadn't checked my phone since Noah picked me up
yesterday and Nina is due to come back this weekend.

Hazel: I'm here.

I waited a few seconds for her response before I realized her message was sent late last night. Packing up, I got dressed and explored a little of Noah's apartment without actually snooping.

An hour later, I was dressed and messaging Marcus to take me shopping. Uncertainty filled my stomach with butterflies. My actions from last night in the car chastened me and I wasn't sure if I could look Marcus in the eye.

When I met him out front, I sheepishly asked if he could just drop me back at my place and I would pick up my own car but he wouldn't allow it. "Noah's orders." He'd said before catching my attention when he didn't quickly open my door.

"Nothing's changed." He hinted. "It would be a shame if you hid your bubbly personality away from me because you assume it has." Saying no more, he opened the door and I climbed in.

My first stop was out for coffee and I forced myself to invite Marcus to join me. He is right. I can't let my insecurity speak for Marcus's thoughts. After a few awkward starts, I confided that I initially thought Noah was a criminal when we first met because only criminals had drivers and it was the first time I had ever caught Marcus in a surprise laugh.

Tensions eased and I stayed away from asking him about his past as he usually ends up effectively changing the subject anyway.

By the time we left the coffee shop, I felt more confident in my friendly relationship with Marcus.

Wanting to make sure I wouldn't be late for lunch, I

asked Marcus to take me to a shopping area near our restaurant. It gave me more time to look around.

Boutiques and salons lined the streets and I wandered around, getting lost for over an hour before finding this little clothing store tucked away. It carries more of a trendy style than high fashion and I could spend hours looking through the hats alone.

Having a steady income and one that is more than my debt load eases my stress considerably and this is the first time in a very long time I will buy my clothes outside of a second-hand store. It feels empowering to finally be ahead of my bills for once.

"Hey, Hazel." My own name surprises me and I jump. "Sorry. Didn't mean to startle you." Cassie smiles from the entrance. "I was just window shopping and I thought that was you."

"Hey. How's your summer been? Are you back already?" I ask, folding the clothes over my arm and moving closer to her.

"I got back last week. I'm here until Monday, then I leave again. Having divorced parents living on opposite sides of the country sucks. I just want my own summer vacay." She glances over her shoulder, waving to some people on the street and walks in, closing the door behind her. "How are you?"

"I'm good. I'm going to try to go home in a few weeks to see my mom for a bit, too." She smiles and nods for a moment and I notice a hesitation.

She isn't saying anything, but she also isn't leaving.

"I was meaning to message you." She starts before pausing again. "Hey, I was out with some friends a couple of nights ago. Um, is everything okay with you?" Cassie lowers her voice as she asks her question

"Yes. Why are you asking me like that?" I step closer as though we are about to share a secret.

"Well, Paul was out with all of us and he was drinking. He started saying things."

It takes everything I have not to blurt out everything that happened but I don't want to start a war among our close knit group.

"Oh? What did he say?" I turn my eyes down to the clothes in my hand.

"He started telling our group that you two started dating but you cheated on him and your new boyfriend is kind of abusive. At first he made it sound like he was concerned for you, but then his story kind of changed and he said you were into some really kinky shit." My stomach instantly turns on itself and I'm not sure I'll be able to eat lunch today.

How could he do this? He couldn't take away my internship so now he's trying to take away my support network. I try my damnedest to smile evenly while she speaks but inside I feel assaulted all over again.

A tinge of guilt registers but I push it back down. Just because Paul says those things, it doesn't make them true.

"Wow. That's kind of hurtful." I mutter. "What did you say?"

"I told him to leave our core alone or get out." She answers firmly.

"Our core?" I raise my eyebrows.

"Yeah. I may not get along with many people, but this," she motions between us, "Hazel, you're good people. You and Nina and our group are my core people. I know everyone sees me as a flighty party girl, but I know who really has my back. You don't fuck with that."

My chest tightens as she explains. I could cry.

"Thank you, Cass."

"Yeah. Listen, I've gotta run but I'm here if you want to talk. I'll be honest, if you've got a guy, I want to hear about him but I won't bug you. Maybe we can grab a coffee before I head back out and chat. As your friend though, I need to ask; are you okay? I just need to know if there is any truth in there because I am worried for you."

"I'm good, Cassie. Better than good. Thank you. Coffee sounds good. Text me."

Cassie is already blowing air kisses as I answer and she turns to leave, catching up with her friends who just wandered down the street.

With no one around, my face falls. I had always considered Paul to be a good guy, a friend. His side of how everything is playing out isn't my understanding at all and I make my way into the change room while I play everything over in my mind.

Every conversation, text and confrontation runs through my head like the recap of a movie. I can't reconcile it against the stories he's telling. And involving our group like this makes me feel ostracized. He's trying to separate me from my own friends.

I pull my phone out to see if Nina has responded yet, suddenly feeling like there might be more to her 2am message than I first thought.

Nina: Hey. Got a minute?

Hazel: I'm here now. What's up?

Unlike before, she instantly starts typing.

Nina: What's going on with Paul?
Nina: I got some weird messages from him last night.

Hazel: I can guess. I just ran into Cassie and she said he was out drinking and saying some things about me.

Nina: Did something happen since I've been gone?
Nina: He's saying he's done with you.
Nina: It doesn't make sense. I thought you broke things off.

Hazel: I did. I don't know where this is coming from.
Hazel: He's been different.
Hazel: I'll tell you about it when you get back. Still Saturday?

Nina: Yes.
Nina: My flight lands in the morning.
Nina: I have so much to talk to you about. And now this.

Hazel: I'm working on Saturday but I'll come home after.

Hazel: We can catch up.

Hazel: Stop in at the Building Assistant office. I'm leaving a new key to our place there for you. I had the locks changed.

Nina: Sounds good. Are you okay?

Hazel: I am. I just hope all of this with Paul goes away.

Nina: Well, you've got me. We'll figure it out.

We text our goodbyes and I take a deep breath before turning my attention back to the pile of clothes in the change room. I need to let this go. He tried to drive a wedge between my school friends and my two closest ones stood by me without knowing my side of the story.

Paul probably had too much to drink and was lashing out his frustrations with how everything ended. If I was in his shoes, I'd feel embarrassed by my actions and maybe he's taking Cassie's words to heart right now.

Then I shake my head at myself. I should be angry. I have a right to be upset. I won't make excuses for his behaviour based on the type of person I am. The truth is, I have no idea what is going on in his head. At the same time though, I won't let it ruin my day or my night with Noah.

I make the decision to tell Noah about all of this tomorrow. I'm looking forward to our lunch and our date tonight and I won't allow Paul to interfere anymore. He has nothing left to take away. My work, my school, my friends and Noah are all solid and his lies won't shake any of it.

I smile into the mirror. I finally feel like I have my place. I'm moving along with my life and it isn't leaving me behind.

42

NOAH

*L*eaving without waking Hazel up this morning was pure torture. The memory of her sleeping soundly beside me makes me impatient to see her again. Her soft breathing followed by the occasional snort of a snore spoke to the deepest part of me, beyond the lust and more complex than my desires. The tenderness in the moment made me weak. I want every morning to start exactly like this, except maybe now and then there could be sex and giggles, too.

Work moved along at a snail's pace, so when Joshua and Emilia stopped by to pick me up for lunch 15 minutes early, I didn't hesitate. I'm still snickering at our text messages from earlier.

Noah: Want to grab lunch? Hazel will be joining us.

Joshua: Yes. Absolutely. Can't wait. Let us know where.

The reply was immediate followed by one five minutes later.

Joshua: Sorry about that.
Joshua: Emilia got a hold of my phone while I was in the shower.
Joshua: We'll be there. Because I said so. Not her.

I've already taken a screenshot of the conversation. I'll save this one forever.

The three of us just get settled into our seats when I see Hazel walk through the front doors and check in with the hostess. Emilia stands as they get closer to the table and circles us to give Hazel a hug and I watch Joshua smile as we both stand, and he extends his hand to greet her.

Hazel's eyes settle on me and I notice the beautiful scarf wrapped around her neck, hiding my mark. She must have picked this up this morning. Leaning in for a kiss, I pull out her seat and gesture for her to sit before joining her at the table, giving her a moment to get comfortable before I reach across and hook my finger along her neck and into the wrap at her throat.

Pulling the downy fabric from her and into my lap, I run my fingers along it's woolen threads remarking to myself loud enough for her to hear me. "Beautiful." I make no move to give it back to her and she knows better than to ask for it.

A soft blush fills her cheeks as she remains still, showing

off the mark I gave her and Emilia can't help the smile on her face as I watch both her and Joshua take in my good girl. The shade of her hickey has deepened and there is no doubt what it is.

She is mine. I've never craved a public display of ownership like I do with her. I catch a glimpse from Joshua and he raises an eyebrow before taking a sip of his drink, smirking like an asshole.

"Do you want a glass of wine? We got a bottle for the table." Emilia asks and Hazel picks up her cup, nodding.

"How was shopping this morning?" I ask, turning the conversation to Hazel and her face falters for the fraction of a second before she answers me.

"It was fine." Her response seems lacking and aloof but I let it go.

"Did you get that scarf today?" Emilia points at my lap where it rests while asking and Hazel nods before she continues. "I want to see everything you bought. Maybe we could go shopping sometime."

During lunch, the conversation settles into an easy flow and even Joshua comes out of his shell asking Hazel questions about the wildlife sanctuary and how we first met.

I catch the waiter's attention after our plates are cleared to order a second bottle of wine when Joshua starts telling stories about our time in high school, eliciting tears of laughter from the women.

While Hazel and Emilia are making plans to get together at a later time, Joshua excuses himself from the table before it is time to head back to the office. I take the time to watch Hazel come out of her shell with Emilia. She hasn't once fidgeted with the mark on her neck and I'm happy she is comfortable being herself around Joshua and Emilia.

"Funny running into you here." I instantly feel a sick pit in the bottom of my stomach at the sound of Paul's voice.

"I thought we made it clear—" I lift my napkin from my lap, placing it on the table in case I need to stand up quickly but I decide to remain seated because it places me closer to Hazel who has now gone eerily silent beside me.

"Relax." He scoffs, cutting me off without taking his eyes off Hazel. "I'm having lunch just like you, with *my girlfriend*." He tilts his head behind him to show a timid woman standing quietly as she follows his lead. "Hello, Hazel."

His tone sounds creepy; like he's trying to inject himself into something he has no right nor is welcomed to.

She takes a few seconds to respond and I see Emilia shifting uncomfortably while she looks toward the back of the restaurant. I know what she's doing. She's looking for Joshua because if he comes back and sees this, there is a good chance he'll lose his shit in the middle of the room. I know because I'm barely keeping my own shit in.

"What happened to your eye?" Is all she asks. She doesn't sound concerned though. I think she just has nothing else to say to him and I catch her eyes as she shifts between the both of us.

Suddenly, I see a change in her. If I knew her better, I'd think there was something she wanted to tell me.

"Ask your keeper." Paul sneers, jabbing a finger in my direction and I roll my eyes.

He seems to enjoy playing the victim and I won't allow it. Instead I speak as though he hasn't said a thing. "Your table is ready." I say coldly, pointing at the poor hostess who has had to stop to wait for him to catch up.

Before he steps away completely, a flash of anger crosses

his face and he steps back into place. Glowering, he squares himself on Hazel. But he isn't looking directly at her. It takes a moment for me to realize what he's looking at.

My mark. He's looking at her neck and he knows full well, the hickey is from me; it's my claim over her.

The lack of eye contact has hit Hazel, too and her fingers slowly lift to her neck as she tries to nonchalantly shield herself from his glare and he smiles a sickening smile before I push myself out of my chair. This has gone on long enough. Stepping beside Hazel, I place a hand on her shoulder to show her she isn't alone. "Take your girlfriend and go sit down." My voice is calm but there is no misunderstanding, it is a threat.

"Or what?" He speaks in a hushed tone, finally turning his attention on me as he takes a step back before abruptly stopping to see who he bumped into.

Emilia sucks in a deep breath as Joshua towers over Paul and even his new girlfriend has the common sense to cower, taking a step back.

I brace for a physical altercation, but nothing happens. Joshua remains resolute, silently challenging Paul to take action or leave and I follow his lead.

Turning to the poor thing who now has to eat lunch with him, he grabs his girlfriend's wrist, pulling her toward the hostess and I breathe a sigh of relief when I see them walk out of our line of sight.

Joshua and I exchange a glance before we both sit back down and our table is silent for a long minute before Joshua speaks. "So what did I miss?"

He's looking between the women at the table. He knows he'll get a straight answer out of me later, he wants to hear from them, and his question wasn't optional.

"How do we always run into that guy?" Emilia leans into the table and Hazel shrugs mutely at her question. She looks deep in thought.

"Are you okay, Hazel?" I ask, staring her down. She's looking at her half-emptied glass as she answers.

"Yeah." She lifts her glass to her mouth, drinking slowly in an effort to end her answer.

She's attempting to avoid answering me fully. There is something else she isn't saying.

"Um, I'm not complaining, but I totally thought you were going to pummel him." Emilia says to Joshua and I continue to watch Hazel out of the corner of my eye. She looks relieved the conversation has moved away from her.

"I'll be honest. I really wanted to, but look at me evolving. Besides, I've recently discovered how scary I am when I do nothing but stare. I figured it out during a meeting with our accounting team. Terry looked like he was going to shit himself." He winks at Emilia. "Just you wait until next time you get in trouble with me, young lady." Emilia laughs nervously as Joshua helps her into her coat.

"I'll catch up with you. Hazel and I need to have a talk." I wave Joshua and Emilia off and they take the hint, leaving us quickly.

Turning my attention back to Hazel, I brush her hair away from the mark on her neck and she watches me closely. Without a word, her lips thin and she offers me a submissive smile. She knows I know something and I know she won't hide it from me if I ask.

"You're going to tell me what happened." I observe her in silence. She nods immediately but takes a moment before speaking.

"I was going to tell you. I just wanted to wait until

tomorrow. I wanted to enjoy our day before I bothered you with it." While I appreciate her trying to look out for me, she needs to understand how this works.

"Nothing pertaining to you is a bother. Go ahead." I make no move to offer her comfort or to punish. I wait and I listen.

"I found out Paul has been spreading some lies about me. He was talking to my friends and telling them I cheated on him." She looks around the table. Recalling what was said is hard for her.

"How did you find out?" I ask. As far as I know, she hasn't spoken to many friends outside of her time with Emilia.

"I ran into Cassie. One of my friends from school. She said Paul was out with her a few nights ago and he was saying all kinds of bad things. And I got a text from my roommate today asking me the same thing."

"Give me your phone." I extend my palm and she instantly lifts her phone off the table and places it in my hand.

I'm happy she still has a passcode on her lock screen and I enter the code she shared with me before pulling up her texting app.

I read back to where the conversation started last night and I feel my own resolve begin to crumble. Had I known about this when Paul first came to the table, I would have beaten him until he was out.

Hazel is right, this bothers me; it angers me. But where she is wrong was keeping this from me.

"Hazel, you have to know this is weak." I lift the phone to indicate what Paul is doing. "He isn't able to control you through work or school any longer so he's trying to control you through your friends." I place the phone back on the table. "That being said, this is information I need to know when it happens. I can't keep you safe if I don't know there's a threat."

"Cassie said he was drunk. I just thought he was...I don't know."

"Exactly. You don't know. You have a big heart, Hazel, and you assume that everyone else plays by the rules you set for yourself. But that's not how this world works."

"You're right. I still want to believe I'm mistaken or I've taken something the wrong way. If he wasn't close to my friends, it wouldn't be this hard to write everything off. I should have told you right away. I was worried if I told you, it would ruin tonight." As she confesses, I keep my features steady. It warms my heart that her first concern is for me, even over herself but she's going to get hurt if she keeps doing this.

"Hazel, do you understand that this was something you should have told me? And when you didn't, you knew you would be going against what I would have wanted?" I force her eyes to stare into mine.

"Yes. I knew I shouldn't have kept it from you and I did anyway."

Reaching to my glass, I down the last gulp of my wine. "Thank you for your honesty. It isn't going to change a thing about tonight, but it is going to add a punishment."

"I understand." Her eyes meet mine.

"Good. You have Marcus for the remainder of the day. I want you to enjoy your shopping but keep him close. I'm going to have a word with him before you leave." I stand, helping Hazel into her coat before stepping aside and leading her out of the restaurant and toward the car.

"As for your punishment, you will be with Marcus when he picks me up from work tonight. We're making a stop on the way home. You're going to help me pick out some items to punish you with. Then you are going to show them to Marcus and tell him what each one does."

"Doesn't he already know what those items do?" Her question is sincere.

"Of course he knows. It's part of your punishment. Your failure to communicate something so simple to me means you now have to communicate something of a more sensitive nature with him. And trust me, I won't allow him to go easy on you. He'll have questions that you will answer clearly and loudly so we both can hear you. Do you understand?" I stop at the car and Marcus joins us, opening the door and Hazel lifts up on her toes to give me a kiss goodbye.

"I understand."

She shoots Marcus a sideways glance, already preparing herself for what is to come before her head disappears into the car.

"Can I have a minute?" I walk around the front of the car to update Marcus. "Any news on Paul yet?"

"Nothing yet, but I don't expect to hear anything until Monday or so unless something urgent comes up. Everything okay?" He asks.

"No. We just had a run in with him in the restaurant." Marcus glances over my shoulder in the direction we came from as I speak. "Just stay close to Hazel today but don't make her feel it. I want her to be able to enjoy her day off. There is one more thing. Hazel has a punishment coming for not communicating important things to me in a timely manner. As part of her punishment, you'll drive her to pick me up after my work and I'm taking her shopping for some sex toys. She'll be communicating what each one does in graphic detail with you later."

The corner of Marcus's lip turns up in a grin. "You're quite creative. That should drive your point home."

I chuckle. "Don't take it easy on her. Ask her questions and make her uncomfortable. I'll let you know when she's had enough. She needs to come out of this knowing it is easier for everyone if she just communicates with me in the first place."

"Got it."

43

HAZEL

"What was that about?" I attempt a nonchalant tone from the back as Marcus gets into the driver's seat.

Instead of answering over his shoulder while he starts the car, Marcus turns to face me, making eye contact and I already know he knows.

"What was what about, Hazel?" His question sounds like a challenge. The smallest hint of amusement barely registers behind his expression and I slink further into my seat in embarrassment.

"Uhm," I feel my confidence abandon me, "everything okay?" I hear my own voice rising. "I mean—" Clearing my throat, I try to sound more confident than I feel. "What did Noah want?"

Marcus pauses for a hot minute, assessing my question and making me simmer in my shame.

"I understand we're all going to have a little talk later, Hazel." His features, unreadable.

"Oh, right." I back off. I am clearly out of my league.

I realize that my punishment isn't starting when Noah gets off work. It's starting now because I know Marcus knows and he knows I know; and I have to spend my afternoon trying to communicate through all of this awkwardness because I didn't communicate earlier.

Defeat washes over me as I drop my eyes down and give him the name of a few stores I want to shop at; and he turns to drive, granting me the temporary seclusion I was hoping for.

Over the next few hours, I gradually descend into my guilt. In between the respite of the stores I escape into, I find it harder to hold a conversation with Marcus and instead choose to sit in silence, missing the easier flow of our conversation from the morning.

I end up finding some clothes for me as well as a pretty necklace for Nina before Marcus announces that he's received a text from Noah.

He's ready to be picked up.

My stomach flutters with butterflies for the entire drive to his office and I don't entirely detest the feeling. The anticipation is unlike anything I've felt before and, while this is still a punishment, the thought of making this right between Noah and I settles my nerves.

"Hey, Baby." Noah joins me in the back as Marcus returns to his seat and pulls into traffic. I assume he already knows where we're going as Noah doesn't give him an address in front of me. "I missed you this afternoon."

My butterflies flutter away as he leans over, gripping my chin between his fingers and pulling me into him for a kiss.

He asks me about my day and I tell him about some of the stores I went to. After a while, I notice the car is moving in the direction of Noah's place and I wonder if he decided against our little side trip. My hopes are dashed when we pull into the lot of an obscure building with nothing more than a business name above its opaque windows.

I felt Marcus's eyes on me as we got out of the car but I couldn't bring myself to look up until I was alone in the store with Noah.

I capitulated instantly. Resigned to the punishment I know I deserve, I followed him up and down the aisles like a puppy. I listened intently as he pulled out each item and told me what they did and how he would use them on me, only nodding and holding out the little basket for him to place them in before we made our way to the front to buy everything.

In the end, I am grateful there are only four things in the bag Noah made me carry back to the car but I have no idea how I'm going to get through talking about these with Marcus present. As the car pulls away from the curb, I get an idea.

Setting the bag on my lap, I dig deep and pull out my first item, prepared to get this conversation over with while Marcus needs to look ahead to concentrate on traffic.

Gathering all of the confidence I have, I hold the first toy up and open my mouth to speak but strong fingers, wrap around my wrist, pulling everything back down to my lap as Noah commands my attention.

"Patience, Baby. Marcus will be joining us for a drink upstairs. You'll have your chance to share everything then." His eyes devour my modesty whole.

I feel the expression on my face falter before smiling to accept my punishment and I nod. I can't bring myself to hold much of a conversation and eventually Noah allows me silence, only drawing circles on my arm with his fingers until the car stops and we all get out.

Once we step into the elevator, I sense Marcus is off the clock as their conversation becomes more casual and I continue to decline joining in, instead choosing to mentally run through everything Noah told me about each of the toys he bought today.

Noah and Marcus both remove their jacket as we walk across his apartment to the kitchen and I leave mine on. Somehow the extra layer feels like a shield of sorts.

As the men continue to make small talk, I walk over to the couch and place my bag on the table. My mind jumps from everything in the bag and what I'm going to say to how I'm going to look both of the men in the eye when I speak and I fail to hear the guys as they join me at the table.

I startle as Noah leans around me, placing a bottle of water down before turning me to face him so he can unbutton my jacket, removing my false layer of protection.

"Have a seat, Hazel. Here, in the middle of the couch." It isn't a suggestion and I sit myself down, waiting for both of them to sit on either side of me, but they don't.

Marcus moves to one of the chairs facing the couch and Noah to the other and I feel even smaller than I did, all alone on the big sofa.

Their conversation has stopped and both watch me intently as they sip from their beer bottles.

"Now, Hazel. Why are we here?" Noah leans back in his chair, crossing his ankle over his knee as his face warms and my eyes jump between them.

"I, um, I have a punishment." I look both of them straight in their beer bottles as I speak like the coward I am.

"You have a behavior that needs to be redressed." He

confirms. "And what is it? Kindly look us in the eyes as you answer."

I close my eyes, taking a deep breath to prepare myself before meeting their stares and answering.

"I need to communicate better. I need to tell you things instead of waiting."

"Good." Noah's voice comforts me as Marcus observes me silently. "Why don't you show us what is in the bag and tell Marcus what we'll be doing to address my concern. I'll give you a moment to get started."

The men sit in rapt silence as I take a sip of my water before picking at the bag, sliding it to the side of the table as I move myself closer to the edge of the couch.

I wrap my fingers around the first surface I touch and pull it out of the bag. I imagine my eyes have bugged out of my head. It's the one I most don't want to talk about and I attempt to try for a different item before—

"Start with that one." Noah's tone is firm.

Reading the package, "Okay, so this is, um, a p-plug." I hold it up in front of my face trying to hide my line of view but it's futile.

"What kind of plug is it, Hazel?" Noah's tone is stern.

"It's a, um, butt plug." Either this couch is growing in size or I'm shrinking.

"Tell Marcus what you do with it." Noah prompts and I turn my attention to Marcus.

"Well, you—you put this in your—ah—butt." Both men look at me in silence before Marcus responds to me.

His tone is confused and slow. "*I*," he points at himself, "put that," he points at the plug, "in *my* butt?" Then points at himself again and I feel my face fall while I struggle to clarify.

"N—no. Noah is going to put this in my—um—butt." I whisper the last word before clearing my throat and Marcus nods in understanding.

"It's not just a plug though is it?" Marcus leans closer to get a better view.

"No, it vibrates. Noah thought I would enjoy this one more while..." My words trail off. I shouldn't offer so much information freely, I tell myself before I realize this is exactly why I'm being punished, so I finish my thought, "...while he is spanking me."

I feel my cheeks warm as I offer the information.

"Take it out of the package. I want to see the size of it." Marcus asks, leaning back in his chair.

I pull at the sides of the package and it falls into my palm. I take a good look at it as I hold it out between us and Marcus leans forward once again while Noah stays still, his eyes never leaving me.

The plug was the smallest one on the shelf but it still looks intimidating to me. The temperature in the room seems to rise as Marcus examines the item and I realize that I've just told him this thing will be in my ass in less than an hour from now.

I place the plug aside and reach in the bag a second time. My fingers graze against leather and I pull out the next toy.

"This is a paddle. Noah will be using it to, um," I make a lame swatting motion with my hand, "spank me." I'm not sure what else to say about it so I meet Marcus's stare to see if he has any questions.

"Did you pick this one out or did Noah?"

"Noah let me choose from the leather ones. I've never been—p-paddled before so I chose this one." I answer, dropping the plain paddle to the table.

I take a quick glance at Noah who smiles at me to let me know I'm doing a good job and I sheepishly smile back as I feel a rush of pride swirl in my chest. Reaching into the bag one last time, I pull out the last two items since they seem to go together.

My jitters get the best of me and I forget what Noah called these so I read from the tags as I spread them out across my lap.

"These are wrist to ankle restraints and a ball gag." Marcus straightens as I dangle them.

"And how do these work?" Marcus, again with the questions.

Remembering my lack of clarity on my previous response, I opt for a forthright answer.

"These attach my ankle to my wrist on each side. Noah will lay me on my stomach. He'll attach my ankle back to my wrist and I won't be able to move while he disciplines me with the paddle." Then, motioning to the ball gag, I continue, "And this is so I can't speak. He's using it to show me only he decides when I don't communicate."

"And is this the end of your punishment?" He asks.

I abandon the restraints on my lap and reach for the bottle of water to quench my thirst as my mouth feels like it's suddenly dried up.

"N—not exactly. Um..." I breathe steadily through my mouth trying to get the courage to tell Marcus that Noah is going to fuck me after he spanks me.

But instead I sigh and search for mercy in Noah's eyes.

"Baby, I'll remind you. Had you simply told me what happened, when it happened, we wouldn't be here right now. Answer his question and then we are done with this part of your punishment." I nod and he touches the tips of his index fingers together in front of his lips in wait.

Just say it, my voice scolds me.

"Noah is going to keep me gagged and restrained and he's going to climb on top of me and fuck me while the butt plug vibrates in my ass—and I'm going to love every moment of it." I answer to a silent room and both men watch me, intently slack jawed. I don't think either of them thought I had it in me and I take a swig of my water while they compose themselves.

Marcus shifts his attention to Noah and they each nod before Marcus finishes his drink and Noah stands.

"I'm proud of you, Baby." He walks around the table, hovering above me to place a soft kiss on my head.

Marcus joins him with a look I don't recognize on his face. I remain seated, only lifting my eyes to meet them.

His eyes search my face as he formulates his thoughts before speaking to me. "If you want my honest opinion, Hazel, you're getting off easy on this infraction. Communication is paramount. If it was someone who was mine, the butt plug would be at least three times as big and I'd be using a wooden paddle on your ass until you cried followed with an edging like you've never experienced." My brows knit at the term. I'm not sure *edging* is but, judging by the serious look on his face, I don't think it's something I'd enjoy at all. "That being said, you embraced your discipline with grace. You and Noah are lucky to have found each other. This changes nothing between us. I hope we can remain as we always have."

I smile and nod but I don't feel strong enough for words with him right now and he allows it; turning to Noah. "Thank you for the drink. Message when you need me."

Their voices fade as Marcus grabs his jacket and the two of them walk toward the elevator as I sit with my thoughts, going over our conversation.

Now everything I described will play out and I'm sure Noah will find a few more things to add to make it more interesting.

I jump in my seat as Noah rests his hand on my shoulder.

"I didn't mean to startle you, Baby." Then extending his free hand, "Come." I take it and rise to take a step toward his room before he stops me. "Don't forget your new toys." His smile is hungry and I feel my stomach twist in depraved excitement at the thought of my atonement as I stuff everything back into the bag and pick it up, following him toward the bedroom.

44

NOAH

*W*aking up on Friday morning with Hazel's thoroughly used body wrapped around me is my new definition of heavenly. After Marcus left last night, I punished her, then used her just as she had described, all the time reminding her she told Marcus this was going to happen to her.

Shame, when used properly, was the most powerful tool I used on her and she gave herself over to me effortlessly.

She stirred beside me, only tightening her grip around my midsection and my first instinct was to take a vacation day and spend the next few hours in bed, but I knew I couldn't.

Hazel's roommate flies back tomorrow and Hazel wanted to tidy up their room and pick up some food and drinks for both of them.

I feel relieved that, after today, Hazel won't be alone at her place. And, as much as I don't want her out of my sight, time away from each other is also healthy.

So I left her sleeping, went into work yesterday and made myself busy today. Hazel normally works a solid Monday to Friday, it was a requirement of her internship, but she is permitted to cover other shifts if needed and she agrees, which is what she's doing this weekend to cover for a coworker's vacation.

It's just before dinner and Hazel has a couple of hours left on her shift before she heads home to catch up with her roommate. The elevator dings and Joshua saunters out, briefly glancing around the apartment before meeting me in the kitchen.

Outside of Marcus, Joshua is the only one with keycard access to this floor.

"It's looking really good in here." He pauses, lifting his face to the ceiling and breathing in, "It smells like sex though." Then he winks like and ass.

"Jackass. Here." I hand him his beer and he takes it before turning his back on me and wandering toward one of the empty areas.

"What are you going to do with all of this space?" His question would have left me pondering if he asked it before I met Hazel. I wasn't sure what the hell I wanted to do with all of it.

Since she became mine, I have a growing list of ideas.

"Well, I was thinking of getting a pool table for this area. I have a few other ideas; I need an office space and possibly a workout or yoga area."

"You do yoga?" Joshua cuts me off.

"Well no, but maybe Hazel does. She's really limber." I reply and Joshua chuckles.

"Interesting. And what else?" He asks and I decide to let his comment go, for now.

"Well, I was thinking we might get a dog." I shrug, taking a sip of my beer.

"*We?*" Joshua raises a brow.

"Or a cat. I don't know but Hazel likes animals so it's worth talking about, you know, down the road." I shrug and attempt to walk toward the deck but I stop when I realize Joshua isn't following me.

"So it's getting serious then?" The look on his face tells me he already knows my answer.

"I don't want anyone else, Man." I say frankly. "It's only her. I have everything I want."

"It's a good look on you." He smiles.

"What's a good look?"

"Domesticity."

"You're an asshole."

"I never claimed I wasn't. Seriously though, Emilia and I are happy for you both." Joshua raises his glass in a cheers gesture and I respond in kind.

"Speaking of Emilia, where is she tonight?"

"She's out with Rosie. Apparently the water cooler gossip at work is off the hook and Rosie found out the new sales guys are joining us soon. One of them was her biggest competitor from Drakus and they need to talk or something. So lucky you; you get me all night."

"Well, the game is starting in a bit. Marcus was supposed to be here already but I guess he's running late. Let's get some food and set up the tv. I moved it out to the deck so we can enjoy the game out there." I continue walking toward the doors leading outside and Joshua follows, grabbing some snacks off the counter.

It's Saturday evening and the streets are getting crowded so the noise from the game isn't going to bother anyone.

Between the nice weather and my company, I should be able to keep my mind off of Hazel for a few more hours.

"Hey, I have an idea for your empty space. You could make a sex dungeon", pointing into the room he continues, "right back there." He laughs, searching my face for signs of annoyance, but I'm one step ahead of him.

I've already thought of that.

"Actually, I have something I'm working on." My confession surprises Joshua and he cranes his neck, searching the room for something he missed. "It's not on this floor. The third floor in this building is empty as well. I was thinking of creating a play space down there. I already have a small set up."

"What does Hazel think of it?" His eyes are wide with curiosity.

"I haven't shown it to her yet. I moved my things down there a few weeks ago and it's in the planning stages right now. I'm going to show it to her this weekend and gauge her interest. The third floor isn't accessible by anyone other than myself and Marcus in an emergency so it would be private and it's also out of sight so if friends or family ever came over, I don't have to worry about hiding anything."

"Marcus is here." The elevator chimes and I stand to wave him onto the deck, dangling a beer in my hand.

As he jogs through the kitchen, I can tell by the look on his face, something is wrong.

"Sorry, I tried to text you." He's out of breath.

I look over his shoulder at my phone sitting face down on the counter. I didn't see a point in checking it every five minutes for a message from Hazel when I know she's working.

"Oh, I turned it—"

"It doesn't matter. I think Hazel is in trouble." He cuts me off and my world instantly freezes.

Joshua stands to join us and there isn't anything for us to say. We just let Marcus speak and he hands me some papers.

"I found out Paul only started at Hazel's school this last year. Before that, he went to Stanford. He was almost arrested for stalking but his father paid his way out of it and brought him closer to home." Marcus speaks quickly as my eyes scan the papers before they land on a photo on the third page.

"Why is there a picture of Hazel in here?" Joshua asks, looking over my shoulder, but already, something isn't right.

"This isn't Hazel." I answer.

"Right." Marcus confirms. "This is the woman who was stalked and assaulted by Paul at Stanford. There is an eerie similarity between everything that has happened to Hazel, too. Including him starting out friendly, to asking her out. When she rejected him, he began showing up everywhere she just happened to be without explanation and there is also mention of a slashing of tires."

"Shit." I look at Marcus and he nods.

"Exactly."

"What am I missing?" Joshua asks.

"The first night Hazel came over to my place, a tire on Marcus's car was slashed. I wrote it off as being from Brent or Sean since their trials were underway." I explain.

"Shit." Joshua mutters under his breath.

"What happened to this one?" I hold up the photo.

"There was never a police report, but I did find a campus report. It's on the last page." I jump to the end to read it as he recaps the details for Joshua and I. "He attacked her on school grounds. She was working on a final project and her professor gave her access to their lab so she could complete it and he showed up without warning and assaulted her. He beat her up pretty bad but he was interrupted by a custodian who heard her scream."

The paper trembles in my hands as I imagine what might have happened to Hazel had we not met the day she spilled coffee on me. She would have been here this summer all alone.

Darkness creeps in along the edges of my vision and the room slowly fades out. The need to protect her surges to the surface.

"So he was stalking her?" I ask.

Marcus has been an acquaintance of mine for a long time. If anyone knows how these things work, it's him.

"I think he still is. Here, read this part of the report." My eyes follow his finger to the middle of the page and I pick up reading the sentence he's marked with an asterisk.

Two days after the assault, Bethany discovered a tracking app on her phone that was sharing her location information directly to Paul Davenfield's phone.

My face heats up as Marcus asks, "Does Hazel lock her phone?"

"She does now, but she didn't before I told her to do it."

A stern look crosses Marcus's face. I know that look because it's the same one I had when I realized she didn't lock her phone.

The morning we met with Paul and his father at Ravenous crosses my mind. Paul was convinced Hazel was hiding in the back room but she wasn't there. I was, however, carrying her phone by mistake.

"I'm going to call her. I need to see her and her friend

tonight." I make a straight line for my phone and turn it over, seeing the urgent text messages from Marcus.

The phone rings twice before she picks up and my body relaxes only a fraction when I hear her voice.

"Hey, I wasn't expecting your call." She starts but I cut her off.

"Hey, Baby. Is this a good time? I need to talk to you for a minute." Joshua and Marcus enter from the deck but both stay by the door.

"It is. I'm just walking back to the main building. What's up?" Her voice is carefree, it pains me to tear a bit of this innocence away from her.

"I found out some information and I need to speak to you tonight. I'm coming to your place for a bit and I'd like to meet your roommate." I don't ask for permission, I will be going over.

"Is everything okay?" Her concern is evident.

"I need to talk to you about Paul. Some things have come up you need to be aware of." I'm not sure how much I want to share over the phone.

"Oh, sure. I'm off in a few hours. Nina should already be at home. I tried to call earlier but she didn't pick up. She's probably unpacking. Do you want me to text you when I'm off?" She asks.

I open my mouth to answer but her voice cuts me off.

"That's odd." I get the sense she's talking to herself and I notice the guys, waiting patiently by the door. I activate the speakerphone and hold it out.

"What's odd?" The guys take a step in to listen.

"One second. The backdoor is open." The sound of the wind echoing in her phone cuts out and I assume she's stepped inside the building. "The raccoon is gone. I think he got out. I need to find Jeff. Give me a moment."

"Hazel, is it just you and Jeff tonight? Maybe Marcus and I will meet you out there and drive you home." I look at Marcus who nods in agreement but she doesn't answer.

After a minute, I hear her calling Jeff's name but she sounds far away. She must have placed her phone down.

A couple of quiet minutes later, I hear a distant scream followed by someone thumping closer to wherever she placed the phone.

Everyone around me jumps as the sound of metal items crashing to the ground pierce the room through the phone.

"HAZEL!" I yell into the phone, hoping she hears me.

"He's here. NOAH! PAUL, NO!" Hazel's still distant voice sounds petrified as more things crash through the receiver and I hear the back door fly open.

Marcus is already running across the room to the door as I grab my keys and follow behind. Just as the elevator doors open, I'm chilled to my core as I hear a male voice yell.

"NOAH WON'T SAVE YOU NOW. I WILL FIND YOU, HAZEL!"

45

HAZEL

"The raccoon is gone. I think he got out. I need to find Jeff. Give me a moment." I answer Noah as I scan the area.

The room is already too quiet so I lower my voice as I make my way to the other side to check out our animals. The cage where we held our recent rescue, a malnourished and wounded raccoon, is open and so was the back door so either the animal got out and Jeff ran after it, or something is wrong. Unless the rescue is prepped for surgery, this is the only room it stays in for all of its recovery.

Placing my phone in front of the abandoned cage, I grab a pair of gloves in case I need to help Jeff apprehend the little escapee and make my way into the hall toward the front of the building.

"Jeff?" My voice is just above a whisper now as I see the door to our supply room is ajar. There's no response.

I decide to check Shana's office first when I hear a muffled groan through the crack in the door to the storage room. Pushing it all of the way open I step inside to a mess. I first see a pile of boxes knocked over before another moan calls me closer to the table in the middle of the room.

Peering over the top, I'm temporarily stunned still. Jeff is propped up against a wall, his legs splayed out in front of him and he's almost unresponsive.

"Jeff. What happened?" I ask, rounding the table to help him up. He looks dazed as his eyes widen when he sees me. Then I notice his arm.

Two needles hang from his limp body as his head dips to the side.

He grunts, trying to speak and I don't understand him before another sound catches my attention. The door from Shana's office rattles then opens and I take three quick steps back as Paul walks into the room.

"What are you doing?" I ask as I turn to look at the medicine cabinet we always keep locked only to find it wide open.

Looking back to Jeff, my mind swirls as I examine the needles once more. They aren't needles; they're ketamine darts. These are the darts we use to subdue wildlife when needed.

Paul doesn't answer, he doesn't speak. Instead, he raises his hand and I notice the tranquilizer gun but it's too late. Firing off one shot, he hits me in the upper arm and I fly backward toward the wall behind me dropping the gloves I was holding. My adrenaline instantly kicks in, overriding any fear I should probably have and I feel a surge of strength push me back up.

Think, Hazel, think.

I take a step toward the door, grabbing the body of the syringe and yanking it out as hard as I can but the tranquilizer we use in the darts is already drained and spreading into my system.

Remembering my education, I know I have anywhere from three to ten minutes before I lose consciousness based on the dose. I'm not getting out of here but I can get to my phone.

Where did I leave it?

I answer my own question as Paul reloads then points the gun at me a second time and takes a step over Jeff to follow me into the hall before I see him go down, taking a set of trays off the table with him.

Jeff must have been able to trip him up and I want to run over to help him, but I'm losing seconds, so I turn to run toward the room at the back. Falling over my own feet, I burst into the back room, slamming into our observation table and more items come crashing to the floor, but I don't waste a second.

I left the phone across the room by the cage, I can see the display lit up on my screen from my spot near the entrance. I think the call is still on but I can't get to it and get out in time as I hear Paul struggling to get into the hallway behind me.

The drugs are getting into my bloodstream. I know because I don't feel as scared as I should and I yell at the phone while I run straight for the back door.

If I can just get out of sight before Paul gets outside, I might be able to hide myself before I lose consciousness.

Luckily, the treeline to the forest is only a dozen feet away from the back steps. I run straight into the cover of the leaves then make a sharp turn to the left thinking he only has a 30% chance of going in this direction and finding me on the first try then I run as fast as I can until my legs give out.

"NOAH WON'T SAVE YOU NOW. I WILL FIND

YOU, HAZEL!" His voice sounds manic and it takes everything I have not to scream for help. There's no one out here anyway.

A burst of energy pushes me on and I try to run faster as he hollers but instead I trip, sluggishly slamming my shoulder into the trunk of a tree before pushing myself up in one final attempt at escape.

This is it.

I won't make it much farther before my body gives up on me.

Now I have to hide.

The ground expands and contracts in front of me and I'm shutting down. I take a few more steps before falling into a small rut in the ground and decide to stay here, stilling myself as best as I can.

I try to curl my legs up to make myself as small as possible so there is less of me for him to find but I have no idea if I succeeded as my limbs are no longer cooperating with my brain.

Birds singing from the trees catch my attention and their song sounds sad. As if offering a chorus to their trilling, the wind blows one beautiful long wave, rustling through the leaves as my eyes grow heavy.

My shallow breaths should concern me, but they don't. Instead, I lie still on the forest floor, staring all of the way up the tall trees that surround me to the heavens above and the sky looks like it stretches on for an eternity. The longer I stare, the darker everything becomes until I imagine I see deep into the cosmos.

My body feels numb, even the pain in my arm from where I tore the syringe out has vanished. At least I don't feel the fear I should.

I hope Noah heard me. I hope he's coming to save me but I know he's at least half an hour out. How long can I hide in plain sight like this?

I suck in a deep breath as the snap of a twig startles me.

Paul is coming.

'But so is Noah. Hold on, Hazel.' I tell myself.

The footsteps are too close now. He's going to find me. I need to try to run. Even if I get caught. I need to run.

All of my hopes are dashed as I attempt to lift myself up one final time. Paralyzed, the drug has claimed its victory over me.

The branches of the last tree I hid beyond are brushed aside a few feet away from me and I already know my luck has run out. The only thing moving across my body is a lone tear rolling off my face and into my hair.

For a moment, there is no movement so I stay quiet hoping it is just a wild animal. Then his laughter rattles around my head.

"I told you I would find you." He steps into my line of sight, glaring down at my motionless body. I fight to stay conscious as he kneels beside me with the most unhinged sneer I've ever seen in my life and reaches out for my neck.

'This is it.' I tell myself, *"He's going to strangle me."* I'm thankful I'm so drugged up that I don't register the level of terror I should. Instead, I feel sad. I won't see my mom, Noah or even Nina again.

My head bobs as he yanks my scarf off reminding me of the marks Noah left on me and the way Paul looked at them like he wanted to cut them out of my throat when I saw him in the restaurant.

"Fucking bitch." He spits his words into my face. "You're going to wake up with my hickeys on you. NOT HIS."

I'm not sure if he knows I can still hear him as I dance dangerously close to oblivion but he continues to speak as he stands.

"Where were we? Oh yes." I feel a dull pinch in my thigh and I already know it's over. He shot a second dart into me. "It's time to get you somewhere where we won't be disturbed. Then I'll take my time with you. Oh, and I almost forgot. I have a little surprise for you."

I drown out the remainder of his words as I attempt to do the math in my head of how many darts I can take based on my weight before it becomes deadly but I come up with nothing. All of my education has been dumbed down by the new rush of drugs entering my system and I've got no fight left in me.

"I have to hand it to you, you're a fast runner. You might have gotten away from me if I hadn't gotten a dart in you first. I think I'll call you my little rabbit. You know why? It's because, if you ever try to run from me again, I'll break your legs just like I broke that bunny's."

Then, darkness...

46

NOAH

"*Try* again." Marcus urges from the driver's seat.
A helpless feeling has already sunk into the pit of my stomach but I try anyway because that is all I have left.

Navigating through the city on a Saturday evening was a nightmare but, once we hit the open road of the country, Marcus has been more than making up for lost time as Joshua checked out every car we passed for signs of Paul or Hazel and I tried to get her back on the line.

The screen on Marcus's phone lights up and he grabs it off the dashboard as we get closer to the sanctuary.

"Yeah—I have a situation. Unconfirmed 207 and a possible 10-57." Marcus stops talking in between his codes and I exchange a glance with Joshua, only hearing one side of the conversation as he continues. "I'm a couple of minutes out—I'll get you the address. Hold—"

Handing me the phone, his eyes stay on the road as I see the first sign of lights from the rescue shelter come into view.

"Just tell him the name of the place, the address if you have it and hang up. He'll know what to do."

I start rattling off as much information as I have but the person on the other end of the line hangs up on me after I say the name of the sanctuary and Marcus breaks hard, kicking up dust in the parking lot.

Paul's vehicle is nowhere to be found.

I don't wait for anyone to catch up as I jump out of the car and run to the front doors as Marcus and Joshua hurry behind me.

"HAZEL?" I yell, uncaring if anyone thinks I'm crazy at this point.

The only thing echoing back at me is my own voice and I take off down the first hall I see, pushing doors open as I go. The second door reveals a disaster and it's the confirmation I need.

Hazel is in trouble.

I step back from the door, allowing the guys entry and Marcus kneels beside the guy lying unconscious on the floor.

Hazel isn't in the room so I leave Marcus to do what he does best and I turn to continue kicking open doors before I get to the last one. It's wide open and equipment is all over the place; the door leading out is ajar.

The instant I meet the crisp air of the evening, I call her name again.

Nothing answers back.

In a futile attempt, I dial her phone one last time as I turn and join Joshua in the room and our attention is caught by something off to the side as I see a phone on the counter light up—at the same time I'm trying to reach Hazel.

"Shit." I mutter, crossing the room and picking up her

phone. I have no idea how I'm going to reach her now and the shared look in Joshua's eyes tells me, he knows it, too.

Our only hope is passed out on the floor in the other room. I return to Marcus and he's made some progress as the man is slowly coming around. He seems to be slurring something to Marcus and trying to move his limbs on his own.

"He's drugged. Darts." Marcus updates me. "I have a call in. The police are on their way to help him."

"What about Hazel?" I feel like an ass, skipping over the well being of this guy on the floor, but she is my priority.

"I have a call in about that, too. Joshua, can you stay with Jeff here?" Marcus asks and Joshua answers by taking his spot on the floor.

"What did you find?" Marcus moves me into the hall.

"Her phone." I hold it up as I continue, "There was a scuffle in the other room, the back door is open. Do you think she's out there?"

"No. Paul is unhinged. There are a boatload of criminal offences here. This was his only chance at taking her. I think he either has her, or he's out there looking for her and his car is gone." He lets the insinuation linger before finishing his thought. "Give me her phone."

He taps the front screen. "Do you know the passcode?"

I reach over and tap out four numbers and her phone unlocks as we both stand around it.

"What are you looking for?" I ask as Marcus quickly searches all of her folders.

"The report said he downloaded a tracking app on the other woman's phone. I'm just checking." I join in to see if there are any icons I wouldn't recognize as I hear sirens off in the distance. "We're running out of time. Listen, when the cops get here, don't fight them. I know you want to find Hazel and I have someone on the way who will get us out of here. Trust me on this." His attention lands on something in Hazel's phone. "Hmmm, there are no tracking apps downloaded. One second, I'm checking one last thing." He mutters the last part to himself.

"GOT IT!" He holds the app up to my face. "He used the location feature the phone came with to connect to his own phone and look, he doesn't know exactly how it works because it's tracking his location back to hers."

"What does that mean?" If my heart could literally jump out of my chest, I feel like it is going to happen any second now.

"It means, if he doesn't turn his own location off, this is where he is right now." I join him, staring at the screen. They are only 15 minutes away from us and they aren't moving.

"Can we just show this to the police then?" I ask, full of hope and Marcus's face falls.

"No. They are bound by procedure. It's my opinion that it would take too long to get to her and, unless he is caught off guard, he may kill her. Follow my lead." Marcus pockets her phone and walks out of the room with me following behind.

I can do this for Hazel. I can be calm and wait.

Joshua and Jeff are already sitting outside on the front steps when we get there and one cruiser is pulling into the lot. I realize Marcus is right, they would have to secure the area, take statements and radio everything in for back up. Somewhere along the line, wires could get crossed and they could drive out to where Paul is, sirens wailing, and get Hazel killed if she is still alive.

The last thought hits me like a ton of bricks. I'll kill Paul myself if he hurt her.

Marcus starts talking to Joshua, pulling me out of my thoughts. "At some point, Noah and I are going to just leave without saying anything. Are you able to stay behind and give them all of the information they need? Have them search the grounds on the slim chance she is out there." Joshua nods without asking any questions. "Here's the old report from Stanford so they have it. And one last thing." Marcus looks at Joshua waiting for him to make eye contact before continuing, "Hazel's belongings are fun the backroom, but you can't find her phone."

"I understand." Joshua answers, taking the papers from Marcus as the men in uniform approach us as one more car pulls in behind them.

"Gentlemen, keep your hands where we can see them. Anyone care to tell us—"

"I've got it." An abrupt voice from behind the two officers speaks up as both startle then immediately relax before taking the steps back to join the third person out of earshot.

The guy looks between the two officers at Marcus as he speaks to them and Marcus points a finger at me before the three of them go back to their conversation. Marcus nods at me once and I assume this is the guy he's talking about.

As the trio breaks apart, the two officers join Joshua and Jeff as the third waves us over.

There are no formalities, no introductions when the stranger speaks. "You've got an hour. Make contact ASAP." Pointing to the road leading away from the sanctuary."

"Thanks, Kill." Marcus speaks over his shoulder as he

heads for the car and I make my way to the passenger seat before he hands me Hazel's phone.

As the center lights are swallowed up by the surrounding trees, I watch Marcus scan the display of the phone in my hand as we drive in the direction of Paul's location on the screen.

"His name is Kill?" I ask.

"Cillian." He clarifies.

"I don't want to know how you know him, do I?" The severity of Hazel's situation slowly sinks in.

"No, you don't."

We drive for five minutes in silence before I ask the question I've wanted to since I heard Hazel yell into the phone.

"Do you think she's okay?" I instantly don't want to know the answer as guilt settles into me.

This escalated because of me. Hazel's safety has been compromised because I took her. I took her to the club when he found her; I removed the scarf from Hazel's neck before he approached us and saw my marks. I was so overwhelmed with claiming her that I didn't notice how I had provoked Paul.

"Don't do that." Marcus keeps his eyes forward.

"Do what?" I clear the lump out of my throat.

"There are no scenarios to play through in your head but the truth and you don't know anything yet. Don't beat yourself up over the possibilities. This", he points at Hazel's phone, "is the best thing that could have happened for us. We'll be there in less than five minutes. Do you know what is out there?"

I look over the area and I instantly know where we're going.

"Paul's father has a resort near here but it'll be crawling with summer tourists. I remember him saying he owned a lot of the land around the property that was undeveloped."

I open my own phone and pull up the property to keep my mind off of Hazel. Just the thought of her hurting sends me into a mental tailspin.

Before long, we drive through the front gates to the resort and it is alive with activity for a Saturday night. Paul's location on Hazel's phone indicates we still have some distance to cover and Marcus drives slowly around the lot, looking for a way toward the back of the building when a staff entrance catches his attention.

The bustle is lowered back here and he continues to drive toward the back of the employee parking lot, not stopping when the paved road turns to gravel, then dirt.

Turning off his lights, our speed slows considerably as we creep down the overgrown path as branches scrape along the sides of the car. I roll down my window in the hopes I'll hear something, anything, but there is only the sound of the waves coming off the lake.

As the dot on Hazel's phone almost completely covers Paul's location, we drive into an opening and I finally see it, Paul's car.

Marcus pulls up and parks as close to his car as possible, trapping Paul's vehicle between us and the trees in front before we get out to examine the area.

"His phone is on his seat." Marcus whispers from the driver's side as I turn to look around.

Other than the full moon's reflection on the water peeking through the trees, there are no lights this far out on the property.

Marcus circles his car to the trunk and pulls out a flashlight before turning it on to scan the treeline. "There are three trails leading away from here. I don't like this, but we need to split up. Take this," he hands me the flashlight, "and message me if you find her, I'm sending you my phone's location, accept it and I'll be able to track you like Paul tracked Hazel."

I drop Hazel's phone into the trunk and pull my own out, accepting Marcus' request before turning toward the closest trail. I decide to start by turning off the flashlight to get my eyes accustomed to the dark surroundings and to lessen the chance of Paul seeing me coming. After a couple of minutes, I turn the flashlight on to find where the overgrown path picks up before turning it off and walking deeper into the woods.

I have no idea how much additional property the Davenfield's own out here. For all I know, I could be at the start of an hour long hike and, without Paul's location, we've got nothing.

We are literally just running around a forest at this point. I push down the urge to start yelling out for Hazel in the hopes she can scream loud enough to tell me where to go, then I see a light through the trees.

Noah: Checking out a building.

I message Marcus then pocket my phone before approaching the wooden shed. Low light shines through the only window and I scan the area before my fingers tighten on the window sill.

There are two women inside.

One is on the floor, propped up against a post. Her head

hangs forward, she isn't moving and her hands are bound behind her back.

I'm sure the other is Hazel. She's also on the floor, facing into the room, auburn hair covering her face and I notice her hands aren't tied. She's either unconscious or she's—

A sharp pain in my ear drops me to my knees as my world tilts on its axis and—

47

HAZEL

*D*ammit. Everything hurts and what doesn't hurt is achingly cold.

Muffled voices fill my head as I open my eyes, keeping the rest of my body still and the first thing I see are wooden crates. I'm no longer lying in the forest, and I'm not alone.

The room smells like it's been neglected over the years, a combination of old leaves and sawdust. As muted sounds continue to gain in clarity around the room, I move my hands just enough to discover I am not tied up.

"Who is that, Paul?" The voice sounds a lot like Noah but it can't be. Still I don't move to check it out in case Paul is watching me, waiting for me to wake up.

I can't have been out for long. The doses we use are low enough to incapacitate animals and, if he didn't use a second dart on me, I'm not sure I would have lost consciousness.

"Someone in the wrong place. Shut up." I hear the thud of an impact followed by a groan and I take a deep breath, opening my eyes once more as I strain my neck up. Paul has his back turned to me and I look just past him to the person bound on the floor.

It is Noah.

My first instinct is to jump up and run to him but Paul is the only one with an advantage right now. Noah is tied up and, if I stand up to take Paul on, no one will be able to back me up.

Questions hit me all at once; starting with where are we? And how did Paul get us out here? He must have carried my dead weight at least some of the way and if he's that strong, there is no way I can fight him one on one by myself.

A softer groan catches my attention and I follow it to— Nina. What the hell is she doing here? She's supposed to be at our place unpacking.

Paul turns to watch her stir and I go limp, closing my eyes and breathing steadily to buy myself enough time to formulate a plan.

"You can't possibly think this is okay." Noah speaks again, drawing Paul's attention back to him and I open my eyes again in time to see Paul has turned his attention back to Noah and is facing away from me as he responds.

"I said shut up or I'll shoot you with a few of these." He rattles the tranquilizer gun in his hand. "I don't want to knock you out, but I will. I prefer you to be lucid when Hazel wakes up. I want you to see the marks I put on her neck." My eyes shut once more as he turns to point in my direction.

"Jesus, Paul. Then what? Have you thought any of this through?" Noah asks and I open my eyes once more to see him trying to stall Paul, and his expression is indomitable.

As Paul rambles on, becoming more unstable with each word, Noah finally looks in my direction and I connect with the eyes I thought I'd never see again. His face falls suddenly, his bravado twisting into terror and Paul stops mid sentence as I close my eyes and still my body.

"J-just don't hurt them. You can let them go and keep me here." Noah pleads as I feel a shift in the room.

Paul isn't responding. Instead, I hear the scrape of his shoes on the dirt floor as he nears, the scent of his pungent cologne as he kneels beside me and his awful breath on my face as he scans for signs of life.

I suppress my natural reflex to swallow the spit building in my mouth and it drips out of my parted lips, down my cheek and onto the floor. He lingers for a few seconds longer before he lifts himself back up and leaves me be.

"P-Paul?" Nina's voice almost startles me to a sitting position but I continue to remain where I am. "What's going on?"

With his attention now on the two of them, I open my eyes just enough to watch what's happening in my direct line of sight. I can't see Nina now but I can see Noah and Paul. Noah remains still, his eyes occasionally land on the door to the cabin. Paul towers over Noah, not turning to make eye contact with Nina.

"I didn't realize you were coming back today. I had no choice."

"What—is—is that Hazel?" Her voice is louder and I assume she's looking in my direction as she speaks and I quickly close my eyes, not moving a muscle.

I half-wish he'd come over here and jam another one of those darts in my arm as the pain is slowly beginning to scream into my body.

Nina must already know the answer because she doesn't wait for Paul to reply.

"You leave her alone. Don't hurt her, Paul." She orders and I hear the fear behind her brave words.

The shuffling of feet concerns me. Paul is becoming more erratic as our time goes on and if he makes an attempt to harm either of them, I will have to defend them with what little I have.

"You know she isn't yours." Noah taunts him.

What? My eyes shoot open at his direct challenge. Noah must sense Paul is losing control of himself, too. Whatever happens is going to happen soon and I open my eyes to confirm Paul is consumed by Noah's statement as he turns his body away from Nina and squares himself on Noah.

"She's mine." Paul declares.

Noah retorts, incredulously. "She isn't a sandwich."

As Noah holds Paul's attention and their conversation continues its back and forth, I shift, making eye contact with Nina, silently shushing her to keep quiet and she slumps in her binds.

"You know what? Fuck it. I don't need you awake for what happens next." Paul raises the gun, pointing it at Noah's chest "She should have been mine. This is all your fault."

"Wait." Noah begs and I have no other options. I decide in this second, I have to try.

Lifting my hands and placing them on either side of my body, I push myself off the floor and my entire being screams at me to stay down. Everything in me wants to curl up and cry in pain. Everything—except my heart and that is what I listen to.

"You know Hazel was never yours." Noah holds his attention as I take a step further behind Paul so he can't see me out of his peripheral vision and reach down, lifting a two-by-four off the ground. Nina holds her breath as I line myself up behind him and out of the corner of my eye, I see Marcus' face peek in through the window. "And neither was *Bethany*."

Who?

"What?" Paul tilts his head.

Two of the three most important people to me are in this room and I take one step forward before I swing with all of the strength I have, no longer caring if I kill him or not and the action reminds me of my high school days on our softball team.

"It's pardon me." I growl as my swing connects with his skull. The impact is instantaneous and Paul drops the gun a split second before his feet leave the floor. The only door to the room we are in bursts open and Marcus runs in before Paul's body bounces off the ground.

I hear Nina gasp then cry behind me and Marcus moves to Noah, untying him and I just now notice the dried crimson on the side of his face as he sits up.

Paul looks like he's trying to stand but his feet only flail out from under him as he attempts to roll over and Marcus moves swiftly behind him, securing him in a grip as he groans, his hands holding his head.

"You cunt." He howls and I've had it. I have no empathy left for someone who has none to begin with.

Dropping the piece of wood, I bend over and retrieve the tranquilizer gun with the dart originally meant for Noah. Without a second thought, I aim it at Paul and pull the trigger. The dart hits him in his upper thigh.

"Hurts, doesn't it, fucker?" I yell at him as I drop the empty gun to the ground. He winces and chokes out a groan.

I'm angry. I'm so angry.

I almost lost everything all over again and I want to cry.

I jump out of my skin, ready for a fight as Noah's arms wrap around me and he pulls me against his chest.

"You're okay now, Baby. It's over." He says into my hair as he kisses the top of my head. "You saved us."

"The police are on their way." I hear Marcus behind me and I close my eyes, a flood of tears rolling down my face.

"Who's Bethany?" I feel like I'm on a delay and my brain is still catching up to all of the events that happened. I look back at Paul on the floor, pinned under the weight of Marcus's body with a dart sticking out of him.

"Later, Hazel."

"Jeff—do you know if he's alright?" I grip the sides of Noah's shirt and his gentle eyes settle on mine.

"He's okay. Joshua is with him. You can stop fighting now. Just let me take care of you."

His permission wraps around me. I don't have to be the only one in charge anymore and I feel my chin quiver as I surrender to my feelings.

"I never thought I'd see you again." My words turn into a long string of blubbering cries as my body heaves uncontrollably in his arms and he only holds me tighter, telling me that he's here with me and I'm going to be okay over and over again.

I fail to notice I must have sunk to the ground as I open my eyes to Noah rocking me in his arms from a seated position.

"I'm so proud of you, Baby. You were so brave." His hands cup the sides of my face, lifting my attention to him and I absorb everything I can. Every pore, his smile, the glint in his eyes, everything consumes me before he leans over, claiming my lips with his own and I go all in, wrapping my arms around his neck and kissing him back like my life just depended on it.

"Hazy?" I had almost forgotten where I was when her voice startles me and I jump to my feet, spinning to where she was tied but all that's left are the ropes on the ground.

"Nina. How did you—you're here?" She hurries over, tears staining her cheeks and hugs me, pulling me the rest of the way off the ground.

"It was awful. I caught him in our room when I got home. He gave me some lame story about you asking him to be there. I told him I was going to call you and that's all I remember. Then I was here. I don't think he knew I was coming home, Hazy. I think he was waiting for you." She bites her split lip then winces as she opens the cut and a trickle of blood runs down her chin.

"Oh, Nina. I'm so sorry. I had no idea."

"Noah, why don't you escort these ladies back to the car. Help should be arriving any time and they'll need to get checked out." I notice Marcus tip his head in my direction. He's probably concerned about the ketamine and I nod, linking my arm with Nina's and heading to the door. "I'll stay here until Kill arrives. Send them my way."

I don't think I've ever appreciated the feel of cool air on my skin as much as I do at this moment.

"I'm not sure I want to tell my family what happened here." Nina speaks as Noah shines a flashlight in front of us and we move carefully in the dark.

"You think you'll be in trouble? Why?" I ask.

"Oh, it isn't them. It's Luca." I stop us both and look at her, silently asking her to explain. "He's the one I told you about—my family's security. He's kind of—well, this might send him over the edge. I wouldn't be surprised if he told me he'd be moving in to keep an eye on us." She smiles for the first time and I smile back.

"Well then, he'd have somewhere to stay because I'm not so sure Hazel should go back there ever again." Noah mutters behind us and Nina and I exchange a secret glance with each other.

"Are you asking Hazy to move in with you?" Nina looks over her shoulder.

"No—I'm telling her." His answer is cocky.

"What?" My voice is an octave higher than normal.

Turning to meet Noah's stare, I realize he's smiling before I notice my mistake.

"Oh, Doll. Just wait until you get a clean bill of health." He winks and I feel my body melt.

This was exactly what I needed to release my pent up nerves and I swivel my head back to continue walking, catching Nina side-eyeing me with a smirk before we continue on in silence.

I take the time to reflect. I used to wonder why we bothered to make plans at all because life always has a way of showing us who is really in charge. But now I realize, it isn't about who is in charge or the curve balls we are thrown. It's about enjoying all of the little moments with the ones that matter because they are the ones who will fight with us during our setbacks.

And I'm going to start making plans—lots of plans.

As we break through the trees to a sea of flashing lights, I know Noah is right.

This time, I'm going to be okay.

48

NOAH

azel spent a night in the hospital under observation to monitor her vitals as the drugs left her system. After Nina was checked out and bandaged up, she joined me at Hazel's side while she rested.

The bruises from the darts looked extremely painful and Hazel asked for a moment alone with me after she noticed the purpling on her neck. Paul had ended up giving her numerous hickeys while she was out and she wasn't prepared to handle the sight. I sat with her while she cried, the severity of her earlier situation and *what could have happened* finally sunk in.

The initial shock from earlier didn't wear off until the nurse gave her something to help her sleep and Nina finally put her head down on the bed from her seated position and fell asleep with her. I know because I was on the other side of the bed until Hazel's mom showed up and asked me if she could take over.

"She took care of me when I needed her. Please let me

help take care of her. She's all I have." She pleaded with tears in her eyes.

Pulling a chair in from the hall, I watched Hazel's best friend and mother surround her as if creating their own fortress around her, keeping watch over her while she rested.

Two hours of silence passed as I sat in limbo, listening to the distant echo of an intercom and the beeping of machines in the room until the light from the hall was all but snuffed out, drawing my attention to the door.

A large, muscular man peeked in, making eye contact with me and I expected him to move on before his gaze landed on the bed and I stood protectively, crossing my arms and stepping in between him and my sleeping beauty.

"Nina Beckett?" Speaking low, he dipped his head toward Hazel's friend as she slept.

I only nodded, not wanting to wake anyone up but the damage was already done.

"What are you doing here?" Nina hissed a whisper as the mystery man straightened, narrowing his eyes on her.

Throwing my hands up between the two, I pointed to the hall in an effort to keep Hazel and her mom sound asleep and Nina considered my request before staring down the big guy and walking out in front of him.

Once in the hall, I learned who Luca was. The tension between the two was thick. Now I understand why Nina mentioned she didn't want to tell her family what happened.

It turned out okay, right?, she said last night.

"What are you doing here?" Nina asked again.

"I should ask you the same thing." He responded coolly, arms crossed.

"My friend was in an accident." Nina answered and I

tried not to let my confusion show as I noticed Luca's expression grow predatory.

"Really? Just your friend? Is that really the only information you want to share with me?" He challenged her directly and she didn't back down.

"I said what I said." Defiant, she crossed her arms.

I remember thinking to myself that her argument might have held water if she wasn't speaking through a fat lip.

"Then explain to me how your beaten face and split lip is all over the news—Kitten." He lowered his voice at the end and Nina deflated instantly at his name for her while she glanced nervously over her shoulder toward Hazel's room.

"I thought so." Luca looked like he was barely holding his anger in. While they bickered, I took a moment to examine Nina's injuries for the first real time that night.

While Hazel had the wounds from the dart gun, Nina's were physical. If that was Hazel's battered face I was looking at, I'd be primed to kill.

"Your father is the damned governor. How did you not think I would find out about this?"

"Can we not do this here?" Her subdued tone was a complete contrast to the one she started out with.

"Gather your things. I'm taking you to your place."

"I don't have anything. He kind of just took me when he —um—knocked me out." She shrugged while she looked up at him with big eyes and I watched as the muscles along his jaw clenched. "Um—this is Noah. My friend's boyfriend."

"Another time, Nina. Let's go."

I made sure Nina felt safe leaving with Luca before promising I would tell Hazel where she was when she woke up then I took up the chair she left vacant and sat with Hazel until she woke the next day.

When the time came for her to be released, I had suggested she move in with me and even offered to give her one of the rooms in my building so she would always have Marcus or I close by, but she had refused saying she could do it on her own.

I allowed it while she recovered.

Driving up to her dorm, I noticed a journalist and cameraman on the steps of her building. Before letting her go, I offered one last time and told her we would wait until she was inside before leaving if she changed her mind.

I could see it in her eyes. She didn't want to be here anymore but she wasn't ready to accept it yet. She wasn't ready to be vulnerable.

So I let her go.

As if sensing their target, the two rushed Hazel and her mother, getting in front of them and pushing the camera into her face before I saw Gina, Hazel's mom, take charge, whispering something to her daughter before they turned around and got back in the car.

Hazel's mother was a big help over the coming days. She helped me get Hazel settled into a spare room on the second floor and she moved in with her to help take care of her while I attended some meetings of our own both with Joshua to discuss our future with the Davenfield's as well as with Ravenous to discuss one of their members covering for their child's destructive actions.

The week following the attack was a series of police interviews and witness statements. It turns out there was a limit on Mr. Davenfield's loyalty to his son. After Marcus located some other women who provided their statements, a pattern had emerged and Timothy declined to bail his son out this time, instead opting to protect his family name over the family itself.

Hazel's work gave her a mandatory two-week wellness leave which I agreed she needed. She was the only one who thought she should get right back to work. And I allowed her delusions while she dealt with her trauma.

I ended up taking two weeks of vacation time to be near her and after the first week, Gina had to get back to her own work, leaving us to ourselves for the first time since Paul took her.

I knew her first night on her own would be hard on her so I asked her to move in with me for as long as she needed. She declined but she took a key card for my floor in case she needed it.

I woke up the next morning with her body wrapped around mine and this is where she slept for the rest of the week.

Now, it's Friday afternoon. Our two weeks together is almost up, she goes back to work on Monday and her new school year starts in another couple of weeks; and she knows all of this. I think it weighs heavily on her and I see her deep in thought much more than usual.

I've allowed many things over the last couple of weeks I wouldn't normally have and it's all about to come to a stop.

For the last day, she's been slowly pushing her boundaries, testing the waters and she knows I've been lenient in some areas that would have otherwise gotten her a punishment.

She is subconsciously seeking the discipline she hasn't admitted she needs and she's pushing my buttons. Recognizing her behaviour gives me strength not to overreact though but this in itself brings its own punishment for her.

I won't allow her discipline to come easy for her. I'll make her face it, then ask for it.

I've told her how important communication is between us and this is just another lesson she'll learn.

"I thought we'd go out for dinner tonight, Baby. We haven't been out in almost two weeks." I test her.

"What?" She knows what she just said, she spoke with complete clarity and now she waits for me to take the bait, but I won't.

"I said, we haven't been out in two weeks. Maybe we can ask Joshua and Emilia, or Nina to join us." I answer indifferently, ignoring her infraction but counting it mentally.

"I don't feel like going out." Wrapped in nothing more than a short satin wrap, she turns toward my window, looking out at the city.

I'm about to suggest inviting friends over to continue this little back and forth when I see her tilt her head up toward the ceiling. Her shoulders rise with a deep breath before her head bows forward in silence and I stay still on the couch, leaning back with a beer in my hand.

As I watch her contemplate, I take a deep sip, setting the empty bottle down on the table and the sound makes her cock her head to the side.

I consider challenging her directly, but she isn't in trouble.

She's hurting. So instead I wait for her to tell me what she needs; I'll sit here all night if I have to.

Silence is a difficult thing to navigate when there is an elephant in the room and she only uses a few more minutes of it before she turns to face me and speaks.

"Noah, I need help. I'm not doing as good as I say I am."

She twists the end of her belt in her fingers. "I want it to be like we were before this happened but I don't know how to just—get back on that bike."

I waste no time getting up to join her. "We are exactly the same, Baby. Between us, nothing has changed." I turn her to face the window once more. "You just need to tell me what you need and I'll take care of you."

She knows I'm not talking about comfort and hugs. We've been doing more than enough of that over the last 12 days.

Brushing her hair off her shoulder, I reach around to her front, pulling on the thin belt holding her robe closed from me. Exposing her shoulder, I feel the deep breath of air she takes while my lips graze over her shoulder toward her neck.

We've both been needing this for a long time.

The marks from Paul faded completely a few days ago and I've been eager to claim her once again.

"I—I want you to—um—" Her hand tentatively caresses over mine and I feel the hesitation in her touch.

"Put your hands on the window and keep them there until I say." Her fingers press against the pane as I pinch either side of her robe between my fingers and run down its length until I am half way down before opening her wrap wide, exposing her little nightie to the city in front of us.

"Do you want me to spank you, Baby?" Kissing her neck, just below her ear. "Do you want me to make you cry?" Sliding my fingers between her thighs. "Do you want me to take care of you?"

"Yes. I need you to take care of me." Dropping her head back, her thighs part just enough and I slide my fingers over the thin piece of satin fabric that is keeping her from me.

"I know, Baby. Come with me. I want to show you

402 | RUN WILDE

something." I stay where I am, giving her the chance to steady herself before she takes the hand I've extended.

Leading her into my room, I pass through it to a small hall at the back. Until today, there was a locked door at the end. Now, it opens easily and I walk through to the staircase behind it.

Hazel follows quietly, only the occasional murmur telling me she's still with me.

I descend the set of stairs, then turn to face her and I know I can't hide my excitement. I wanted to bring Hazel down here two weeks ago, before everything happened. Since we've been at my place, I've been sneaking away while Hazel has had her mom or Nina over and I've been coming here to make this area more usable.

It's far from complete, but it is a start. I had the staircase built, linking both floors awhile ago when I first got the idea. Since the stairs just go down into the empty apartment below my bedroom, I have full access to the bathroom and a kitchen as well.

The only thing different is that I've had some of my items stored down here and now I've brought them all out to show Hazel.

The first room we enter into is just the living area. I have an old sofa down here but eventually, I want to upgrade it to a deep comfortable leather couch we can get swallowed up in. I'd like to make this a place where we can come just to hang out and unwind.

Hazel's deep breath tells me she likes the idea of a secret room and I stay at the door, allowing her to walk into the place on her own.

"Wow. What is this?" She asks as she circles the couch heading to the temporary fridge I have in the kitchen.

"This is for us. Somewhere where we can leave the world—out there. I still have a lot of work to do. This would be just a resting area." I answer, following her toward the first bedroom.

The dimmed room is painted a dark stone grey and the furniture is a combination of old wood, leather and metal. I watch Hazel's mouth drop open as she eyes the heavy suspension bar hanging from the ceiling then the bench off to the side of the room and her face warms with a pretty blush when she turns to look at the large four poster bed adorned with rings and restraints.

"Is this?" She notices the area where I have my rope stored. "Um are we going to—"

"Strip, Doll. You and I have some unfinished business and we're not leaving here until I decide we're done."

49

HAZEL

The last time I felt this overwhelmed was when I was a kid and my parents took me to the fair and told me I could pick which ride I wanted to go on first.

I wanted to go on everything at once.

I don't even know what half of the things in this room do and that is part of their allure.

Then I see the rope.

"Is this? Um are we going to—"

"Strip, Doll. You and I have some unfinished business and we're not leaving here until I decide we're done."

The deep masculine scent of leather mixed with Noah's promise makes me lightheaded. My anxiety over going out in public and returning to work takes a back seat as I run my fingers up the cool satin to the straps on my shoulder. The robe and nightie hit the floor in unison taking my inhibitions with them.

The room is completely sealed off from the outside. There are no windows; or, if there were, they're gone now, replaced by hooks, cabinets, toys and mirrors. Everything outside of the door feels like an eternity away.

Noah watches me as I shuffle in place, my eyes darting all over the walls, before he pulls his shirt out from the waist of his jeans and over his head in one smooth motion.

"I'm going to show you pain, but no punishment." Noah points his hand to an odd seat in the middle of the room and I take two steps, meeting him on the opposite side of it.

"This is a spanking bench." My eyes shoot to his as he speaks then I avert my stare like the mouse I am. "Climb on." He offers his hand and I take it, allowing him to move me over the bench, face down.

My midsection rests along a soft leather section and I kneel both legs into the spread reverse stirrups. His body brushes against mine as he binds a strap around my calves, buckling them at the back.

Noah bends my first arm at the elbow and secures it into place on a rest near my upper body and I move my second limb into place for him, earning myself a kiss on my bare back.

"You asked me to spank you. Pain can be cathartic, it can feel like a deep release and it doesn't always have to be delivered as a form of punishment, Hazel."

His use of my name feels profoundly personal. When he calls me Baby or Doll, I've always been able to compartmentalize that personality away from my own by labelling it as a part of me. Not all of me. Using my real name brings my entirety into the room with us.

"Do you like this, Hazel?" There's my name again. This doesn't feel like a coincidence.

I look up to examine his face. His features hide his

secrets well as his fingers tickle along my back, distracting my senses.

"I—yes. I like this." Something on the wall behind him catches my attention and my eyes jump over to take a closer look when he turns to follow my line of sight.

"Those are some of my toys. They're mostly for spanking or sensory play. I'm going to use some of them to play with you."

"Are all of these going to feel good?" I ask, resting my cheek on the headrest while still keeping an eye on Noah.

"Most do, but everyone reacts to each item differently. I'll find out which toys you enjoy." His fingers continue to caress my skin, dropping lower and tickling between my bottom cheeks.

"And you'll get rid of the ones I don't?"

"No. I'll set them aside for another type of play. Knowing which toys you have an aversion to will come in handy the next time you have a punishment." I want to show him my defiant face but all hope is lost as his fingers reach the slick area at the apex of my thighs. My rebellion comes out in an indecent groan and I hear him chuckle softly to himself.

"See. I knew you'd like this, Hazel." His tone is lowered and I arch my back, shamelessly offering more of my sensitive core to him. Dipping his head, his lips tickle along my ear lobe. "Tell me, Doll. What do you want me to do to you?"

"I want you to spank me—hard. I want to feel pain and—oh—I want you to ffffuuuu—keep touching me." Slurring my words, my hips buck as I turn my head toward the floor, allowing myself to fall limp for him on the bench but I don't stay in that position for long.

His first spank is sharp and the sting burrows into my body. Taking a deep breath to center myself, the scent of leather from the headrest fills my nostrils giving me an idea.

"Your belt." His hand settles on my back as he leans over my body, brushing the hair over my shoulder.

"Pardon me?"

"D—do you have a—can you use your belt?" Since Noah first punished me in the alley behind the restaurant, I've wanted more. I've wanted to escalate it and I've found myself wondering what a belt would feel like.

"You want me to strap you?" His voice is curious, probing without judgement.

"N—not hard. I just, I want to know what it feels like."

Without a word, he moves away from me and I hear him near the wall I looked at earlier; the wall with all of those items on it. I don't turn my head to look, instead, I close my eyes and listen. The occasional chain clinks against itself, then he's back at my side, his free hand gliding down my back to notify me of his presence.

"Just say *yellow* if you want me to ease up. Remember *red* to stop. Understand?"

"Yes. Thank you." I whisper my thanks, feeling a little embarrassed I'm asking for this.

I imagine the first swing is going to sting and I feel my muscles tighten in anticipation, but it doesn't come. Instead, the smooth leather travels gently over the curve of my ass before I feel Noah's fingers reach under the bench, sliding over my mound and searching for its way between my lips and I bow my hips forward to connect with his touch.

"Relax, Baby." His breath follows his words and I shiver, feeling his exhalation against my skin. "I'm going to make this feel good." Goosebumps swell down my arms at his promise.

Lifting the belt off my skin, his first few taps with the strap are tender while his fingers continue to explore my folds and I wriggle my hips to offer myself to him.

A groan surges out of my throat as his next hit lands on the fleshiest section of my bottom. I can't imagine this is anywhere close to his full strength but the sting and slow burn of his marks are creating a layered sensation that is only compounding on itself.

Fingers knead into my reddened ass as he spreads me open and I hiss through the headrest before floating away on a drawn out moan as the warmth of his wet tongue licks along my pussy before sucking my clit into his mouth.

Releasing my sensitive sex, another smack lands and I grind myself into it as a thin thread of drool escapes over my lips for the ground below.

"You still with me, Doll?"

"Hhhholy—yes."

"Good. Open your mouth." I lift my head at his order and twist to face him as he rounds the bench, standing beside me. I follow his muscled torso down to his erection and I must have zoned out for a bit because I don't recall him removing his jeans before now.

My mouth has been watering since I climbed on this contraption and spit coats my lips and chin. Craning forward, I stretch out my tongue to taste the salty droplet on his tip and his fingers snake into my hair as he pushes his way into my mouth.

"That's it. Just follow my lead." He guides himself in and out in steady movements and I hum around him as I try to keep up. His fingers tightening in my hair make my eyes roll back. The thought I am causing his pleasure gives me an intense release of my own.

Pulling out, his fingers stay locked in my hair as he leans over, claiming my mouth in a heated kiss before lowering my head back to the rest and returning to his place between my legs as another slap lands and I cry out.

I won't use my safeword though; they aren't tears of pain.

"Please, Noah. I want to feel you inside of me while you spank me." My fingers dig into the leather padding my arms are strapped to.

I've needed this release for a while now. I don't know why I didn't just tell Noah I needed this sooner but now I feel like I can't wait any longer.

Answering my wish, I feel the head of his cock slide into my wetness toward my core and I pause, waiting for him to push himself all of the way in.

His fingers and the leather of the belt draw down the length of my back before his hands on my hips lift me up and open for him and he pushes all of the way in in one long motion. We moan in unison as he pauses, giving me a moment to settle myself around him.

His pace steadily picks up until he is fucking into me at the pace we both need. The time for being soft is gone, replaced by an intense ache to simply claim and own. I'm vaguely aware of his fingers sliding up the back of my neck into my hair as they clench in a fist at the base of my skull and he carefully lifts my head up, facing me forward.

"Open your eyes, Doll." His growl is the only warning I need and my eyes focus on the mirror in front of us.

I hadn't noticed its placement before. Now I see myself, spread and bound on this bench with Noah behind me, fucking me as he raises his other hand holding the belt.

"Yes." I hear myself beg as his hand drops, cracking the leather across my ass and the delight plastered on my own face surprises me.

Watching him riding me, claiming me, makes my head spin. My face, contorted in ecstasy stares back at me, challenging me to deny this is who I am and I can't.

"Fuck. I'll never get enough of you, Hazel. I feel you, Baby. You're close." His voice comes out in raspy breaths.

I barely hear him over the moaning in the room before I realize the sounds are coming from me.

"Please, don't stop. Just—like—tha—" The syllable of my last word is lost on a scream as I arch my back, releasing myself to him. My orgasm punches into me, the binds are the only thing still holding me on the bench as I writhe under him while he continues to thrust into me.

The sharp snap of his strap against my ass draws out my euphoria on a second strong wave. The sound of the belt hitting the floor catches my attention as his hands grip my waist. Leaning over my body, he joins me in oblivion, latching his lips onto the back of my neck and sucking hard.

A new mark just for me.

The gesture is entirely encompassing. I know he left a mark on my neck and I can't wait to see it, I think to myself as my arms vibrate loosely, still secured to the bench.

Noah works quickly, first unfastening my arms so I can steady myself, then moving to my calves. He braces me while I put my weight back onto my own two feet before swooping down to pick me up, walking toward the large bed.

The moment I hit the soft sheets, I slide myself across the king-sized mattress and Noah follows me, swatting at my hands as they try to grab the covers to hide myself.

"None of that. I want to see all of you." His fingers tickle my midsection just enough to coax out another rash of goosebumps and I giggle. "I'm scoping out all of the places I still have to mark." Dipping his head, the warm ridges of his soft tongue glide over my breast before he sucks me into his mouth, his teeth clamped lightly around my hard nipple as his eyes stay locked on mine.

"I want this all of the time, Baby." My breast bounces gently as he releases his grip.

"So do I." I smile.

"No. I mean, I want you to consider moving in here, with me." My heart swells as he speaks but I can't find the words to answer him. "Before you decide, you can take the apartment on the second floor if you still want to have your own place. Even though I would rather have you in my bed every night, I understand if you want to take it slow."

After my father passed away and I moved my mother into her new apartment before going to school, I've missed being at home. Home is a place, but it isn't a building. I love living with Nina, but I never made it my home because I knew it was temporary; eventually we would both graduate and move on.

"I don't need to think about it." I finally find my words as tears sting the corners of my eyes. "I feel at home when I'm with you. There's nowhere else I would rather be." Before I finish my sentence, he has his arms wrapped around me in a bear hug while he plasters kisses onto my face.

"Well, then. I can't wait to fall asleep with you, Baby." He smiles.

"Me, too. Should we head upstairs?" Noah's expression turns serious as I ask my question. "What's wrong?"

"You don't think we're done here, do you?" His wolfish smile tells me this is most likely a trap.

"Huh?" Raising my eyebrows, I squeak and he continues as his fingers pinch my nipple.

"I told you we had unfinished business and I'm far from done with you, Doll. I haven't shown you your new nipple and pussy clamps yet."

"WHAT!?!"

ACKNOWLEDGMENTS

I wrote Run Wilde during the 2020 pandemic and posted each rough draft chapter as it was finished on the Radish Fiction reading app. I'd like to thank everyone at Radish Fiction for reading it and commenting or motivating me to continue. I'd also like to acknowledge the creators and staff at Radish Fiction for granting me their platform as an outlet for this story.

I've had the pleasure of connecting with many of you on my various social networks and I want to thank all of you for taking the time to read, share, comment, review and support my writing.

Until next time...

Printed in Great Britain
by Amazon

83092611R00243